AMERICAN ROYALTY
BOOK TWO

T0357799

Her Darling
MR. DAY

GRACE HITCHCOCK

BETHANYHOUSE
a division of Baker Publishing Group
Minneapolis, Minnesota

Published by Bethany House Publishers
11400 Hampshire Avenue South
Minneapolis, Minnesota 55438
www.bethanyhouse.com

Bethany House Publishers is a division of
Baker Publishing Group, Grand Rapids, Michigan

Printed in the United States of America

Library of Congress Cataloging-in-Publication Data
Names: Hitchcock, Grace, author.
Title: Her darling Mr. Day / Grace Hitchcock.
Other titles: Her darling Mister Day
Description: Minneapolis, Minnesota : Bethany House, a division of Baker
    Publishing Group, [2022] | Series: American royalty ; book 2
Identifiers: LCCN 2021031569 | ISBN 9780764237980 (trade paperback) | ISBN
    9780764239830 (casebound) | ISBN 9781493436026 (ebook)
Subjects: LCSH: Romantic suspense fiction.
Classification: LCC PS3608.I834 H47 2022 | DDC 813/.6—dc23
LC record available at https://lccn.loc.gov/2021031569

Scripture quotations are from the King James Version of the Bible.

This is a work of fiction. Names, characters, incidents, and dialogues are products
of the author's imagination and are not to be construed as real. Any resemblance to
actual events or persons, living or dead, is entirely coincidental.

Cover design by Create Design Publish LLC, Minneapolis, Minnesota / Jon Godfredson

Author is represented by The Steve Laube Agency.

Baker Publishing Group publications use paper produced from sustainable forestry
practices and post-consumer waste whenever possible.

22   23   24   25   26   27   28   7   6   5   4   3   2   1

For Cora Belle,
My Little Flower

He healeth the broken in heart, and bindeth up
their wounds.
He telleth the number of the stars; he calleth them
all by their names.

Psalm 147:3–4

One

It had taken some of her best work to convince her parents and four sisters to summer in New Orleans instead of in their mansion in Newport, but with Teddy Day *finally* a bachelor once more, Flora Wingfield wasn't leaving anything to chance. She leaned against the polished rail of the steamboat, gripping her chapeau as she peered down at the muddy Mississippi River, attempting to catch a glimpse of life below the surface, but she doubted that if she stuck her hand in the water, she would even see her own fingers. Instead, all that greeted her was the blurry reflection of her cream hat peeking over the side of the boat.

At the *Belle Memphis*'s jarring whistle, she straightened and pulled at her high collar, the thick air leeching upon her skin. The hum of the levee workers greeted her as the boat's paddle wheel slowly churned into port. As the landing stage swung into position, Flora was jostled against the crowd pressing with the rest of the passengers to disembark at long last. She clutched her beaded reticule to her chest, having been thoroughly warned against pickpockets by Father after losing her pin money on the journey here.

She at last ambled down the landing stage and broke free from the group. She pushed back her golden curls from her face and, with her hands on her slim hips, whirled around and around, drinking in the city from the waterfront. Craning to see over the hundreds upon hundreds of bales of cotton and countless wooden barrels being stacked and readied for shipment, she made out the distant spire of a church above all else in the clear sky. While the New Orleans port was not quite as deafening as New York's, the cadence was different with drawn-out words, dipping and swaying in an unfamiliar, lovely pattern. "Beautiful," she whispered. And what was even more beautiful was the thought that Teddy Day was in the same city as she for the first time since—well, she wouldn't think about *that* part.

She turned back to the steamboat and strained her neck, searching for her family and spotting Tacy's orange gown almost at once. It was a rather hideous gown, yet her sister was not one to hide herself in a crowd, and as a close friend of the Vanderbilts had commented that Mrs. Vanderbilt hinted it was to be the hue of the season, Tacy had immediately ordered a fleet of orange gowns from Worth.

Flora lifted her handkerchief and waved it above her head, but instead of garnering her family's attention, she was met with that horridly familiar grin beneath the thin greasy mustache of Mr. Grayson, who lifted his cane in greeting. She at once shifted her gaze and to her relief found Father stepping onto the dock, extending his hand to Mother and leaving it there for Ermengarde, Olive, Tacy, Nora, and finally cousin

Cornelia, who kept her hand splayed against her back, supporting her ever-growing girth. The family had been a bit uneasy when Cornelia had requested to summer with them while her husband was in Europe so she wouldn't be alone for the remainder of her pregnancy. But in the end, Father shrugged and acquiesced, for what was one more female in their troupe?

Even from yards away, Flora could hear the high-pitched complaints already flowing from her younger sisters. She gritted her teeth and moved to join them. Before any petulant comments could be directed her way, she lifted her hands in hopes of warding off an attack. "Now, I know it may not be as cool of weather as I initially promised, but I am certain once we reach Auntie's mansion on St. Charles Avenue, it will be *much* . . ." But of course her words were lost in the cacophony erupting from the group. Flora pinched the bridge of her nose and inhaled. An hour longer and she would have the privacy of walls to separate herself from her three youngest sisters with whom the only things she had in common were their mother's clear blue eyes and Father's golden hair. *This will all be worth it when Teddy and I are walking down the aisle at summer's end*, she reassured herself, chanting, *A bride by fall. A bride by fall.*

Olive gave her a sympathetic smile. "Here, use this." She whipped out her fan, handing it to Tacy in a vain effort of ceasing the flow of complaints regarding the palpable heat.

The group came to a halt as Mother bade farewell to the two families they had become acquainted with during the journey, promising to stay in touch, even though Flora knew well and good that Mother had no such intention.

They were merely friends of convenience, and they were no longer convenient.

"Mr. Wingfield?" A middle-aged man with wisps of graying hair in a canary-colored livery approached them, hat in hand. "I'm Peterson, a footman to Mrs. Dubois, and I've come to fetch you to the lady's residence."

"A bit old to be a footman." Father eyed him and gestured to the mountain of Louis Vuitton flat-top trunks that were still being unloaded from the steamboat. "See to collecting our things at once. I wish to be seated for dinner as soon as possible."

With a grunt surely aimed at the shameful amount of luggage, the servant showed Father and Flora to a wagonette while a second, younger fellow in the same yellow livery began loading the bags and trunks into another wagon.

Mother emerged through the crowded docks with Flora's sisters and cousin trailing behind in a burst of vibrant brocades, cotton sateens and bustles, her brilliant smile fading on sight of their transportation. "A *wagonette*?" Mother narrowed her gaze at the driver, who quickly busied himself assisting the servants loading the tower of trunks. Having no one upon whom to bestow her ire, she whirled to Father, whispering, "This is beyond humiliating. Your aunt should have sent us two open carriages, Florian. But no, instead we are to be treated like a group of country servants, seated atop benches for all the world to see. What a fashion to enter into New Orleans society."

Father ran his hand over the back of his neck, concern flickering through his features. "Yes, we do seem rather exposed. Anyone could recognize us . . ."

Flora twisted her hands. This entire situation was unraveling far sooner than she had anticipated. "I'm certain Auntie Violet did not mean any disrespect, Mother. Surely, when she read how many were in our party from my letters, she thought it would be easier on the servants to drive us—"

"We are *knickerbockers*, Flora. That should count for something." Mother huffed and climbed aboard, settling her voluminous brocade skirts about her while the rest of the exhausted company piled inside, Father taking his seat beside Mother, Ermengarde and Nora behind them with a birdcage between her and Cornelia, leaving Flora, Olive, and Tacy to scrunch together on the last bench seat.

Despite their outlandish appearance, Flora sat straight and gripped the open windowsill of the wagonette and observed the flurry of activity in the French Quarter. Between the shouting vendors, tourists, and street musicians performing on nearly every corner, the streams of people weaving through, she was beginning to worry that the tranquil summer she had promised Father was not actually going to happen when they pulled onto an avenue dripping in low-lying branches of majestic oaks, and the din faded into the background.

"How much farther?" Tacy shouted to the driver.

Flora flinched. *How does someone so slight have that much nasally power in her voice?* She resisted rubbing her ear, as she knew Tacy would take offense in an instant and another fight would ensue.

"Little over a mile, Miss Wingfield," the driver called over his shoulder, the footman nodding his agreement beside him on the front seat.

"Thank goodness for that." Mother's fan slowed.

And with Tacy slumping back in her seat, Flora sighed at

the few moments of blessed silence as they passed mansion after graceful mansion on St. Charles Avenue that made their brownstone home in Gramercy Park seem plain in comparison to the opulent Corinthian-columned verandas. Flora reached for her reticule, itching to use her white pearl opera glasses in an attempt to catch a glimpse of the interiors in passing. She rubbed the outline of the lenses inside her bag and decided that instead of earning a reprimand from her mother for being so obviously nosy, she would keep alert for the numbers over the doors of each mansion to discover which belonged to Teddy and if she could make him out in the parlor window. If only she could actually *use* her opera glasses, she probably could catch a glimpse of him, satiating her aching soul for only a moment. She shook her head at the ridiculous wish. Teddy would be at the office at this hour or perhaps just finishing a meeting at a client's residence. It was for the best she didn't see him, for if she did, she wouldn't be able to sleep tonight with thoughts of their contrived encounter that she had been planning for weeks.

"Why, isn't that Theodore Day on horseback? What are the odds we run into him on our *first* day in New Orleans?" Tacy exclaimed loud enough to raise the shades of St. Charles Avenue.

Flora craned around Tacy. She would recognize Teddy's broad shoulders and striking form anywhere. "Yes," she breathed, longing to call to him after the two months apart. Had he missed her as much as she had him? Or was he simply glad to be away from New York after being jilted by her dearest friend?

"Mr. Day!" Tacy crooned, waving her lace-trimmed handkerchief to the figure ahead of them at the corner they were very rapidly approaching.

"Shh." Flora clapped her hand over her sister's mouth, ducking down, praying that he would not see her, but it would take a miracle for Teddy not to hear her sister's shrill call. "I did not journey *hundreds* of miles to have him see me for the first time all covered in the grime of travel." She bit her lip as she realized she had said the wrong thing, as all in the wagonette turned in their seats to stare at her.

Father set aside his paper, narrowing his gaze, a smirk appearing at the corner of his mouth. "You mean to tell us that all those long speeches you gave us over a month and a half of dinners on the magnificent education the girls would receive being immersed in the grand architecture and rich interiors of the city with its French and Spanish influences, its culture, food, and music were all a ruse?"

"You knew?" Flora pressed the back of her hand to her flaming cheek. She had *purposefully* not mentioned the Day family in all her hours of convincing, except briefly during her presentation of the advantages of the variation of high society in New Orleans.

"Of course." Mother dabbed her handkerchief over her forehead. "Do you think I would have dragged my girls anywhere besides Rhode Island for the summer season if there were not ample bachelors to choose from to make you all suitable husbands? The Day family is one of the only families in New Orleans with knickerbocker roots. And we heartily approve of the Day brothers, especially with the wonderful press Theodore has been receiving after Willow Dupré's competition to find a husband ended in April. Securing the affections of a man who was jilted by the famed sugar queen is worth a summer in this oppressive humidity."

Flora dropped her gaze. *Of course, that was the only presentation Mother found moving.* When it came to young men paying court to one of the Wingfields' five daughters, especially the eldest, Mother would move heaven and earth to make a favorable match. Not that Flora was against the idea of marriage, as it was the motivation behind this whole scheme, but she was only open to the idea of marriage to one man in all the world. And that man just happened to live on the opposite side of the country, who was now literally within reach.

"This trip is about acquiring husbands for you all," Mother continued. "Well, minus Nora . . . though I suppose sixteen is old enough to secure a promise of a marriage to occur in a few years."

"Flora? Is that you?" Teddy called from atop his ebony stallion as their wagonette slowed. He grinned and swept off his broad-brimmed hat, revealing a ring of matted blond curls he had cropped much shorter than he usually kept them, and he now sported a closely shaven, blond beard that complemented his russet eyes.

Flora straightened, quite aware of her chapeau's undignified, squished state between two sisters and the sheen of perspiration dotting her forehead and the seven pairs of relatives' eyes fixed upon them. "Why, Teddy Day, what a wonderful surprise!"

Tacy snorted, and Flora gave her a sharp jab in the corset stays, keeping her smile firmly in place.

"It is delightful to see you all! Good afternoon, Mr. and Mrs. Wingfield. Ladies. What brings you to the illustrious Crescent City?" Teddy tipped his hat in greeting to the rest in her party and adjusted the leather strap across his chest, attached to a narrow leather tube upon his back, which no doubt housed his latest steamboat designs.

A chorus answered him, and Flora gritted her teeth. This was not how their first meeting was supposed to transpire. She had planned to happen upon him in her darling new, striped cream walking suit, perfumed in what she believed was his favorite scent of gardenias, completely unaware of his beauty, and *alone*—not with her entire family looking on as she stumbled through her explanation of their unexpected appearance in her wrinkled rose-colored suit. Thank goodness she had worn her new hat.

He laughed, clearly enjoying the chaos. "Do you have accommodations?"

"We are summering with Great-Auntie Violet," Flora interjected before anyone else could speak over her.

His brows rose as he tugged his ebony planter hat back into place, his horse prancing to the side as a carriage rolled past. "Violet *Dubois*? How did I not know she was your relation? Why, her mansion is but a ten-minute walk from my residence." He gestured to a two-story, pale-blue mansion on his right with scrolling Ionic columns and a modest veranda adorned with potted ferns on either side of its ornate front door. "Would you care to take a stroll with me, Flora?" He looked to her mother. "If it is agreeable with you, Mrs. Wingfield."

Her heart leapt, and Olive squeezed her hand, knowing the full extent of Flora's desire to be with Teddy. Flora regarded her mother, desperately attempting to conceal her excitement, for it would not do for him to recognize the depth of her affection so soon.

"She would be *honored*, sir." Mother flapped her hands at her youngest daughters to move them to the side and make room for Flora to pass. "Tacy and Olive, follow along behind them. It will do you all a world of good to walk after being cooped up since the train ride to Illinois and then the everlasting steamboat route to the port."

"Wonderful!" Teddy dismounted, then drew the reins over the horse's head and led him to the gate, handing his mount off to the waiting stableboy.

With a romance on the line, Tacy for once did not complain but instead followed Olive out of the wagonette. And as Flora passed Cornelia, her cousin pressed her own lovely Parisian lace parasol into Flora's hands. "Breathe. All will be well."

Flora smiled, hopped from the wagonette, and placed her gloved hand in Teddy's, the touch sending a pulse through her body. Mother sent her an indiscreet wink and motioned the wagonette onward, Father returning to today's copy of the *Picayune* without a second glance to Teddy.

Her sisters slid past them, pointing at things that caught their eye, giggling and completely aware of their oldest sister's tumultuous heart. While Tacy's favorite pastime was husband hunting, Flora had never before attempted to capture a young man in the net of matrimony, but Teddy was not just any man. At least she was wearing a gown that would bring out her blue eyes and that she knew for a fact was his favorite color on a lady. As she opened the parasol, momentarily blocking herself from Teddy's view, she quickly turned her head and sniffed her puffed sleeves and winced. She should have dabbed on more perfume this morning. If only Father hadn't insisted on scrimping and providing a single maid for his daughters for the entirety of the summer, she would have fresh clothes daily.

Flora rested the parasol on her shoulder and smiled. "Teddy, it really is marvelous seeing you. I haven't heard from you since—" She clamped her mouth shut and kept her focus on the front-yard landscapes. *Since the night of the ball when I stole Cullen into Willow's suite to convince her to marry him instead of you.*

"Since our dear Miss Dupré jilted me at our own engagement party?" He laughed, kicking at fallen, shriveling yellowed gardenia on the sidewalk. "Well, my hiding has been intentional."

"Is that why you have changed your hair and grown that?" She pointed to his jaw. While she normally did not favor beards, she found it suited him and hardened his boyish lines and accentuated his fine jaw.

He laughed, absentmindedly rubbing his hand over the thin beard. "Indeed. I stay buried in my work most days, as I find it helps in avoiding thinking about Willow, but whenever I resurface, I am at once reminded of my rejection."

Her brows rose. "Oh? But your courtship took place in New York. What reminds—"

"Why, Theodore Day." A fiery-haired woman in the same shade of gown as Flora's, but pressed and trimmed in gold cord and puffed to perfection, hailed them with her magazine from her veranda, leaping to her feet and sending her golden, curly-haired lapdog rolling down her skirt and yipping to the floorboards in her haste. "What fortune it is that you happened to walk by while I was taking in this lovely breeze."

Lovely breeze? Heaven help me if she is serious. Flora seized Teddy's momentary distraction to dab at the sweat

15

beading above her lip with her cuff as the woman reached the wrought-iron gate that bordered her home.

"It truly is a rare summer's day," Theodore agreed, sending Flora's stomach to plummeting at the thought of all her promises of fine weather turning out to be false and the ramifications that would fall upon her head for unknowingly misleading her sisters. "Miss Penelope, allow me to introduce you to one of my oldest friends in the world."

Penelope? They are on a first-name basis? "Oldest? Surely you haven't forgotten that I'm quite a few years younger than you." Flora bumped him with her shoulder. "I would prefer you say I am one of your *closest* friends, Teddy dear."

"An older acquaintance than me?" Penelope's bottom eyelid twitched, Flora's use of his pet name bringing about the desired irritation. "I do not recall you ever mentioning *her.*" She flicked her magazine back and forth, looking Flora up and down in a slow deliberate fashion, the wafting of her makeshift fan filling the silence. "How nice, Miss . . . ?"

Before Flora could answer, a flock of women rounded the corner, their eyes widening at the sight of him, all in various shades of rose, save a blonde in a trim walking suit of cobalt. But instead of walking around them, they flew up to Teddy, fans and eyelashes fluttering, creating an *actual* breeze. Her sisters paused behind the group, looking back to Flora as bewildered as she felt. One of the young ladies, with limp brown curls and wire-rimmed glasses, narrowed her gaze at Flora's proximity to Teddy and promptly pressed her heel into Flora's thin shoe. Flora yelped and scrambled back to free her toes, the woman using this time to thread her hand through Teddy's arm.

"Mr. Day, when are you going to come to dinner? Mother

won't be kept waiting much longer, and Father is most anxious to discuss his purchasing a steamboat from you." She blinked her stubby lashes at him.

Flora squelched her retort, gripping the delicately carved handle of the parasol and fighting the urge to wallop the toe stomper with it. If this parade of Southern belles was how it had been since Teddy had returned home, she had more competition than she realized. Irritated that she hadn't thought of the notoriety of Willow Dupré's competition bringing more potential brides to his side, she glared at her assailant. She would simply have to adjust her plan after this development.

Teddy's jaw fell open. "I had no idea that he was ready to purchase, Miss Pimpernel. I thought he was still thinking about it."

"Father listens to Mother." She allowed her painted fan to slowly draw across her cheek. "And his daughters."

Flora stifled a gasp. She had enough romantic ladies in her home to know of the famed Parisian fan maker Duvelleroy's pamphlet on the language of the fan and their scandalous meanings. *Is she truly hinting that she is in love with Teddy?* She pursed her lips, thankful of Teddy's obliviousness to that little piece of coquetry.

"And we insisted a steamboat was something we need if we are to maintain our high standing in society, and that you are the only one we wish to design it," Miss Pimpernel finished.

"Then I shall send round a note, and perhaps we can arrange a meeting for this coming week. If your mother and father are agreeable, of course."

At the lift in his shoulders and bright response, Miss Pimpernel must have taken it as a sign of fondness for her as she clutched his arm. "Our mother is always agreeable, isn't that right, Mathilda?"

The lady in blue with a slight resemblance to Miss Pimpernel nodded but kept silent, her lovely green eyes wide, taking in the conversation. "Yes, Josephine."

Miss Josephine Pimpernel tossed her wilted curls and cast the other three young ladies a triumphant grin as the raven-haired one in the group with a perfect figure, minus an unfortunate chin that seemed to wish to double, chose that moment to pop open her parasol, sending her rivals skittering to the side to avoid losing an eye.

"Sandrine," Penelope chided, rolling her copy of *Harper's Bazaar* as if she wished to throttle someone with it.

At the sharp elbow in her ribs, Flora yelped and lifted her parasol to ward off another belle, only to find Olive giving her a telling lift of the brows and miming grabbing Teddy and pointing away from the group. Knowing Olive would not rest until she acted, Flora cleared her throat, hoping to garner Teddy's attention from the ladies, but that just served to bring a few snickers from the women surrounding him as they took yet another step closer to him, further blocking Flora from his view.

"So desperate," whispered Miss Josephine to Miss Penelope, who hid her laugh behind her magazine before Miss Penelope tapped Miss Sandrine on the shoulder, forcing the curvaceous lady to surrender her hold on Teddy.

"But I do believe I asked you the moment you returned to port, Mr. Day, and you still haven't given me a firm date, as you stated you did not have your diary with you and could not promise anything as yet. So I think it is only fair that you attend me before the Misses Pimpernels and Sandrine Fontenot," Miss Penelope cooed. "Steamboat order or not."

"I'm afraid I must attend to business before leisure, Miss Penelope and Miss Fontenot." He tipped his hat to each lady, which Flora supposed was meant to be reassuring. Yet poor Miss Josephine Pimpernel looked as if she were about to cry at the unintentional slight, while Penelope smiled sweetly through gritted teeth.

Flora twirled her parasol impatiently, earning protests from the women about her as they gripped their chapeaus and scuttled closer to Teddy. "Come on, Tacy and Olive," she muttered, sauntering down the sidewalk. Even though she had chased Teddy Day all the way to New Orleans, her pride wouldn't allow her to chase him further . . . well, not today at least.

Two

Theodore Day was not prepared for his heart to beat again. Flora was the last person he expected to see, and while her presence ripped him back to the very near and painful past, he was thankful to have an old friend in the city, one that did not have any romantic entanglements up her puffed sleeve, which would certainly help him in getting his heart and head straight. A fellow should only have to endure one broken heart, and yet he had *two* broken engagements following him through life and at only six and twenty years of age. He would be a fool to allow himself to fall in love again . . . especially since it had been only two months since Willow had ended things.

Tactfully extricating himself from the untimely ambush, Theodore adjusted his jacket, gripped his leather strap securing his sketches that he had forgotten to hand the footman, and jogged down the street after Flora and her sisters, his breath catching as he drew closer to his childhood friend. "Flora!" He called as loud as he dared for fear of summoning more eligible ladies from their front parlors.

She looked over her shoulder to him and twirled the handle of her frilly parasol so that the tassels fanned out around her, the sun catching on her loosed golden curls from beneath her chapeau. While disheveled from her journey and glistening, he liked this unkempt version of the usually polished Flora Wingfield.

"Sorry about that." He released a short laugh to dispel his unease, rubbing his unusually sweaty hands over his jacket.

"Quite the little club." She smiled softly, keeping her gaze on her sisters, who were hurrying toward the wagonette that had at last turned onto Mrs. Dubois's drive. "If they are the reasoning behind your attempt at changing your appearance, your disguise is not working."

He brushed his fingers across his stubble. "A club *not* of my choosing, let me assure you. I'd much rather focus on my family's business, but alas . . ." He shook his head, adjusting his broad-brimmed hat that had shifted in his bolt for freedom. Ever since Willow Dupré's outlandish competition where he had "won" the coveted place of Willow's fiancé for all of half a week, he had become the most sought-after bachelor in the city with a continuous parade of women catching him unawares about New Orleans. And now he could not even go for a walk on his own avenue without tripping over a belle at every corner, a fact his older brother, Carlisle, teased him mercilessly over, which was even more tiresome given that Carlisle was always attempting to take control over every aspect of the family business based solely on the grounds he was the eldest. Theodore was just as capable of closing the deal as he was designing and overseeing the building of the luxury riverboats, if only Carlisle would cease this relentless pursuit of power and give him room to grow. Age and line in birth had nothing to do with his capability. "If it were up to me, I'd remain a bachelor after what Willow put me through."

Flora shook her head. "I cannot imagine the pain of being jilted."

Twice, he added silently, cringing at that ugly word . . . but what other would do? Rejected. Scorned. Abandoned. Unloved. No, jilted was the least horrible description. "I would not wish it on anyone."

She paused in her promenade and rested her pale hand on his arm, her brilliant blue eyes betraying her pity. "But would you really have wished to marry a woman who loved another, despite her unfortunate timing of coming to that realization?"

Theodore shoved his hands in his pockets and sighed. He had forgotten how direct Flora could be. "In the two months since Willow turned me away, I have mulled over that very question, coming to a different conclusion each time it seemed, but now, with clear vision, I can say that *no*. I would not have wanted a bride who wished for another groom."

"Well, thank goodness for that," Flora admitted, almost sounding *relieved*? She looked up to the oak trees, a new light in her countenance, and continued their walk.

He scrunched his lips to the side. Was she happy that he was healing? Or was she happy for another reason entirely? He thought of the time they spent together during Willow's competition, as friends of course. Flora had always looked out for him and even championed him to Willow, but during that brief time of his engagement, Flora had disappeared and he hadn't seen her since that fleeting moment at the announcement ball where she hadn't been able to look him in the eyes. He had briefly wondered at the time but did not put much thought into it, as his mind was on Willow and their future and how to release his own dream of shipbuilding to support his bride. Yet after that horrible night of being released instead of his dearest desire coming true, he had scrutinized every conversation between their engagement and leading up to that night in hopes of finding closure. Flora had never been anything but a friend to him, so her sudden change toward him had confused Theodore to no end, *unless* she had known what Willow had been about to do and was unable to warn him. And if that were the case— Theodore shook his head free from that dark evening. "So, summering in New Orleans, what brought that on?"

"I suppose it is rather surprising." Flora's focus fixed on a magnolia tree at the corner, where two boys were busying themselves climbing to the top. "But, uh, I wanted a change of pace from the usual Newport scene and crowd. Coincidentally, Father is looking into making an investment with your company, as well as a few others, of which I'm sure you are aware."

His brows rose at that. He certainly would have written Flora if his father or Carlisle had informed him about a business deal with the banker, known among his peers as having the Midas touch. To have garnered Mr. Wingfield's interest in the Days' luxury riverboat company would mean their business would likely double in size by the end of the year.

"No, I hadn't heard," he admitted.

She lifted her gloved fingers to her lips as she paused outside the Dubois residence. "Then I shouldn't have said anything. I'm certain Father will be approaching Mr. Day as soon as we are settled, if he hasn't already."

At the shrieks coming from the Dubois estate, Flora laughed as Tacy and Ermengarde pushed through the group on the brick path leading to the steps and rushed inside. "My youngest sisters are no doubt hurrying in an attempt to claim the best rooms for themselves after they greet my great-aunt."

"Then I'm afraid you will have the smallest room in the estate, and I will be to blame for keeping you." He chuckled and leaned against the short black iron fence bordering the property.

"It doesn't matter to me which room I get," Flora replied, closing her parasol.

"So how is she anyway?" He coughed as the question that had been plaguing him spilled out.

Flora dropped her gaze, worrying her bottom lip, surely knowing how much the question cost him. "She is happy. I'm certain you've read the papers on her nuptials to Cullen back in April?"

He nodded, the burn returning to his stomach at the humiliation of being jilted and then having his fiancée marry someone else the very next day. He supposed, though, Willow's hasty marriage was better than Bernadette's cruel elopement with his chum *before* breaking it off with him.

Flora brushed her fingers down his sleeve, bringing him back to the present. "Teddy, please don't pretend with me that it hasn't affected you. Has it been so very difficult recovering from Willow's rejection?"

Willow. The name did not cause him such sharp pain as it had in the first few weeks, and now that it had been two months, he was surprised to find that his heart had been slowly mending despite the yearning to call Willow *his* darling Mrs. Day. But that would never be, and after such rejection two times over, Theodore doubted he would ever call someone his own who did not have any design on being with him other than just loving him. He gestured to the knot of women behind them, who were still staring after him. "As you can see, I am reminded of my loss at every turn by the single, female residents of New Orleans. With you here, however, I might be able to move past it."

Her eyes widened. "Oh? How so?"

"Well, for one, I don't have to worry about your misinterpreting our friendship and trying to entrap me in the net of matrimony." He laughed and pulled a small cluster of blooms from a lantana bush and crushed it between his fingers, the red-and-yellow petals staining his fingertips, leaving behind a delicate, sweet scent.

Flora pulled a lace-trimmed handkerchief from her sleeve and dabbed at her cheeks that seemed a tad brighter than only seconds prior. "Is it always so warm here?"

"There's a breeze today." He suppressed his laughter at her look of incredulity. "It is a cool day for June."

She sucked in a breath. "I had hoped Miss Penelope was merely jesting. My family is never going to forgive me for dragging them here for the summer."

He shifted the narrow leather tube. "I wish I could see you inside, but my brother is awaiting these sketches for a meeting with a potential buyer this afternoon."

She straightened at once. "Please, do not be late on my account. I well remember how Carlisle could be when he grew impatient as a lad. Is he still the same?"

"Worse." He chuckled and bowed. "Until tonight then, Miss Wingfield."

"Tonight?"

He grinned. "I will, of course, be attending your aunt's ball. My mother will be thrilled to know that it is a welcoming party for you and your family. She adores your mother."

"Which will come as a pleasant surprise to my family, as well. You had best be on your way, because I need to greet my aunt and, apparently, ready myself, and that will take some doing with only one maid between five sisters and a cousin." She curtsied and started up the brick walkway.

"We will send over an invitation for dinner this week," he called after her, but before she could reply, he set off at a jog, knowing that time had gotten away from him again. He did not need to give Carlisle any more fodder for treating him like an errant employee.

He trotted up the front steps into his family's residence on St. Charles Avenue. While it was not the grandest of houses on the avenue, he preferred their smaller, more modest two-story to the expansive mansions continuously being added to the avenue as New Orleans's most wealthy joined their ranks. He tossed his hat onto the hall tree and shrugged off the leather strap.

As expected, Carlisle stormed out of the study, fists on his hips, his chest pulling against his silk waistcoat, sleeves rolled to the elbows, sweat coating the fabric under his arms. "Where have you been? Did you finish those sketches yet? Honestly, I do not know why you have to seek inspiration at the dock office when you have a perfectly good desk here. I have reserved a table at *Antoine's* for my meeting with Mr. Hebert, which is in half an hour. You know I like to get there early, and now I am already late."

Theodore held up the cylinder containing his sketches and shifted past his brother into their shared office. "All here. Seems to me that if he is *your* client, as you so often remind me, *you* should be the one designing everything for this order."

Carlisle snorted, snatching the cylinder from Theodore, sliding open the top and shaking out the papers, unrolling them atop his Brazilian cherrywood desk. "It's called delegating. And as this will be *my* business one day and not yours, all intellectual property of my employees belongs to me. Work shrewder, not harder, is my mantra."

Theodore folded his arms at this and leaned against the doorway. As usual, he did all the work, while Carlisle received the credit from Father and the clients.

Carlisle sent him a grin as he unrolled his sleeves and buttoned the cuffs. "Oh, don't sulk, little brother. You know that as head of the company, it is important for me to spend time with each of our clients to make them feel heard and their opinions valued, which in turn will bring more business and a higher sale's price."

"*Future* head." Theodore pushed off the doorframe, refusing to allow his brother to manipulate him into recanting the way he felt. "I don't see why the business defaults to you on the grounds of your being a few years older. I am just as qualified as you."

"Of course you are." Carlisle winked and grabbed his coat off the back of his chair.

"Well, if that's how you really feel, my boy," Father called from behind in the doorway, "I think it is time to tell you both what I've been mulling over for quite a stretch now and have just finished writing up the documents supporting my decision." Father moved to his desk and drew out a thick stack of papers, dropping it on his desk. "We shall have a competition to set aside this argument once and for all. It isn't healthy for you two to have such a thing between you."

Carlisle and Theodore shared a worried glance. Father and his competitions were always tricky and were rarely worth the effort of going through for the prize that almost always turned out to be some sort of character-building lesson instead of something tangible. But, as it had been years since their last little competition, Theodore supposed it was time for another. Although he was rather taken aback that perhaps he had not hidden, as well as he had thought, that the future of the company had been a source of contention between himself and Carlisle since Theodore's return from Paris, if Father had gone through all the trouble of having papers drawn up.

Theodore suppressed a sigh. "What do you have in mind, sir?"

Father leaned over Carlisle's desk, nodding over Theodore's work. "Excellent lines, Theodore. I think Mr. Hebert will approve."

Theodore's chest swelled at this unexpected praise.

"He will if I make it to the appointment on time," Carlisle muttered, rolling up the plans and slipping them inside the leather tube.

Father steepled his fingers, trilling them together. "Let's say that the brother with the most sales at summer's end shall be named the new head of Day's Luxury Line, a fitting way for me to retire."

"What?" The brothers gaped at their father.

"I know I have only mentioned retiring in passing, but it seems most of the gentlemen my age with sons are taking a step away from—"

"Father, you cannot be serious." Carlisle paused in shrugging on his morning coat. "It is absurd to make up such an outlandish plan, not without putting serious thought into the ramifications of such a scheme."

Theodore nodded. He did not like the idea of being pitted against his brother for something so important. No matter Carlisle's authoritarian, overbearing nature, he cared deeply for his brother and did not wish for Carlisle to feel ousted of his inheritance, even if the idea of the eldest receiving the lion's share was an archaic practice that his French aristocratic mother saw as the natural order of things, who claimed that it had nothing to do with favoritism or love. It was simply how things were done.

"Actually I have given this serious thought, and there is no avoiding it. A kingdom cannot survive under the rule of two kings, and one way or another, you boys will have to deal with someone taking the head position, so why not a joust of wits like kings of old to claim your land?" Father looped his thumbs into his vest pockets.

Carlisle crossed his arms, fury lining his features.

"But instead of winning all or nothing, which would hardly breed familial goodwill, the profits will be split with my taking a thirty-percentage stake, the head fifty percent and the remainder goes to the vanquished. In any event, you both will be taken care of with a generous share of the company, but the head will be running the business and therefore will receive over double the profits for his guidance."

The vein in Carlisle's neck throbbed. "I have devoted *my life* to this business, Father. It has always been implied that Day's Luxury Line would be mine someday." He ran his fingers through his dark-blond hair. "And are you just going to forget that Theodore has been out of the picture for months with that ridiculous trip of his to New York?"

"It was the *only* break I have had from company business in years," Theodore interjected, irritated that his brother kept bringing up the issue whenever it suited his point, which made him wish to agree to this scheme all the more. "What do you think I was doing in Paris? I was studying interiors, architecture, and European steamboats in order to bring a fresh perspective to our industry. Or have you forgotten the dozens of new designs I sent home to you that resulted in a surge of interest in our business, even garnering notice from the Anchor Line? Which is no small feat. I have a bid in with them right now to build a boat for their route to Vicksburg."

"And we appreciate your efforts, Theodore, because while New Orleans is no longer the hub for riverboat building like it was when I first began, our line remains the most coveted in America thanks to *both* of your efforts." Father lifted his hands. "Still, this challenge is not to be disputed. My decision stands. The brother with the most riverboats on order by the end of summer—without the aid of offering steep discounts—will be named the head of the company. And as for the ready-made model boats, you will each be given two with which you can design the interior and sell while securing orders for more." Theodore made a move to reclaim his sketches, but Father stepped between the brothers. "*After* today's sale, obviously, which will *not* be counted toward the competition."

Carlisle gritted his jaw, the muscles in his face tightening. "Very well. I will win this company fair and square, and *when* I do, I don't want to hear another word of complaint from you, Ted."

Theodore grinned, clapping his father on the shoulder. "Thank you, sir, for this opportunity to prove myself. Now, if you'll excuse me, I have a lot of planning to do." He started up the narrow stairs to his room to commence sketching, then snapped his fingers as he remembered his hasty invitation to Flora. Turning on his heel, he took the steps two at a time. He poked his head into the parlor. "Mother? The Wingfields are in town for the summer, so I invited them over for dinner this week. Can you send them an invitation for whatever night works best for you?"

"Theodore Pierre Day, I have guests," Mother scolded, setting down her tea and gesturing to Mrs. Pimpernel and her daughters, Josephine and Mathilda, who both straightened at the sight of him. "Who have already informed me of the Wingfields' arrival in a wagonette, no less."

How did they get here so quickly after cornering me?

"Teddy, what an unexpected pleasure to see you twice in a single day." Miss Josephine smiled at him, dipping her head in what he assumed was supposed to be a demure fashion.

Is it? But he returned her smile with a bow. "My apologies for the unseemly interruption—"

"Nonsense." Mathilda blinked her lashes at him. "We were just discussing your coming to dinner as you promised, so I hope you will attend us before extending an invitation to Miss Winfield."

"*Wingfield,*" he absentmindedly corrected, the competition fresh in his mind. Carlisle might think he had an advantage with his being chummy with the businessmen of New Orleans, but Theodore had an even more unique opportunity to secure sales thanks to Willow. He grinned at the Misses Pimpernels. "How does tomorrow work for your diary?"

"Perfect!" The ladies fanned themselves at Mrs. Pimpernel's answer.

"Then I shall see you all at eight." He bowed once more and, before Mother could invite him to join the husband hunters, darted up the stairs to make a list of New Orleans's most wealthy, starting with the Pimpernels, and how to get them to spend a small fortune on a luxurious boat that they surely did not need.

Three

A regal woman with snowy hair arranged in an old-fashioned rolled coiffure stood in the great hall that was decorated in burgundy rose boughs with massive floral arrangements atop gold draped tables lining the chamber. Despite her hair style, Great-Auntie Violet was dressed in a fashionable gown of lavender brocade and yards of creamy lace, petting something small and fluffy in her arms, a long ear draped over her satin sleeve. *A bunny?* Flora repeatedly poked Olive in the arm against the unbidden laughter swelling her throat.

"Florian! Hyacinth! It's delightful to see you, my dears. It has been far too long." The grand elderly lady swept her arm wide, the action jarring the rabbit, sending it leaping from her arms, its nails scraping against the hardwood floor as it flopped about trying to secure a foothold in a desperate attempt to scurry through the open front door to escape the influx of people. Yet the butler was faster, slamming the door and barring the rabbit's flight.

Great-Auntie Violet beamed at them as if nothing were

out of the ordinary and turned to a large, gilded cage replica of her mansion, set in the corner of the room, and from its second story she withdrew a second rabbit with a mottled coat of gold, brown, and cream, and resumed her stroking. "My dears, please make my home yours while you are here. I want none of this formal *great-aunt* nonsense every time you address me, as you so often do in your letters. You may call me as your father does, Auntie Violet. And while you are here, your parents have charged me with finding suitable husbands for all, besides Nora of course." She paraded down the line of young women, appraising them with a pleased smile. "With your fortunes, though a miserly sum in New York"—she looked pointedly to Father—"and lovely appearance, I believe you will have your choice of offers."

Mother clasped her hands to her lace jabot. "You hear that, my dear Florian? Grandbabies are not so far away after all."

Father gave her a halfhearted smile in return and checked his pocket watch.

"And to begin, I have summoned the most elite New Orleans families with eligible bachelor sons for an intimate ball tonight."

Mother's eyes widened as understanding flooded her features. "*Tonight?* As in a few hours?"

"Yes." Auntie blinked as if Mother was suffering from the heat in making her repeat her statement. "You will have ample time to dress. And it is not as if you piloted the boat into port, Hyacinth, so you shouldn't be too exhausted from your travels to dance."

Father took Mother's hand, and Flora knew he was gently squeezing it as he answered, "Your generosity is touching,

Auntie. After all, the sooner we marry off Flora, the sooner I can return to my office in New York."

Flora chewed the inside of her cheek against the sting of his words. He had never acted as if she were a burden before this summer. But in recent weeks, she had noticed him growing steadily more and more vexed, snapping at the servants and occasionally her should she ask him a question while he was in his study. And every time he received a telegram, he would reach for the port, which led to far too many dinners passionately discussing his daughters needing to marry and begin their own families, leaving him in peace.

Auntie Violet tenderly patted Father's cheek. Olive elbowed her so hard, Flora fairly gasped. No one ever treated Father like a lad. Not even Flora's grandparents had done such a thing when they were living. "Remember, Florian, returning to New York at this time is not wise, especially after that dreadful business with—"

"Let us not speak of it." He sent Auntie Violet a sharp look, cutting her off.

But instead of cringing like most from his strident tone, Auntie Violet patted his cheek once more. "You poor dear. You're much too stressed. Well, maybe this summer you will learn to decrease your frenetic pace enough to savor life. For what is the use of all that money you keep piling up in that bank of yours, if you do not stop to experience its benefits every now and again?"

"Really, Auntie Violet." Mother's cheeks brightened, glancing toward the servants bustling about, readying the house for the ball. "Such a topic is not appropriate."

"Nonsense. It's only inappropriate to discuss money when one does not possess it, which is not the case with our party."

With a kiss to each cheek, Auntie Violet sent the daughters up the winding staircase to claim their chambers on the second and third floors and to dress once their trunks had been delivered to the appropriate room.

Tacy surged ahead of the girls and took the stairs in a surprising burst of speed, Ermengarde and Nora on her heels, birdcage in hand with the poor bird squeaking in protest, flapping its wings to balance itself while Olive and Flora gripped Cornelia by each elbow and helped drive her up the stairs, poor Cornelia's panting growing by the step.

"Never fear, Cousin, for if those girls take the last guest room on the second floor, I'll have words with them. You will not be made to climb to the third floor for the entirety of the summer," Flora assured Cornelia at the landing.

Cornelia, unable to speak, nodded and patted her brow with her silk handkerchief as Flora and Olive each took an end of the hall, searching for the rooms with blank name cards in the bronze holders affixed to the guest-room doors. At the pounding of feet coming from above and the bickering down the far hall, Flora grinned, knowing Tacy and Ermengarde were too busy arguing over a room while Nora was endeavoring to find the best one upstairs, which meant there was at least one left to be claimed that wasn't allocated to Mother and Father. She found the room and, not daring to leave it unguarded, waved Cornelia over, who waddled down the crimson carpet, the floorboards squeaking slightly under each step.

"Thank goodness you found one," Cornelia murmured, her hand on her abdomen. "My mother says that women in our family have the good fortune to have our bodies expand to appear full term by the time we are only six months with child." She snorted. "Good fortune indeed to be nine months pregnant in size for the whole of a Southern summer."

Flora laughed, then smothered it at Cornelia's glare. *It seems my sisters aren't the only ones put out over my exaggeration of the pleasant climate, but the novels set in New Orleans that I've read made little mention of the heat.* "Take a seat on the bed while the girls are distracted. Ermengarde and Tacy will soon see where arguing gets them in about a half hour when there are no rooms on the second floor to be had." Patting her cousin on the shoulder, Flora and Olive climbed the stairs to the third level.

Knowing better than Nora than to choose the largest of the rooms to avoid a fight with the losing sister of the second-floor battle, Flora continued to the far end of the hall and pushed open the final door, smiling at the lovely wall covering pattern of pink roses, emerald ribbons, and little blue birds. Light streamed in from the trio of windows in the corner turret, the branches of an oak tree reaching the panes. A small writing desk sat under the far right window that would most certainly prove a most delightful place for her correspondence with Willow. A quaint fireplace that looked like it hadn't hosted many fires was on the interior wall that most likely shared a chimney with the next room. Atop the mantel sat a small fancy silver-and-bronze clock with bronze statues of a gentleman and lady playing croquet on either side of the timepiece. The bed, though small, had mahogany posts that supported the yards and yards of netting that, when released from their tiebacks, would form a cage over the sleeping occupant. She sucked in a breath. Were the mosquitoes so numerous that it required netting to keep them at bay? *Tacy is never going to cease plaguing me over this if she gets bit on her face.*

In a flurry of trunks arriving, unpacking, and shaking out of dresses and overskirts, without the assistance of a maid, it was a miracle that Flora had finally been allowed into the shared bathroom before it was time for the guests to arrive. But, having been the sole advocate for this trip, Flora had acquiesced to being the last to use it between her sisters, though her patience was beginning to wane with Tacy's and Ermengarde's constant bickering that could be heard from under her third-floor bedroom floor, as it turned out there was no fourth bedroom upstairs to be had.

Dressed in a wrinkled gown of canary yellow, Flora flung open the middle window of the turret to escape the arguing and, pressing her hands to the sill, leaned out to examine the oak tree's graceful branches that bent right up to her window, forming a wonderful place to perch—if one wasn't afraid of heights. At the sight of carriages already lining the avenue, none of which bore the Days' family crest, sending her racing pulse into a thud of disappointment, she lifted her gaze to the stars peeking through the leaves and drew a deep breath of the thick evening air devoid of the afternoon's oppressive heat. *Lord Jesus, you know that deep in my heart I never thought it was possible that Teddy could see me . . . until Willow chose Cullen for her husband.* As always, she felt a twinge in her gut, remembering that she was the reason Cullen had been able to convince Willow of his affection and thus being the direct reason for the jilting and Teddy's humiliation. *Would it be too much to ask for Teddy to realize that I am more than a friend? And if he does, help me to tell him the truth as to how Willow changed her mind on whom to marry.*

Cornelia's steady huff sounded behind her. Flora pulled back inside as her cousin lowered herself to the narrow bed, resting her hand on her peach satin ruching that did little to disguise her swollen abdomen, a sheen of sweat already covering her temples, matting her rich russet hair as she lifted her swollen ankles atop a pillow, muttering, "I will never forgive my husband for taking a business trip and leaving my side." She reached out her hand to Flora and sighed. "I know I shouldn't complain so. Thank you for convincing Aunt and Uncle to take me under their wing. I couldn't imagine doing this without you all by my side to distract me until the baby arrives."

Flora sank down on the hardwood floor beside her cousin. "From my years being Willow Dupré's dearest friend, I know providing for family can be a test. I am certain your husband would rather be at your side, seeing you look so lovely, than in Paris, overseeing the setup of the Duprés' new factory."

"As long as he returns in time for the birth of our first child in September, I suppose I *will* forgive him, especially since he is bringing me a fresh wardrobe from Worth for after the baby." She sent a longing look at Flora's gown trimmed in lace and bustle with its matching clusters of silk yellow roses. "Speaking of gowns, you are resplendent and are certain to turn heads tonight." She grinned, adjusting the tulle about Flora's shoulders a hint lower. "So, how are you going to have that contrived magical moment with your darling Mr. Day tonight?"

"How indeed." Flora laughed, if only to cover her growing anxiety. For the past two months, she had planned their reunion to the minute, but she had planned on it happening when they were *alone*. And now that the moment had

39

finally arrived for her to attempt to garner his attention and redeem her appearance from earlier today, her mouth grew dry even as her palms began sweating through her gloves. At the sound of rattling carriage wheels pausing at their drive, she flitted to the open window, searching and hoping for a glimpse of Teddy. "My plan will likely have to wait, because judging from the line of carriages continually growing along the avenue, this is no intimate ball that Great-Auntie Violet assured Mother it was. She is not going to be pleased."

"Indeed. Still, there is one certain way your mother will forget her irritation. Simply fill your dance card with eligible bachelors."

"Yes, but I don't wish to dance with just any beau tonight." Flora helped Cornelia to standing, adjusted her cousin's bustle, and the pair of them took the corner stairs to the second floor before descending the massive, curving stairs to the great hall that served as Auntie's ballroom, which was already filling with guests, dressed in only the latest of fashions.

It was quite disconcerting not recognizing a soul among the masses. After years in New York's Four Hundred club, she knew most in her set, while here she felt curious eyes turn on her for the first time since her debut. And that was *before* word circulated of her father's peculiar view on his daughters' inheritance and the curiosity evolved into apathy.

"They are staring at us," Flora whispered to Cornelia, pausing under the stained-glass window at the landing, her hand resting on the Flemish oak rail.

"Correction, they are staring at *you*, my dear," Cornelia said, her eyes sparkling in the candlelight. "You and your sisters' arrival is probably the most exciting occurrence in New Orleans high society in a decade."

Her mother caught sight of them, flicked her fan open, and motioned for them to take their places in the greeting line in the grand foyer beneath the copper chandelier, a single brow lifted in warning not to dawdle further. Flora swept past the onlookers and stood at the front of her sisters as the eldest and curtsied to the guests, who continued to pour into the foyer, handing their wraps to the butler and footmen, greeting Auntie Violet and continuing down the endless line that was the Wingfield ladies and then on to the great hall, where more footmen swarmed about with silver trays of refreshments.

Flora attempted to focus on each guest introduced to her, but her attention kept returning to the arrivals that flowed out to the sidewalk, waiting for admittance. Her stomach flipped at the thought of Teddy taking her hand when it was his turn. Lord help her if he kissed it. She might actually swoon for the first time, as she had far too much time on her hands waiting for the bathroom and had picked apart their chance meeting earlier. And the more she had dwelled upon it, the worse she seemed. She must follow through with another chance meeting to erase any doubt in Teddy's mind that she was to be more than a friend to him.

"Miss Wingfield, a pleasure to see you again so soon." Mr. Grayson pressed a kiss to her hand before she even had a chance to register that he was holding it, his thumb grazing back and forth over the top of her hand as he leaned on his cane.

She pulled it back, grimacing at the mark he had left on her gloves from his mustache pomade. "Mr. Grayson, I had no idea you were acquainted with my great-aunt."

"I'm not. I am a guest of Mr. Bridgewater." He gestured to the man Father was greeting, drawing Father's gaze.

Father stepped beside Flora, his hand on her elbow, guiding the three of them from the receiving line. "Ah, Mr. Grayson. It was sly of you not to mention aboard the *Belle Memphis* that you are the vice president of Wellington Sugar. I have been attempting to meet with you for the past two months, after I discovered how amiable you were to signing over Wellington's Parisian factory to Mr. Dempsey for a mere pittance, for I thought you would be more open to a discussion."

Flora stiffened at the name of Willow's former competitor that had also been her husband's, Cullen Dempsey, former mentor. Because of Wellington's Machiavellian need for power, he had forced Willow's board into giving her an ultimatum—marry or hand over the company to her cousin. He had almost succeeded in destroying Willow's reign, but because of Cullen's decision to garner information for the Pinkertons, Wellington was now under house arrest while he awaited trial for dozens of crimes, including manslaughter.

Mr. Grayson shrugged, fiddling with the carved cane head. "I preferred to retain my anonymity as I needed to become better acquainted with your family before I decided to meet with you and see what you could possibly do for me that Wellington could not." His gaze lingered on Flora for a moment before returning to Father. "Besides, that sale was approved by the former vice president. I was swiftly promoted and replaced the defector after that incident and was warned by Wellington not to betray him, which made me hesitant to meet with the man who had undercut my boss on multiple occasions."

Father gave his business chuckle, as if his past actions were of little consequence to tonight's goal. "He understands why I did what I did."

"Yes, well, be that as it may, I don't like to announce my position, especially in light of recent events, what with Heathcliff Wellington being falsely accused and imprisoned in his home while awaiting trial."

"I wouldn't say 'falsely,'" Flora muttered. *Cullen's findings are enough to see Wellington behind bars for the rest of his life. All of America knows that it is only the man's interminable wealth protecting him from jail at the moment.*

Father squeezed her arm. "Well, those events, be they false or not, were not by any fault of yours. A man with such means does not become so without making a few enemies along the way. So, tell me what brings you so far away from Wellington's headquarters?"

"Yes, well, as Wellington cannot leave the house, he sent me to New Orleans for a few weeks to meet with our suppliers, namely the Bridgewaters, as their sugar plantation is by far the largest in the area." Mr. Grayson narrowed his gaze. "Which I have heard that you are attempting to capture . . . an odd turn of events, as you do not have a hold in the sugar world."

Father shrugged. "If you had met with me, perhaps this challenge could have been avoided. Regardless, I am certain we can come to some sort of arrangement now that I know you are staying with the Bridgewaters, but we mustn't keep you, Mr. Grayson, eh, Flora?"

I wasn't . . . "Of course." She curtsied to the gentleman, who, with a chuckle aimed at her father, slipped into the crowd.

"If he asks you to luncheon, accept," Father commanded under his breath.

Flora blinked. For a man who never approved of any

gentlemen for his daughters, especially one only wishing to acquaint himself with the family because of their holdings, Father was approving the unctuous, smarmy Mr. Grayson? "But—"

"He represents Wellington Sugar, and his amity is a vital component in my procuring the Bridgewaters' cane sugar supply."

"You are going against Heathcliff Wellington?" Flora gasped. From what Willow had divulged to her, no good came from an alliance with that man, and if one was going against . . . Flora shuddered at the potential ramifications. "Whatever do you want with him?"

Father strained his neck to see who was coming through the door. "I bought out Mr. Crain at an exorbitant sum, after he realized Miss Dupré—I mean, Mrs. Dempsey—wasn't stepping down, and I am now a member of the board for Dupré Sucré."

"Surely Willow would have told me if she had sent you on such a dangerous mission."

He snorted and reached for his pocket watch. "That child doesn't even know the real reason why I am here. I have decided, for the good of the company, that I need to secure Dupré Sucré as the Bridgewaters' new refinery."

"But—"

Father snapped the gold watch shut with a grunt. "Flora, I have been more than generous with my time in explaining things that no woman needs to understand. So, for once, do not argue, and see to it that you do as I say," he said over his shoulder, returning to Mother's side.

"Yes, Father," she whispered, resuming her position beside Olive, who quirked a brow in question. Not daring to anger

Father further, Flora merely shook her head and smiled at the next guest, trying to dismiss the horrid feeling of Mr. Grayson's gaze. She looked again for Teddy, but as the line receded, there was no Day family member in sight. Auntie ushered the family into the ballroom, where the guests and several gentlemen continued to swarm about her.

Between tête-à-têtes, Flora surreptitiously glanced over her silk fan in an attempt to spot Teddy's arrival when Mother poked her in the corset stays, jarring her back to the present to find that Mr. Turner had departed, and in his place stood Mr. Grayson.

"Our dear Bradford asked you how you were enjoying New Orleans, Flora."

Flora blinked at the grinning, gangly gentleman before her, his eyes wide in rapt attention. The man had gone from unnoticed to *dear* Bradford simply because of Father's next business deal? "My apologies, Mr. Grayson. The carriage ride from the dock gave me a glimpse into the wonders New Orleans has to offer, and I look forward to exploring more of this illustrious city." *There. That should save me from a scolding, as I could have pointed out that I have not had time to explore, for I just arrived on the same boat as he.*

His smile broadened to reveal his molars. "Illustrious indeed! I have visited here once before and would love to explore more with you, if you wish?"

Oh no. She kept her smile firmly in place. Had she successfully avoided his requests for the whole of the steamboat ride to the port of New Orleans only to fail now in a moment of reckless distraction?

"Provided we have a chaperone, of course," he supplied, as if *that* were the reason for her hesitation.

"She would be delighted to accept, Mr. Grayson," Mother interjected before Flora could form an excuse. "Let us say . . . next Thursday?"

"That would be lovely," he replied, whirling his cane in a flourish and almost whacking the bustle of a nearby belle, whose husband scowled at Mr. Grayson. "And may I have the honor of the opening dance? Miss Bridgewater has told me so much about you, Miss Wingfield. I feel as if we have been acquainted far longer than a boat ride down the river."

Ignoring the odd comment, her fingers tightened around her dance card.

Mother pressed her lips into a smile, tugged the card from Flora, and moved to hand it to Mr. Grayson.

In a desperate attempt to liberate herself, she brushed her hand on Mr. Grayson's sleeve, keeping him from flipping open the card and claiming a spot. "As you are staying with Miss Bridgewater and her family, perhaps it would be advantageous to offer her the first dance?"

"Nonsense, I've done business with them for years in one capacity or another. Besides, she is far more interested in Mr. Theodore Day. In fact, Mr. Day called on Mr. Bridgewater merely an hour ago and spoke with Miss Bridgewater prior to his meeting. They were discussing you at great length." He scribbled down his name for the waltz and the Esmeralda polka, his presumption in claiming two dances irking her, and handed it back.

Despite her first dance being taken by the grimy fellow, warmth flooded her being and she dipped her head to hide her smile. "Mr. Day has spoken of me?"

"Oh, yes. He told us all about how you have been such good friends since childhood." He glanced over his shoulder toward the foyer. "He and Miss Bridgewater should be arriving at any moment."

Well, there goes that dream. She held her smile at the information of Teddy escorting another woman to a party in *her* honor, allowing her mother to steer the conversation.

"Why, if it isn't Miss Flora Wingfield. I haven't seen you since you were a girl, building sandcastles on Bailey's Beach." A deep voice called from behind her, saving her from further conversation.

Flora turned to find a familiar gentleman, who possessed impressive broad shoulders and a small gap in his front teeth, his golden-flecked amber eyes giving him away. There was only one lad she had ever met who possessed such eyes. "Carlisle Day." She dipped into a curtsy, noting his gaze trailing over her for half a second. "I thought we might see each other tonight."

"Thought but not hoped?" He grinned, a far cry from the serious young man she recalled who was always too busy studying for Teddy or his friends.

She ran her fingers along the perimeter of her dance card, not knowing how to respond to that bit of nonsense that bordered on flirtation. "How have you been, sir?"

"Busy. Overseeing a steamboat business never ceases, night or day. And now I am quite grateful that Mother insisted I put aside my designs and come here tonight, as I would have missed seeing you looking so grown up and exquisite in that lovely shade of yellow."

Flora barely kept herself from glancing over her shoulder to see if he meant her. Carlisle had never strung so many words together directed to her before, much less in the form of a compliment. He had always been exceptionally kind to her, but certainly not *so* kind. "Thank you. I, uh—"

Olive grasped her elbow, saving her from forming a reply, and whispered, "Have you seen Teddy?"

"I believe his group of lady friends seized him upon sight and dragged him away, though he doesn't appear to be suffering." Carlisle chuckled and gestured with his glass to the piano in the corner of the room, where Teddy leaned against the top of the piano hemmed in by ladies on every side as he accompanied the hired pianist and sang Tchaikovsky's "None But the Lonely Heart," which had the ladies practically swooning at his feet as he reached the refrain, "'None but the lonely heart knows what I suffer, alone and parted far from joy.'"

"No, he doesn't appear to mind the attention," Flora murmured, casting a furtive look in Teddy's direction. It was difficult seeing him so, obviously still pining for Willow if he was performing such a ballad. And what was even more difficult was the fact of his being surrounded by so many ladies. But she supposed that when one was written about with such romantic flare in articles across the country, one was bound to attract every eligible lady in the area.

You are from one of the most elite families in New York. Hold your head high and approach the gentleman. She gritted her teeth, waiting for courage to fill her veins at her mother's familiar speech. Nothing. As much as Flora had planned on winning Teddy's heart, she had not thought of the humiliation of actually *chasing* a gentleman. She was the daughter of Florian Wingfield. She shouldn't have to resort to chasing. *And yet . . .* She worried her bottom lip. *It is Teddy.* And the last time she had waited for him to approach her, he did not but instead almost marched down the aisle with another. Flora shook her head. No. She could not

48

afford to do so again, unless she was willing to settle down with whatever bachelor her parents deemed worthy after Teddy married, leaving her with only her memories and her broken hopes of a future with him.

Carlisle's booming laugh brought her back to the present, and she gave a little laugh along with Olive, hoping that her distraction had not been too evident. When Carlisle was at last called away, Olive and Flora sauntered toward Teddy. Pausing in his line of vision, Flora pulled Olive close, her fan flapping wildly and lifting her golden curls from her shoulders in her frazzled state.

"I don't think I can do this," Flora whispered, her voice growing higher with each word.

"Mother has trained you to be a husband hunter. Are you going to stop now with your prey merely yards away, after dragging the family across the country for the entirety of the summer?" Olive returned from behind her own fan. "You will never forgive yourself if a Penelope of this world manages to snag your dream gentleman simply because you were too afraid to actually follow through on your plan." She crossed her arms. "You pretend to be brave in private, Flora, but words mean precious little if you cannot act."

Flora groaned through pressed lips. This was the worst part expected of a husband hunter. All of her sisters, even Olive, were shameless in their attentions, while Flora had always been more reserved. "If I must."

"You must, but first . . ." Olive plucked at Flora's puffed sleeve, her nose wrinkling. "You are perspiring far too much, and that color will not disguise it for long. Perhaps you should take a moment in the powder room prior to capturing Teddy before it stains your gown?"

Heat flooded her neck, which most likely did not help the situation. Without another word, Flora rustled out of the ballroom. She paused at the foot of the stairs, glancing about for the powder room, as Auntie's house was unlike the mansions she had grown accustomed to, where the ladies' powder room could be found on the landing between the first and second floors. She meandered down a second hall and opened a few doors, at last finding a small, dimly lit powder room. It was positively cramped inside, but she snatched a few toilet sheets from a wicker basket atop the marble vanity and dabbed away under her puffed narrow sleeve, dropping the soiled squares into the wastebasket below the vanity. She adjusted the tulle at her shoulders, leaned over the counter and drew a steadying breath, staring at her reflection in the gilded looking glass.

"You can do this." Yet the flushed blue-eyed lady in the glass looked anything but confident. With a grunt, she spun away, her bustle catching on the marble counter and her hem getting wrapped around her feet. She kicked it away and bumped into the doorframe on her way out. She paused in the hall, rolled back her shoulders, and assumed a confident air before swaying into the ballroom to find that the piano had been commandeered by Tacy, who hit multiple discords, her high voice dropping notes at every turn. Flora swallowed back a cringe at the performance, but it could not be helped. Whenever Tacy spotted a pianoforte, she could not be dissuaded from playing. *Mr. Vanderbilt compliments her talent once, and now she acts like the next Jenny Lind songbird.*

Sauntering about the great room, Flora noticed guests turning her way. Well aware of how her skirts were trailing behind her in a buttery cloud of tulle and rosettes, she lifted her head, proud of her Worth gown fresh from Paris. While some knickerbocker families felt the need to allow their gowns to season for a year in trunks in the attic to avoid seeming vulgar with their wealth, Flora was thankful that her mother did not follow that ridiculous practice. At a woman's tittering behind her, Flora turned, brows raised in question, but the woman only hid behind her fan, giggling all the more to her friend.

"Flora." Teddy appeared at her elbow.

"Teddy!" Her breath caught at his nearness. "I was just on my way to find you."

"Thank goodness for that, because I'm afraid . . . uh, you have a fragment of tissue stuck, um, under your, uh, your . . ." He scratched his temple with his forefinger and looked anywhere but at her.

Flora tucked her chin in and gasped to see a toilet sheet tucked under her arm, still gathering her perspiration. She snatched it out, but bits of the sheet were still adhered, eliciting more giggles from nearby belles. Fleeing the room before anyone else witnessed her demise, Flora ducked into the shadows of the vacant hall and rubbed off the remaining bits of toilet sheet, cheeks flaming. This was it. This was how she perished. She buried her face in her hands for a soundless scream.

Four

Cornelia rustled around the corner, pale even in the shadows. "Flora, you *must* return. Recover now or all is lost. I want you to laugh it away, or this summer is over before it has begun. The daughter of Florian Wingfield will not be brought down by a couple of sheets of toilet squares."

"A couple?" Flora gasped as she frantically looked to locate the second traitor.

Her cousin grimaced, placing a hand on her stomach. "Your foot, dear."

"How am I going to live past this?" Flora kicked the offending bits away from her precious silk slipper, a whimper slipping from her lips.

"Flora?" Teddy called, advancing down the hall toward them.

"Laugh. You must laugh." Cornelia squeezed her hand and slipped past Teddy on her way back to the party, leaving them alone.

Flora gave a shaky laugh that had Cornelia halting her

departure to roll her eyes and gestured behind Teddy for Flora to try harder.

He took her arm, leading her beneath a crystal sconce and turning the gaslight on brighter. "Are you well?"

"You mean despite my recent humiliation?" She returned the gas to its previous flame, pressing her hands over her cheeks. "You don't need to turn that up to see my blush, I assure you."

Teddy wiped his hand over his mouth, his grin spreading despite what seemed to be his best efforts to squelch it.

Flora dropped her arms and released a genuine laugh. "I know. It is a ridiculous situation to find oneself embroiled in, so I will forgive you for snickering just this once." She waggled her finger at him. "But, after tonight, you can *never* bring this up again."

"May I ask *how* you came about having toilet sheets stuck to your underarm in the first place?" he choked out, his deep laugh filling the dimly lit hall.

She could flee now and return to New York. Surely the *Times* would not run the story, not if she paid off the right reporter so no one at home would ever know her shame. "No, you certainly may not!"

He threaded her hand through his arm. "I'm sorry. I won't laugh anymore."

She looked up into his brilliant eyes, her resolve fading. "I think it is plain that this New Orleans climate is trying to best me, but it will take more than a few sheets of toilet squares to send me running home to New York."

"That's my Flora." He winked, patting her hand. "Now, let's dance the next three pieces, and I guarantee you no one will remember the toilet sheets tomorrow, for all that they will be discussing is the beauty who has captured the elusive Mr. Day's attention."

"Elusive?" She snorted. "You had *five* women surrounding you at the piano."

"Whom I escaped to rescue you." He grinned, leading her onto the parquet dance floor. "Which means I am exceedingly gallant, knightly even." He bowed to her.

Standing beside the belles of the South, Flora lost her witty retort and focused all her efforts on willing the trembling in her hands to cease as she curtsied. She stepped into his arms for the Esmeralda polka, and soon the vigorous hopping-and-whirling dance dispelled her mortification from moments before as Teddy placed his hand on her waist and, using her right hand to brace against his, lifted her into the air, smiling up at her, making a spectacle of seeing only her. They then placed their hands at their hips and began the series of chassés and heel-to-toe steps toward one another, whirling away once more. As the strands of the polka drew to an end, instead of following the other couples off the floor to seek new partners, he bowed to her again. As predicted, the giggles ceased, and fans about the ballroom fluttered to life like a mob of incensed butterflies as the society matrons and their daughters whispered away as to what was the meaning behind Teddy's deliberate action.

"Thank you for rescuing me," Flora whispered, dipping and swaying in time with the waltz.

"Anytime." He smiled, pulling her closer. At her quizzical look, he whispered in her ear, "We have to make my infatuation appear *genuine*."

Which is no trial on my part. She dropped her gaze lest Teddy read the desire in her eyes.

He laughed softly, completely unaware of her inner turmoil. "Though I should be thanking you too, since you are rescuing me by keeping me from having to dance with the others at the moment. I cannot say for certain, but I think the women are organizing against me, forming some sort of diabolical plan to ensnare me once and for all."

She giggled. "Against? Never." *For you? Absolutely.* Having been trained in the art of husband hunting, she knew a hunter when she saw one, or in this case an entire pack of she-wolves.

The pair flowed into their third dance, but the galop's rapid chassé and hopping heel click left little breath for conversing. She performed it without a single blunder, laughing with Teddy as the dance progressed, earning glares from Miss Penelope Bridgewater, Miss Fontenot and the Misses Pimpernels, until the pair concluded the dance with a final whirl.

Teddy led her to the refreshment table, threading her hand through his arm, keeping his other hand possessively over hers. "That should do the trick."

"Thank you, Teddy, but"—Flora nodded to his mother, who was waving him over—"duty calls, Mr. Day."

"I'll be back for you to conclude our saving you from scandal," he whispered, handing her a glass of punch, his gaze wandering to a group of gentlemen nearby who were eyeing Flora. He leaned toward her, capturing her hand in his and pressing a kiss atop it. "And this is to keep you safe until then. Now, if you need aid in keeping your admirers at bay, signal me."

"Shall I flutter my fan at you?" Flora snapped open her fan and batted her lashes at him.

He pressed his lips together. "No, there are too many fans

in one ballroom to do much good in getting my attention."
He snapped his fingers. "I know! Just stick some more toilet
sheets under your arm and I'll come running."

"Very droll." She rolled her eyes but couldn't keep her
laugh from escaping at his ridiculousness as he ambled away.

"I took the liberty of fetching you a refreshment after
all your dancing, one set of which belonged to me, but as
you never left the dance floor, I was unable to claim it." Mr.
Grayson held out a glass of raspberry lemonade to her.

"My apologies for missing the opening dance as well as
the polka. I did not mean to snub you. Mr. Day and I simply
got carried away." She accepted the glass, scanning the room,
desperate to find an ally. But her sisters were all dancing, and
Theodore was surrounded by belles once more.

"So it would seem. Though I see he is entertaining Miss
Bridgewater again. Prudent move."

She gripped the crystal between her hands, keeping her
voice light. "And why is that a 'prudent move,' as you say?"

"Because her family owns one of the largest sugar planta-
tions in Louisiana, which as you know is the supplier for my
company." He lightly sipped his glass.

"Wellington's company," she corrected.

"Yes, well, details. She has a dowry nearing twenty million, a sum that rivals many in New York, I believe. And then
there is your father's obvious interest in procuring her family's sugar for himself rather than for my employer, which
makes a connection with Miss Bridgewater even more desirable for a local suitor who will not only obtain her money
but also secure a foothold in your father's court."

The pinch in her stomach was making it hard to breathe.
Did Teddy desire a connection with Penelope over herself?

If he could have a connection with her father while still marrying someone from his own city . . . why wouldn't he?

"Has your father mentioned what he intends to offer my supplier in order to woo them away from Wellington Sugar? I would be surprised if he didn't wed one of you to the Bridgewaters' son. Or perhaps Mr. Wingfield is considering a buyout, though I didn't know the man had an interest in the sugar industry until just recently, so I doubt he is willing to take on the growing of sugar cane . . . only the refining of it."

Flora blinked, not caring to follow along with his stream of thought when all she could consider was losing Teddy *again*. "My father doesn't discuss such matters with the women in the family."

His eyes gleamed. "Does he discuss anything challenging with you?"

Flora's cheeks heated, and she hid behind her drink, taking a long enough draft to compose herself. *Of course he does not. And what is Father doing with sugar now?*

"Forgive me." Mr. Grayson swept her hand into his and was about to kiss it when they were surrounded by four belles whom she recognized from her walk with Teddy.

"Of course." She pulled her hand from his, willing it to cease its shaking. The man positively unnerved her.

"Excuse us, sir, but we must steal away Miss Wingfield," Miss Penelope said with a smile, wrapping her hand possessively about Flora's arm.

The action surprised Flora, nearly as much as the fact that Penelope had left Teddy's side to speak with her.

Mr. Grayson gave a nod and bowed. "I shall return to secure a dance with you, Miss Wingfield, in restitution for the one stolen from me by Mr. Day."

"I'm afraid I have promised the rest." Flora's hands wrapped around her card. She would return to the powder room before each dance for the rest of the evening if she must so as to avoid dancing with him, or excuse herself to her chamber with a sudden headache. Not waiting for his reply, Flora drew Penelope farther into the corner near a dessert table, the Misses Pimpernels and Miss Fontenot clustering about them. "I trust you are all having a pleasant time? Auntie outdid herself, did she not?"

"She certainly did." Miss Penelope's smile did not reach her eyes as she folded her gold gloved hands before her copper silk skirts. "You remember Miss Josephine Pimpernel." She smiled to the lady nearest her, whose gown was an unfortunate shade of bright pink. "And her sister, Miss Mathilda Pimpernel." She nodded to the tall blonde in green that perfectly matched her eyes, then gestured to the raven-haired lady of their troupe with a perfect, curvaceous figure. "And, of course, Miss Sandrine Fontenot."

"Yes, lovely to see you all again." Flora dipped her head in greeting as if they had not all *just* seen one another this very day.

Penelope closed the gap between them to create an intimate windmill, their bustles and trains keeping all other guests at least three feet away and giving them a modicum of privacy in the crowded ballroom. "Let us begin as we mean to continue, shall we?"

Flora paused in her perusal of the croquembouche tower of what appeared to be cream-filled profiteroles covered in spun sugar and edible flowers, unsure as to what the woman could possibly mean. Had she been less than friendly? Flora pulled a profiterole from the tower and took a bite, closing her eyes at the delightful burst of flavor.

"You danced many times with our Theodore Day tonight," Josephine Pimpernel interjected, pressing her thumbs into the crevice of her open dance card that held a surprising number of blank entries. "And I happened to be saving a dance for him." Her attention darted to the dance floor, where he was whirling about with another socialite.

Penelope patted her hand. "Speaking of which, this dance should have been yours, Fifi. I will be speaking with Angelique as soon as she steps out of our Mr. Day's arms."

"*Your* Theodore Day?" Flora giggled, but at their austere expressions, she suppressed her mirth, pressing her hand to her lips. "Oh, forgive me, you are serious."

Penelope narrowed her eyes, the red curls framing her face atremble. "Quite. Now, as you have only just arrived to New Orleans, we feel it is our duty to save you from certain heartbreak by explaining the situation to you."

"I beg your pardon?" Flora set aside her glass on a passing footman's silver tray and reached for a second profiterole.

"We are referring to New Orleans's dearest, dreamiest bachelor." Miss Sandrine Fontenot giggled into her blue silk fan that accentuated her wide eyes and rested it above her ample décolletage. "You see, while Theodore would not agree to our casual proposals for a competition for his heart, much like the one Willow Dupré hosted this spring, we decided what better way was there for him to move on than to fall in love with one of us?"

Flora dug her fingernails into her gloved palm. "And who exactly is *we*?"

"The high-society belles of New Orleans." Mathilda blinked behind her delicate glasses as if it were obvious. "Who else?"

"I see," Flora murmured, certain at this point that socialites across the country would be flocking to be a part of this inane game for Teddy's hand if word ever escaped.

"And so"—Penelope snapped her fan closed into her open palm—"to avoid his being overwhelmed with too many options and choosing no one in the end, we have taken the liberty of narrowing his options to a list of the most elite women in New Orleans—a list, my dear Miss Wingfield, which frankly does *not* include you."

Flora plucked a narrow pastry dipped in chocolate on both ends from the table and took a bite, nodding her understanding. *These women actually think they are a part of an exclusive competition for Teddy's hand. But he is not some prize to be fought over and won.*

Penelope squeezed her arm and bestowed a brilliant smile upon Flora that had the others following suit. "I knew we all could be friends. I am *so* glad you agree. We only want what is best for New Orleans's best bachelor."

Flora swallowed her treat. "Pardon me, you misunderstood my nod."

The women halted in their warm acceptance of her, their smiles frozen in place as her words set.

"Whatever do you mean?" Sandrine gripped her fan much like a saber.

"I meant that while I understand you, I do not agree. You see, I never did care much for lists and rules." She lifted her pastry to them. "Happy hunting, ladies. May the best socialite win." *And for Teddy's sake, let's hope it is not Penelope.*

"I heard their father is the wealthiest gentleman in America," Theodore's chum and recently appointed New Orleans

Pinkerton Agent, Gale Thornton, commented to the crescent of gents, all eyes upon the Wingfield sisters, a fact Theodore did not appreciate.

"Then how have they remained single for so long?" Mr. Bridgewater asked, reaching for another cup of chicory coffee from a footman in the Dubois family's signature yellow livery, handing a second to Bradford Grayson.

"Those New York fellows must not be looking hard enough. I must send them each a note of thanks." Gale laughed, finishing off his drink. "Beautiful, knickerbockers and rich. My mother actually fainted when she learned the family was here for the summer and, the moment she roused, begged me to woo one of them."

"And as there are five of them, you may do just that, especially after the rumor I heard," Mr. Grayson interjected.

"What rumor?" Theodore's stomach turned, knowing all too well how much idle gossip could damage a person.

"Oh, nothing of a nefarious nature, I assure you." Grayson laughed, lifting his coffee in salute to the group before reaching into his jacket and retrieving a flask, pouring a generous amount into his cup and Bridgewater's. "Only that their father is highly motivated to marry them *all* off, which means we won't have to fight amongst ourselves for a hand and should have little trouble procuring the blessing of Mr. Wingfield." At the stir this caused, he added, "And just to inform you, gentlemen, I've already secured an outing with the eldest."

"From knowing the Wingfield family as well as I do, I would be wary of following that bit of gossip. And as the youngest is only sixteen, there are only four daughters of marriageable age," Theodore corrected, irked that Bradford Grayson had approached Flora.

"Still plenty to go around, eh, Teddy?" Gale clapped him on the shoulder. "Not to worry. Unlike Grayson, I know better than to chase the eldest."

At that, Theodore opened his mouth to protest, but the group was laughing too heartily to hear a protest even if he could formulate one.

"You would allow Ted's preference to keep you from paying call to Miss Flora?" Carlisle joined the group, straightening his lapel. "She has become quite the beauty, and if she is as sweet and diverting as she was years ago, you would be fortunate to secure her hand for more than just her wealth."

Theodore glanced sideways to his brother at such praise. *Does Carlisle admire Flora?* The thought was so preposterous, it brought forth a chuckle.

"Yes, well, there is only one eldest daughter. If I wasn't clear, *I* already have a call with Miss Flora scheduled for Thursday." Mr. Grayson stared at Theodore as if challenging him to his right to an outing with Flora. "I have worked for days to secure it, too."

"Fortunate fellow indeed to have had the opportunity to travel in the same steamboat as the daughters of Midas down the Mississippi River." Mr. Bridgewater stepped between them, clapping Theodore on the shoulder. "Any of us fellows would be fools not to endear ourselves to the Wingfield ladies, seeing as that would allow us access to Florian Wingfield."

"And his millions upon a union." Mr. Grayson threw back his drink, hissing at the heat.

Not caring for the direction of the conversation, the mere idea of Gale or one of the others pursuing Flora not at all to his liking, Theodore skimmed the room to spy Flora lifting her cannoli to the group of belles he had only recently escaped. Even though he had run into them this morning . . . and most of the mornings before that, they continued to flock to his side. And despite his brother and friends' teasing, all he could think about was spending more time with Flora. He had missed her. No one could make him laugh as much, albeit no one in his acquaintance had ever waltzed into a ballroom with toilet sheets stuck to them.

"Excuse me, gents." Theodore snatched a savory tart appetizer from a footman's tray and popped it into his mouth, striding across the room to steal Flora away from the ladies, the men crowing all the while behind him, Mr. Grayson looking more than a bit nettled. "Miss Wingfield, I—"

"Teddy Day," Penelope crooned. "I'm eager to see your ensemble for the upcoming ball." Penelope fluttered her fan and lashes in remarkable unison with Miss Sandrine and the Misses Pimpernels.

"Ball?" Flora asked, her wide eyes fixed on him. "Are you hosting it?"

"It is Miss Penelope's annual ball next month," Miss Mathilda supplied.

"Yes, it is one of the most anticipated parties of the summer. Certainly, Miss Penelope has informed you of it?" He tilted his head to Penelope, giving her a dimpled smile that he knew would bring about a happy outcome for Flora.

"I was about to inform her when you joined us that, uh—" her smile faltered under his gaze—"that although I am giving the party, I am afraid that a month is less than ample time for Miss Wingfield to have a costume completed."

"It's a costume ball?" He sucked in his breath. He'd have to throw something together, as it was far too late to order a costume from his tailor, who would surely be overwhelmed with orders for the ball.

"I *love* costume balls. I knew I should have packed the gown from the last one I attended just in the event I was invited to one here." Flora finished off her pastry in a dainty bite, eyeing the table for more. "It is not every day that one can reuse a costume."

"How fortunate that you would deem it well done to wear a *used* costume to my party. However, it is a pirate-themed party, so I doubt anything you would have brought would fit the style I have in mind," Penelope replied with half-closed lids.

Theodore's brow furrowed. "Pardon? Did you say it was a pirate-themed party?"

"I have never heard of such a ball," Flora commented, jotting down a note on her dance card, though he did not see how she could possibly forget a theme so bizarre. "Still, I think I can manage a costume in time if I can find a seamstress who can take on the project."

The Misses Pimpernels whispered in Penelope's ears, but she batted them away with her fan. "Yes, it is unique, yet I couldn't throw my annual ball without some sort of novelty, not after Mrs. Vanderbilt's costume ball this spring that was said to have been the greatest party society has ever seen. I'm certain you have read about it, my dear Miss Flora. Only the most elite members of New York society were invited."

Theodore wasn't certain if he could take much more of her condescending tone to Flora. He glanced down to his friend, who seemed unbothered as she nodded, not revealing the one little detail that would cease Penelope's rant and secure her place in New Orleans society.

"Well, then you know my ball must be done with the greatest care, expense, creativity, and above all, *exclusivity*," Penelope continued, flipping open her fan in a little wave to emphasize her words. "So, by extending an invitation to you, and so late at that, I'm afraid I would have to cut a dear friend. And if we follow Mrs. Vanderbilt's guide, you see that I cannot invite four hundred *and one* guests."

That did it. Theodore drew Flora's hand through his arm. "We certainly are aware of Mrs. Vanderbilt's standards, as we were in attendance that night, along with *fifteen hundred* other guests. I was King Arthur to Willow Dupré's Guinevere, while Flora donned the most enchanting blush-colored fairy queen costume I have ever beheld."

Flora's cheeks spotted as Penelope's flared, who turned to glare at Miss Josephine, but he suspected the cause for Penelope's coloring was for entirely different reasons.

"B-but I read the *New York Times* and *Godey's Magazine* multiple times like you asked me, and *she* was not mentioned," Josephine murmured to Penelope, who flicked her hand, silencing the poor girl.

Flora shrugged. "Not everyone was mentioned, as it would have overtaken the entire morning paper, but I didn't wish to speak to reporters that night and managed to slip inside without much ado, as I was in the carriage following Willow Dupré's, who eclipsed many of the elite knickerbocker families, including myself and my sisters."

"Knickerbocker," Penelope muttered out of the corner of her mouth to Josephine.

"Yes," Josephine whispered to Penelope. "Which of course means she would have been invited, since her family would be a part of the Four Hundred set as Knicker—"

Penelope pinched the bridge of her nose. "Enough, Fifi."

"You may have heard of her father, Florian Wingfield, one of the wealthiest men in America? If her father had been in attendance, I am certain the reporters would have taken greater care to mention Mr. Wingfield's daughters."

Flora turned to him, eyes wide in exasperation. Though he could not determine why when he was defending her.

Mathilda leaned over and whispered into Penelope's ear, who at once paled and nodded.

She smiled at Teddy. "Forgive me, but it entirely slipped my mind that Alice Summerton wrote to me only yesterday that she will be traveling to Newport and cannot attend, so—"

"Why did Alice write when she could have simply walked next door?" Miss Sandrine gasped. "Is it because she had a cold? When I visited her a few days ago, she insisted it was only from the change in weather, but—"

Penelope's glare could dry a swamp, but it was effective in silencing Miss Sandrine at once. She turned a gracious smile to Flora. "If you would like to join us, Miss Wingfield, we would love to have you."

Sensing a polite refusal forthcoming from Flora, Theodore squeezed her elbow. "She would be honored."

"Of course, I would love to attend. Thank you for the invitation." Flora dipped her head.

Penelope blinked as if she too had been expecting a swift refusal after it had been made clear that Flora was not welcomed and was merely an afterthought. "Well then, I have great expectations for your ensemble, Miss Flora. My party will most certainly be covered in the papers, so see you do not disappoint either, Teddy." Penelope turned on her heel, her entourage following suit, though Mathilda did send Flora a sympathetic smile.

Flora whipped around to him. "Really, Teddy. Do you wish for me not to make any true friends while in New Orleans?"

"Am I hindering you from making friends?"

"You are giving these women the impression that I am some American princess." She scowled. "No one wishes to be friends with an heiress just for the sake of friendship. There are *always* ties."

"My apologies. But I do not think Miss Penelope Bridge-water, nor her friends, will be so quick to dismiss you in the future." Theodore led her through a set of French doors, out onto the veranda facing the avenue. The full moon cast the evening in an ethereal air, lending a glow far brighter than the gaslights flickering along the walkways. Carriages rolled slowly past as the passengers craned their necks to make out the *joie de vivre* within the estate.

"I'd rather lose a few dinner invitations than get the reputation for being supercilious." Flora pulled away from him, crossing her arms.

"Then it might be best to avoid using such words as *supercilious*." He laughed, drawing a reluctant smile from Flora.

She lifted her gaze to the stars peeking through the live oaks and leaned back on a column. "But, despite *how* my invitation was extended, a pirate-themed party sounds like great fun. I think even Willow would enjoy it. Cullen has worked wonders in peeling back those serious layers she affixed to cover up her playful nature in the business world."

Theodore scrubbed a hand over the back of his neck at hearing his ex-fiancée's name and her husband in casual conversation, but the more Flora brought her up, the less and less her name stung each time. "I believe she would have, as well. And since there haven't been any river pirate attacks in New York's Hudson River or our Mississippi River in years, I suppose *fun* could be considered the correct term for someone who doesn't remember them or wasn't directly affected by them." He shifted in his jacket, the heat drawing his clothes tight against his chest, making the evening even muggier with the notion of being strangled in one's own suit.

"Oh. I hadn't thought of that. Father still tells tales of the New York river pirates wreaking havoc on shipments and how the Steamboat Squad managed to quash them at long last." She shivered. "Honestly, it *did* sound terrifying, but then Willow gave me the most romantic dime novel about a river pirate and a lady falling madly in love."

Theodore grunted. "Utterly nonsensical. A pirate romance, much less a pirate-themed party, seems to be a strange form of entertainment . . . celebrating something that was once so terrifying for hundreds, if not thousands, of travelers along the river."

"But oddly still romantic," she added and turned a smile up to him, sending his heart to pounding.

This was not good. He could not allow himself to be distracted by another potential love during his competition with Carlisle, especially with Flora, who surely had no designs on him, which would inevitably lead to disaster. The music began again, and he extended his hand. "Shall we have the last dance?"

"Always." She fitted her hand in his, and he at once found the fault in his using a dance to distract himself.

Miss Sandrine flounced in front of them, blocking their entry to the ballroom floor with her voluminous bustle and train filling the narrow French doors. "Mr. Day, I was wondering how long it would take for you to approach me after our own little tête-à-tête on the veranda." She sniffed at Flora on his arm before remembering to smile. "I thought that you would be a little more enthusiastic about securing the sale of a steamboat?"

"Miss Sandrine, it is a sorry thing that I did not seek you out sooner, or we could have danced." Even though he had originally thought to use his connections with the daughters of the buyers, he had balked at outright flirting with a particular lady. No matter the sales that would come from such actions, it did not settle right with him to use a lady thus.

Her eyes brightened and she leaned to him, displaying her assets. "There is still this last dance."

He coughed and looked at once to Flora, silently begging her to save him.

"Which, I'm afraid, he promised to me," Flora replied, patting his arm and chasséing around Miss Sandrine with him in tow.

Twirling Flora into a waltz, he made certain they were away from the belles before whispering, "I wanted to tell you something before the night was over."

"Oh?" She grinned. "Well, you best tell me at once for fear Miss Sandrine will cut in on our last dance of the night."

"Even she is not so bold." Excitement swelled his chest at his secret hope of running the company potentially coming to fruition. "I was presented with a rather odd opportunity this afternoon, and if it wasn't for your presence here tonight, I would have stayed holed up in my room and missed the ball." And with that confession, he confided of his father's competition.

"Teddy, do you know what this means?" Her hand tightened around his. "You have a *real* chance at last. As long as I've known you, you've always dreamed of running your own company. After all those years studying your father's craft, and then with your travels to Europe, examining the finest interior designs in Paris, the stunning architecture and their steamers, what better company is there for you to run than your family's?"

"And what of Carlisle?" He didn't want to ask it, but he knew if anyone was going to give him a direct answer, it would be Flora. "Am I being selfish by accepting this challenge?" *Even though Father would have eventually mentioned it, even if he hadn't overheard our quarrel earlier.*

She leaned toward him, and he bent to catch her hushed words. "You were made for this profession. Carlisle was simply *born* into it, and it is time that sort of outdated thinking has been eradicated. And to do so, I think you must participate to prove who is the better head of Day's Luxury Line. If anyone can do it, it's you."

Theodore stared down into her brilliant eyes, nearly stumbling over his next step at the confidence in him found in her gaze, for she was not one to flatter. "When you say it, I can almost believe it to be true."

"Then believe it." Flora squeezed his hand. "For by believing, you are that much closer to realizing your dream."

"Mind if I cut in, Brother?" Carlisle's hand rested on his shoulder. "You have kept our beautiful Miss Flora to yourself for far too long." He flipped his palm out to receive Flora's hand. "And unlike you, I have years' worth of discussions to catch up with her."

With a smile to Theodore, she relinquished her hand before

he could protest. Stepping off the dance floor, he watched Carlisle whirl away with her, which left him with more than an ounce of annoyance, the feeling giving him pause. The four dances they shared so far were supposed to benefit Flora's time in New Orleans, but here she had been telling him things he had longed to hear for years. She believed in *him*.

"Why, Mr. Day, you came to claim me for this last dance after all, didn't you?" Sandrine Fontenot trailed her hand down his arm, sending a look of triumph in Penelope's direction.

Blast. He had gotten too lost in thought, but being the gentleman his mother raised, he squelched his sigh and instead bowed and extended his hand to her. "May I have this dance?"

"You already have my heart, so of course you may have my hand." She fluttered her lashes and slipped her gloved hand in his.

He paused mid-bow, uncertain he had heard her correctly. "Pardon me?"

Her eyes widened, and she giggled into her fan. "Oh, Teddy, you take everything so seriously. Now, shall we dance before the waltz is over?"

While that statement did little to alleviate his horror, he pasted on a smile and led her onto the dance floor, his eyes seeking the woman in the pale-yellow silk.

Five

Flora drew a steadying breath underneath her blush parasol, loving the breeze created by the open carriage as she rode back from her shopping on Canal Street. Last night's unfortunate incident, as it forever would be referred to and never spoken of, had almost destroyed her, but thanks to Teddy's quick thinking, she would be accepted in New Orleans society for another day. And today, Flora would at last have that enchanting encounter, which would surely drive Teddy into her arms and leave any haunting memories of his fiancées behind him forever.

Having overheard him discuss his meeting schedule for the following day with his father at the party, Flora planned for Auntie's carriage to bring her shopping and leave her along the route Teddy traveled home, a spot where no Penelopes could spy them from the parlor. The carriage rolled to a stop, sadly bringing the breeze to an abrupt end. Flora glanced at her ladies' watch pin at her waist. Teddy should be coming down St. Charles Avenue at any moment. She swept down from the carriage, clutching her sketchbook in one hand

and reticule in the other, and motioned the driver onward. "Thank you, Bryson."

He chewed the inside of his cheek. "Miss, I don't think your family would take kindly to my leaving you in the middle of New Orleans without protection."

She gestured to the row of elegant houses on either side of the avenue with their rich landscapes behind heavy wrought-iron gates to keep any undesirables out. "Bryson, this is the Garden District, not the French Quarter. I will be completely safe. Besides, Olive knows where I am, so please do not feel the need to gossip about me to my parents or any of the staff. If you could have my maid bring my purchases up to my room, I'll see to unpacking them." She trilled her fingers at him, motioning for him to continue on his way.

"Very well, Miss Wingfield, but I won't be held responsible for nothing." He huffed and snapped the reins, sending the pair of dapple-gray horses into a prance, leaving her in a cloud of dust.

Flora coughed and batted away the dust with a gloved hand, relief settling over her at being alone, for she feared that if the driver had stayed nearby and she had a means of escape, she would not follow through with her bold plan that she and Olive concocted in the wee hours after the ball, which sounded so much saner in the dark, but now . . . *No going back.* She smoothed her darling walking gown's brocaded grenadine mantle that fell to just above her elbows, straightening her matching blush chapeau to a jaunty angle that would allow him to see it was her while still shielding her from the sun. The cream-colored egret feather charmingly embraced her cheek, which was always rosy now thanks to New Orleans's sultry air.

Where is he? Flora tapped her foot against the minutes that dragged on and on. She longed to use her opera glasses tucked inside her reticule to pass the time, looking inside each home, but didn't dare take her eyes off the avenue for fear of missing him. She paced beneath the graceful boughs of the massive live oaks lining either side of the avenue to keep from being too noticeable and watched as a team of horses drew an emerald streetcar down the patchy grass in the middle of the avenue. A few men leaned out of the car's open windows, brazenly nodding to her, one of them wearing a garish plaid suit and sporting a thick greasy mustache and familiar chipped tooth beneath a straw boater hat. Her heart leapt into her throat. How did Mr. Grayson keep appearing wherever she was about the city? She refused to admit that she had spotted him by nodding a greeting in return. She could not allow him to approach her. He would not only ruin everything, but his presence made her unsettled and, she had to admit, a bit frightened.

Before Mr. Grayson could disembark and approach her, she spun around and dashed around the corner and away from the passengers of the streetcar. But she found it to be not as populated with homes as fine as the mansions on St. Charles Avenue. She pulled out her heavy opera glasses and clutched them, comforted that she could wield them like a club if need be. Now that they were in hand, however, she glanced about the homes to see which one had the shades raised. She peered through her glasses at a few and bit her lip at the interiors. They were no mansions, and those men from the streetcar might live in them . . .

She was beginning to agree with her driver that she shouldn't be unescorted in an unfamiliar city, and yet she didn't want to miss this chance to be alone with Teddy. And if she stayed away too long from his route, she could miss him, but if she returned too soon, she might run into Grayson. She had to chance it. She paused by a hedge of azaleas with a few late magenta blooms adding a burst of much-needed color on the dreary street and dared a glance around the corner. Grayson was nowhere to be seen, and the streetcar had long since departed.

"Excuse me, miss." A man in a worn suit with a limping gate approached her.

Her heart hammered in her chest. Why hadn't she listened to Bryson? She gripped the glasses by their handle. It would be better for her to return them to her reticule and use it as a mace, but that would mean she would have to open her bag, which contained all her remaining pin money.

"You dropped this," he said and held out a grimy handkerchief that certainly was *not* hers.

But, knowing to argue would prolong the interaction, she accepted it with a nod. "Thank you, sir."

He grinned, revealing his perfect teeth. The sight was so startling that she forgot she was supposed to be frightened.

At the sound of carriage wheels approaching, she squinted and barely made out Teddy driving a two-wheeled buggy, drawn by a single white horse. She turned to thank the man, but he had already limped on. She stared at the disgusting handkerchief and didn't have the heart to cast it aside after all the man's efforts to be kind. She shoved it inside her reticule and turned back to the buggy, a brilliant smile in place, ready for Teddy to greet her.

But it didn't slow. It was almost as if . . . he didn't see her on the corner. As she stepped closer to the road, the buggy seemed to gain speed. This wouldn't do. *What would Mother do if she were me?* Flora worried her bottom lip, considering waving him down, but that would be too obvious for what she was attempting to accomplish. *I could pretend to be crossing, forcing the gig to slow lest it run over me.* She gritted her teeth. *That's what Mother would suggest to do if she were here.* And that was what she had to do. Taking a deep breath, she stepped off the walkway into the path of the oncoming buggy.

"Watch out! Get out of the way, miss!" Teddy yelled, pulling back on the horse to slow his rapid approach. But she lifted her opera glasses to her nose and pretended to be overcome with the architecture across the street—an unremarkable three-story mansion—before whipping about for Teddy to see it was her.

He shouted again, pulling against the reins as the horse reared its head in protest and stubbornly barreled toward her. Shrieking, Flora scrambled back, dropping her sketchbook in her haste and stumbling over her skirts, falling hard on her derrière, the wires of her bustle failing to collapse. She threw up her hands to shield herself from the horse's hooves, and then all went black.

The muffled rumble of a familiar voice and the vigorous shaking brought her back. Was she being dragged under the carriage by her bustle caught on the axle? Was this how she would die? Father would hate the headline. Most definitely worse than death by toilet sheets.

"Flora. Flora!"

She fluttered her lashes and found him peering down at her, the sun filtering through the leaves of the oaks, forming a soft halo over his golden curls. If she hadn't known every line of his face, she would have thought an angel had come for her. She blinked again, the halo vanishing.

"Flora? Can you speak to me?"

Her tongue was not working properly. Too dry. She coughed, spewing a cloud of dust into Teddy's face. He wrinkled his nose against it, but his hold did not falter.

"Keep coughing." He patted her back.

She rolled to her side, coughing, and caught sight of the crowd disembarking from another streetcar, craning their necks in her direction, two of them in matching gowns of chartreuse silk.

"Let's get you into the buggy before the Misses Pimpernels descend upon you," he murmured, scooping her into his remarkably solid arms and depositing her onto the tufted leather seat before going back and snatching up her reticule, opera glasses and notebook, tossing them on the seat beside her. Then he snatched up the reins.

Her hand went to her hat, which was listing dangerously to the side, discovering that her beautiful feather had been broken in half. No matter, for she was alone with Teddy Day at last. She would have smiled up at him, but she was fairly certain her teeth were caked in dirt.

"What were you thinking walking out in front of the carriage like that?" Theodore fought to keep his voice low, but the sight of her crumpling to the ground before his horse . . . He shook his head, trying to dispel the image. He snapped the reins, inadvertently passing his own home, but he had no thought other than Flora's well-being and controlling his anger. "You could have been killed."

"Well, I wasn't killed, thanks to my quick footwork. And really, your horse should be better trained, lest next time he *does* trample someone in its path." Flora whacked the dust from her gown.

Theodore rubbed a hand over his chest, his racing pulse paining him. He knew he wasn't truly angry with her as much as he was terrified of almost losing her. Without drawing his eyes from the road, he clasped her hand in his, stilling her dusting, and exhaled again. No, he was not angry with her. At the feel of her head on his shoulder, he jerked his neck back to look at her, at once tightening his grip on her as she seemed to be listing to the side. "Are you feeling faint?"

"A little," she murmured.

He draped his arm around her shoulders, foreseeing her tumbling from the buggy if he did not. She stiffened for a moment before relaxing into his side.

"I'm sorry for frightening you, Teddy."

He grunted. "I'll say. Now that I know you are well, you owe me three years that your actions have shaved off."

She had the audacity to laugh. "How about a pastry instead?"

"Try a dozen beignets *and* a café au lait at Café du Monde," he countered.

"Done." She pulled the pin from her chapeau, letting the hat rest on her lap, and with a sigh tugged out the broken feather and let the wind carry it from her fingertips. Her fingers wove through her locks, twisting and tucking each strand back into place before affixing her hat once more. "So, how was your meeting?"

"Abysmal." He slumped into the bench seat, flicking the reins unenthusiastically.

"That bad?" She shifted, lifting her face to look at him.

He clenched his jaw and nodded. He had let his hopes get too high, but this contest would not be easy. If it were, Day's Luxury Line would already be overflowing with orders. For the business wasn't like the bygone years of his father's time when New Orleans was *the* port for building riverboats. Now most everyone who had survived in the business had moved to the more central location of St. Louis to build for Anchor Line and their fleet of steamers traveling up and down the Mississippi River. It had helped in the beginning to lessen the competition between companies, but buyers were more inclined to go elsewhere, unless they felt luxury and price were no object. And that was where the Day boat-builders stood out. They could secure most luxury products, though today the gentleman was more concerned for his new bride's comfort than most costumers, which had resulted in the sound rejection of Theodore's proposal.

At the shifting beside him, Theodore found Flora leaning over the side of the carriage, one hand gripping the sideboard and the other her chapeau, peering at a passing mansion in rapt attention.

"Flora!" he shouted, startling her. He grabbed her wrist lest she fall out and pulled her back down into her seat. "Honestly, you will be the death of me today!"

"Sorry. Sometimes I get so overwhelmed with the beauty of unusual designs that I quite forget myself," she replied, breathless, eyes bright.

Honestly, has she never ridden in a gig before? Does she not realize that it is pulled by a horse and therefore dangerous and unpredictable? Yet scolding her would only bring about a fight, so he swallowed his retort. "Where were you off to alone that was worth risking your life over? I can escort you because I find that I don't necessarily wish to return home yet after all." Why should he return only to hear of Carlisle securing a client, possibly two, when he had none to speak of?

Flora lifted her sketchbook that bore a muddy imprint of a hoof on the cover. "Despite the heat, I thought I'd find myself a cup of tea at a café and sketch in Upper City Park."

His brows shot up at that. "That actually sounds delightful. Though quite the walk from where I found you . . . . which was in the opposite direction of the park."

Flora laughed. "Was I? Well, I'm glad you came along, then. You may join me if you wish."

"Don't mind if I do." Theodore flicked the reins again, passing Penelope's and then Flora's homes, and directed his horse to a little tea shop within walking distance to the park. Tying the horse to a post in front, he slid on the leather strap to the tube securing his drawings onto his back.

"You don't wish to leave those in the buggy?" Flora gestured to the tube.

He shook his head, keeping a firm hand on her elbow in case she grew distracted again and decided to walk out into the street. "While I trust no one will risk the punishment for horse thieving, the leather case is another matter entirely. And who knows, maybe Carlisle will recognize my horse and take a look at my sketches."

She pressed her lips together as they stepped into line at the tea shop. "While unlikely that would happen, Carlisle does not strike me as a fellow wishing for an unfair advantage."

He clutched the leather strap, the press of the cylinder against his back, reassuring him that his drawings were safe.

"I have been designing all the models *without* any input from him for over a year, which is partly why I was so surprised that I was turned down this morning. But, despite that fact, I think Carlisle might find himself scrambling for decent modern designs that incorporate traditional pieces as well, and with the head position at stake, I have a feeling he might try anything to keep it."

"Ah. I didn't know that." She leaned around the line, peering at the front door. "How long do you think we will have to stand outside before we are seated?"

Flora's fan never ceased its rhythmic, steady pulse, flipping the curls framing her face out to the brim of her chapeau, barely giving them time to settle before the next flap lifted them again from her flushed face. He had never noticed how blue her eyes were before.

"Teddy?"

He blinked at her eyes narrowing as she tugged off her left glove, the back of her hand going to his forehead. The touch brought him back at once. "I'm well." He stepped back from her as an elderly lady gave him *the look*, the one that said she saw no ring on either of their hands. "This is a popular tea shop. Are you certain you wish for something hot? Perhaps something iced would be best? There are vendors in the park for that, as well."

"I hadn't counted on there being a line, but now that I am thinking about it"—she adjusted under her frilly mantle, which had to be stifling—"I am far too disheveled to be seated in public. So, yes, something iced sounds lovely." She shifted her notebook from arm to arm, as if even having the leather book against her sleeve was confining her.

He lifted it from her hands as they crossed the street into

the park. "What are you sketching? The ducks at the pond, I'm guessing? Perhaps the swans swimming about? Or handsome fellows who caught your eye?"

"Very funny." She moved to take it from him, but he raised it above her head, laughing at how endearing she looked when irritated. "No, not ducks because, firstly, wildlife is extremely difficult to capture, so unless they are a part of a design I am creating for a gentleman's study, I avoid them. Most girls sketch landscapes, or graceful creatures such as yourself, but I prefer the beauty of opulent rooms."

Theodore paused in opening the book. "Did you just say you sketch *rooms?*"

"Yes. It has become quite the obsession for me, especially in recent months. Which is why I chose Upper City Park, for the unobstructed view of the mansions lining the park that Auntie Violet told me about on Exposition Boulevard." She gestured to the row of fine homes on their right. "And if you were not with me, I do not believe I would have found the boulevard, for it is in actuality a sidewalk?"

"For now, but they are adding shells to create a makeshift boulevard for the Cotton Centennial Exposition next year," Theodore supplied.

"It's a shame that the fair is not sooner, or we could have spent the whole of summer examining the wonders of the exposition." She shook her head as she headed toward the boulevard, weaving through the live oaks, the Spanish moss wafting dangerously close to her head.

"Take care or you will be picking lice out of your head for the whole of the summer," Theodore chided, her hand jerking back from her examination of a gray clump of moss that had fallen to the ground.

"Anyway, Auntie mentioned that most leave their front windows open with the shades lifted, because they are proud that their address has become so desirable owing to the location of the exposition, giving *me* the opportunity to take a glimpse inside."

His mouth fell open, recalling he had scooped up opera glasses off the avenue but had been too distraught earlier to comprehend or ask why she had them on her person. "You cannot be serious? You actually traipse about strangers' front lawns in order to peek inside their homes and sketch the design of the inner rooms?"

Flora snorted as she stepped over a large root of a massive oak, her fingers trailing over the scaly ridges of the dark-brown bark. "Of course not."

"Thank goodness for that, because—"

"I use these." She fished out a pair of fine pearl-encrusted opera glasses. "Interiors are my passion, but as I cannot rightly knock on every door and study people's interior designs without sounding like someone who has escaped Blackwell's Island Lunatic Asylum, I content myself with peering through windows. Do you have a handkerchief?"

"Flora." Theodore ran a hand over his face and handed over the cotton square. "You cannot continue doing that. You will be arrested."

She wiped the lenses, blowing on them for good measure, then offered back the soiled handkerchief. "The police wouldn't dare."

"And why not? You are not above the law. Being the daughter of a multimillionaire will not save you."

She lifted her chin. "It already has on several occasions. I am a socialite, and as such, I am allowed certain privileges."

"Maybe as a socialite in New York, but as an unknown socialite in New Orleans, dressed in a gown currently sporting horse droppings on her back hem—"

"What?" She gasped, bending over backward to see for herself.

"You didn't expect it was *all* mud caking your person?"

"Of course I did. I would have returned home at once to change instead of sitting beside you and allowing you to smell—" She pressed a hand to her mouth and looked at her hem again in disgust, holding it away from her.

"It's not all that bad." Theodore grinned and flipped open her notebook. "And all of these, I am guessing, are your collections of snooping on every poor soul who happened to leave open their window shades?"

She pursed her lips and rolled her eyes, tugging him to the side to allow a mother pushing a pram past. "Not *every* page. Most are the rooms I designed myself based off what I think they should look like, as well as the layout." She gave a short laugh, shaking her head, continuing their walk. "Though I doubt I will ever get to use my ideas until much later in life. I have designed my entire mansion room by room that I plan to have built someday once I come into the first part of my inheritance. Father promised me that if I was not wed by thirty, I could have the amount he set aside for my dowry as well as half the fortune he will leave me upon his passing."

"Six years is a long time to be dreaming of a home that will take years to have built."

"A dream that is worth anything is worth waiting for to come true."

He paused along the path beside a vendor parked under

a magnolia tree and ordered two lemonades and a bag of peanuts.

"Wait, sir, before you fill a tin." She dug into her bag and removed a small, gold collapsible cup and handed it to the vendor, whose eyes widened at the piece.

Theodore rubbed his forehead and chuckled. "Not only do you carry a collapsible cup, but a *gold* one?"

"Father requires all of us to carry one, and as such, Mother had them designed for us." A hint of a smile appeared at the corner of her mouth as she accepted her cup with a nod of thanks and rotated the front of the cup to Theodore. "See, my initials are engraved. And as Mother knows Father's sobriquet is Midas, the gold is a nod to him."

Theodore laughed and accepted the tin provided by the vendor, downing it quickly and handing it back and accepting the bag of peanuts while Flora slowly sipped from hers, ambling along.

She took another sip and made him wish he had a cup of his own to linger over in the summer heat. "And I must say, Teddy, I'm impressed that you recalled my age."

"Hard to forget the little girl trailing behind myself and Willow all those summers."

"You make it out as though I were a babe." She helped herself to the peanuts. "I am only two years younger than you."

"In my defense, when one is twelve, two years feels like a *significant* age gap."

"And now?" She looked up at him through her long lashes.

Her brilliant blue eyes pierced him, for now he saw no little girl. He hadn't for some years. Shaking himself free from the fleeting thought of her lovely, slender form on the dance floor last night in Carlisle's arms, he gestured to a bench beside a patchy flower bed to the left of the path, facing a winding, narrow pond where mallards were swimming, a swan gliding out from beneath the branches of a weeping willow toward them.

But instead of following him, she gasped and pointed to a mansion lining the park and retrieved her opera glasses. "Such understated magnificence."

Theodore lowered the glasses from her nose and placed her hand over his arm, guiding her to the bench. "Before you begin sketching private rooms again and get arrested, I'd love for you to take a look at my designs and tell me why you think Mr. Thompson turned down my proposal."

She blinked. "You want my opinion on business matters?"

"You seem to know interiors, so I welcome your insight."

She sank down beside him as he slung off his leather case from his shoulder, painstakingly slid the papers free, and slowly unfurled them before Flora, gripping the sides as if the nonexistent breeze could send them into the duck pond. *Perhaps they do belong in the duck pond for all the interest Mr. Thompson showed.*

"Lovely," she murmured, skimming her fingers over the main sketch with the layout of his latest steamboat, pausing when she came to a rough sketch of the interior design of the one room that had eluded him and he knew kept him from securing his bid. She pursed her lips, wrinkling them to the side, a gesture he well knew.

"You have an idea?" He nodded to the powder room page. "I cannot seem to master this one element. The banker wished for his young bride to feel as if she had never left her home, making the traveling upriver to see her family in St. Louis not only convenient but comfortable. I spent hours on this room and I am baffled by what more a woman could want."

Flora withdrew a pencil from her reticule. "May I?"

"Anything would be an improvement." He gestured for her to draw on his precious finished page.

Flora pressed her hand to her jabot and laughed. "Why, thank you for your confidence in me." With her sketchbook beneath the page, Flora bent over the paper, adding a second vanity, arched doorways, beautiful moldings, and a crystal chandelier with a fresco above it, all with deft strokes before adding lovely wall-covering patterns, a rug, more gilded mirrors, and little touches over the entirety of the room, noting which color each item should be, even going so far as to detail the silver toiletries atop the vanities. Sitting back on the wooden bench, she held out the drawing with so many novel features, it had Theodore squinting trying to make them all out. "There."

"How on earth did you come up with this in the span of a few moments?" Theodore traced the drawing with his fingertips.

She shrugged. "It only needed a touch of opulence, along with the comforts of home. I know you were only thinking of her comfort in the designing, but if she wished to bring a companion, she would not want to share her vanity while enjoying her friend's confidence as they had their hair dressed."

"All of these things are in a lady's dressing room?"

Flora shook her head, looking for all the world as if she was holding back her laughter. "And much more. You said 'comfort,' and for any lady of fashion and means, comfort *must* also mean luxurious. Would you like me to jot down a list?" She flipped open her sketchbook. "Yes, you need a list."

"Comfort meets luxury. Another form of exclusivity," he murmured.

"Exactly." She grinned, pointing at him with her pencil. "And I have a few more ideas throughout that you can add that may change Mr. Thompson's mind. Of course, you will have to charge him more for all the furnishings and tidbits and bobbles I will add to the list, but I *know* his wife will love the outcome."

"This is marvelous, Flora. How were you able to see the colors so quickly?" He set to rolling the papers. She had done so much with a single room . . . An idea began to form, his heart racing, knowing that most of her ideas had never been done by the line before. *With Flora, I could beat him.*

"I have always had an eye for it." She dropped her pencil in the spine of her sketchbook, marking the page. "Design is everywhere if you know where to look." She bent over and plucked a marigold from the clump growing alongside the bench, twirling it slowly by its stem. "See how the brilliant gold against the emerald stalk and pointed leaves is so beautiful in the sunlight? The same goes for interior design. Some colors naturally go better together, are more pleasant to the eye than other color combinations, such as for a chamber. We get those patterns from the first designer, God."

"This is incredible, Flora. You have quite the gift."

She lowered her head, clutching her hands on her lap, and whispered, "Like I said, I see things differently than others."

At the tears in her eyes, he leaned toward her and rested his hand over hers. "Have I said something? What's wrong."

She cleared her throat and swiped her fingertips under her lashes. "I have only ever been told that designing was a waste of time. Once, I stupidly mused to Father that if any universities had a class on design, I could formally develop my skills, but alas, Father thought it a misuse of money, for by the time I would have finished studying, I most likely would've missed out on my chance to ensnare a desirable husband." She blew her nose into Theodore's offered handkerchief, her eyes rimmed in red that matched her nose. "But the jest is on him. There are no classes for me to attend, and yet I still do not have a husband."

He scowled, not enjoying the picture of Flora married to another, nor her father scorning her obvious skill. "Education is never a waste."

She shrugged and rose. "Maybe he is right. Even if I had the opportunity for formal training, no one would hire a woman when they could have a man who, in their mind, could do it three times better."

"Then they are missing out on treasures like the one you just provided." Theodore tucked the designs into the tube. "What would you think about taking a look at *all* my designs and adding your own touches? Or even start a room over should it fancy you? I would love to hear any and all suggestions. I need to make each room so opulent that it is impossible for Mr. Thompson, and every gentleman after him, to refuse me. And, in return, I will pay you handsomely for your time and list you as my partner in design."

She pressed her hands to her mouth. "Truly?"

He lifted the tube. "You have given me more ideas in a quarter of an hour than I have had in weeks."

"Then I would be honored. But listing my name alongside yours would be payment enough."

"We may have our first disagreement there, but thank you." He secured the carrier tube to his back and jumped to his feet, extending his hand to her. "You don't know what this means to me, Flora. And if you refuse to accept your fair compensation, I will find some way to repay you that you cannot decline."

"Your delightful company is enough," she replied, accepting his hand. "So, when shall I tour one of your steamboats? I think it would help me envision our project better by starting with the baseline of what you offer to your clients."

"I have a better idea than just showing you our model. I think it is time I hosted a dinner aboard my family's private steamboat to demonstrate to my potential clients the lifestyle that comes with owning a boat from Day's Luxury Line. What do you say, Flora? Would you and yours like to while away an evening on the Mississippi River next week?"

Six

The day had gone more perfectly than she could have ever dreamed. Though even in her wildest of dreams, she had not thought of having to throw herself in front of a racing buggy to capture Teddy's attention. Stepping into the grand foyer, Flora stripped off her kid gloves and rumpled hat and shed her mantle that would take the maid some time to restore to its former beauty, grateful for the reprieve from the extra layer in the heat.

Olive poked her head into the hallway. "Did you see him?" Her gaze rested on the dirt marring her gown. "What on earth happened to you? You look like you were trampled." She held her hand to her nose and warily eyed her sister's hem. "And that's not dirt, is it?"

Flora lifted her skirts to keep the hem from dragging on Auntie's floor. "Only that splotch on the back isn't. But never mind that. I *did* see him and do not fret—"

"No, you don't! Do not say another word, Flora Wingfield, until you are at my side." Cornelia called from the room Olive had just vacated.

Flora threaded her arm through Olive's who chasséd away from her.

"No touching *anything* until you bathe and I have that dress burnt." Olive waved her hand in front of her scrunched-up nose. "Please tell me that you did not get near Teddy while smelling like that."

"Stop it!" Cornelia shouted. "So help me, do not make me get up from this chaise lounge."

Laughing, Flora waltzed into the parlor to find Cornelia had taken up residence beside the open glass French doors, fanning herself with a novel. Despite Auntie's massive house, the room had been arranged in an intimate fashion with the Louis the XIV chairs cloistered together atop a Persian rug across from the chaise lounge, with the floor-length windows opened wide to allow a gentle breeze to flow through the sheer curtains that helped to keep the mosquitoes at bay.

"Do *not* spare any details, Cousin." Cornelia rested her open book upon her stomach, folding her hands atop it.

"Well, let's begin by saying that all did not go according to plan." Flora kicked off her shoes and in her stockinged feet paced before her sister and cousin, regaling the story, the ladies gasping and sighing appropriately. It was a rather dreamy story, she had to admit, with a runaway horse, fainting, and Teddy seeking *her* help in his hour of need.

Cornelia reached behind her head for her box of chocolates on the tea cart, the empty wrappers rustling until her fingers found an uneaten chocolate. "I still cannot believe that a scheme you made up on the spot actually worked. You could have been *trampled*, Flora."

"But she wasn't, and Mother would be so proud." Olive giggled. "Ever since Flora became of age, closely followed by myself, Tacy, and now Ermengarde, Mother has constantly been on the husband hunt while training us to be the most accomplished of wives. Even Nora spends hours each day learning the art. Though I do not quite see the point anymore, as Father seems not to approve of any of the gentlemen Mother selects, despite complaining of the drama that comes with having so many women in his home, as we have yet to secure an engagement."

Flora snatched the remaining pastry left on the tea cart behind Cornelia.

"I was saving that," she protested around her mouthful of chocolate, her hand on her widening girth. "This child is starving me."

Flora sighed and surrendered the scone, pouring a cup of tea instead. "Or, more than likely, the suitors we might have catch wind of Father's idea of only bestowing a few million on each of us for a dowry."

Olive threw up her hands. "Father makes us paupers in comparison to most of the American heiresses out in society by keeping our full inheritance until his passing instead of presenting them to us and our husbands upon marriage like the rest of society."

"Well, that was *New York* high society," Cornelia reminded her and pinched off a bite of the scone. "Here, your family is the wealthiest in the city, and the pile of invitations that have appeared on your tray after a single party is testimony to the weight of influence your knickerbocker heritage and inheritance carries. You are American royalty. The men here seem to have gone senseless to know that a family of *five* daughters have three million *apiece*, with more to come."

"That we will collect in about forty years," Olive corrected with a laugh. "Yet I can't imagine needing all that money by then if my husband is well established."

While they both did not care about the money as much as Tacy, Flora knew just about every bachelor who had been attempting to court her in the past eventually *did* when they discovered it was a stipulation carved in stone. Why all the young men coming courting thought they could change Florian Wingfield's mind was beyond her.

"Nonetheless, the Wingfield sisters are quite the buccaneers in New Orleans." Cornelia brushed off her hands and slid her swollen ankles from the pillow. "And as we each only have the one shared bathroom per floor upstairs, we best prepare for the ball tonight at the Musgroves'."

"Tonight? And who are the Musgroves?" Flora straightened from her post at the tea cart. If she had any hope in bathing, she had to move if she wished to have the bathing chamber before Nora, which was irritating as Nora wasn't even out yet in society and yet was allowed to attend the balls and parties right along with her older sisters. When Flora was sixteen, she had *begged* to go to society events, but no, Mother had to do everything that was proper. And by the time Ermengarde was fifteen, Mother had relented in her strict rules until they were practically nonexistent for Nora, save for the stipulation that, of course, she could not marry until she was eighteen.

Olive slipped an arm about Cornelia's waist, helping her to standing. "Yes. They apologized for the lack of notice, but since they only just met us last night and they have an eligible son, Mother overlooked the departure from etiquette and sent along her acceptance."

"Only eligible?" Flora peeled off her stockings for good

measure, not wishing to leave a trail in her wake, and grabbed her reticule from the side table. "Tacy won't approve of that."

"We can't be greedy and expect handsome *and* eligible, Flora."

Cornelia shook out her skirts and popped the last chocolate of the box into her mouth. "Well, I waited and I acquired both."

The clock chimed five times, and as if on cue, Mother burst into the room and directed all to the poor maid. Hearing the pounding feet on the staircase, Flora shook her head over her younger sisters dashing to use the shared bathrooms first and therefore have the maid's attention before the rest of them. Father's penny-pinching made no sense. Why should they have to overwork one poor girl when they could easily hire a maid for each in their party?

Instead of joining the others in the queue for the bathroom, Flora kept to the hall, running her fingers across the chair rail until she reached the study where her father was likely hiding behind his books, ledgers, or papers. She tapped on the door with her fingernail, knowing how he detested loud noises, which was rather inconvenient as he had an aunt, five daughters, a wife, and a niece living under the same roof, and not one between them seemed to possess a demure nature in private.

"Enter." His voice cracked through the empty hall.

Flora peeked inside and stood on the threshold, again acutely aware of how singularly different Willow's life was from hers. Willow was always welcomed in the study with her father, until she was eventually given the crown of the sugar empire, while Flora was seen as a nuisance. "Father, I wanted to ask you something."

He did not look up, his pen moving steadily across the page before him, which was probably for the best given the state of her gown that would no doubt lead to questioning and then a reprimand for being seen in such disarray. "Yes?"

"Well, I know how you detested using the shared steamboat from the port in Illinois to New Orleans and . . ." She swallowed. Ever since Teddy had mentioned needing clients, her first thought was to ask her father, but it would take everything in her to convince him.

"What you are about to propose sounds expensive." He set down his correspondence, his eyes widening. "Flora. What on earth? You were not seen in public with that hem, were you?"

"I had a little accident and am waiting for the use of the bathing chamber." She took another step toward him, her hands folded around her bag in front of her soiled skirts. "But, as I was saying, my idea could prove economical in the end."

A hint of a smile appeared at the corner of his lips. "Oh? Pray, go on."

"I know you are thinking of investing in the Day family business, so why don't we commission a riverboat from Teddy Day to help you in your decision?"

Father rolled his eyes and stood, patting his vest pockets for his glasses. Flora pointed to the top of his head. He fitted the wire-rimmed glasses over his ears. "Flora, I know you are fond of this fellow, but we do not *need* a riverboat for the few trips a year we take as a family. And besides, I do not need one of their boats to know if I wish to invest in their business. If I had a product for every business I invested in, I would be swimming in items that we simply do not need.

Money breeds money. Spending money on things is a detriment to that cause. I am investing a large sum with the Day business because not only will it provide *free* shipment for all the raw sugar I'm sending to the Duprés' factory—which will be a significant savings if I can secure the Bridgewaters' sugar along with the rest I have already contracted—but I also see it as lucrative with the percentages I would receive with each sale. If I wanted a boat, they would simply give me one."

She paused in her speech. She hadn't thought of that, and from his tone she could tell he was growing more and more annoyed with her apparently silly line of reasoning. "You're investing that heavily?"

"Not that it is any concern of yours, but yes. I have a desire to increase my Southern holdings as the East is conquered for me. I would take on the West, but your mother detests the idea of traveling to San Francisco, and as she asks for so little in regard to my business traveling, I agreed to her request of not pursuing it." He waved her off. "We do not *need* a steamboat, Flora, and that's that."

"But if you are going to the South on business more often, you could use it all the time. Or if you didn't wish to travel the Mississippi River, imagine, in the summers you wouldn't have to take the public line to and from Newport and the New York offices."

"I do not mind the public luxury liner, and if I desire privacy, I always have my Pullman car for *any* line I wish to travel, which is far more *economical* than what you've proposed. Next time you think of interrupting me while I work, do not do so unless you are bearing a tea tray and a dime novel to keep you quiet." He motioned for her to exit the room, leaving the door ajar. "Now, if you'll excuse me, I need to dress for this evening."

Blast. She should have gone through her mother. If Mother wanted it, Father would consider purchasing it. *Neophyte mistake.* His comment about the novel should have stung, but she was too used to it by now. She was *never* wanted in his study.

Flora waited for the main stairs to creak before she returned to his office desk and flipped through his New Orleans correspondents, and as he would not have any gentlemen in his address ledger with anything less than five million in his bank account, she read through the names of the men who would have ample funds to purchase a riverboat. Footfalls sounded in the hall, and she froze at the desk, spying a flash of black skirts as the maid, Becky, flurried past with a stack of soiled gowns. Flora exhaled and jotted down a few of the trickier names. She stuffed the paper into her reticule, pausing on sight of the rumpled handkerchief from the well-meaning stranger.

With the tips of her fingers, she pulled it from her bag, causing it to unfurl, revealing a perfect black spot in the center of the cotton. She dropped it. Her heart thudded. How many pirate romance novels had she read of someone receiving such a sign—a mark of promised death. She shivered. "You are being ridiculous. No one uses that sign anymore, if they even did in the first place."

Footsteps sounded in the hall once more, heavier this time, and lest Father catch her, she abandoned the unnerving handkerchief and dashed out to select her dress while she waited for her turn with the maid. Father's sharp intake of breath brought Flora to a halt on the stairs. She was torn whether she should tell him. Deciding he would be less annoyed with the strange object than if she admitted to snooping in his office, she fled.

Once more, Flora was the last to use the shared facilities, resulting in a rather wet, plain braided bun with a few curls to frame her face and the last one into the carriage, which had all scowling at her. She pretended not to notice and patted her low coiffure, praying she had set the pins firmly in place.

Within moments they were filing out of the carriage, as it seemed every fine family had their residence on St. Charles Avenue or in the French Quarter. Before she even had a chance to descend the carriage, Teddy was there, smiling up at her, offering her his hand. He would be her darling Mr. Day before summer's end.

Seven

Flora stifled a yawn as she picked up a warmed china plate at the buffet table that held an impressive array of breakfast meats, quiche Lorraine, tiers of pastries, and pots of chocolate, tea, and coffee. While the aromas drove her mouth to watering, Flora couldn't help but think the food would be even more enjoyable in bed after such a late party and her near-death experience that had left her bruised and stiff. Yet Great-Auntie Violet insisted that all join together at breakfast instead of taking trays to their rooms. Though the initial change in habit had been rather disastrous with getting so many women dressed and downstairs in time, after staying up for parties every evening since their arrival, Flora and the young ladies mastered it after yesterday once they discovered Auntie Violet had all the remnants of food sent away to the kitchens and the pantry locked after the appointed hour, leaving them famished until teatime.

Thinking of that hunger-filled morning, Flora lifted a second golden puffed square dusted in powdered sugar with the silver tongs, smacking her lips in anticipation as she set it on her gold-rimmed plate. After tasting it for the first time with

Teddy yesterday for the apology treat she had promised him, Flora could not get enough of them. Between this treat and chicory café au lait, she could grow quite plump this summer.

"Really, Flora," Mother chided, reaching for her teacup, eyes half closed.

"Excuse me, Mrs. Dubois, but there is a gentleman caller here for Miss Flora," the butler announced, holding a silver tray in one hand, his other tucked behind his back.

Flora blinked at the butler and dropped her gaze to the plate in hand. *But my beignets.* If it was Teddy, perhaps he wouldn't mind her bringing her plate along, especially if she brought him a couple extra. She reached for the tongs and balanced two more on her plate as the butler handed the tray to Flora, which held the gentleman's calling card.

Tacy straightened, pinching her cheeks. "Who is it, Flora?"

Flora swept it up and read aloud, "Mr. Clancy Drake. Does anyone know him? Father?"

"I do not." Father lowered his copy of yesterday after-noon's *New Orleans Item*, the shuffle and snap of pages being folded betraying his agitation at the interruption. "And so it begins," he muttered, reaching for his coffee cup and lifting it to the footman to refill.

Mother stirred her tea, clanking the silver spoon against the china. "Begins, Florian? It already began the moment Flora became of age. But because you never think of any man good enough for your daughters and have yet to budge on her dowry, we now have *four* marriageable daughters with another closely behind them."

"Nonsense," he retorted, stuffing a forkful of andouille sausage into a croissant.

"Florian, you must be flexible lest our daughters become

the most famous, wealthiest spinsters in America." She tapped her forefinger nail on the table linen, revealing her annoyance. "If Flora was not so pretty and from such a fine family, she would be labeled a wallflower and forgotten, which is *why* I agreed to this trip in the first place. Here, there is not much competition in dowries, and the young men think our daughters' three million each is generous."

"It *is* generous," he snorted, then took another draft of his coffee. "If our daughters cannot make a life with three million apiece, they should not be wedding said gentlemen."

Mother flung up her hands. "Really, Florian."

As the verdict on whether or not she could receive Mr. Drake did not appear to be concluding anytime soon, Flora slipped into her seat and took a bite of the golden cloud. Aunt Violet sent her a wink and lifted her own beignet in a silent salute before doing the same.

Father sighed and pinched the bridge of his nose. "Hyacinth, you know I love you and our daughters, but you have to trust me that I know what is best. For if no man would have them as a pauper heiress, they do not deserve to have my millions upon my death, making them the wealthiest women in America, for by then I plan to have long surpassed the Dupré family." He turned to stare down the line of women. "Do you girls understand?"

The siblings nodded, except Tacy, while Cornelia kept her eyes fixed on her plate, her cheeks reddening from the topic of money. Though unheard of in most households, money was discussed quite frequently at the Wingfields' table, because Father did not wish to shield his family from the motivations of the world. How could his daughters defend their hearts if they did not understand the power of money?

"Some of us need more money than others," Tacy dared to voice, moving food about her plate without eating.

"There is more to life than a pretty face, Tacy, and if your caller does not find you attractive, you do not want him for a husband," he replied, his gaze still on his paper where he did not see Tacy's color fall, tears welling in her eyes.

Mother reached for his hand on the table, squeezing it, murmuring something that only he could hear. His brow furrowed at Mother for half a second before he realized his inadvertent insult.

"That is not to say you don't have a pretty face, my dear Tacy, but fair looks are not everything," Father added, reaching for another croissant. "Take care you remember that when choosing a spouse. I want more in a son-in-law than a handsome dandy." He pointed his fork at his daughters. "And I *do* want sons-in-law by summer's end or I will be decreasing your dowry."

Flora stilled. *Why would he threaten to lower our dowry? Why the haste?*

"What? Father!" Tacy's voice rose to glass-shattering proportions. "You cannot just demand such things."

"I believe I just did."

Mother patted his hand. "While I understand your motives in keeping the dowry so modest, you must be more open to the young men who wish to pay call. Promise me you will at least consider them before dismissing them as dandies? They cannot help being handsome."

Father snapped his paper open again. "Very well, but they could at least allow us to finish our breakfast in peace and call at two of the clock, as is proper."

Auntie Violet reached for her napkin and dabbed her lips.

"If you are done with your little tirade, Florian and Hyacinth, I think we should not keep the young men waiting as *I* invited them."

"You what?" Father and Mother exclaimed.

Flora and her sisters' gazes went to the four vacant place settings. "Them?"

Auntie's eyes widened in a show of innocence that Flora was beginning to recognize as anything but innocent. "Well, Florian, you were not giving the poor fellows the time of day at the ball I threw for you all, and they just looked so darling in their coattails and efforts to obtain admittance to pay your daughters call, I couldn't resist helping them out."

"Them?" Flora and Tacy repeated above the din of her father's protestations of the way things were done.

"Yes, them. Now, girls, leave a place between you for a gentleman to sit beside you. Harold, rearrange the plates, would you?" She motioned to the butler, who surged forward into motion with the footmen to move the ladies' plates. Auntie Violet patted Cornelia's hand as she moved to vacate her chair. "Not you, dear. You stay beside me."

"How many are coming?" Mother gasped, half rising from her chair, her napkin falling to the floor. A footman swept it away and promptly replaced it with a fresh folded linen beside Mother's plate as the girls rushed about in a flurry of lace, silk, and ribbons.

"Four, maybe five." She flipped her hand dismissively and tapped her spoon atop her hard-boiled egg. "Enough for Olive, Tacy, Flora, and Ermengarde to have their pick and solve your little problem, Florian, of having so many unwed daughters. Though I still do not see the problem of them remaining unmarried when you possess funds enough to care for you all until the end of time."

Nora crossed her arms. "I am nearly seventeen. You girls don't need all five men, so I'll take one off your hands."

Flora's heart clenched at the thought of the youngest out in society. She did not approve of her being admitted to balls before her New York debut, but to have her husband hunting before her debut? Scandalous. "Nora, you *know* you cannot seek out a husband."

"Auntie, that is not how things are done," Father groaned, ignoring his daughters' little quarrel as he usually did. "What will New Orleans society think of us coming into their city and disregarding etiquette by extending an invitation to these men for *breakfast*?"

"*I* extended the invitation. The society matrons will overlook any sins I commit because of my wealth and age. And besides, I am offering their sons the chance to be wed to a daughter of *the* Florian Wingfield and establishing a lifelong connection with one of the greatest titans of our day."

Father narrowed his eyes at her blatant flattery. "You know I am immune to your toadyism, Auntie."

Auntie lifted her chin and her cup. "I haven't the slightest notion what you are on about. The moment I received your letter stating your wish to come for the summer, I held a little tea with a choice few matrons of society and casually mentioned who you were and perhaps what you are worth and what you are offering as a dowry for each of your girls." She chuckled into her napkin. "After that little earth-shattering announcement, you should have seen the callers I had prior to your arrival, all clamoring for an invitation to your welcoming ball. Why, my butler had to turn away callers at one point."

Father muttered something into his hand, which had Mother patting him on the other.

"It *is* what you wished for, dear," Mother whispered. "And isn't it safest for the girls?"

Safest? Flora quirked a brow to Olive, who shook her head in bewilderment.

"Let's not keep our guests waiting a moment longer." Auntie nodded to the butler.

The butler's departure sent Tacy scrambling for the looking glass above the mantel, smoothing her hair into place while Olive straightened her lace jabot and moved down a chair, as did Nora, who drew herself up to display her favorite assets, which had Tacy pulling at her own neckline.

Ermengarde rolled her eyes. "There is more to life than securing the hand of some gentleman. And so what if Father takes away our funds? We have minds, able bodies, do we not? We can work."

"Ever the suffragette," Nora giggled.

Flora shoveled down her beignets before Mother could make a comment about a lady's consumption of large quantities of food before suitors.

Auntie Violet lifted her brows at this, her wrinkles prevalent around her pursed lips, but Flora could tell she was hiding her smile. "And, Flora, do look after Mr. Drake. He was unable to attend your welcoming party, but Clancy is a favorite of mine. I knew his mother well. Poor dear lady spent years trying to return to New Orleans, and the year her mansion on St. Charles was completed a few summers ago, she passed during a yellow fever outbreak." She shook her head. "Terrible time."

At the footfalls outside the breakfast door, the group rose

and Flora smoothed her pretty gown of blue silk with its embroidered clusters of pink roses and assumed a cheerful expression for Auntie's sake, her smile faltering the moment the gentleman she assumed was Mr. Drake strode into view. His dark locks, perfectly chiseled jaw, and muscular shoulders were too manly to bear gazing at for long. Unfortunately, her reaction did not go unnoticed by her sisters, eliciting giggles from Tacy and Nora as all curtsied besides Flora, who remembered at the last moment to bob into a curtsy. Mr. Drake bowed to the group, sending a perfectly coiled curl springing from his pompadour to his forehead.

"Positively dashing," Tacy whispered to Flora.

Though he was no Teddy Day, *dashing* was the only way to describe him, but she couldn't allow her sister to know that lest Tacy use it against her. "I suppose so."

Tacy rolled her eyes. "Then I shall have him. One dowry in this family is as good as the next to woo a Southern suitor."

"Clancy, my dear boy. Come give your Auntie Violet a kiss." The elderly lady beckoned him to her side with both hands, the joy in her countenance testament to her love of the gentleman.

She couldn't contain her smile at Auntie's happiness. If a gentleman could garner such affection, to be treated as more of a son returning home than a friend, there must be something special about him.

Tacy elbowed her. "What are you doing? Are you only smiling now because I laid claim to him? Cease that or he will notice."

Beaming, Mr. Drake bent down, giving her a resounding kiss on her withered cheek. "Thank you for the invitation to join you, Auntie."

Auntie Violet patted his cheek. "Oh, you know that you never need to wait for an invitation to join me for a meal. Florian, ladies, allow me to present to you my friend, Clancy Drake, one of the wealthiest railroad barons in the States."

Mr. Drake gave a deep, booming laugh that brought Father's attention from his paper. "Now, Auntie, is that any way to introduce me to your guests? Listing one's status before we have even exchanged greetings?" Father chided.

"As I am determined to match him with one of my great-nieces, *yes*. I want them to know exactly who Clancy Drake is and what he can offer to a marriage." She lifted a pointed brow to Father. "Especially now that you seem so keen on marrying off your daughters at long last."

"I thought you Southerners were supposed to be painfully subtle," Father said as he reached for his coffee.

"Most are." Auntie shrugged. "I, however, am originally a New York knickerbocker. And of course you must make allowances for my age. One of the greatest gifts time gives us is the ability to spout off one's opinion without being judged too harshly." She winked at Flora, which drew Clancy's gaze.

Something flashed in his eyes, and in that moment she felt her heart dip, followed at once with guilt at thinking of a gentleman being attractive when she had her heart set on Teddy. *But it is not as if he sees me in that light.* She smiled and then focused on the back of her chair, waiting for her confusion to abate, when behind him two gentlemen appeared that she had met that first night—a Mr. Ward, who seemed rather winded, as if he had run to avoid being late, and the handsome gentleman she recognized as Teddy's friend, Mr. Gale Thornton.

Curtsies, bows, and pleasantries exchanged, Auntie clapped

her hands. "Clancy will be sitting beside Flora. The rest of you gentlemen, please choose your seat."

Tacy, having a sparkle in her eyes directed toward Mr. Drake, elbowed Olive into switching places with her before the men joined the table, placing Mr. Drake between Flora and herself. Across the table, Mr. Thornton sat between Olive and Ermengarde, whose cheeks were flushed a pretty pink, while the paunchy Mr. Ward took a seat beside Nora, which had her at once relaxing her pose and drawing a long-suffering sigh. She downed her hot chocolate before glaring at Ermengarde, as if any gentleman in the world was preferable to Mr. Ward.

Mr. Drake swept Flora's hand into his and pressed a kiss atop it. "It is an honor to meet you at long last, Miss Wingfield."

Flora dipped her head. "Mr. Drake. I hope you are well after your travels?"

Before he could respond, two other male voices sounded in the foyer, the butler appearing with Teddy, in a striking burgundy morning coat with a matching cravat and gold brocade waistcoat, and Carlisle in tow. Nora brightened considerably as the only two vacant places were on her side of the table.

"Ah, the last of our party has arrived. I wasn't certain you would be joining us." Auntie Violet called to the brothers, motioning them to their seats as the footman brought the trays around the table instead of the buffet style they usually breakfasted. But as this entire breakfast was unprecedented, Flora did not hesitate at the chance of securing another beignet with Mother being too preoccupied to comment.

Flora nodded her greeting to the late arrivals, her heart

stammering, when Teddy glanced between her and Mr. Drake. His closely trimmed beard truly was becoming. As Teddy was seated at the far end of the table with Nora, and Carlisle with Mother and Father, she turned to speak to Mr. Drake before Tacy ignored poor Mr. Ward completely. "With a name like Clancy, I would think to find you in the Wild West, not at my aunt's table."

That rumbling laugh from Mr. Drake drew all feminine eyes to him. "I actually *am* from the 'Wild West,' as you call it. My mother married a railroad man, who had us spending many seasons away from New Orleans, and I have only recently returned to my fair city."

"Which is why he was not at your ball," Auntie interjected from across the table, her gaze flicking to Father. "After the untimely fatal accident of his father, Clancy now oversees the railroad expansion all over the country, a prosperous endeavor for such a young man."

Father straightened at this. "What lines are you overseeing currently?"

"We have just completed a few transcontinental routes, including one from Los Angeles to New Orleans. And we are currently working on a line from New Mexico to California, which should be completed by August."

"And how do you secure so many projects when you are working with different lines?" Father queried, setting his fork down, a sign of his interest that usually turned into his investing in a new venture.

"I'm an independent contractor who presents bids the lines cannot refuse, and my late father's and my track record are golden, as our fleet of workers are fairly compensated and therefore reliable." He took the tongs from the tray the footman held and selected a variety of pastries, settling them beside his quiche. "Though, after the completion of the line in August, I intend to oversee from afar as I have recently come into some holdings this spring in New York City, and I must attend to them in person."

Mother's brows lifted at this. "So, you will be taking up residence in New York?" She sent Flora a wink, humming around her mouthful.

"If I can find a property to suit me on Madison Avenue, I plan to set up residence there by Christmas." He smiled down the table to Auntie. "Rest assured, I will not be selling my mother's dream home here, for I intend on keeping it as a Southern base for all the visiting I will do with you, Auntie."

She lifted her spoonful of egg to him in a salute, whispering loudly to Mother, "Such a good fellow."

The barrage of questions after that bit of news was dizzying, and when Father finally turned to speak with Carlisle, Mr. Drake leaned to her. "So, Miss Flora, what is it that you do?"

Having taken an unfortunately large bite, she worked to swallow, lifting her hand to conceal her full cheeks. "What I do?" she managed around her beignet, her neck flamed at the puffs of powdered sugar that sifted through her lips with each word. At home, no one would think of asking. She was a socialite, and everyone knew what that entailed.

Teddy chuckled at her spewing powdered sugar. Flora couldn't help but be pleased that he had noticed her from across the table for a second time. Perhaps being seated apart would prove advantageous in sparking something within him. Mr. Drake's eyes brightened at her misstep, but being a gentleman, he refrained from bringing attention to the powdered sugar now sprinkled on the front of her floral gown. While Mr. Drake was painfully handsome, she would not flirt with him only to make *someone* jealous.

"Yes." He leaned toward her as if she were the only one in the room. "What are your interests, hopes, and aspirations?"

"That is quite the question for a single breakfast." Flora sipped her water and speared a pineapple cube from her crystal fruit cup.

"Then you must allow me to see you to luncheon to hear the answer. Perhaps something can be arranged for this week, if your diary allows, and I can show you about the city? I know that it can be daunting to be in a new place for the summer season, but I assure you, there is nowhere I would rather be, no matter the heat. Would that be agreeable?"

Flora froze, realizing her mistake in her leading answer as the table quieted at that moment, Tacy's slim chest heaving with suppressed fury at being excluded from Mr. Drake's invitation, Mother's gaze eager, Father nodding approvingly, and Teddy scowling . . . and she rather liked him scowling over her. *No flirting. Be direct.*

"She would be delighted," Mother answered, lifting her glass to Mr. Drake. "How kind of you to escort my eldest to your favorite places."

"Oh, wonderful!" Auntie Violet clasped her hands to her lace jabot, her eyes shining.

"Yes," Flora choked out. "And Cornelia, Tacy, and Olive must attend as well since they know so little of the city. We will make it quite the merry party."

Teddy frowned, but as he did not interject, Flora felt her pride and resolve strengthen. If he wished to court her, wouldn't he have spoken out before now? He certainly had ample opportunity.

"Very well." He turned to the ladies. "What say you, Mrs. Rosings, Miss Tacy, and Miss Olive?"

Tacy rewarded him with a brilliant smile, displaying her slightly stained teeth. "A merry party indeed, Mr. Drake."

Theodore attempted to engage Flora in conversation, but every time he inclined his head toward her, he found Mr. Drake and Flora engrossed in a lively discussion that would inevitably turn into bouts of laughter. He could save her from that outing if only she would *look* at him instead of being so friendly to the man. But Flora was nothing if not friendly, always wishing everyone to feel at ease.

He took his last swig of coffee. While he had accepted the invitation with hopes to persuade Mr. Wingfield to purchase a boat from him, despite his brother being invited as well, Florian Wingfield wasn't giving him a moment of time and seemed as enthralled with Mr. Drake as the rest of the women, leaving Carlisle to Mrs. Wingfield and him to Nora, who had more interest in fluttering her lashes at him than conversing, an action that had him adjusting his now-tight neckcloth. He coughed and turned to Cornelia. "You are looking healthy these days, Mrs. Rosings."

Her brows rose. "And by healthy I am assuming you are attempting to politely avoid addressing the amount of weight I have put on in recent months?" She pursed her lips and set down her forkful of food.

"Uh." That had certainly *not* been his intention, and besides, how could he possibly be thinking of that since he had only met the woman once in society years ago before she had married and then briefly at the ball?

"I will have you know I have only gained what the doctors have deemed necessary for the baby." She stabbed at her fruit cup. "And I think it is abominable for you to even venture on such a delicate topic while my *husband* is abroad and cannot defend me."

He cleared his throat. "Mrs. Rosings, please, I meant no offense. Truly—"

"Teddy dear, how is your mother?" Mrs. Dubois's shaky, age-worn voice pulled him from his stupor but did not distract Flora from her suitor.

He glanced sideways at Mrs. Rosings as she finished her fruit and began consuming her grits with gusto. Deciding that he could do no more damage than he already had by letting the misunderstanding lie, he turned to Mrs. Dubois. "She is well and enjoying the season. Thank you for inquiring, Mrs. Dubois."

She shook her finger at him. "That is an answer you give when you do not wish for further inquiries. I have known you since you were in dresses, so the least you can do is answer me."

"A practice that I will never understand. Why on earth do women put their boys in dresses when babies?" Theodore queried, hoping to distract her. Mother had taken his jilting just about as well as he had, but he would never admit that his mother was secretly mortified over her son's public shaming and was doing everything in her power to see him happily married by summer's end and mend his heart. Another engagement was the last thing he desired, yet he would not burden his mother with his decision to remain single until she had recovered from the latest disappointment.

"Babies crawl and dresses keep babies from crawling

away." Mrs. Dubois laughed. "Though I do remember your mother wishing to keep you dressed as a baby longer than Carlisle."

This turned the conversation into snorts from the gentlemen and giggles from the ladies, except Flora, who well knew his discomfort of his mother's doting upon him in public.

"Speaking of my mother." Theodore adjusted his collar again. "Mother is planning a dinner for Saturday and wishes for me to extend her invitation in person." He withdrew a card and presented it to Mrs. Dubois, thankful for a topic to keep her occupied.

"We would be honored if you all attended," Carlisle interjected, his gaze flitting toward Flora's end of the table.

Mrs. Dubois pored over the invitation before handing it to Mrs. Wingfield, who nodded with approval and smiled.

"A steamboat dinner. How unique. Please tell your mother we accept." Mrs. Wingfield passed the note to Mr. Wingfield. "Florian, be certain to mark your diary."

"It would be foolish of a potential investor not to attend," Father replied, turning his attention to Carlisle. "And I have heard from others of your competition for the head of the company."

"Yes, this dinner will announce it to the public, as the Day family will be having society touring our personal steamboat. While it was Theodore's idea, Father decided it was only fair that *both* of the brothers attend in an attempt to garner sales," Carlisle explained.

"I see." Florian placed his napkin atop his plate, the footman whisking it away at once. "I worry about your family's divided attention . . ."

Theodore pulled his shoulders back and looked directly at

Mr. Wingfield. "If anything, sir, I believe it will double our sales this summer through healthy competition."

"And afterward we expect the sales to continue to climb with the help of your investment," Carlisle added.

"This is so exciting!" Tacy lightly clapped her hands. "I'll have to write my friends in Newport and tell them all about your quaint riverboat dinner. I had thought when we left for New Orleans, we would have to sacrifice our habits of multiple parties a week, but now this will be our third since arriving. How unexpected!"

"As it should be. The Wingfield sisters are the toast of New Orleans." Clancy smiled at Flora, sending a blush up her neck.

Theodore refrained from rolling his eyes at Clancy's obvious attempts to garner affection from the Wingfield ladies.

"And if you will forgive me for being so bold, I would be honored to sit beside you at the Days' dinner, Miss Wingfield," Clancy said, his eyes on her.

Too far. At the growl swelling in his chest, he looked to Flora, desperate to make eye contact and signal that he was ready to save her, but at the nod she gave Clancy, he stabbed at his now-cold breakfast. *What is the matter with me? What do I care if a gentleman is paying call to one of my friends?* But at the morsel of rubbery egg wedging in his dry throat, Theodore found that he did care who Flora was seeing. Very much.

Eight

Flora leaned over the hedge of azaleas as far as she dared, its sharp branches piercing her sleeves as she perched her opera glasses on her nose and thrust her head through the wrought-iron fence. She adjusted the lenses to view a beautiful portrait of a young woman from the early eighteen hundreds, judging from the fashion of the model's hair. "Oh! I think it is an original Thomas Sully painting. Did you know he painted Queen Victoria's portrait? And would you just look at that gorgeous imported rug? Though the color does tend to clash a bit with—"

"No. Because polite people do not peer into others' houses before being invited inside!" Teddy hissed. "Now put that down before you get us both arrested."

"But I don't know the owners and will likely never receive an invitation. How am I supposed to capture the essence of New Orleans interior designing if I do not study it first-hand?" Flora replied, adjusting the focus of the right lens to a collection of porcelain birds mounted on decorative blocks on the far wall that rose to a point above the fireplace mantel. "Bizarre."

"Flora," Teddy groaned out her name.

"Shh. Someone is coming," she squealed, then leapt off the two-foot brick wall onto the sidewalk as a servant came running at them with what appeared to be a closed umbrella in hand.

"Off my lady's lawn, you oglers! Hooligans!" the man-servant shouted, which unfortunately caught the attention of a policeman standing at the corner of Prytania Street.

"Run!" She grabbed Teddy's hand and pulled him around the block, laughing at how nervous the poor man appeared. But the policeman was surprisingly fast, and her laughter turned into gasps for air. She pushed Teddy through an open gate and sank to the ground, the gravel biting her shins, with Teddy squatting down behind the hedge. She held a finger to her lips until the policeman's pounding footsteps faded. She sighed and leaned against Teddy's shoulder. "That was close."

"Flora Wingfield. I told you—"

"I know. But I had to see, and I am so glad I did because, Teddy, an *original* Thomas Sully!" She fanned her cheeks with her handkerchief. "Mother will definitely want to make the owner's acquaintance."

"Which you cannot do, may I remind you, because that butler will recognize you in an instant!" Teddy returned.

Flora clapped her hand over his mouth. She almost jerked her hand back from the spark that traveled through her arm, but the fear of the lawman hearing him kept her hand steady until she was certain they were safe. "I'm going to let go now, but please do not caterwaul your displeasure at being silenced."

"So, you *are* frightened of being caught." He grinned and swiped his cuff over his brow. "And where was all that bravado about your being a socialite and therefore above being arrested?"

She dared a peek over the hedge, whispering, "I didn't want Father to be alerted again."

"Again?"

"Well, I said I have never been *charged* with anything. I have, regrettably, been taken down to the station more than I care to admit. And while I am a well-known socialite, there has been occasion for Father's pocketbook to make an appearance or three."

Teddy sagged into his drawn-up knees, his shoulders shaking. "I hope it was worth it." He chuckled. "You ran faster than one of Mrs. Dubois's rabbits for the front door."

Flora giggled, muffling the sound at once with her hand for fear the man would hear. "Well, it was worth it. For now I know just the color scheme I wish to incorporate in the master bedroom for the Thompsons' steamboat."

At the gonging of a nearby church bell, Flora's breath left her. "Is it really two of the clock already?" After a morning of tea and scones and redesigning Teddy's steamboat for the Thompsons, she had decided they required a break for inspiration, but as it always did with Teddy around, time had gotten away from her.

"Why?" He smirked. "I thought your outing with Mr. Drake wasn't scheduled until after my steamboat dinner?"

Flora rooted around her reticule for her pocket mirror. "It isn't, but I have my outing with Mr. Grayson in a quarter of an hour."

"Bradford Grayson? Why are you seeing him?"

"Because he is eligible and he asked me to tea," she retorted, holding up the silver rectangle looking glass, smoothing back her hair and biting her lips for added color before dropping the mirror back into her bag. She gave the bag a shake to allow the mirror to settle into the bottom. Of course, she had only accepted Mr. Grayson because he had asked her in front of Mother, and Father had demanded she accept, but Teddy did not need to know that.

Teddy held his hand out to her. "If you are getting tea, then we best get you back home before he cancels."

She jutted out her chin, ignored his hand, and strode out onto the sidewalk, the scent of a sweet pie wafting on the air. "Gentlemen never cancel on me. And I'm not returning. I'm meeting him at the Bridgewaters' home now." She turned to find the source and discovered the pie was cooling on a rear open windowsill of a lovely home with Doric pillars that had her reaching for her opera glasses.

"And your *mother* approved of this little arrangement? A gentleman requests to call upon you and yet *you* are the one who travels to see him?"

"She was the one who arranged it," she murmured from behind the lenses.

"That is hardly proper. And please do not pull those glasses out, and before you argue with me, you don't have time to snoop."

She sighed and returned the opera glasses. "Mr. Grayson and I are taking a stroll to a tea shop."

"Without a chaperone?"

"Well, unless you are willing to act as one, then yes." She crossed her arms and lengthened her stride. *Really, if Teddy isn't going to ask me to luncheon himself, he shouldn't be so bothered.*

"If you had told me, I would have canceled my next meeting. You shouldn't be alone—"

She stepped aside to allow a couple to pass and held up her hand to Teddy. "If Mother and Father approve of Mr. Grayson, then I'm certain it is fine."

"No, you don't know him. No one does. Doesn't it strike you as rather strange that a man no one truly knows suddenly has your father's attention?"

She clutched her hands over her reticule to stay her trembling. Bradford Grayson did not sit well with her, but her father did not care to listen to her many protests, simply citing that it was her duty to comply. She was pretty weary of doing her so-called duty, yet Teddy had no place questioning her father's discernment. "Father approved this outing and therefore I *must* go. I'll see you tomorrow for our meeting. Excuse me." She brushed past him.

He caught her elbow. "I'm sorry. You're right to be angry with me, but at least let me walk with you. For while the Garden District may seem safe, thieves and panhandlers lurk in odd places."

Great. Now he is escorting me to my outings with other gentlemen. She sighed and took his arm. *Perhaps I should allow Clancy Drake to pay a call to me after all and put an end to this charade in my heart.*

Theodore trailed behind Flora and Bradford down Louisiana Avenue, unwilling to leave her alone with the fellow. From what he had gathered, Bradford Grayson had visited the Bridgewaters only once before when Grayson was but a manager for Wellington Sugar. *And now Grayson just happens to return to New Orleans with the Wingfields?* Theodore stuffed his hands into his pockets, his gaze never leaving the pair. *Why is Mr. Wingfield open to him, of all gentlemen, paying call to Flora?* He had seen suitors try for her hand before, ones with far greater credentials than Grayson. One would think that with his holding such a close connection with that cad Wellington, Mr. Wingfield would steer his daughters in the opposite direction.

Theodore paused on the street corner, watching through the window of an old mansion that had been converted into a tea shop as Grayson held the chair for Flora, his hand lingering too long at her shoulders. She sent him a scowl and moved away to what Teddy assumed was the powder room, leaving behind her reticule atop the linen. Grayson took his seat and reached across the table linen and popped open the beaded reticule, slipping out a coin purse and withdrawing a folded bill before replacing the coin purse inside.

Theodore's neck heated. *Mr. Wingfield trusts his daughter with this man?* He clenched his fists. If the man was too busy to look after his daughter's well-being, then it was up to Theodore to expose this man for the fraud he was. He charged inside, ignoring the garçon.

"Bradford Grayson." Theodore greeted him with a smile so as not to draw unwanted attention and sank into Flora's vacant seat. "I suggest you return Miss Wingfield's pin money."

Grayson looked down his nose at Theodore and trilled his fingers atop the table. "What on earth do you think you are doing here?"

"Looking out for my friend."

"Well, she does not wish it or she would not have come here alone to meet with me." He smirked. "And what makes you think I am stealing from her?"

Theodore nodded to the vest pocket where he had seen the money disappear. "Are you going to confess to her or shall I tell her?"

"Tell me what?" Flora asked from behind him.

The men stood at once. Theodore glared at Bradford and waited until the waiter approached.

"Shall I be fetching a third chair, Mr. Day?" he asked, one hand behind his back, the other gesturing to a nearby chair.

"Yes," Theodore replied, glaring at Flora's suitor.

"No," Bradford growled. "Mr. Day was just leaving."

"Would someone please inform me as to what is going on?" Flora whispered, eyes on Theodore.

"Grayson stole from your reticule," Theodore answered without taking his gaze from Grayson.

"Teddy!" Flora grasped Theodore's arm, pulling him away from the table with a smile to Grayson and the waiter. "You are behaving irrational and making a scene. Why would Mr. Grayson take money from me?"

"Go ahead and check your bag, Miss Wingfield," Mr. Grayson called, gesturing to the purse on the table and earning the glances of nearby guests, eager for a diversion.

Flora's cheeks brightened. "That is completely unnecessary, sir. I'm certain this has all been some terrible misunderstanding." She glanced at Theodore, eyes wide. "Still, perhaps it is best if Mr. Day joins us and so put to rest the tongues of bystanders."

"Well, that is a relief that you believe me, but I refuse to

stay here and be insulted by Theodore Day with his belliger-
ent allegations." He nodded to the garçon and handed him
the very bill Theodore witnessed him taking from Flora's
reticule. "Miss Wingfield? Shall we?" He motioned for her
to join him.

Flora gave Theodore's arm a squeeze. "I am certain an
apology would go a long way toward repairing the damage—"

"Certainly not. I *saw* him, Flora. Why don't you believe
me?" Theodore whispered before glaring at the man. "And
you are officially uninvited to the dinner aboard the *Lark*,
Grayson."

Grayson clutched at his heart. "I'm wounded. How will I
ever survive missing a dinner party on a *boat*." He snorted
and took Flora's arm, who hesitated.

"Miss Wingfield! If you stay with Mr. Day, you will be
joining him in the insult, and if you do, I am afraid I cannot
do business with a family who would believe such slander-
ous lies," Grayson hissed and plunked his hat on, the action
making his ears poke out from the brim.

Reluctantly, Flora took Grayson's arm and allowed him
to lead her outside.

Theodore followed them out, unwilling to let the matter
rest. "Flora!"

She glanced over her puffed sleeve and shook her head,
continuing on her walk.

He shoved his hands into his pockets. How could she refuse to believe him when he was only trying to protect her?
He kept to the opposite side of the street of them, but as
they were all traveling in the same direction, he couldn't help
but notice when Flora paused, fishing about in her reticule,

her eyes on a house across the neutral ground. Her opera glasses. Theodore ran a hand over his face, shaking his head. *Let Grayson stop her.* He continued down the walkway when he saw the officer they had narrowly avoided being arrested by rounding the corner.

He didn't dare shout a warning. With a grunt, Theodore casually jogged across the avenue, moving diagonally toward her as if avoiding the oncoming carriage. "Flora!"

She gasped and whirled around, her incriminating opera glasses swinging around on their handle in her grasp. "Ted—"

"I say!" Grayson blustered.

He grabbed her wrist, turning her back to the policeman. "That officer. He is behind you."

She paled, her grip slacking on the glasses. They tumbled to the ground as the officer was passing. He at once paused and scooped them up, holding them for her, when he recognized them.

"You!"

Grayson reached for the glasses from the officer. "Thank you, sir."

"Oh no. These are staying with me. They are evidence."

"Evidence?" Mr. Grayson looked to Flora. "Why would Miss Wingfield possibly possess something of interest to you?"

"Miss Wingfield, is it?" He reached into his coat and withdrew a notebook, jotting down her name.

"Sir, it wasn't what it looked like." Flora gave a shaky laugh, glancing to Theodore.

"It looked like you were breaking the law, Miss Wingfield."

"I'd hardly call it that," Theodore interjected.

"What is going on?" Mr. Grayson shouted.

"These two were caught peering into Mr. and Mrs. Austen's private residence, using these very glasses. You two will have to come down to headquarters with me."

"Henning!" An officer rode up to them, accessing the scene. "What's going on?"

"Caught that peeping Thomasina." He pointed with his baton at a blushing Flora. "And her Tom."

"He isn't *my* Tom. And his name isn't Tom. This is Theodore Day, and I'm Flora Wingfield, a socialite from New York City, and—"

"Mr. Day?" The officer on horseback pushed back his cap, a grin spreading. "Officer Henning, I've known this gentleman and his family for years. He ain't no ogler."

"Oh, thank the good Lord." Flora leaned against Theodore's arm.

Theodore found himself wrapping an arm around her waist to keep her steady, earning a glare from Grayson.

Henning scowled at Flora as if to melt her into silence. "You didn't see the Austens' butler chasing after them, Knox."

Knox waved him off. "It is a classic case of one man's word against another."

"And are you saying a gentleman's word is greater than the butler's?" Henning crossed his arms.

"I didn't say that." The officer lifted his hand.

"And I didn't say we didn't—" Theodore started, but Flora elbowed him in the ribs.

"Mr. Day is innocent," Flora interjected, lifting her arms in front of her, wrists up as if readying herself for the cold embrace of handcuffs the moment the words fell from her lips. "I am the one you want! But let the record state that I was not *ogling* anyone. I merely wished to see the beautiful interiors of New Orleans before I returned home."

Mr. Grayson took that opportunity to take her hand and thread it through his arm. "Yes, my dear. Interiors are so diverting. Now, Officer Henning and Officer Knox, you must forgive Miss Wingfield, for she, as a feminine tourist socialite, suffers from overwhelming sensibilities that cause her to take leave of her senses, and we gentlemen were only trying to prevent and *not* aid her in her endeavors."

She gasped. "I do not suffer from sensibilities!"

Mr. Grayson shook his head. "You see, sirs, she is overwrought. Allow me to bring her home to her father where she will be thoroughly reprimanded."

Flora opened her mouth to protest, but this time it was Theodore who sent her a warning look to remain silent as Grayson masterfully appealed to the officers, eventually winning them over and even going so far as to secure her opera glasses on the promise she would not peer through others' windows ever again.

After the officers bade them farewell, Grayson bowed to her, presenting her with the opera glasses.

"I thank you, Mr. Grayson, even though your defense was rather an attack on my femininity," Flora muttered, dropping the opera glasses into her bag, sounding for all the world as if she would rather be carted off to jail than be indebted to Mr. Grayson.

"Miss Wingfield, we have lingered too long in the street. I best see you home. It is almost four of the clock."

Flora gasped, whirling to Theodore. "Your meeting! Teddy, you missed it . . . because of me." She rested her hand on his sleeve and whispered, "You worked so hard."

Theodore shrugged, swallowing back his disappointment. This meeting was hard enough to reschedule, and now that he had kept Mr. Thompson waiting without a reason, he would be that much further behind Carlisle, for his brother would likely hear of the debacle and offer the man a deal he could not refuse—well, as much a deal as the rules allowed. "We can still use the design for someone else. Besides, you needed me." He winked at her, whispering, "Even if you didn't want my help."

"Miss Wingfield! Any more lingering and I am nearly certain that I will *not* be doing business with your father."

"Mr. Wingfield will not desire to do business with a black-mailer," Theodore retorted. Something about that man did not sit well with him.

Mr. Grayson paled. "What did you say?"

Flora patted Theodore's arm. "Thank you for everything, but Father will be angry with me if I cause his dealings to fail." She slipped away from him, sending him a smile that made his missing his first big sale worth it.

Well, almost. Theodore had his work ahead of him if he had any hope in claiming the throne of Day's Luxury Line.

Nine

As she stood on the upper deck, the gentle wind sweeping her curls off her shoulders, Flora knew there was not a vessel in Newport to rival the beauty that was the Day family's personal floating palace. It seemed as if the Days had taken one of the elites' cottages in Newport and set it afloat with a giant crimson paddle behind it.

"What keeps the boat from running aground on sandbanks constantly?" Ermengarde called out to Teddy, then leaned over the rail to study the hull as the Wingfield family paused in their private tour for a clear view of the thirty-foot pair of decorative smokestacks.

"Our hulls and paddle wheels are designed to be wide and, more importantly, flat in order to travel the Mississippi even when the river is low," Teddy explained, excitement brewing in his eyes. "But even with the best design, a boat is only as good as its river pilot. As the river is always changing with every storm or drought, the pilot must stay alert at all times, even when traveling down a river he has traversed a hundred times."

Flora glanced to her left and could tell from Father's expression that even he was impressed by the sheer opulence, yet Flora knew she had best not push her father after her little incident that almost landed her in prison. If it hadn't been for Bradford Grayson, Flora was certain she would be on a boat heading up the Mississippi to the Illinois port, where their private Pullman awaited them to take her home, in shame, to New York City. If only Mr. Grayson had kept his mouth shut when he left her at her auntie's instead of bragging to her father about how he had saved her from scandal, Father would still be speaking with her, and Mother would not have insisted on having Mr. Grayson join their party, which led to some fairly smug glances from Grayson to Teddy as the group continued to the interior of the boat.

"Every few years, Mother would have us design and build her a new riverboat and sell the previous, making her our most challenging client to please," he admitted with a grin, pausing next in the grand salon as the girls openly admired the gilded room with its six crystal chandeliers cascading down the long, wide hall over a massive mahogany table. In the corner beside the piano was a string quartet, along with potted palms, clusters of yellow roses and red hibiscuses.

Mother gave a knowing laugh, patting Mrs. Day's arm in a show of camaraderie.

"Until at last, Mother fell in love with the *Lark*, the first riverboat I designed on my *own* five years ago." Teddy spread his arm wide for them to take note.

"And this is the one Mrs. Day has kept longer than all the rest?" Father looped his thumbs in his vest pockets, rocking back on his heels, a sign that he was calculating something. "That *is* an accomplishment. My question to you, Theodore

Day, is why hasn't your company become more famous for your designs? You should be swimming in orders, no?"

Teddy motioned the family down the hall. "While we are profitable, I have asked myself that very question. I believe that if we could have someone credible and in high standing in New York championing our line, our profitability would triple within a year."

Father merely nodded, continuing his study.

"It's a masterpiece, Florian," Mother murmured, her hand on Father's arm, worrying her bottom lip, her eyes bright with possibilities. She wanted it.

Flora grinned to Teddy from behind her father, pride bubbling inside her. But before she could whisper her encouragements to him about the possible sale of a boat with Mother's interest, the hum of guests arriving abruptly ended their tour, as Teddy had to excuse himself to greet them with the rest of the family. Flora gripped Olive's arm. "Should I ask Father what he thinks? It is agony not knowing what he is intending."

Olive placed a hand over Flora's. "We both know that when Father is thinking, we had best leave him to it." Her attention shifted to the entry, her cheeks tinting. "Besides, Mother will be the one who decides this purchase in the end, so you had best focus your tactics on her."

Flora turned to find Mr. Thornton approaching the door, Carlisle at his side, explaining something with enthusiastic gestures. *Olive likes Mr. Thornton?* She took in the broad-shouldered fellow with his voluminous brown curls as he flashed his dimpled grin to her sister, or was it directed toward her? Carlisle and Mr. Thornton bowed to Mother and Ermengarde while keeping their shoulders inclined toward Olive and Flora.

"What are you waiting for?" Flora teased, giving her a little shove. "Make yourself indispensable."

"I intend to." She ran her hands down her peach overskirt. "How do I look?"

Flora reached up and adjusted Olive's gold, diamond-encrusted tiara that sparkled in the candlelight. "There. We must keep up appearances."

"Always. And if we cannot have the gentleman of our dreams, let us thank heaven for handsome alternatives," she replied and twirled Flora to face Mr. Drake.

"Miss Wingfield." Mr. Drake bowed to her, looking quite dashing in his evening coattails.

"Flora." Carlisle appeared at her elbow, taking her hand in his, pressing a kiss atop it. "You are lovely tonight, as always."

"She is at that," Mr. Drake agreed, taking her other hand and kissing it as well. "And I was hoping, before you take dinner with me, that you would care to take a turn on the promenade deck? I have spent the majority of the day indoors working on new developments for my properties in New York, and it surely would be a sin to neglect such a fine night."

Flora opened her mouth to refuse, but Mother was at her side in a flash of satin, whispering, "He is one of the few deliciously handsome men your father has approved of in years. Go," she commanded through her smile, practically shoving Flora into his arms.

"I think a breath of fresh air is just what is needed." Flora nodded, sending Carlisle an apologetic smile, once again wondering why her father was suddenly interested in her having a beau. At least, though, Mr. Drake was eligible and attractive, unlike Grayson who was merely a business deal.

Bowing to Mother, Mr. Drake extended his arm to Flora, and settling her arm through his, she found he was quite solid. Cheeks heating, she was thankful he did not linger inside but instead led her around the deck to the staircase and up to the promenade deck, where Flora could see the line of guests on the dock as they drove to the two rows of torchlights that formed a path to the partitioned landing stage and on to the receiving line. She only recognized a few guests, including Penelope Bridgewater with her family, pausing to greet the Days. While she could make out Mr. and Mrs. Day receiving, she did not see the Day brothers.

She tugged up the neckline of a gown she had chosen because it was Teddy's favorite color, a brocade and satin *merveilleux* rose gown with a daring off-the-shoulder cut. Even though Teddy had acted nobly in saving her from being arrested and informing her of Mr. Grayson's stealing, which did indeed turn out to be true, nothing in his countenance revealed anything other than a true friendship for her.

A cacophony of squeals rippled through a cluster of women on the dock, all leaning toward a single gentleman, and that man was not looking tortured in the least with the grin he sported. Apparently, *his* receiving line started in front of his parents. She gritted her teeth against the idea of Teddy enjoying the belles' attentions and returned her own to Mr. Drake, who was leading her around the curving deck.

She skimmed her finger along the pristine white rail of the boat as they walked, enjoying the steady lapping of the river against the boat. Great bursts of steam sent her leaning into Mr. Drake's arm as she moved her hands to her ears.

Clancy laughed, his hand on her elbow. "Steady there," he cautioned, raising his voice to be heard.

"Whatever is it?" she called over the commotion, pressing her hand to her chest. "Why, it sounds like an organ?"

"It is only the calliope. I'm guessing it means all the guests have arrived." And at her confused look, he grasped her hand in his, pulled her to the rear of the boat above the crimson paddle, and pointed to the organ pipes mounted on the upper deck. "It's a steam-pressured organ that steamboats use for both entertainment and to alert any towns of the boat's approach." He grinned down at her, still holding her hand in his instead of sliding it into the crook of his arm as was acceptable. "I gather the steamboat you arrived on only used it for signaling and Mr. Day did not reach that part of his tour with you?"

"I would have made him play it then and there for me if he had." She squealed as more bursts of steam floated out of the calliope as it began the next tune and allowed Clancy to pull her away once more, running away from the near ear-bursting song.

Halfway around the deck, he slowed their flight. She refused to allow the pinch in her side to make her gasp and leaned her hand against a column to gather her breath, then looked up to find not the popular gingerbread molding of so many riverboats, but an opulent molding, almost Corinthian in nature, which complemented the thicker columns. Teddy's touch was all about—from the colors he selected to the very last detail overhead and underfoot. Even if she would have done a few things differently, she had to admire his craftmanship. She folded her hands against the column as she leaned into it, taking in the lovely city as the riverboat churned farther into the Mississippi River. Soon the calliope was replaced with the delicate singing of violins and the sound of the waves lapping against the hull. It was rather pleasant at night, and in the middle of the river there was no hum of pesky mosquitoes, though she supposed they would descend upon them the moment they docked. She sighed.

Mr. Drake leaned against the rail, staring down at her, cutting quite the figure in the moonlight. "Do you ever grow weary of this constant rotation of dinner parties, tea parties, balls, and the endless pursuit of entertainment?"

She shifted her back to the column, her fingers sliding along her pearl necklace to the sapphire pendant in its center. No one had ever addressed her like Mr. Drake in their few moments together. It was as if he had not read the same etiquette book as everyone else in society, the thought bringing a smile as he most likely did not out in the West. "I—"

"I know, you are a socialite." He smiled, stuffing his hands into his pockets. "You can admit to loving it and I wouldn't judge. I sometimes miss the simplicity of life in a tent."

"You didn't live in a Pullman?"

He threw back his head and laughed. "Is that what you have been thinking? No. When I didn't sleep under the stars, I was beneath a canvas tent avoiding the rain, snow, and sometimes even wild animals."

"Well, we may not have tents, but perhaps marriageable women out in society on the prowl for husbands will remind you of wild animals." Flora flicked open her fan in her left hand, holding it still in front of her face.

"Yourself excluded, of course." He chuckled.

"Didn't you get my message?" She laughed, gesturing to her fan. "Nearly every gentleman I know has studied the language of the fan."

He drew his brows together, resting his chin on his fore-finger and thumb. "Pray, teach me."

"When I hold it open, thus, it means 'desirous of acquaintance.'" She felt her cheeks heat. She had meant it in jest, but the way his eyes sparked, caused her stomach to dip.

"As do I." He grinned. "Your aunt has mentioned you to me many times over the years, and as I traveled more to Chicago and New York City for business, I had heard tales of Mr. Wingfield's comely eldest daughter. I must say they were grossly inadequate."

She froze. Not once in her four and twenty years had a man ever insulted her looks. "Excuse me?"

His gray eyes widened. "Oh no." He lifted callused hands. "No! That is not what I intended to convey. That was supposed to be a compliment! I meant that you're a classic beauty."

She crossed her arms and raised a single brow.

"Miss Wingfield, I truly meant no offense." He sighed, his shoulders caving. "I have never attempted to court a young woman before and I am making quite the mess of it, aren't I?"

Court? She leaned back on the rail, suppressing a smile. However unlikely it was that this striking man had not courted before, she couldn't help but believe him, for he wasn't like most who had paid call to her . . . though, now that he had stated his intentions, she needed to somehow tactfully clarify that she was not available for courtship without insulting him in turn. *But if Teddy doesn't ever come calling, who will Father ask me to marry at summer's end?* She studied him in the moonlight, mulling over their odd tête-à-têtes and knowing that if she could not have Teddy, perhaps Mr. Drake could be someone she respected enough to wed. She loosened her grip and dropped her fan.

He scooped it up and handed it to her, his contrite expression enough to bring forth her giggles.

"You, sir, really must study the language of the fan. By dropping it, I have declared that 'we will be friends.' I'll forgive you this once, but the next time you compliment a lady, maybe ponder it for a moment before saying the first thing that comes to mind."

"That's the trouble. I did," he admitted, shaking his head as they both laughed. "Back west, I never had the time to court, but now that I am settling my affairs here before making my move to New York, I would say that I will practice with other young ladies. However, no other lady has caught my eye like you have, and it would feel unchivalrous to flatter other ladies when no other will do." He leaned down and swept her hand into his, pressing a kiss atop it. "Is there a fan sign for that?" he whispered.

Oh my. Flora's stomach twisted as she pulled her hand from his. She wasn't used to eligible gentlemen, much less such handsome gentlemen, paying her compliments, as they reserved those for women with better dowries. "Yes, but I shan't show you tonight, Mr. Drake."

A muffled, slow clap from behind broke the silence. Tacy swayed toward them in her new crimson Worth gown with its outrageously low neckline, her stuffed, hidden powdered puffs doing their best work to support her charms. "Now, *that* is how you compliment a lady, Mr. Drake." Tacy lowered her fan, arching her back coyly, drawing a blush from Flora at the show of décolletage. "But, if you would like to practice with another, I can offer my assistance." She wove her arm around his, lifting her brow to Flora, her meaning clear. *Leave.*

"If you'll excuse me, I must find a friend of my father." Before Clancy could object, she hastened to the stairs to escape Tacy's shameless flirting and Clancy's confusing compliments. She did not have time tonight to allow a gentleman to flirt with her, no matter how attentive or handsome he might be. She had a job to do. Pausing outside the grand hall by the coatroom, she pulled the slip of paper from her bodice and once more reviewed the names she had scribbled down in her father's study. The trick would be in finding the men who matched the names, as she had no idea what they looked like.

Lord, please let this work. Let Teddy see me as an asset to his work, she prayed as she collected her journal from her reticule that held her carefully laid plans for the interiors of several of Teddy's model steamboats with her most lavish touches. She paused beside the footman at the grand hall's entrance. "Excuse me, do you know where I might find a Mr. Bartholomew Radcliff?"

"Of course, miss." He gestured to a group in the far corner of the room just outside a row of open French doors, which would be such an obvious trek for a lady to sojourn unescorted. "He is the, um, larger gentleman in the group, the one with the pipe."

Ah. She had not counted on his being surrounded by other men, and the thought of approaching him while he was smoking . . . she suppressed a shudder when a new thought formulated. "And what of a Mrs. Thompson? I believe she is new to this area."

"Ah, yes. Mrs. Delia Thompson. She is the one in the

orange gown, Miss Wingfield." The young man gestured to a lady standing alone along the wall, a half-empty glass in her hand.

"Thank you," Flora said. She maneuvered through the guests, pausing beside Mrs. Thompson, folding her hands around her sketchbook in front of her overskirt, and dipped into a curtsy. "Good evening, I'm Flora Wingfield. I know we haven't formally met yet, but may I join you, Mrs. Thompson?"

The young woman straightened, her eyes widening, and smiled as if surprised by the attention. She returned Flora's greeting with an infinitesimal curtsy. "From the sound of you, I assume you are not from the South?"

Flora smiled. "New York City."

The woman's lips curved upward as she inclined her head. "Two ladies in clashing gowns speaking to each other instead of mingling with anyone but each other? Whatever will people say."

"Perhaps we are such an enchanting tableau that they overlook our faux pas," Flora replied and shook her head at the passing waiter, rejecting the refreshment. She would need both hands to showcase her idea.

She laughed. "Delia Thompson of St. Louis."

"I've heard of you."

"Oh?" Mrs. Thompson stiffened, her gaze flickering toward Penelope and her troupe of belles. "What did you hear?"

How on earth could she transition gracefully? *Do it. For Teddy.* "Only that you were rather lonely in your new home, so I thought I might show you something that could help."

She pursed her lips. "The only reason I am lonely is that

dreadful Penelope Bridgewater had her sights on my husband before he met me in St. Louis at Christmas, and she cannot bear that she lost him to a woman of modest means."

Flora snapped her jaw closed before Mrs. Thompson could notice. "She was interested in Mr. Thompson, too? She is so devoted to Ted—Theodore Day—that I wouldn't have thought her capable of wavering so."

"These society women like to keep their men to themselves and resent any outsiders from marrying into their set." She lifted her glass in salutation. "You have been fairly warned, my dear."

Flora's cheeks flamed before she could remind herself that no one here could possibly know of her affections besides her family. "One could say the same for New York society."

"Forgive me. I see I've made you uncomfortable." She returned Mrs. Day's wave from across the hall, smiling as if all in the grand hall were her friends. "Must never let the others see how their words affect you. Now, tell me, how can you make my transition into wifehood easier?"

Flora flipped open her journal and spent the next half hour speaking with Mrs. Thompson and praising Teddy's work. Eventually, they abandoned the grand hall in favor of a self-guided tour of the *Lark*, which landed them in a mahogany-lined chamber with heavy emerald curtains that while immaculate for the showing, the hint of sandalwood confirmed her suspicions at once. *This is Teddy's room.* Her well-rehearsed speech died on her lips as she trailed her fingers over the intricately carved bedpost, her eyes lingering on the pair of Scottish dirks beside the books lining the single built-in bookshelf.

Flora picked up a metal figurine from Teddy's desk of

a knight who was missing part of his helmet, most likely having been chipped away long ago judging from the faded paint. She set it down alongside the inkwell with an oversized quill beside it. *How romantic of Teddy to still write with a quill.* She took up the antique telescope that rested on a display stand at the front of the desk, opening and closing it, admiring the craftsmanship before returning it.

"My husband would love a room like this," Mrs. Thompson said, breaking her reverie.

Flustered, Flora jerked her hand from the telescope as if it were a hot curling tong and wrapped her hands safely about her journal. "We can certainly accommodate any request, and I think that with the changes you proposed to Mr. Day's original sketches, we could have you in a boat come summer's end, ready to travel to St. Louis for a much-needed visit."

Delia sighed. "That would be marvelous. The trip down here . . ." She shuddered. "Well, let's just say there are some riverboats that should be burned rather than be allowed on the Mississippi River. I know Felix will happily purchase a boat from Theodore Day for me if I insist I wish for a Wingfield and Day design. And I *will* insist."

"You will?"

Mrs. Thompson laughed. "You don't think I would have followed you about the boat only to be polite, do you? Do you think you can have the sketches and papers drawn up for me in two days' time, and you can come present them to us at teatime?"

Flora nodded, clutching the journal to her chest, speechless.

"Wonderful. I'll send a card with my address to your aunt's. And my dearest friend in St. Louis, Mrs. Tyndall, has mentioned to me on numerous occasions that she wishes to purchase a steamboat in order to come for a visit whenever she'd like. I wonder, do you think you could send her a copy of the plans? She may wish to have a smaller one built for her. It is a shame you don't have one ready-made. She isn't as picky as I am but still needs a luxurious boat for herself."

"O-of course. And we actually do have two ready-made boats available that we can customize for her."

"Marvelous. Please bring sketches and layouts for both, and I will send them to her. Now, I must go find my husband for dinner and tell him all about your sketches, which are so much better than the others he has found for me since meeting with your Mr. Day and Mr. Day's inexplicable cancelation."

"He isn't *my* Mr. Day," Flora sputtered, her cheeks heating again. If word traveled around to Teddy that Flora was insinuating . . . She swallowed back a grimace.

Mrs. Thompson rested a hand on Flora's. "Excuse my assumption. You speak of him with such fondness and familiarity that I think, if he is not your beau now, perhaps he may well become yours soon. It is not every day a gentleman finds a like-minded woman with beauty *and* a brain." She winked and swished out of the room.

Ten

Flora's heart swelled. She had never given much thought to her designs ever being used beyond her own home one day, but with Teddy's request and Mrs. Thompson's enthusiasm, perhaps she could be known for something more than being the eldest, *unwed* daughter of Florian Wingfield. She refrained from releasing a squeal and instead gave a little twirl. *I just sold my first design!* She sank down in the chair behind Teddy's oversized desk and spotted a sheet of paper sticking out from under a stack of books on the desktop, the titles ranging from steamboats to French architecture.

She tugged on the edge of the paper and gasped to find a sketch of a woman. Though rough and in an unpracticed hand, it could be no one else but Willow. *He hasn't gotten over her yet.* She traced her finger along the delicate charcoal strokes, the action smudging it. He was still in pain and *she* was the cause. She set it on the desk, crossing her arms and scrutinizing the sketch. *Would he wish for my help if he knew I was the one who assisted Cullen in stealing Willow away from him?* At the time, she had tried to convince herself that she was only doing so out of concern for her friend, but now, as the panic of Teddy's impending marriage had dulled a bit, she realized she had acted out of selfishness as well. Yes, she did love Willow and wanted the best for her dearest friend, yet Flora was still very much relieved that she did not have to think of Teddy as a friend for the rest of her days . . . well, until his *next* engagement, and Lord help her if he chose Penelope. She would never see him again. The thought knotted her stomach.

Voices sounded outside the door, and Flora darted to her feet, knocking the inkwell over and onto the sketch. "No!" Flora groaned, flipping the inkwell upright. "Who still uses an inkwell?" She slid the sketch from the mess, but it was clearly ruined. "Oh!" She flapped her hands, trying to find something to blot the desk before the next tour group opened the door. She ripped off her gloves and scrambled to sweep the sketch and ink into the wastebasket, leaving a long, dark smear on the desktop and the wastebasket bottom ruined. Groaning again, she drew open the closet doors and pulled out the nearest shirt from its hanger, praying it wasn't a favorite, and wiped the rest of the mess from the desk as the door opened. Having no other means of escape, she seized her gloves and kept the ruined shirt pinched between her fingers at arm's length and dove into the closet. Quickly she drew the doors closed, leaving a narrow crack for her to spy through, and tossed the shirt into the back corner.

"And as you can see, we have personalized each family member's private quarters," Teddy explained as the Pimpernels and Bridgewaters entered the room. "This is my room while aboard, and as you can tell, I've kept to the traditional masculinity while my brother's room, which we just saw, has a tad more luxuriousness to it." His gaze landed on his desk, and a hint of confusion passed through his eyes.

The giggles of the Misses Pimpernels filled the room, and Flora for once could not blame them. To be in a gentleman's private chamber was unheard of, but in the name of showing a boat, it was *maybe* acceptable with the large party. As the guests milled about the room, Flora took a step farther into the closet, Teddy's shirts enveloping her, their scent filling her head. Was this what it would be like, swept in his embrace? The closet door shut, waking her from the enchantment in one horror-filled moment.

The instant the group moved along, Flora ran her hand over the door, desperately trying to find the knob. She didn't dare try to ram her way out, which would only turn her battered. She buried her face in her hands. Just once, she'd like a dull evening.

Just when she was feeling as though she was going to die a slow death from suffocation from the scent of sandalwood, the next group arrived, led by someone who sounded like Carlisle. She suppressed a whimper and looked to the beadboard ceiling and waited for the footsteps to file out. Then, knowing Carlisle would likely be the last to vacate, Flora tapped on the door. Nothing. She tapped again, harder this time.

It flung open, and she blinked in the gaslight. "Thank goodness," she whispered.

"Flora? What on earth?" Carlisle gaped at her.

She shook her head. "It would take too long to explain. I'll wait until you leave to make my departure."

"But you *will* explain?"

"In due course." She shoved him through the door and tugged on her gloves to hide the ink staining her fingertips and stole away before she could be caught again. Figuring one sale was enough for now, and not having the courage to pursue more, Flora deposited her journal with the rest of her things and returned to the grand hall to give Teddy the good news before dinner.

Nearly a hundred guests swarmed about, the room humming in a multitude of conversations. To avoid the crush, Flora pressed against the wall and drew a deep breath, her fan fluttering as she looked about for Teddy. While a floating palace would normally be pleasant with a breeze flowing in from the river, there was no such draft in the swarm of guests. At high-pitched laughter, she spotted Teddy in yet another cluster of young women, Miss Penelope clinging to his arm and every word.

Flora frowned. Here she was spending the evening trying to garner business for Teddy, and what was he doing? *Flirting.* She crossed her arms, fighting the jealousy building within. *He is not mine. No matter what I might wish. Teddy Day is not mine . . . and he very well may never be mine.* Against her will, an image of Teddy standing at the altar with another on his arm flashed through her mind. She moved along the wall, thinking she could make a hasty exit, when she recalled that as a river party, there was no escape until the appointed departure hour. She would have to endure watching Teddy flirt and be flirted with until she could make her escape. She spun away from the painful scene of Miss Penelope wooing her Mr. Day with all her charms and instead focused on Ermengarde cornering Clancy Drake, laughing with abandon as Tacy strode across the room toward them, fury in her eyes directed toward their younger sister.

"A blossom as lovely as you should never be left with

the wallflowers." Carlisle greeted her, breaking her morose thoughts as he bowed to her, extending his hand.

Wallflowers? She cast a glance where she had stopped to watch Teddy in the flock of girls. Along the wall sat Miss Bennett in her lavender gown, Miss Smith with her graying curls, and three other ladies she had yet to meet. Her mother would *never* forgive her for standing here if she were spotted by the society matrons. She shoved off the wall and placed her hand in Carlisle's, allowing him to lead her away as the pianoforte sounded and Tacy pulled Mr. Drake into a Viennese waltz.

"We shouldn't let them dance alone." Carlisle extended his hand to her. "Shall we dance before we sit for dinner? That way you can tell me why exactly I found you in my brother's closet."

"I do not remember your asking to sit with me," Flora laughed. "And I'm afraid I already have an escort for dinner."

"One does not need to ask when one is a host and can simply have the butler rearrange the place cards." He winked, sweeping her into his arms, the crowd of guests looking on with interest at the impromptu dancing.

"But, as I have already promised to sit with Mr. Clancy Drake, you will have to switch the cards *back*."

"You still haven't answered my question."

Flora gritted her teeth. "If you promise not to tell a soul . . ."

"You'll find I am good at keeping secrets," he replied.

And so she told him, and to her surprise, Carlisle did not chide her but merely laughed and twirled her about the room, accepting her. And in their dancing, she found he was as agile a dancer as Cullen with Willow. She shook *that* thought from her head. There was no comparison really.

Carlisle was merely being kind after her mishap. She glanced up at Carlisle and found nothing but admiration in his eyes and inadvertently spied Teddy behind him, whirling on the dance floor with the lovely Miss Penelope in his arms. The moment he turned, he would see her, so Flora brightened her smile at Carlisle into one she reserved for Teddy. *Let Teddy think something is going on between us.* Teddy clearly did not care if she was here or in New York so long as he had her assistance with his contest. Well, she would make him care.

For the duration of one dance, she flirted with Carlisle, laughing at his jests, batting her lashes, and generally acting as if he were the only man in the room . . . until she noticed Teddy had departed the dance floor to speak with the butler, who was holding a padded mallet and a small bronze gong that hung from two knotted golden ropes that formed a triangle handle. Carlisle, however, was too animated to notice her change of heart as he bowed to her, awakening her to the fact that the dance had ended.

The gong sounded once, and the butler bowed. "Ladies and gentlemen, please take your seats."

Carlisle threaded her hand through his arm, led her to the table, and held her chair for her near the opposite end from where Teddy was seated. "I wasn't intending on asking this, but when will I be seeing you after tonight?"

Flora blinked. Surely he did not think one dance—no, Carlisle had always been aloof, older, above anything the trio of friends were up to in Newport. "I'm always about. I'm certain our paths will cross sooner than you would think." She sank into her chair, feeling a sting for using Carlisle so, even if it was only for a dance.

"What the blazes?" Carlisle murmured, lifting the place card at the setting beside her. "I'll be back directly."

She turned her attention to the line of guests taking their seats, her gaze immediately finding Teddy with Miss Mathilda. *This was a terrible idea to come to New Orleans. If he had liked me in that way, he would have sought me out.* She blinked back tears at her stupidity.

"I was afraid you had changed your mind about my sitting beside you for dinner when Mr. Day escorted you to your seat," Clancy said and took the seat to her right.

"Of course not. I promised you." She whipped open her fan to blink behind it for a second to compose herself under the guise of needing cool air. "Though Mr. Day did mention that he switched your card with his." She leaned over her plate and found Carlisle four seats down from her own, scowling. "But it appears he has been relocated." She lifted her brow at Clancy. "I wonder how that came about?"

"A gentleman never reveals his secrets." He winked as the footman placed the first course before them.

"He doesn't look happy," she murmured into her soup, giggling at Mr. Drake's audacity to move one of the host's place cards. She enjoyed the fact that he would breach etiquette to sit beside her and felt more than a little guilty that Carlisle looked so put out by it.

"Then he should have taken the seat on your other side instead of attempting to rid himself of competition and placing me so far away."

She glanced down the table to see if any of her sisters were near, but alas, the only one she spied was Olive across from Carlisle, seated next to Gale Thornton. *One would think that with four sisters, there would be more of us about.*

"Miss Flora?" Mr. Drake queried, the back of his hand brushing hers.

Her senses sharpened at his touch, and she was at once aware of Tacy's glare from down the table. *Of course Tacy would see this.* She pulled back. "Sir?"

"I asked if you had a moment yet to sample our city's fine cuisine."

"Forgive me. I was lost in thought. But no. I mean, there is an Italian cook and a French baker at my great-aunt's residence, and they have prepared delightful foods that hold far more flavor than our usual fare at home, as Father likes his dishes plain, though I may have to convince him into allowing our dear cook to experiment more with spices after this trip."

"I was hoping you would say no, because I want to bring you to Antoine's for our dinner." He paused, taking her hand in his. "That is, if you are still willing to go to dinner with me. You never gave me an appointment."

"Didn't I?" She bit her lip, the New Orleans fare tempting, and yet she didn't wish to hurt him if her heart would not release Teddy even if she wished it to after tonight. And besides, she had a steamboat to design with every spare moment she could find, even if said design did not end with a wedding band as she had originally hoped. "I believe luncheon would be better, sir. As you may remember, I will be bringing my sisters along. How does tomorrow sound?"

He grinned. "Perfect. I have just the tearoom in mind, which is quite popular."

Theodore gritted his teeth. The Wingfield family was already crossing the landing stage, Mr. Clancy Drake in the midst of them, his grip possessively on Flora's elbow as she glided her hand over the burgundy twisted rope rail, giggling as her foot caught against the carpeted stage and Clancy helped right her. "Flora, wait!" he called over the rail of the second level, sprinting for the stairs.

Miss Sandrine flipped open her fan like a threatened peacock. "Mr. Day, you promised me a turn about the deck," she cooed.

"And I would be honored, but I must bid my friends farewell. Excuse me." He disentangled himself from her clasp and darted around the guests. "Flora!"

At his second call, those lovely blue eyes pierced him, her lips pursed. And in that single glance, he could tell she was angry with him, despite her trying to mask her feelings. He motioned for her to wait for him, but she shook her head and continued toward the line of carriages at the Day dock, her escort pausing to speak with Mr. Wingfield. With a grunt, Theodore wove through the guests disembarking, and as she lifted her skirts to enter one of the two Dubois carriages, he cleared the landing stage and grabbed her wrist, pulling her around. "Flora, don't be upset."

She stepped aside to allow her sisters to pass and clenched her gloved fists at her sides. "Why do you think I am upset? Do I look upset to you?"

This felt like a trap. He chewed the inside of his mouth, but her eyes did not waiver from his, her little foot tapping beneath her yards of pale pink skirts. "Because I did not spend much of the evening with you after the tour?"

"Do you think I was just sitting around waiting for you?" She snorted. "I kept busy."

He ran his fingers through his hair, the pomade making

the action difficult. "I really am sorry I wasn't able to speak with you after our initial tour with your family. However, I spent the evening attempting to garner more business through the daughters."

"Through the daughters?" She folded her arms across her chest. "Is that what you would call *flirting*?"

He did not like where this was heading. "Do you have any better suggestions?"

"Yes. I went directly to the wives, and now I have the Thompsons ready to meet with us to discuss purchasing a boat," she said, her hands wrapping around her beaded reticule, the outline of her journal distorting the bag. "Along with a friend of Mrs. Thompson in St. Louis, who may be interested in one of the ready-made boats. You would have to deliver it to the port in St. Louis, but I daresay you will, what with Carlisle already gaining the lead."

His jaw dropped. "But Mr. Thompson rejected my proposal. How—?"

"As I said, I went to the wife. He may be the head of the family, but she is the neck who can turn his head and redirect his attention. Our meeting is in two days, and we have not one but two unique masterpieces to create and refine."

"That's marvelous. Shall we meet up tomorrow sometime to solidify our plans?" He rubbed his hands together, pausing only when he did not see his enthusiasm mirrored in his friend's expression. "What's wrong?"

Flora's bottom lip trembled. "We are supposed to be friends. Be my friend. Don't call on me when it suits and then ignore me when it doesn't." She lifted her lashes, whispering, "Like you did after Paris."

Paris. He recollected their chance meeting before his courtship of Willow with fondness, never stopping to consider how such an abrupt farewell had seemed on her end. He groaned and muttered, "I cannot bear this, Flora."

"Cannot bear what?"

He spread his arm wide despite his hushed tones. "To be the center of all these women's attention any longer. I did not sign up for a second competition, and I certainly do not intend on marrying anytime soon—not after suffering *two* broken engagements."

"I see," she whispered.

Theodore was stunned to find tears lining her eyes. What had he said now?

Mr. Drake finished his conversation with Mr. Wingfield and appeared at her side. "Shall I assist you inside, Miss Flora?"

Without a second glance at Theodore, she placed her hand in Mr. Drake's and vanished into the carriage with her mother and Tacy, followed by Mr. Drake, sending a pang through Teddy as he vividly recalled Willow leaving with gentleman after gentleman every morning, afternoon, and evening. He shook himself from the memory. Why should he feel so about Flora?

They had always been only friends. Well, except that one week . . . that one fleeting week before all this nonsense Willow Dupré's competition had created when he had run into Flora in Paris, merely weeks after Bernadette had eloped with his chum. Yet neither Flora nor himself had admitted to feeling any attraction, so he thought it was all an ephemeral infatuation that came with his heart healing, because then he had fallen for Willow. And now, like before, Flora was there to help him through the pain of his latest heartbreak.

He stuffed his hands into his pockets as the carriage rolled away. It seemed whenever his heart had been broken, Flora was there to pick up the pieces. He turned to find Mr. Wingfield lingering outside his carriage with Mr. Grayson, deep in discussion.

"Mr. Wingfield, that is quite the offer, and I would love to accept it," Grayson replied.

"Wonderful!" Mr. Wingfield clapped the man on the shoulder.

"But"—he pulled an envelope from his pocket—"I cannot make such a massive decision on my own. My employer included this note in his letter to me. It is sealed, and I have no idea what it says, but he was insistent that I gave it to you. He fears the post these days, what with his house arrest and all."

"Wellington would keep his business partner in the dark?"

Grayson shrugged. "I'm used to his ways by now. And besides, I'm not a partner, just the current acting head. And as I'd like my head to stay on my shoulders, I will abide by whatever that letter states."

Theodore watched for a hint of teasing in Grayson's words but found none. Mr. Wingfield slowly broke the seal, and it could just be the flickering light of the torches, but Theodore could swear the man's hands were shaking.

"Preposterous," Mr. Wingfield fairly growled, crumpling the letter.

Grayson's brow furrowed. "Not an acceptable proposition, I'm assuming?"

"*No*. And if this is how he is going to conduct business—"

Grayson held up his hands. "Sir, surely we can work something out that is agreeable to both of you."

"If you knew what the letter contained, you would understand that is not possible." Mr. Wingfield ran a hand through his hair, tugging on his top hat.

"Then I shall ask him to reconsider whatever he is asking," Grayson contended.

"Good evening, Grayson." Mr. Wingfield climbed into the carriage, slamming the door behind him.

And from his place in the shadows, he saw a glimmer pass through Grayson's eyes. He waited for the man to take his place in the Bridgewaters' awaiting carriage and saw Gale Thornton descending the landing stage. He waved his friend over and kept his voice low. "Gale, I need you to look into Bradford Grayson."

"Is it because he is attempting to court your Miss Flora?" Gale chuckled. "You know researching suitors on behalf of jealous friends is not what Pinkerton agents are meant for, right?"

Theodore frowned. "What about thieves and blackmailers? And most likely a few other nefarious activities?"

The humor fled Gale's expression at once. He reached into his coat and removed a small notebook and pencil. "Tell me everything."

Eleven

There were only so many ways a lady could chase a fellow before resigning herself to the fact that said gentleman simply did not think of her as more than a childhood friend. Flora looked to Mr. Drake beside her in the open barouche, with Olive, Tacy, and Cousin Cornelia vis-à-vis. He *was* quite pleasing to the eye, but again that ubiquitous thought rose that Mr. Drake was *not* Teddy and no other man would be. Mother was right. Flora had to set her sights, not exactly lower but elsewhere, if she wished to marry a man of her choosing—mostly her choosing.

If only she hadn't seen Teddy in Paris. If only he hadn't captured her heart then, mayhap she would be free now to fall in love with a kind, adventure-loving fellow like Clancy Drake. That was all she desired—to be loved—and if she allowed herself to truly dream, to design with her spouse's complete support and belief in her work. And now that Teddy had offered to partner with her for the summer, that dream was one of the few that could come to fruition, well, without the husband part. If she couldn't have Teddy, and love did not find her in New Orleans, maybe her dreams of becoming a known authority on interior design and opening a class for other women to learn the trade would be fulfilled in a small way once she came into her inheritance and could open a school or perhaps a class for women. She sighed, glancing sideways. Teddy wasn't her only option, and if she was being honest, he wasn't really even an option at this point.

At a bump in the road, she was jarred from her daydreaming to Decatur Street with the pedestrians milling along the Mississippi River as vendors sang out their wares. The carriage halted at Jackson Square, the beautiful three spires of St. Louis Cathedral visible beyond the small park and above the handful of trees gracing the green.

"I thought a stroll through our square would be just the thing before lunching at the Pontalba shops' teahouse across St. Ann Street," Mr. Drake said as he extended his hand to the ladies. Tacy hastily gripped her orange skirt and stepped down first, tripping into his chest with a tinkling laugh, his hands flying to her waist to steady her.

"Pardon me, Clancy, I lost my footing." She batted her stubby lashes at him.

"Then thank goodness I was here to keep you from marring your unique gown." He smiled, righting her, but she kept her hands affixed to his arms.

"My, did you work on the railroad as well as direct its construction?" Tacy dared to tighten her fingers in an action that had Flora lifting her eyes to the heavens.

He chuckled, gently releasing her. "I believe that a good boss understands what he is asking of his workers, and in order to do so, I did indeed assist with the ties for about a month before rotating to another aspect of the railroad, most of which involved backbreaking work."

Flora's brows rose at that as she closed her pink carnation-embroidered emerald parasol. "What a brilliant idea, and I'm certain it aided in fostering a much-needed compassion that most tycoons lack."

At her interjection, Tacy seemed to fade from his attention as he turned, the action forcing Tacy to release him from her claws.

"I'm pleased you think so, Miss Wingfield. My father made himself from nothing in order to take my mother's hand in marriage, so I never wish to forget what it was like to work with my hands for a living."

"Which explains why they are so callused." Tacy brazenly held his hand palm up in her own and gave a little laugh tinted with desperation.

Seeing as Tacy was not going to relinquish her hold on Mr. Drake, Flora gathered her reticule and let herself down, her foot catching on her hem and, to her horror, sending her plummeting to the stones directly into the path of a fresh patty. She thrust out her arms and closed her eyes, unable to bear the pain of the impact to come.

Mr. Drake caught her in his arms, sweeping her to himself, their faces parallel, his gray eyes capturing her. "Are you well?"

"Yes, quite." *Why am I so breathless? And goodness gracious if Tacy isn't right. His chest is remarkably solid. I suppose one would possess such a physique after working—* At throat clearing, she blinked. Had she been staring into his eyes this entire time? "And you?"

"You weigh far less than a railroad tie." His eyes twinkled.

"I think the only thing that hurts is the thought that I will have to set you down at some point or people will talk."

Her heart tripped. "I think you may be right."

"As you wish, my lady," he whispered and steadied her as if she were dear to him. "But I wish you would call me Clancy."

After all this time spent yearning for Teddy, it felt rather wonderful to be treated so. "Only in private." She smiled, enjoying his hand on her elbow. "And only if you call me Flora."

He grinned and whispered in her ear, "Very good, Flora."

The throat cleared again, and she stepped back, earning glares from Tacy beneath her chapeau while Olive and Cornelia sat, mouths agape. She moved away from him as he helped the rest of their party descend and swept her hand over her carnation-embroidered emerald Marie Antoinette overskirt that pulled back in pink ribboned points below her hips. Aside from a few wrinkles, she was immaculate, thanks to Clancy.

"You *had* to take my moment and make it all about you again, didn't you?" Tacy huffed as Clancy directed them to the open iron gates of the park.

"What does that mean?" Flora righted her chapeau, pleased that *this* fall did not ruin her adorning cream egret feathers. *What has happened to my footing since arriving in New Orleans?* She half smiled, thinking of Teddy's rescue before remembering that she was not going to be thinking of *him* today. "Honestly, Tacy, not everything I do is an attempt to thwart your plans and make you miserable."

"Then leave Clancy alone. He's *mine*," she hissed. "You are already an old maid. Do not make me one, too."

Flora jerked back at her sister's cutting remark. "That has

yet to be proven, and until he *is* yours, he is fair game to the rest of us. And I am not an old maid yet." She snapped open her parasol and lengthened her stride to catch up and claim Clancy's free arm. *Did my calling Willow an old maid on New Year's Eve hurt her so much when I said it?* She would have to write and apologize for that tactless comment. Obviously, her friend was no longer a bachelorette, as Willow labeled herself, but nonetheless, words had a way of lingering if they were not forgiven.

Tacy caught up with her. "We all know that you have your bonnet set for someone else, so do not toy with Clancy. I'm warning you, Flora. If you ruin this for me, you will live to regret it."

Tacy flounced away, claiming her position on Clancy's other arm, when Flora heard a familiar call, sending her heart to skipping wildly despite her morning's resolution to forget Teddy. She lifted her parasol enough to catch a glimpse of Teddy rising from a bench, a half-eaten sandwich in hand.

"Flora? How did you know that I take my afternoon breaks here?" he called, lifting his straw boater hat to her.

Her cheeks warmed as the group paused, all regarding them. "I didn't know you liked to eat here." She gestured to Mr. Drake, who joined her at her side. "Clancy was simply showing us some of the city before luncheon." Her eyes widened at the faux pas of using a gentleman's Christian name, and Teddy's flinch vanished so quickly, she wasn't certain if she even saw it. She felt Clancy's swell of confidence as he took her arm and placed it where Tacy's had been only moments prior.

Clancy nodded to Teddy. "Mr. Day. Good to see you so

soon after your party. I have to say I was very impressed with your steamboat."

"Good to see you as well," Teddy replied, though he did not sound as if he meant it. "Thank you. I'll be sure to let my father know. Luncheon sounds nice. A sandwich is never enough to fill me." He grinned, tugging his hat back into place as if he had already been extended an invitation.

Clancy exchanged niceties with Teddy as Cornelia pulled Flora a few paces away. "Now, I know that you have been waiting for Teddy to show signs of interest, but he ignored you all last night. And while it isn't terribly improper that he is asking to join us, it isn't well done of him that in doing so, he is ruining Mr. Drake's perfectly laid plans to spend a pleasant, thoughtful day with *you*. If Theodore Day wishes to court you, then *he* should be the one inviting you to luncheon, not the other way around."

Flora twisted her lips to the side. "I couldn't refuse him! It would be beyond rude to exclude—"

"Trust me." Cornelia rested a hand on her belly. "I have a husband, and if you want to have one someday, then *you* need to remind him that you are *not* anyone's second choice. *Subtlety.*"

"That's a terrible argument," Flora groaned.

"It was all I could think of to say. Now go!" Cornelia gave her a little shove toward the men.

"So, when shall we be dining today?" Teddy asked, looping his thumbs in the pockets of his silk waistcoat.

Clancy pasted on such a broad smile that Flora had no doubt of his true feelings about Teddy's assumption of an invitation. "Well, uh, I made reservations for the five of us in about ten minutes, but it was only for five," Clancy repeated.

"Perfect. One more seat will make the party complete," Teddy interjected, rubbing his palms together as if that settled matters.

At Cornelia's pinching her upper arm, Flora stepped forward. "I'm afraid we couldn't impose on the tearoom staff, Teddy. Mr. Drake informed me it is quite a popular place to take tea, so I am assuming that means it will be full, and I'd hate to embarrass you like that."

He blinked, clearly taken aback. But Flora kept her resolve and curtsied to him, signaling the end of their dialogue. *Lord, help me to stay strong and forgive me if that was a bit of a stretch.*

"But you will still be able to make our appointment this evening to discuss our plans for the Thompsons and her St. Louis friend's design, yes? With her proposed changes?" He ran his hand down the front strap of his leather case. "I'm to meet with the Pimpernels beforehand, so I won't have time to finish any work that you have not."

Flora's burdened spirit twisted, swathing her in disappointment. Of course, that was all he wished from her. She forced a smile to her lips. She should be grateful at this small offering. If she succeeded in business with him, she could have something in her future besides marriage, though it would be nice to have both. Unlike Willow, she wished for love more and she refused to feel ashamed of that desire. "I will be more than prepared by the appointed hour. Enjoy your sandwich and meeting with the Misses Pimpernels." And with that, Flora turned her attention to the man who was actually interested in her. "Clancy?"

Clancy tipped his hat to Teddy and led her across the square, Flora feeling lighter with each step.

"So, Mr. Drake, do you come to this tearoom often?"

His eyes fixed on St. Louis Cathedral as mass ended, the stream of congregates spilling from the heavy carved doors and down the stone steps. "I used to. When my mother was alive and we were in the city, we would come here every Tuesday, rain or shine, and talk about all the places she wished to visit and revisit from her girlhood grand tour."

She swallowed, the heat pressing down on her neck. She had not expected that answer. "Did you ever get a chance to visit those places with your mother?"

"One." His eyes shadowed. "There is a little town across our massive lake, Lake Pontchartrain, called Mandeville where there is a single live oak that is said to be the largest in the country and over a thousand years old. Its branches are so long they dip to the ground, and when you are beneath it and atop the tapestry of roots and emerald moss-covered soil, you can hardly see the sky for the breadth of the canopy. It's speculated that it was once seven individual oaks that grew into one. Mother had always wanted to travel there to see it for herself, so a few weeks before she came down with yellow fever, I hired a yacht and a photographer and took her there." He smiled, his voice growing rough. He opened his jacket and removed a small picture from his billfold, worn about the edges, where a younger Clancy stood, leaning against the ancient tree, while his mother sat on its roots, her skirts billowing around her in a cloud. "We will never see Scotland together, but it was a perfect day."

"I am so sorry. She sounds like a wonderful woman." Flora squeezed his arm. "Will you visit Scotland still? In her honor?"

He cleared his throat and pocketed the picture. "The week

after she died, I took some time to myself and traveled to nearly every place on our list, besides India, before I had to return and continue helping Father with the business." He smiled. "Father doesn't like to travel, you see—"

"Clancy!" Tacy called, ensnaring his free arm in her grip. "We have hardly had a chance to talk, so we must be seated together. I am excellent at serving tea, so if Flora doesn't mind my taking over, I'll see to pouring your tea and you can see my talents for yourself."

"It would be a relief to have you at my side, for I'm afraid that tea serving is not something I was taught on the railroad and I would make an abysmal mess of it all." He winked to Flora. "And if you would be so kind as to sit at my right, it will make this afternoon complete and my return to the tearoom as wonderful as all the times I've been there before."

Theodore scratched his head as Flora strolled away on the arm of Clancy Drake, her easy dismissal of his clear wish to join them for luncheon irking him to no end. Shoving his hand into his pocket, he removed his sandwich, pulled back the wax paper, and took a bite, then kicked at the dandelions dotting the patchy grass, sending a spray of the white seedlings into the air. She wasn't being coquettish by flirting with someone else, was she? He did not think she could ever be so sly.

He cast a glance over his shoulder to see if she was looking back at him. No. She was laughing at something the gent said. Laughing. Theodore was sidestepping a group of children careening about the square when the awful thought occurred to him that he had never seen Flora so attentive to a gentleman. *What if she marries this Clancy?* What would his life look like without Flora in it as his best friend? He tried to picture it, and the result was not something he wished to contemplate.

He could not lose another woman's heart to someone else again. Reaching out, he tugged a leaf free from a holly bush and rolled it between his fingers, watching the green life ebb from the leaf and stain his fingertips, the sharp tip jabbing his finger. But did he *love* Flora? With Bernadette, it had been blinding attraction, and with Willow, an old dream of a future with her that had made him fall so quickly. But with Flora, it was different. Instead of being swept away, feeling like a dandelion seed caught in the wind, he felt grounded—as if a cinder were lodged in his stomach that, with every day spent by her side, was growing ever more into an inferno that could not be quenched.

He swiveled on his heel and bent to peer through the wrought-iron fence to catch a glimpse of the group as they entered the lower Pontalba building into the tea shop on the corner that he frequented. His stomach rumbled at the thought of the Italian pastries within, yet it would be beyond humiliating to follow the group inside and to sit at a table on his own while Flora was being courted by Clancy.

Theodore checked his pocket watch, running his finger over the engraving inside the lid, remembering the moment Flora had given it to him in Paris for his miserable twenty-sixth birthday. *Some Starry Someday.* When he had first read the message, it had given him hope that perhaps one day he would find a bit of happiness. He sighed. An hour left before his next meeting. Snapping it closed, he pocketed the gold watch and glanced to the river.

Carlisle's dock was nearby. He *could* go and check out the progress his brother was making on his latest order. But there was little spying to be had between the brothers, as all previous designs were available to them . . . unless Carlisle had actually paid attention during his boatbuilding apprenticeship and business classes at Tulane University and could bring something unique to the designs that they had not discussed. While Theodore had studied in Paris, Carlisle probably did have an advantage, having attended classes in New Orleans alongside the sons of clients Theodore was attempting to capture.

He marched up the stone steps toward the river and stared out at the dock, where Carlisle's men were crafting more Day masterpieces. He watched the Italian workers in their positions aboard the boats in various stages of development. One boat was nearly complete with only the interior left to finish, another with the exterior walls going up. The last boat was still in its early stages of construction with a hog-chain system running up and down the skeletal hull, supporting the boat as the substantial engine, boilers, and rear paddle wheel were added.

Theodore studied the boat that was nearly finished and wondered what Carlisle had changed on the interior to give himself a bit of an edge. He shook his head. Best not to obsess over his brother and focus on the task at hand. Despite the sandwich earlier, his stomach rumbled again, reminding him of the tearoom's fare. He sighed. He had better staunch his wailing stomach lest it distract the Pimpernels and keep their focus on feeding him more than on closing the deal.

Purchasing a bowl of jambalaya from a nearby vendor, Theodore promised to return the tin bowl and utensil and took a seat at a vacant bench along the river. He shoveled a spoonful of the spicy rice into his mouth, closing his eyes at the perfectly browned andouille sausage and wondering if Flora had tried it yet. *Flora.* She was always in his thoughts these days, and yet he hadn't even thought of what Willow was doing today. That realization made him straighten. He smiled and took a second bite.

Twelve

The next few weeks were lost in a flurry of activity as Flora had multiple fittings for Penelope's upcoming costume ball and spent many an hour with her sisters visiting with Auntie while driving about the city, taking in all that New Orleans had to offer. But every afternoon when they returned home from their excursions, Flora found Teddy awaiting her in the parlor to discuss his designs. Despite her best efforts to remain logical, Flora could not keep her hope at bay that some small part of their meetings wasn't about the designs. Oddly enough, Carlisle always joined them after enigmatic meetings with her father, which worried her. Had her father softened to the idea of purchasing a steamboat, only to give the commission to the wrong brother? At the slam of the front door, Flora nearly knocked over the enormous bouquet of snowy camellias that she was arranging in the foyer.

Tacy ripped off her chapeau, stabbing her hatpin through the grosgrain band. "I need you to tell Clancy about the dowries at tea this afternoon."

Flora reached for another blossom. "Hello to you too, Tacy."

"Are those from *him*?" Her younger sister's lips pursed. She knew as well as Flora what the blossoms meant from their required study of the language of flowers with its deep green leaves shining against the snow-white bloom. Her gaze landed on the small card that had accompanied the flowers and she lunged for it, but Flora was faster.

Flora tucked the little card up her sleeve with its telling lines and clipped a wayward leaf, the trimming tumbling toward Tacy. "I doubt Mr. Drake truly means that 'his destiny is in my hands,' if that's what you are thinking."

Tacy clenched her jaw as she swiped at her silk tea gown with her lace gloves gripped in her fist, grunting when she did not find a green stain from the wayward stem. "Then why are you hiding the card from me?" Tacy's voice trembled. "Most likely because we both have no doubt he *does* consider you to be in possession of his future."

Flora shoved a stem through the leaves, spacing the flower just so in the cluster, and drew a long breath of its delicate scent, sending her to sneezing into her puffed sleeve before she could draw out her handkerchief. She dabbed at her nose with the corner of her lacy apron and finished the arrangement. "I will tell you again, just as I have hinted to Mr. Drake after our time together, I am *not* interested in courtship at the moment. Why are you so jealous?"

"Because by refusing him now and yet giving him that dash of hope, you made yourself even more desirable. *And* someday obtainable." Tacy crossed her arms. "You have no idea what it is like to be a middle child in a family of all daughters. To him, I am just one of many. The first is always in the spotlight, always paraded about as the perfect example of how a daughter of Florian Wingfield should act."

Flora winced. She had so often felt inconsequential that she hadn't stopped to consider if perhaps her younger sisters sensed Father's apathy toward his daughters.

"Obviously, you are the one he wants. He will never actually see me until you are gone," Tacy muttered, then snapped off a perfect full bloom, spoiling the arrangement. She twirled the stem between two fingers.

Flora refused to react. Instead, she simply removed the stem and shifted a bloom to fill the spot. "Well, if you are waiting for me to be married off, you will have a long wait ahead of you. If you wish to have him as a suitor, I will not stand in your way."

"How generous of you," she crooned, tucking the flower into her frizzled flaxen curls that had doubled in size since her outing, and then reached for a second bloom.

Flora slapped her hand away. "Stop it. If you want him, make him *know* that you want him." *Though I do not know how he possibly could not know about your feelings for him after the way you practically threw yourself in his lap at tea the other day to garner a seat beside him.* She shifted another bloom, stepping back to admire her work and pulling at her apron strings.

"It's not that easy when the Wingfield sister a gentleman wants is you. And they will *always* want you if the suitors here do not know the amount of our dowries are the same. Because if they did know, I'm certain you and Ermengarde would be the only old maids in the family and not drag Olive and myself into your shame."

Flora decided to ignore that barb and turned to her sister as she shed the apron. While she and Tacy had their differences, she did love her sister. If this scandalous notion was what it took to have some semblance of peace or would get her sister married and out of the house, she would have to do it. For once Tacy latched on to an idea, nothing could dissuade her. She sighed. "You want me to *announce* it this afternoon?"

Tacy grasped her hand, hope sparking in her eyes. "It would mean everything to me."

"If you insist on believing I am leading Clancy Drake on by not humiliating myself in naming our fiscal worth, then very well. But if this doesn't change anything concerning his attentions toward you, please cease your plaguing me at every turn."

"Done." Tacy pecked her on the cheek. "If you were this agreeable all the time, we might actually be friends."

"Excuse me, Miss Flora," the butler called from the open door, his arms stiff at his sides, "but the afternoon tea in the garden is ready for you and your sisters. Miss Olive is already entertaining."

"Already?" Flora wiped her fingers on her apron, freeing them from green smudges.

"Yes, miss. Apparently, your aunt thought it would be best to have the gentlemen arrive a half hour early so as not to give you a chance of finding an excuse to leave the premises." The butler sighed. "Mrs. Dubois has always had her heart set on being a matchmaker. If she succeeds with one of you, I fear it will only add kindling to that desire."

"Thank you, sir." Flora paused at the door and ran her hands over her hair, smoothing out-of-place strands.

"Do not forget your promise," Tacy hissed, pushing Flora to the door.

"Seeing as I *just* promised, it is unlikely I could forget it so quickly," Flora said and swept outside, down the steps of the veranda, and around the path to the lilac wisteria-covered gazebo, where Auntie had arranged for a table to be draped in white linen and set with fine china. She found not only Clancy, but Carlisle Day as well. The gentlemen rose and bowed to them as Olive merely nodded to her sisters from her seat.

"My sincerest apologies for intruding upon your teatime, Miss Wingfield. Your father and I had business to discuss, but as Mr. Wingfield is not here at present, your aunt insisted I join you all in lieu of waiting for an unforeseeable amount."

"You could never be an intrusion, Mr. Day," she returned reassuringly. "And we have been seeing you so often here of late, it is not a surprise now. Though I have to admit I am wondering why?"

"You will find out soon enough." Carlisle held the back of a chair beside his, motioning for her to take her seat. "And when did you change from calling me by my Christian name to stuffy Mr. Day?"

"When I crossed the threshold into high society, good sir, which dictates formality when in mixed company." Flora motioned for the men to resume their seats at the round table.

Clancy cleared his throat, shifted his neckcloth, and held the back of a chair, his gaze locked on her, silently asking her to join him. But Tacy took the seat beside Clancy, leaving Flora between her and Carlisle with Olive on his other side.

Flora reached for the porcelain pot to pour the tea, but Tacy's hand shot out first and she secured the handle of the pot, lifting a single brow, laying claim of being in charge of the tea. The rules of etiquette were clear about which

Wingfield sister should serve, though Flora ignored this bit of unseemliness, as she usually did where Tacy was concerned, and turned to Carlisle.

"Mr. Day, how are things progressing with the competition? Should I assume that since you are not down at the dock office during the workday, you are struggling and have decided to surrender the throne to your brother?"

He accepted a cup from Tacy and lifted it up in a toast to Flora. "Do you think if I was overwhelmed, I would disclose such a thing to you, Miss Wingfield, given your relationship with my brother?"

Her eyes widened. *Teddy has spoken of me . . . as a relationship?* "Pardon?"

"You do not have to play coy with me. I know all about it." He reached for a cucumber sandwich.

"Oh?" Her cheeks flooded. "And what exactly do you know?" Seeing as Tacy had forgotten her in the tea pouring, Flora reached for the pot, shooting Tacy a scowl. Her sister was too absorbed in flirting with Clancy to even notice.

"Everything. Your partnership with him to usurp me from my rightful position should make me entirely put out with you." He laughed, mistaking her blush for subterfuge. "Even so, be assured that I feel no ill will, as I know you two have been chums since childhood." He leaned forward, accepting a plate of pastries from Tacy with a nod of thanks.

"So, you have been meeting with my father quite often. Are you building him a steamboat?"

"While I did ask him for the honor at the river dinner party, when I discovered the following day that you were on Teddy's team, I all but gave up on that hope."

"But he went with you anyway," she guessed.

He shrugged. "I was stunned when he awarded me the project. I even questioned his reasoning, given your involvement, and he was shocked that you were trying your hand at designing with Ted."

"Yes, well, he doesn't exactly think much of my designs, so I didn't wish to disclose it to him unless absolutely necessary," she admitted with a laugh to distract from the pain the truth cost her.

"I don't understand why he wouldn't go with you and Ted, for I know having you on his team greatly lowers my chances of success in this challenge."

She stirred a spoonful of sugar in her tea. "I suppose I should be flattered that you do not think my help a hindrance like some may have already suggested."

His brows rose. "Not at all, my dear Flora. I well remember your sketches."

She blinked. *Sketches? The last time I showed him, I was but fifteen.* "How? I only recall showing you my pictures once when you returned for the summer from Tulane."

"And that should demonstrate how much promise I saw in them if I still recall them in detail nearly a decade later."

Her throat swelled. Save for Teddy, Willow, and Olive, no one had ever praised her work.

"But have no fear. I will not use your ideas even though I now have to come up with designs for the four your father ordered and the one for himself."

"What?" Flora and Olive gasped.

"He was so against the one, why on earth would he order *five*?" Flora resisted the urge to scream. Her father might have single-handedly given the competition to Carlisle just to spite her.

"It is a surprise," Carlisle added with a grin.

"A surprise?" Olive shook her head. "Why would five steamboats be a—oh." Her eyes widened, her hand going to her mouth.

Flora felt it in her gut as well. Father really was intending on finding husbands for all four of his marriageable daughters this summer and supplying them and Mother with steamboats to ease their transition by making their visits home as comfortable as possible.

Tacy beamed. "He is the most wonderful man!"

Carlisle chuckled. "Really, ladies, how can you be so certain they are all for you?"

She clenched her fists. *No. There is still time. We can win.* She would not sink into the pit of melancholy over conveying this blow to Teddy. This would only add to their drive to win, to prove that Theodore was the true head of the company . . . She felt something brush against her foot. She moved her skirts. *What is a fur muff doing on the floorboards?* The fur muff nipped her ankle. "Rat!" Shrieking, her teacup shattered on the floor as she leapt to her feet, Carlisle instantly up with her. Without thinking of anything other than escape, she threw her arms around him and lifted her feet, leaving him little choice but to cradle her against his chest.

In a daze, she was dimly aware of Olive, scrambling atop a chair, and of Tacy wasting no time in attempting to follow suit in Clancy's arms. Instead, he bent down and scooped up, not a rat but a black-and-white bunny, its long ebony ears flopping over his hand. "How naughty of you, Hemsworth, to attempt escape and frighten the ladies so."

∞

Plans tucked under his elbow, Theodore was handing his straw hat to the butler at the entrance to the Dubois mansion when an earsplitting scream ruptured the afternoon. He bolted around the house, skittering to a halt on the gravel at the sight of Flora in his brother's arms, her hands wrapped about his neck and Clancy holding a . . . rabbit? "What on earth is going on here?"

Flora loosened her grip about Carlisle's neck as a blush crept over her cheeks and she set both feet upon the gazebo floor, bits of china cracking underfoot. "I do apologize about that, Carlisle. I am not certain what came over me."

"I wouldn't mind it taking over you again if it gets you in my arms and calling me by my first name again." He winked, his hand on her elbow, steadying her.

Tacy seemed put out as Clancy moved to Flora's side and held the rabbit out to her. "Hemsworth won't bite—at least I don't think he will. Though he is no rat, he did kick at me in the most terrifying manner," Clancy teased.

Flora held the back of her hand to her cheek as if to cool it and stroked the animal's ears. "Very funny. I apologize for my outlandish reaction. I had a rather dreadful encounter with a rat as a child. My cousin chased after me with his pet rat, and when I shut myself in the retiring room to escape him, he pried open the door, flung it into the room and then shut me inside with it." She shivered. "It was horrible. I had to scream and scream for help from atop the vanity until the butler saved me."

"Thank goodness it was only a rabbit then and nothing deadly," Theodore interjected, feeling rather desperate to get her away from his brother. At Carlisle's finally releasing Flora's arm, Theodore clenched his jaw. If anybody else in society had spotted them, word would have spread through New Orleans faster than yellow fever.

Flora gave the rabbit a little pat and motioned for the footman to take it. "I thought our meeting was in an hour, Teddy?"

"I came early to discuss a new sketch I worked out for our follow-up meeting with the Thompsons tomorrow morning, but, uh, I see you are busy." He stepped back as if to leave, even though he had no intention of doing so, not with Clancy and Carlisle looking at her as if they would perish should they look away. *What is Carlisle thinking? He has never paid any mind to Flora prior to the party . . . but then she has never been in his arms before either.*

"I'm afraid we will have to wait to discuss it in an hour, but would you care to stay and have some tea?" At his shrugging off his leather case, she requested another setting with a nod to the footman standing just outside the gazebo, along with a tea cart stocked with extra food and place settings.

Theodore moved to take the seat next to Flora, yet Carlisle was faster in reclaiming it, sending him a smirk. Tacy fixed a pointed look at her sister, which caused Flora's color to heighten once more. Flora directed a slight shake of the head to her sister, which made Tacy purse her lips even tighter, turning the rim of her lips white. *What is going on with these two?* The sisters were usually at odds, but this, this seemed another matter entirely.

As the round table was too small for a sixth guest, the footman placed a set for Theodore on the gazebo's bench lining the perimeter that would serve as his table. With a nod of thanks, Theodore looked to the pot of tea and triple-tiered tower of scones, pastries, and dainty cucumber sandwiches that could be eaten in a single mouthful, waiting for someone to offer him refreshments. But with Tacy fawning over Clancy's every word, even though he was directing them to Flora, and Carlisle leaning toward Flora, Theodore was surprised they had noticed him in the first place. Even Olive was distracted. He reached for the pot and poured himself a cup, splashing some into the saucer. It was a little trickier to manage than he had thought, but he dabbed it up with Carlisle's napkin and piled a plateful of sandwiches, followed by a heaping spoonful of salted almonds.

Nora's laugh sounded on the path, and he glanced up to find her beside Mr. Grayson, carrying several hatboxes. Theodore scowled. He had thought Mr. Grayson was interested in Flora . . . unless this was his way of garnering her attention by using her youngest sister as a means to incur jealousy or perhaps instill gratefulness for taking care of the youngest Wingfield.

"Thank goodness we are in time for tea. Mr. Grayson is in need of refreshments after running into me outside the milliner's shop." Nora slipped off her flower-rimmed chapeau and tossed it on the bench alongside the pathway, pulling off her soiled gloves.

Mr. Grayson, however, did not wait for her or for a proper setting, but instead withdrew his handkerchief and helped himself to the array of food.

From where he sat, Theodore could see Flora's shoulders tensing, her knuckles growing white as she clenched the teapot, waiting for the footman to bring two extra cups. "Mr. Grayson, so happy you could join us. What were you doing outside the milliner's?"

Mr. Grayson smacked his lips, clearly enjoying the cucumber sandwich he had taken straight from the tier. "Waiting for the excuse to be invited to the Wingfields', of course." He winked, eliciting a giggle from Nora.

"Nora, you should find Father. He asked about you earlier," Olive interjected.

"I'm certain a half hour more will not hurt," Nora returned.

Mr. Grayson joined Theodore and did not even bother using the plate the footman at once supplied before consuming the four sandwiches in his stained handkerchief and easing himself on the wooden bench beside Theodore, where he began munching away on Theodore's plate of almonds.

The party was growing far too large for an intimate discussion with Flora about sketches, which he had hoped would prove a good transition into a conversation of his growing feelings. Yet how could one approach a topic that had been avoided for the entirety of one's friendship? He supposed Flora would question the state of his heart after two broken engagements, which was why he needed the extra time with her. He swallowed the tea, nearly choking on the bitter, black brew. He had always despised Darjeeling, a fact Flora well knew, which further attested to her distracted state. He discreetly lifted his cup over the rail and poured it into the azalea bushes, wincing at the telling rustle of the tea hitting the dead leaves gathered beneath.

"As my sister was about to mention before you all joined us"—Tacy looked to Flora, who shook her head in quick succession—"some of you gentlemen may not have heard everything about us sisters."

Olive, who had just accepted the empty teacups and saucers from the footman for Nora and Mr. Grayson, cast a glance to Flora, who had relinquished her hold on the teapot and was instead pinching the bridge of her nose, exhaling.

Tacy turned a brilliant smile to Clancy, which did not have the desired effect, given her stained teeth. "For example, Clancy, you have remarked several times on our beauty you've heard of far and wide, but perhaps what you haven't heard is that—"

"Tacy." Flora cleared her throat, eyes pleading, but Tacy persisted.

". . . that our father, being the best of gentlemen, has arranged for his daughters to enjoy equal shares of his wealth," Tacy continued as if she did not realize the stillness of the gazebo as the hum of the cicadas seemed to grow about them into a deafening symphony. "Which means we Wingfield sisters are *all* entitled to the same amount, despite our line in birth, and will all have equal shares upon our father's demise."

Flora took a long draft of tea as if hiding her embarrassment behind her gold-rimmed cup while Olive looked everywhere *but* at the gentlemen, paling at Tacy's declaration, and Nora giggled into her hand and sank down beside Theodore.

"Poor Tacy," Nora whispered to Theodore. "How humiliating for her to have to resort to such measures when I had already hinted at that breakfast with Mr. Drake of the same fact. I'm certain he would have circulated the word himself, if he wasn't so afraid of competition and of losing his chance with one of us."

Theodore popped a cucumber sandwich into his mouth, avoiding searching for an answer to that bit of information.

"Well, Miss Tacy, I thank you for your honesty." Clancy broke the silence. "Being a gentleman of means myself, I do not necessarily need more wealth, though I will not be above saying that the more wealth the merrier. I am happy for you and your sisters that you will not be overlooked simply because you are younger than Miss Flora."

Carlisle nodded, lifting his cup toward Theodore. "We know better than most of the pain of line in birth, eh, Teddy?"

Flora's nervous laughter broke the tension. "Well, now that you all are aware of our worth as daughters of Florian Wingfield, would anyone care for a second cup?" She lifted the pot and spotted Theodore's cup beside him on the bench with the spoon still in it, signaling his wish for more tea, and refilled his cup before he could protest.

"Well, that was strange," he whispered to her.

"I'm only thankful she did not force me to speak it," she said, shooing Nora over in Mr. Grayson's direction and taking the seat beside Theodore on the bench, holding the teapot with both hands atop her skirt.

"What does she have over you?" he murmured, lifting the cup to his lips before he remembered it was Darjeeling. He fought back a gag. *Swallow it like a man, Day.*

She pressed her lips into a thin line. "Only the ability to make the remainder of my summer here miserable, which is more than enough, but I'll tell you more on that score later."

His temperament brightened at this promised confidence, even as Carlisle waved her over and Theodore at last was able to settle back on the bench to appreciate his plate, except for the now-tainted almonds.

The tea seemed to go on forever, during which time he noticed Carlisle and Flora laughing far too much. What was Flora thinking entertaining him? Carlisle was the competitor after all, and Theodore did not think she was capable of acting as a spy. Not that she needed to. Her designs were more original than anything Carlisle could have worked up on his own.

When the party at last broke up with Tacy walking Clancy to the gate, lingering longer than was proper while Nora agreed to a stroll with Mr. Grayson, and Carlisle departing with Olive to speak with Mr. Wingfield, Theodore retrieved his designs.

Flora was by his side at once, taking a chair at the now-cleared table, save for a plate of fruit, in a cloud of blue material that made her eyes far too distracting. "What did you work up?"

"See for yourself." Theodore flipped through the designs with her. She stopped him occasionally, commenting on something she liked and even pointing out aspects she didn't. That was another thing he liked about her. She wasn't afraid of being honest. When he had first seen Flora and her family again in Paris after years of being apart, he had thought she had become like most other girls, only interested in the latest fashions and the next party, but that one week touring with her had proven him wrong. Then she had mentioned a love for interior design, but he'd been too absorbed with Bernadette breaking his heart to press further on the matter. He had found Flora to be caring and kind during that horrendous time, and then throughout his stint in Willow's competition he found a depth in Flora he had not known before—a depth that was being further revealed in her willingness to assist him without compensation.

With the final page of designs, he sensed his courage fleeing. Despite her kindhearted nature, would she also reject him just as Bernadette had? As Willow? And though he knew Flora, he was not sure he could risk his heart again so soon, not after enduring the searing pain of loss twice over. And not until he was certain of her affections. Thankfully, she was here for the summer. Perhaps he could use that time for safely discovering if she harbored any feelings for him under the guise of friendship, or if instead she was simply being kind before turning away from him to accept another—after his heart had been ruptured. His family had warned him of giving his love away too eagerly, but this was Flora . . . and it seemed she had always possessed a piece of his heart. *But a few more weeks of working by her side to ascertain her feelings may save mine from being crushed once more, and from certain humiliation if rejected.*

He returned the designs to the leather tube. "After we secure our first installment from Mr. and Mrs. Thompson and her St. Louis friends, Mr. and Mrs. Tyndall, we can discuss our plans for getting our designs into the hands of more buyers. What do you say to our meeting at the tearoom in the lower Pontalba building every morning after breakfast? Perhaps we could ride there in my gig? It is a far piece to travel every morning by foot." *Even though walking would mean more time with you.*

"I think that is brilliant, but you are going to have to pay. There is only so much pin money Father provides me, and I have spent all mine on a costume for Penelope's party tomorrow evening," Flora replied, snatching a chocolate-covered strawberry and popping it in her mouth.

"Done. And shall I pick you up at seven for the party? I don't think it is wise for a lady such as yourself to ride about the city without an escort." He glanced toward the gate, where Clancy was lifting his hat in salute to Flora. "Unless you have already agreed to go with another?"

"I haven't." She raised her hand, waving farewell to Clancy. "And even though you are leaving for St. Louis to deliver the Tyndalls' steamboat the morning after the ball, don't think you can use the excuse of packing for your being late to fetch me, because I *will* take my carriage without you if you do not arrive on time. I cannot afford to affront Penelope Bridgewater, as my father is now attempting to woo her father into selling their sugar plantation—if Mr. Grayson does not agree to a buyout of Wellington Sugar within the next few days. And as I have already angered Father with that little incident with Mr. Grayson and the policeman during our outing, I don't dare misstep again and ruin a potential deal."

He caught her hand in his and pressed a kiss atop, her eyes widening with his action. While spending every morning together might not have been the most direct way of securing time with her, it was the safest. And that was what he needed right now after everything. He needed to keep his heart safe.

"And Teddy," she added slowly, "there is something you need to know about Carlisle's place in the competition."

Thirteen

"Apparently, if one dons an eye patch, it instantly metamorphoses you into a proper pirate," Teddy explained as he adjusted the patch back into place while the carriage rolled to a stop on Baronne Street outside the imposing Grunewald Hall. "And once I secured the patch, the rest of the costume was simple enough to create by turning my cape inside out to display the scarlet interior silk."

Flora smirked, keeping a firm grip on her cloak to keep Teddy from seeing her gown. "Telling this to a woman who worked tirelessly on her costume, attending fitting after fitting, do you know how infuriating it is that you can get away with only wearing an eye patch to a costume ball?"

Teddy hopped out of the carriage and spread his arms wide beneath his scarlet cape, displaying his riding pants and boots. "Don't forget the rest of my ensemble. It took me all of half an hour to piece together. I had nearly forgotten it was a costume party, as it wasn't mentioned on the invitation."

"You must not have examined it very hard. It was on the bottom under the date and time." Flora took his offered hand and stepped down from the carriage, taking care that her costume did not jingle or show beneath her golden cloak. She looked up to the four stories of the grand hall's windows glowing in the night, and for once, Flora wasn't sweating.

My first party in the city alone. Though her father saw the lack of his being extended an invitation as a slight, she sighed in delight not to have her sisters or parents along, for as much as she loved them, it was nice to be invited for herself only. She extended her invitation to the footman, who bowed, then stepped aside to let them inside.

Her breath caught at the sight before her. The hall, impressive in its own right with its polished floors, glittering chandeliers, and gaslight sconces, was transformed into a panorama of the sea with aquatic vivariums lining the walls, filled with colorful exotic fish swimming about. One tank was filled with lobster, and it appeared that guests were selecting which one they would like to have for dinner. An obliging chef de partie lifted out the unlucky crustacean using a pair of silver tongs, his assistant then labeling the lobster's claw with a tag.

At the center back of the hall, affixed atop a row of three cutout, painted cresting waves that moved on a spigot to aid in the illusion of movement, was a ship about fifty feet in length, rocking back and forth with pirates swarming about the deck.

Flora's jaw dropped at the sight. "I've never seen anything like it."

"Which I'm certain was the point. This must have cost her father a fortune," Teddy muttered out of the side of his mouth as a fellow shouted to him from behind, pulling him from her side, even before the footmen had a chance to gather their outerwear prior to their greeting the Bridgewaters.

Even though she loathed the idea of greeting Penelope without Teddy by her side, etiquette instilled in her since birth kept her in line. She craned around the reception line, waiting to see when the footman would come and relieve her of her cloak, but oddly enough it seemed they were taking off the cloaks after they greeted the hosts.

Mr. and Mrs. Bridgewater greeted her without ado while the son pressed a far too lingering kiss upon her glove. She drew in a deep breath and moved before Penelope.

"Miss Wingfield, so happy you could join us." Penelope smiled, returning her curtsy.

Flora's lips parted at Penelope's gown, a beautiful seafoam-green Worth creation with pearls woven into the tulle about her shoulders, but not at all a costume. "I-I thought you said this was a *costume* party?"

Penelope's eyes widened in a show of innocence as the Misses Pimpernels flanked her on either side, one in a silver ball gown and the other in blue, trimmed in black lace. "Did I? My mistake." She flipped her hand. "A slip of the tongue. I meant to say sea-colored gowns, not actual *costumes*. You didn't take my little jest seriously, did you?"

Flora clenched her hands around her cloak, but she would not give Penelope the satisfaction of a horrified reaction. She stood, stalwart, and gave her hostess a pretty smile. "I'm afraid so, as it was printed on my invitation. But it is no matter."

Penelope pressed her hand to her throat. "My, what a ghastly mistake. And how distressing for you, but you'll have to forgive me for my calligraphist's mistake. He must have overheard my jest when I requested your late invitation." Her eyes glinted, betraying that it was her design all along to humiliate Flora in front of all of society. "Sandrine knows not to believe half of what I say, don't you, dear?"

Sandrine bobbed her head, accenting her double chin. "Certainly. Like when I overheard you were meeting up with Theodore Day for tea and I asked if I could join you. Then you gave me the wrong date and I sat there for the whole of an hour, not even aware that the tea occurred the day before."

Flora tilted her head. "That wasn't a jest—that was simply a misunderstanding. Unlike a printed invitation . . ."

Penelope smiled sweetly. "It is no matter."

No matter? I am the only woman in costume. Flora wanted to scream but instead composed herself with dignity.

"Why, Miss Penelope? Ladies! Why aren't you in costume?" Teddy called from behind Flora, sweeping into their little circle in his scarlet cape, eye patch firmly in place.

Penelope released a high, nervous laugh and seized his arm. "Why, Theodore Day, you dressed in costume as well? I should watch my jests more carefully in the future."

"See? I told you it wasn't on my invitation, Flora." He laughed and flipped up his eye patch. "Well, as long as we stay in costume together, we won't need to depart early to save face."

Even as the prospect of staying with Teddy for the duration of the evening appealed to her, the idea of being mocked by New Orleans society was not something she relished. "Teddy, it will only take a moment to return home and change—"

"And miss all the good food and entertainment Penelope has arranged? We couldn't be so rude." He motioned for her to remove her cape, wiggling his fingers. "Solidarity. You will be fine so long as you are with me. Off with the cloak."

With a sigh, she drew back her hood to reveal the strands of freshwater pearls woven into her elaborately braided locks and released the clasp of her cloak, allowing it to fall into his waiting hands, the ladies surrounding her gasping. She grazed her hand down the gold gown. *Thank you, Lord, for letting Mother catch me before I put in that order for the parrot costume.* She cringed at the nearly diabolical ramifications of that choice Mother had spared her from before Flora had left for the seamstress. Mother had practically had an attack over the vibrant green-and-purple-feathered ensemble Flora had intended to order and set aside her own plans for the morning to redesign a gown worthy of a Wingfield.

"I thought you would dress as a pirate," Penelope sputtered.

"You said 'pirate-themed,' and every pirate needs his treasure, no?" She smiled, running her hands over her gold silk gown that caught in the candlelight, swaying slightly to allow the Spanish doubloons sewn into the bodice to jingle and the interspersed rubies and pearls to sparkle. In her bustle, the maid had sewn clusters of pearls with diamond centers that cascaded to the floor with her trailing hem in a priceless masterpiece. At her neck, she wore a thin, black satin ribbon with a single diamond in the center, tied back, which flowed down her bare shoulders. She cast a glance at Teddy, and at his slack-jawed state, she could not keep her smile from broadening.

Sandrine stepped forward, her fingers outstretched as if she wished to touch it, but at Penelope's elbow to her corset stays, she jerked it back. "You are wearing a fortune. I've never seen anyone wear so many jewels on a single gown before."

"Well, I didn't know what sort of treasure I would be without a fortune. Mother had such amusement aiding me in the design and used the jewels that we usually have sewn into all our ball gowns."

Miss Josephine traced a gold coin at Flora's waist, incredulous. "You usually wear coins?"

Flora giggled. "Of course not. The Spanish doubloons are something unique to this gown. My father enjoys collecting them and was gracious enough to allow me the use of some for this evening, though under strict instructions that they be returned to him on the morrow."

Teddy clasped her hand. "Well, at least now I know that no one will be noticing me, not with you by my side. Thank you for having the most outlandish gown of the two of us." He took her hand and raised it, pulling her into a twirl to display her gown.

She laughed and complied, determined to put on a show of ease to irk Penelope. "I don't know about that. You look like the very pirate waiting to carry off treasure." She spread her arms wide. "Which I am!"

He caught her hand and kissed it. "Then I best stay by your side all night to ensure you are not carried off by another. You are *my* treasure alone this evening."

Flora's heart tripped. Such blatant flattery was not like him. She glanced at Penelope out of the corner of her eye, seeing her stiffen at his words. He could be just trying to protect her from Penelope's enmity, but as the crowd around Flora and Teddy grew, all whispering over her gown, he kept her safely tucked in his arm. While her costume was indeed outlandish, she knew next to Teddy she did not stick out as much as she would have alone. Once again he had saved her.

Penelope huffed and marched away toward the ship, and soon ladies surrounded Teddy, jewels dripping against their ivory skin, though no one would have as many jewels as Flora tonight.

"To how many people did Penelope mention that tonight would be a costume ball?" Sandrine giggled into her fan and pointed to the door.

Flora turned to find a woman in an emerald gown, entering on the arm of a man, both wearing masks. The woman paused, looking about the room, her confusion clear at the attire of the crowd. At once she cast her mask into the hands of a passing footman, closely followed by Clancy's. Tacy's grin spread at the sight of Flora in her gold gown that had caused her sister such envy only hours before when she was lamenting that she had not been invited. Tacy had not taken too kindly to the slight, but apparently she had somehow managed to have Clancy escort her.

"My, aren't we feeling a tad ridiculous in all those jewels?" She flipped open her painted fan.

"I think she looks stunning." Clancy's eyes shone, lingering over the jewels at Flora's neckline for a second too long for a gentleman of good fortune.

"Thank you, Mr. Drake. I did not know you two were coming together?"

"Clancy arrived only moments after your departure. He received your note that your escort canceled at the final hour and was coming to your rescue."

"Note? I didn't send a note." Flora gaped at her sister, but at Tacy's warning tilt of her brow, Flora clamped her lips shut from openly accusing her sister of forgery. "I'm so sorry, Mr. Drake, for the confusion. You must know that I never would have summoned you like that and then not been there to receive you. You must believe me."

Clancy glanced sideways at Tacy, understanding flashing through his eyes as she took a sudden interest in a nearby vivarium. "Well, I must admit that it is rather a relief to hear you say so."

"Yes, well, while he did not rescue the intended damsel in distress, he rescued me by extending an invitation to come with him to Grunewald Hall," Tacy said, beaming up at her stolen escort.

Flora felt her face warm. It was one thing to attempt to make her announce their dowries over tea, but quite another to tarnish her good name in order to gain good standing with a suitor. "Were you ever going to admit that I did not send that note, Sister?"

Tacy gaped at her. "I have no idea what you are talking about."

Clancy leaned to her, whispering, "Do not be distressed. I believe you did not send the note, especially when you were already being escorted." He took her hand. "It is such a relief to know you did not give me the cut direct."

"You know it is ill-mannered to ignore the two of us while you are having your private interlude," Tacy scolded, crossing her arms.

Flora swallowed back her retort that it was also ill-mannered to *lie*.

"Ladies and gentlemen, please turn your attention to the stage," a voice sounded from the rigging of the ship. There, a squat, barrel-chested pirate with a paunch gripped the ropes, brandishing a sword in an effort to gather the guests around the massive ship as it rocked on its base with the line of waves rolling before it, giving the illusion they were sailing the high seas.

From her position at the edge of the crowd, Flora could see enough behind the painted scene to make out footmen working each spigot, sweat dripping from their powdered wigs as each man turned a level of the waves with a partner on the other side.

"I need a volunteer, and since one of you so kindly dressed for the role in a stunning costume, we would like to ask you to play the part of our treasure, my lady." He pointed his sword at Flora, his eyes boring into hers as the gaslights and chandeliers dimmed. Soon the only light in the room emanated from the stage lamps aboard the ship, set beneath the rail.

She swallowed as all eyes turned to her. This would surely be in the papers tomorrow, and she could not afford to have another toilet-sheet moment. It was a miracle *that* disaster had not been written about. She could not balk, yet how was she supposed to board without showing the world her crimson petticoats? As she reluctantly stepped forward, a giant of a man in pirate garb marched down the steps of the ship, disguised as the planked side of the ship.

Teddy's fingers wrapped about her wrist, anchoring her to him. "You don't have to do this."

Penelope patted his arm. "How kind of you to fear for her safety, but the actors are reputable and she is being watched by all, so it is quite unnecessary to put on such a show. Best leave that to the actors."

"My lady." The pirate bowed to Flora, extending his hand to her.

Flora sent Teddy a reassuring smile and placed her hand in the pirate's and boarded the ship.

The pirate lifted his sword to the crowd, shouting, "What you are about to witness dates back sixty years to our grandmother and grandfather, she an infamous river pirate and he a pirate of the Gulf of Mexico, who passed down her stories to her children and her children's children! The lovely lady will represent our grandmother's greatest haul. Many of you may recall *Captain Lavigne the Terrible*. This is the story of how *The Siren of the Mississippi River* and the greatest pirate of the Gulf created an empire of terror."

Flora's knees shook beneath her gown with these men in costume milling about her, but she focused on Teddy's brooding face in the crowd, with Tacy closely behind him pasted on Clancy's arm, her sister's vehement gaze oddly reassuring as it helped to ground her.

"And now we'd like to request a male volunteer from the crowd to play the part of the gentleman pirate sent to retrieve the treasure at all costs," the pirate called.

Teddy's hand shot up at once, but to Flora's irk, Penelope was there at his side and bumped into him, causing him to lower his hand for a second, which was long enough for the pirate to select a gentleman from the back of the hall.

Flora squinted through the lights into the dark crowd, trying to make out who would be her counterpart as he waded through the guests and climbed the stairs where the stage lamps illuminated his smile. Flora gripped the side of the ship. Would she never be free of the man?

Mr. Grayson accepted the wooden sword, painted to look like steel, and was given instructions to hold the sword above his head as if ready for a fight.

"Miss Wingfield? What a pleasure to see you again," Mr. Grayson whispered to her, taking his position as the pirate continued on with his story. "Such a small city this has turned out to be."

As a guest of Mr. Bridgewater, she should have known he would be in attendance. It was a miracle he had not paid her call again with all his attentions toward her on their outing, but perhaps he had finished his business with her father and had no more need of her? *Or maybe he has already made a deal with Father for my hand . . .* The horrid thought was enough to nearly make her sick. "I thought you were here on business—not pleasure."

"When both align, it is the best sort of business."

"Pardon my asking, but why are you here now that enough time has passed for your business to conclude? I seem to recall aboard the *Belle Memphis* your mentioning that you were only in town a short while."

"It is flattering you remembered. I extended my stay as my employer wishes for the Bridgewaters to remember why they do business with him instead of your father." He flipped his hand toward the pirates rushing about the deck. "Because of my employer, Penelope was able to have her dream in hand."

"Heathcliff Wellington *paid* for this extravaganza?" Flora's flesh prickled. Nonetheless, she could not shake the sense of unease that had settled over her heart. Wellington never did anything without a motive, and from what Father mentioned over breakfast to Mother, Wellington was enraged with the Louisiana sugar barons for even contemplating abandoning him. She scanned the room from her place below the mast. But what was the message he was attempting to convey with such a lavish party? She would have to tell Father—if he would ever unlock his study door.

"Whatever is pinned on your gown?" Mr. Grayson pointed to her waist.

She looked down and found a folded, white cotton square. "That's odd."

"And then the mighty hurricane came!" the narrator shouted, cymbals clashing, jarring Flora from her place on the deck.

She slid the pin from her bodice and let it fall to the floor, removing the square, unfolding it to find—she gasped.

The actors swarmed Grayson, making a show of sword fighting with him.

"And to the Siren Queen's horror, the storm swept the treasure, the gentleman pirate, and Captain Lavigne into the mighty Mississippi River, never to be found again!"

The floor gave way, and Flora felt herself falling before her scream could leave her lungs as she plunged into darkness, the handkerchief bearing a black spot tumbling over itself through the trapdoor after her.

Fourteen

The hall was snuffed of light, the ladies in the audience screaming. A single candle flickered to life as, one by one, the stage lamps were all lit again and the play resumed with a weeping pirate queen leaning over her lost love— which would have been far more convincing were the part played by a woman—only to reveal that Flora had vanished from her place at the mast, and Mr. Grayson along with her.

Theodore surged through the crowd, Penelope trailing after him. Flora shouldn't be out of his sight with strange actors roaming about, especially while she was wearing a fortune. *It is one thing to hire actors, but quite another for Penelope to use men who are descendants of the notorious river pirate queen.* He clutched his fists. He would have words with her parents. It was far too soon to make light of the meaning of the word *pirate*, especially in New Orleans.

"Where are you going?" Penelope caught him by his shoulder.

"To find Flora," he grunted, too annoyed with Penelope to coat his words.

"It's a *play*, Theodore. She is well. We wouldn't have brought in pirates who were not thoroughly vetted." Penelope's hand trailed to his arm, but he shrugged her off and took the stairs up the side of the ship two at a time.

"Looks like we have another volunteer!" the pirate laughed. "And he too has been so kind as to dress in costume. What role shall we give him? Is he another pirate coming to woo the Siren Queen? That role doesn't end well either, though," he added, drawing laughter from the crowd below.

Did no one remember the countless pirate attacks on the Mississippi River, many of them from the hand of the Siren Queen, that had plagued his family's business for years? "Enough. Where is she?" Theodore hissed.

"Lover Number Two it is then. Though he seems to be more concerned about his *treasure* than the queen," he muttered out of the side of his mouth. "Trapdoor by the mast. If you ruin this production for me, you'll owe me a hundred dollars for tonight and five hundred more for potential jobs lost. This Miss Bridgewater may start a fad."

Not caring one whit about the man's so-called entertainment, Theodore knelt at the mast and wrenched open the trapdoor, finding the hollowed inside of the ship and the floor of the hall with sacks piled beneath to cushion one's fall. He dropped down, landing hard on his feet and rolling off the sacks. Squinting in the darkness, he heard the boards of the framework creaking overhead and ducked in time to avoid the ship's rocking left and a beam knocking him senseless.

"Teddy." Flora's arms were about his neck before he could even call her name. She pulled him down as the ship rocked right, perilously close to where his head had been only moments before.

On his knees, he held her close, the sweet scent of her gardenia perfume making him wish he could hold her longer, but here in the darkness was not the proper time and place. He helped her to standing, both crouching over to keep free of the ship's movement, obeying its rhythmic sway so as to prevent an injury. "Are you hurt? Those sacks don't seem that effective in cushioning an unexpected fall."

"The fright of free falling was rather terrifying, but I am well."

"I'm surprised I didn't yell myself." A chuckle came from the front of the hull.

Theodore whirled about. How could he have forgotten, even for a moment, of the gentleman with Flora? *Unchaperoned and with Grayson at that.* He tightened his hold on Flora's arm. He would have some very serious words with Mr. Bridgewater, no matter that he might lose a sale for his confrontation. After tonight's party and the new orders he'd secured, he would be tied with Carlisle, with or without Mr. Bridgewater's support.

At the shouts above them and the clanging of swords, Flora ducked into him as the trapdoor opened and a pirate came flying through, landing with practiced ease on the sacks and hopping up at once.

Grayson braced a hand against the ship's frame. "Good of you to drop in." He laughed at his own jest as the actor rolled his eyes. "I wanted to ask why so-called river pirates would choose to use a ship instead of a model riverboat for their play?"

The pirate dusted off his costume. "There was some confusion when Miss Bridgewater ordered the play, and well, by the time she could correct the issue, we had most of it built and no time to start over." He shrugged. "These socialites and their whims. First, she tells us to build a *ship* and then a steamboat and was angry when we lowly pirate actors threatened the success of her night. So she changed every-thing to be a 'pirates on the high seas' theme, following the love story of a river queen—"

"I know, I know. I was right there onstage listening to your never-ending story." Grayson waved him off.

"The play should provide enough cover for us to depart if you are well enough to leave," Theodore whispered to Flora.

"Now, why would she be ill or wish to depart?" Grayson interjected, tugging against the wood frame propping up the deck above. It budged a half inch. "But perhaps you are right about getting out of the bowels of this makeshift ship to view the rest of the play in case they have a shipwreck planned that they did not disclose to us. There is a door at the back we were about to exit when you dropped in and interrupted us."

Flora's hand in his, Theodore brushed past the actor and flung open the door, nearly smacking into the wall behind it. He guided her along the slight gap between the ship and the wall, hesitating at the edge of the crowd, when he spot-ted Mr. Bridgewater. "I should really tell Mr. Bridgewater to keep a better hold on his daughter's ideas, but let's get you home before I embarrass us both," he muttered.

"Speaking of embarrassing myself . . ." She halted. "I need to prove to Penelope and the belles that I am unshaken about wearing a costume to a non-costume ball even due to a so-called misunderstanding, and also that I'm fine with being the center of attention, even after being called onstage for all to see that mistake. If I waiver, the socialites will never let me live it down."

"Why do you care so much about society here? You will be gone by summer's end." Theodore dropped her hand. "And besides, Penelope would not be that petty as to purposefully embarrass you in order to make your time here miserable."

She lifted a single brow. "I know you are not that naïve."

He threw up his hand in defense. "She may come across a bit cold, but I have known her since childhood. We grew up on the same avenue, and I know she is not mean." He studied her, but instead of his words reassuring her, her cheeks brightened. Was she angry?

"When you put it in that light, you most likely know her even better than me." She twisted her hands. "Then I suppose, as her friend, you will be so kind as to convince her to play nice?"

"Absolutely." *She may hesitate, but she will cease this battle with you for my attention.*

"Despite the fact that she set me up for humiliation?" Flora crossed her arms.

"I'm certain it was an honest mistake." Theodore spread his arms wide beneath his cape. "If that were the case, she planned the same humiliation for me, and I can guarantee you she does not wish me ill."

"And you know that because of the way she flings herself in your path at every turn?"

"If that's the definition of a young lady being taken with me, seems as though you fit that description as well." He laughed, recalling her tumbling before his carriage, which was still disconcerting, save for the fact that she was well and whole before him.

Flora screwed her lips together and whirled away from him.

"Flora? What did I say?" he called after her. But the ranks had spotted him and were already closing in on all sides. "It was a jest. Flora, come back!"

Flora pressed her back against the wall of the powder room and covered her face with her hands, attempting to gather her breath. *How could Teddy have said such a thing to me? Has he been laughing at me for the entirety of my visit? Thinking of me as the poor, dear rich girl who is always second to someone. Second to Willow. Second to Father. Second choice of every man in New York because of my stupid dowry. Never good enough.*

She drew in a shaky breath. She couldn't cry and spoil her complexion and let the entire party conclude that she had wept. She rested her head against the wall. *Lord, will I ever be enough? Will I ever be seen as worthy?* Tears brimmed at the harsh hints her father had been setting free at every meal since their arrival to New Orleans. *Am I really only a means to an end for my father's business? Because, at times like these, it's difficult to feel special. To feel worthy of true love—of dreaming.*

She kicked off the wall and ran her fingers under her lashes. "Lord, help me make it through one more night watching him flirt with others, and then help me forget how much I love him and let me find a bit of happiness elsewhere." Straightening her shoulders, she swept into the ballroom as the play ended with thundering applause. She glanced about for Tacy and Clancy, anyone who seemed friendly that was *not* Teddy Day whom she could latch on to for the rest of the evening.

She strolled about the room, studying the ornate wall coverings, the furniture's French influence, and the ironwork gracing each balcony at every French door along the second floor of the hall where the ball was taking place. To her surprise, gentlemen at every turn greeted her with a smile, though etiquette kept them from approaching her without an introduction.

"Miss Wingfield." A tall gentleman in a well-tailored black coat and tails bowed to her. "Beaumont Bridgewater. We met at your aunt's."

She returned his greeting with a curtsy. "Of course, how could I forget Penelope's older brother." She caught sight of Tacy, who was in an animated argument with Clancy in the corner of the room. Though Flora could not make out their words, Tacy's hurt expression and Clancy's annoyance were clear.

"I hope that my relation to her does not count against me?" He chuckled.

Flora laughed before she could stop herself.

"I see it does." He grinned, lifting his glass to her. "She seems to have struck again."

"Pardon?"

He motioned to her ensemble. "We all know she is the reason that you are dressed in costume tonight. Though may I say that you look very fetching. Would you care for a refreshment before dinner?" He lifted his empty glass to a passing footman with a silver tray of drinks.

"Thank you, but I'm afraid I need to return home," she replied, twisting her gold doubloon bracelet, the jingling of the coins bringing a light to the young man's eyes.

"Before dinner? Did you not pick out your lobster?" He gestured to the aquatic vivarium housing the crustaceans.

She folded her hands in front of her overskirt. "A pressing matter has come up and I must see to it tonight."

He caught her hand in his, kissing the top. "Until next time, Miss Wingfield."

Flora looked about for her sister, thinking she would surely wish to have a ride home after such a public disagreement with Clancy. She wove through the crowd, starting at the sight of Tacy handing the lead pirate something that looked like a diamond necklace. "Tacy!" she called.

Tacy spun away from the actor, who shuffled away, stuffing the jewels into the pouch hanging from his waistband. "Yes?"

"What did you just give him?"

She dusted her hands off and shrugged. "Nothing. He dropped one of the stage props for the treasure. I was merely returning it to him."

Flora's brows rose with this uncharacteristic kindness. "Oh. Well, I was wondering if you wished for a ride home. I find that it is far too crowded in here for me."

"Why would I want to leave before dancing and dinner?" She stared at her blankly. "There's *lobster*."

Flora lowered her voice. "Because you and Clancy had a fight."

"It wasn't very gentlemanly of him to react so in public. Mind your own business, Flora, and let me handle Clancy in my own fashion." Tacy straightened her shoulders, hiding her anger behind her fan. "I came with Clancy, and I will leave with him. Where's Teddy?"

Flora gestured to the press of women in the corner. "I decided not to bother him."

"I suppose now you at last know how it feels to be un-wanted and second choice." Tacy's eyes flashed, a smug smile settling into place as she flounced away. "Have a safe drive home alone."

Fifteen

Theodore had searched the length of the hall for Flora twice now and no one had seen her, which seemed odd as the woman was dressed as a treasure. Having no other idea where to look, he trotted outside, the music and candlelight spilling from the windows of the hall and lighting the sidewalk. He swiped off his patch, hoping he would not find her on the streets of New Orleans, and glanced down the line of horse carriages, grunting when he did not see her, uncertain if he should be relieved or not.

"Excuse me, sir?" A groom in a scarlet livery approached him. "May I call a carriage for you, or perhaps have yours brought 'round?"

Theodore pulled off the cape and flipped it over to have the black silk on the outside so as not to stand out in the night crowd. "Do you know if Miss Wingfield departed? She was dressed in a costume, though you may not have noticed. It would be covered in a gold cloak, which would be odd in itself given the heat, but her gown would jingle when walking."

Recognition lit his eyes. "Yes! There was a lady who

clinked as she walked instead of rustled. She left in a rush in the carriage she summoned from my stableboy using the name Mr. Theodore Day, and as she came from inside and the driver recognized her, I allowed her to take it."

His shoulders sagged. She had withstood so much tonight, only to leave because of an offhanded comment from him? Well, now that he thought it over, perhaps it did not come across as intended. "I see."

"Was the carriage not hers for the taking, sir?"

"It is fine." He went to stuff his hands into his pockets, only to recall that his costume sported no pockets, and if he were to hire a carriage to go after her, he would need his billfold . . . which he had forgotten in his haste to meet with Flora. Sighing, he nodded his thanks to the groom and started the long walk home.

"Theodore, you can't leave without asking me for a dance," Penelope stood at the threshold of the hall, dance card in hand.

"I have to—"

"Theodore Day. You do realize that a reporter from the *Picayune* is here, don't you?" Her bottom lip trembled. "I told the reporter this party would be as historic as the Vanderbilt costume ball, and that couldn't possibly be true if guests are seen leaving early, especially if said guest is *you*—New York City's darling Mr. Day from the Dupré competition."

Seeing the tears filling her crystal eyes, he took her hand in his, sighed, and unfurled his eye patch. "Shall I don it again?"

"Yes!" She smiled as she slipped her arm through his, returning inside, the hum of the guests greeting them. "It makes you seem mysterious and not so much like the boy next door, especially with your short beard."

He couldn't refuse her. For no matter her feelings against Flora, she was still a long-standing friend. Leading her onto the crowded dance floor, she melted into his arms.

"You know we could be good together, Teddy—great even—if you would only give us a chance," she whispered, walking beneath the arch their arms created.

He cleared his throat, his neckcloth growing tight at her forwardness. "Penelope—"

"Do not pretend as though you are unaware of my feelings for you," she scolded, her grip tightening on his hand.

"I'm only surprised at your declaration," Theodore stated, "which is not very Southern of you."

She gave him a smooth smile. "Well, when a Yankee is obviously attempting to abscond with you, the time for subtlety has passed."

"You know I was born in New York, yes? And that my father's parents still live there in a brownstone near Flora's?"

"Yes, but you were raised here." She looked at him pointedly. "If you wed me, my father has agreed to help you in any way he can to expand your business. And as he is the nephew of one of the most respected river pilots of our time, he can secure countless contracts for you to fulfill, earning you the position as head of Day's Luxury Line."

Theodore dropped his gaze at Penelope's proposal. She could be good for him. And if his brother was right about his ostensible fickle heart, he could fall in love with Penelope, couldn't he? But looking again into her eyes, her flaming hair caressing her face in soft tendrils, all he could see was Flora. The thought made him break his rhythm and nearly stomp on her toes.

"Well? What do you say?" Penelope asked, her voice strained.

"Shall I inform my father of your paying call tomorrow to speak with him?"

While he had fallen in love with two other women, his family was wrong in that he would not take heed with his heart this time. This time he wouldn't fall in love again without assurances. Flora was different. Unlike the other women, Flora had spent the most time with him and not grown bored, rather more animated, and he with her throughout her time in New Orleans. He looked forward to each morning when he could see her, be with her. If he accepted Penelope, Flora most likely would never cross his path again, and that could not happen. He spun Penelope toward the corner and motioned to Gale Thornton to take over as her partner. "Excuse me, please."

"But—" Her protest died as his friend twirled her away, but her hurt expression seared him.

He strode toward the door, where he found Tacy with tears in her eyes. "Tacy? Whatever is wrong?"

"What's wrong?" She blew her nose into her handkerchief in an unladylike fashion. She folded it and, frowning at what appeared to be the dampness, dropped it into the base of a potted palm near the door. "Clancy has convinced himself that he is in love with my sister, and nothing I can say will keep him from proposing to Flora the next time he pays call."

"And then I dropped through the trapdoor!" Flora sank onto the settee in the front parlor over chamomile tea with Mother, Father, Nora, Ermengarde, Olive, and Cornelia, Auntie Violet having retired to her rooms after dinner.

"Thankfully, by the end of the performance, no one thought any different of my costume."

Mother sighed, pouring a second cup for Father. "Thank goodness you avoided embarrassment. Could you imagine how you would have felt in that ridiculous parrot costume you were going to have designed?"

Olive pressed her hands to her cheeks. "I think I would have fled, no matter how breathtaking the costume."

"I would have enjoyed being the center of attention." Nora closed her eyes and swayed in her seat.

"Heaven help us when your time comes," Father murmured, biting the end of his pipe as he lifted a match to the bowl, lighting the tobacco in a circular motion. He allowed the embers to die before striking a second match and drawing in a breath and a second, bringing the tobacco to life.

Cornelia smiled. "It really is quite romantic the way you and Mr. Day were thrown together for the evening despite *someone's* attempts to isolate you."

"I don't know about romantic," Flora mumbled into her teacup, thinking of Teddy's remark. While he'd apologized, he had cut her deeply, as her affection for him was her greatest secret.

"I agree, Flora." Father exhaled a ring of smoke. "Seems someone wished to make a fool of you, Daughter, and would have succeeded if not for Theodore Day's misunderstanding the invitation as well, though I do not take comfort in that fact as it does not bode well to misunderstand something as simple as an invitation."

"I fear his confusion was due to my misunderstanding, Father, not his. Though I like to think I would have stood my own even without him. But yes, whoever wished me ill"—

209

obviously Penelope—"they were unsuccessful." She sat up straight, remembering the handkerchief. "Speaking of which, the oddest thing happened while I was aboard the vessel. I found a handkerchief pinned at my waist, and odder still, it had a black spot in the center."

Father lowered his pipe, his knuckles whitening as they tightened around the carved bowl. "What did you say?"

"It had a black spot in it like the pirate messages of old. And what's more, it is the second one I have received since we've traveled here."

Father's hands shook as he pressed the pipe to his heart and held the other out to Mother. "Dear Lord . . ."

"I'm certain it is a poor jest, Father."

"Are you?" he whispered. "Yes, one would hope." He took a steadying draft of his tea and stood. "Girls, you best take to your beds or you will miss breakfast come morning."

At the chorus of protests that it was only nine of the clock, he lifted his hands to the group. "I need to speak with Flora, and I'd rather not be interrupted. Go now or I'll be withholding your pin money for the week."

They at once shuffled out, knowing Father was true to his threats, casting Flora curious glances in passing as Father spread his arms wide, herding them out of the room and closing the French doors behind them.

"Florian?" Mother set aside her tea. "Whatever do you think those handkerchiefs mean? No matter Flora's opinion, it worries me. And I noticed another letter was delivered. Was it from him?"

Flora stiffened. She had seen quite a few letters pass into his hands over the summer, but she could always tell when *the* letter came, all postmarked from New York City and sealed with crimson wax. The one that bespoke ill. Though she did not dare question her father, he and Mother had been so mysterious of late, she was beginning to worry as well.

"Rest assured, all will be set to rights. I have Pinkertons in New York working around the clock to locate the last of his minions." He rested a hand on Mother's shoulder, bending down to kiss the top of her head before straightening and puffing his pipe for a full minute before the open window, the sheer curtains rippling from the light breeze as thunder rumbled in the distance. "Flora, it is no secret as to why your mother and I agreed to come on this trip."

"Husband hunting," Flora supplied, folding her hands on her lap.

"Yes, but do not be so vulgar. It is not becoming for a young lady to be so blunt about such matters." His scowl deepened. "And after recent events, I have decided that it is high time you marry."

Flora laughed, reaching for the teapot, as this would most likely be a long lecture. "Yes, I am inclined to agree with you, but I am afraid it is a little more complicated than your deciding I should marry. A young man, who values my opinions and dreams, must first propose marriage."

"Your opinions and dreams?" He snorted. "Come, girl. You really must have a realistic expectation or you will die a maiden. Set aside your ridiculous standards and choose one of the perfectly good bachelors here that I have approved."

Flora lowered her cup to the side table, anger rising. *And yet it is perfectly fine for you to be perfectly blunt regarding my lack of a perfectly good suitor.* She drew a breath and rubbed a doubloon at her waist, attempting to suffocate her retort.

Mother rose and joined her, putting her hand on Flora's. "Florian, I wish our daughter to marry as much as you, but why the sudden need?" She gave him a pointed look. "Is it because of last night's letter?"

He rubbed his chin. "That and people are beginning to talk about Flora."

What letter? Flora rose from the settee, thinking at once of Penelope's grudge against her. "What are they saying about me?"

"That I spoil you and you are not fit to be a wife because of it." He tapped the remainder of his pipe tobacco into the fireplace, its sweet scent filling the room as the embers died in the cold hearth. "I cannot have the reputation of allowing my girls too much freedom."

"Yes, heaven forbid we have freedom in America," Flora murmured, but not low enough, as her father's scowl burned into her.

"Do *not* make light of this, Flora. I've had several investors on this trip express concern about my judgment because of my long list of unmarried daughters. And so, as the eldest, you must marry by summer's end, closely followed by Olive, Tacy, and Ermengarde. I cannot return to New York with you unattached."

Mother gasped. "Florian, you sound as if you are banishing her from New York."

"I think that's rather dramatic. I merely wish for her long-time hope of marriage to come to fruition sooner rather than later."

"If there is someone in this room to blame for her unwed state, it is *you*. You are always sending away suitors because you refuse to budge on *your* principles of keeping her an heiress pauper. Do not punish her for *your* standards." Mother huffed. "And if people are insulting my daughters, they are insulting me, so you best tell me at once *who* is brewing such outrageous rumors against my family."

"That I will not and cannot disclose." He waved her away.

Flora warmed at her mother's defense. In all her years observing her parents' happy marriage, Mother had only stood up to Father twice. The first when she refused to send her daughters away to boarding school as children, and the second when Flora expressed a wish to travel to Paris and Father did not wish to pay for it.

She squeezed her mother's hand. Perhaps Mother could keep her father from tossing her into the arms of the next man who asked for her hand. She knew her father had not placed much value on her, but to call her a burden? To cast her away by forcing her to marry in New Orleans and be left behind, separated from her sisters? *Does he even love me? He would never do this to Nora.*

Father rested a hand on Mother's shoulder, waiting for her to calm before replying in a low voice, "Do not get me wrong, my darling. I desire Flora's happiness, but I cannot have her feminine sensibilities hindering the building of my empire. The sugar barons like to do business with strong men, and a man ruled by his daughters will not woo them away from Wellington."

"What are you doing in the sugar business?" Flora groaned. *Don't you have enough money? Why do you need more? And at the expense of my happiness?*

"What I always do—making a deal. Since Wellington's imprisonment at his home, I have been slowly working away at the man's holdings, buying out his suppliers for Wellington

Sugar, weakening his fortune until I cripple him to secure another holding for our family as well as our safety. If he does not have funds, he will not have minions out to destroy us and the Duprés. That crippling, however, has caused some adverse reactions, but I am dealing with them."

Mother looked to Flora, twisting her hands on her lap. "And those suppliers live in southern Louisiana, which is how I convinced your father to agree to our summering here for your pursuit of happiness with Theodore Day."

Flora didn't trust herself to thank her mother for her surreptitious support without her voice breaking but merely squeezed her arm, careful not to crush Mother's brocade, puffed sleeve. "And do those letters have anything to do with that adverse reaction? Are you being threatened, Father?"

"No need for you to worry." He crossed his arms as he lifted the pipe to his mouth before recalling it was empty. "It is time we return to the matter at hand."

"You always change the subject when I attempt to ask about your business or your welfare. Heaven forbid that your family is actually informed."

Father narrowed his eyes at her tone. "Yes, because the security of one's family and business are indeed a man's game, no matter what Willow Dupré-Dempsey leads you to believe. When it became clear that I would not have any sons, I made my peace about running the business alone and without help, but if you cannot perform the single duty expected of you since birth, then what is the point of my having given you the best tutors to make you clever enough to become a business tycoon's wife?"

Mother's grip tightened on Flora's waist as tears filled

Flora's eyes. "So, you are saying, Father, that my only worth to you is an advantageous match?"

"I'm certain he doesn't mean that, my dear," Mother whispered. "What he *should* be saying is that we have always hoped for you to marry well, what with you being the prettiest of all your sisters."

"Perhaps that was a little harsh." Father sighed. "I love you, Flora, but your greatest value to me would be to marry a tycoon and give me a grandson—someone I can leave my empire to, someone who could at last become the wealthiest man in America. I could leave the business to one of your sister's future sons, but as they are receiving equal shares of my money, I feel no qualms in keeping to tradition and giving the eldest child's son the business and keeping that side of things intact."

Her tears spilled. Of course she wished to marry, and yes, have many children someday, but to say that was the sum of all her worth? That if she remained alone, she was worth nothing to him? It was not to be borne. She tore away from her mother and took the stairs, tears clogging her throat as she reached the second-floor landing.

"Your father wouldn't know treasure even if it was dropped at his feet in a gilded jewelry box." Auntie Violet stood in the hall in her dressing gown. At Flora's confused look, she added, "The tubes throughout the house allow me to speak with the servants, but they also provide a unique method of eavesdropping. Your father's shouting awoke me, and then of course I had to press my ear to the tube to listen to find out what on earth was happening. I am appalled by what he has told you." She lifted her arm, wiggling her fingers. "Come with me, my dear. The third floor is no place for you right now."

Too hurt to protest, she allowed Auntie to pull her into her suite, which held the faint odor of animal fur and wood shavings. Blinking in the dim candlelight, she found three gold-plated metal bunny mansions dotting the corners of the room, each resembling different homes on the avenue. It was a miracle the chamber smelled as little as it did. Auntie patted the back of a settee in her private parlor, and Flora numbly sank into it as Auntie glided to one of the cages and returned to set a brown rabbit with long ears in Flora's lap.

"Pet her. Tiffany will help."

Flora lifted a brow at the name.

Auntie smiled. "She was a gift from Clancy for my birthday a few years ago. He asked if I wished for a Tiffany's jeweled confection or another bunny, thinking he'd know the answer." She stroked the rabbit. "I chose a bunny. You should have seen the look on that dear man's face."

Cracking a smile, she stroked Tiffany as Father's shouts floated up through the tubes. "I cannot believe Father could say those things to me." She attempted to swallow back her pain, but it burst through the walls she had spent years constructing in a wail, sobbing out, "But now I know I am nothing in his eyes. Nothing but a bargaining chip to garner more wealth, and if I cannot even do that simple task . . ."

Auntie reached a withered hand to Flora's cheek. "You are young and have so much life in you. Marriage with the right man is a dream, but I know from my parents that a marriage of convenience or infatuation to the wrong person would prove a nightmare." She sighed. "I was engaged before I married my Ulysses, you know."

"What?" Flora gasped. "I had no idea."

She traced Flora's cheek with the back of her hand. "I was nearly your age when my father promised me to Simon Blum, but by then I was so in love with my Ulysses, I couldn't go through with it, no matter how much it hurt me to go against my parents' wishes."

"But wasn't Great-Uncle Ulysses wealthy?"

She nodded. "But his parents did not approve of his marrying a Yankee and they cut him out of their hearts, while mine disinherited me." She rose and went to her desk at the window and removed a card from one of the drawers. "It wounded me to the core to be separated from my brother and parents, but I knew in my soul I was supposed to be with Ulysses and so I married him." She clutched it to her chest. "And one Christmas, after five years of marriage, I learned my father was ill and I tried to return home to see him." She swallowed, eyes brimming after all this time. "And I was barred from the door. My brother wanted to see me, but Father held the purse strings until the end. And so my Ulysses gave me this to remind me of my true Father. One who would never turn His back on me. One who valued me." She handed it to Flora. "I have kept this to myself as a reminder for nearly fifty years, but I think it is time I share it."

Flora turned over the worn card and read the faded black ink in a gentleman's hand.

Auntie Violet closed her eyes, reciting it from heart. "'But now thus saith the LORD that created thee, O Jacob, and he that formed thee, O Israel, Fear not: for I have redeemed thee, I have called thee by thy name; thou art mine. When thou passest through the waters, I will be with thee; and through the rivers, they shall not overflow thee: when thou walkest through the fire, thou shalt not be burned; neither shall the flame kindle upon thee. For I am the LORD thy God, the Holy One of Israel, thy Saviour: I gave Egypt for thy ransom, Ethiopia and Seba for thee. Since thou wast precious in my sight, thou hast been honourable, and I have loved thee: therefore will I give men for thee, and people for thy life.'" She looked up at Flora.

"Even though I did not have the blessing of my earthly father, nor his love, I had someone who paid a ransom for me. Someone who called me precious in His sight. Who gave all for my life." She reached for her comb on the side table, sinking down beside Flora and unpinning her hair, slowly allowing the golden locks to fall to her waist and drawing the comb through in gentle, deliberate strokes. "I pray that this truth will bring you as much comfort as it has me."

"I will guard it and return it to you," Flora whispered, still tender.

"Guard it, yes, but do read the verses before bed each night until it begins to make sense, my dear. And if you ask God to reveal its meaning to you, it *will* make sense, and with that knowledge your entire future may change."

"I will," she promised, enjoying the comforting pull of the comb until the clock sounded the late hour.

At Auntie's smothered yawn, Flora kissed her withered, age-spotted cheek. "I best let you rest."

"Flora?" Auntie called just before Flora closed the door. "Your father really does love you and may come around yet. Do not lose hope."

Nodding and bidding Auntie a good night, she clutched the card over her heart and slowly climbed the stairs at the far

218

end of the hall to the third story, thankful to find that Olive must not have overheard the shouting and had not waited up.

"Miss Flora?" Becky called from the bathing room. "I took the liberty of drawing a bath for you. I thought you might want to rest after your long evening."

Flora's eyes filled at the sight of the rose petals floating atop the steaming water in the wood-encased tub, knowing the three flights of stairs must have taken the maid a half hour to complete. "Becky, you are too good to me. Please don't wait up for me to finish."

Sixteen

After a long soak in the tub spent in prayer, Flora tugged on her dusty rose dressing robe, pulled her damp braid over her shoulder, and silently padded back to her bedroom with her kerosene lamp to guide her, as the gaslights had all been extinguished. Unwilling to sleep in the dark where her thoughts would surely come for her, she turned up the wick and returned the lamp to the windowsill, set the card on her vanity, and crawled into bed, attempting to finish a romance novel in the flickering lamplight.

Just as the villain was about to capture the damsel for the fourth time in a single novel—which normally would have made her toss the book across the room, but as she did not have a second readily available, she gritted her teeth and read on—a *plink* on the turret windowpane nearly gave her an attack of the heart and sent her book tumbling to the floor. She waited a few seconds before snatching it up, thinking perhaps some cicadas had hit the glass and knocked themselves senseless. She settled back into her feather pillow, but then a second *plink* stopped her heart altogether.

She darted to her feet and stayed close to the shadows, peering out the wavy panes to the lawn below, when a hand shot out from the darkness and tapped the left windowpane. Her knees weakened and her scream died of fright in her throat. Then she spotted the fiend's scarlet cape caught up in the leaves behind him. She threw open the window. "Theodore Pierre Day! What on earth are you doing? You'll fall out of the oak tree to your death, and I'll be forced to watch."

"Well, what was I supposed to do when your butler said you had already retired and refused to bring you my note until you awoke?"

"Wait until morning, perhaps?" she offered, moving to close the window.

Teddy's hand splayed against the glass, keeping it open. "I can't, not with my callous comment between us."

She dropped her gaze and, realizing she was in her nightgown, whipped around with her back to him, quickly pulling on her dressing gown again.

"Are you not going to speak with me even now?" he whispered. "I'm in a perilous position, and your last words to me could be silence."

Flora rolled her eyes and returned to the sill, keeping her arms firmly crossed in front of her. "Very well. Let's speak. You hurt my feelings in a way that only you could."

Teddy shook his head. "I'm sincerely sorry for the pain my offhanded comment caused you."

"It didn't seem offhanded," she mumbled. After her father's blunt tête-à-tête over the state of her confirmed spinsterhood, she was raw. There was nothing left for her to hide behind.

Teddy adjusted his seat on the branch and teetered for half

a second, sending Flora lunging out the window, snatching his cape's clasp.

"So, you do care for me." He grinned, his hand covering hers. "Please believe me that it was careless. I know you are not like those other women, Flora." He slowly reached out to her cheek, brushing a curl from her face.

"For goodness' sake, hold on to the branch, Teddy," she reprimanded, attempting to pull away from him. Yet his hold on her hand only tightened.

"Not until you hear me out. I have been hiding something from you for the past few weeks."

She swallowed, once again wondering if he knew of her secret involvement in the breaking of his second engagement and was surreptitiously angry with her. "Oh?"

He nodded. "I have come to the conclusion that my heart has healed significantly since your arrival."

She stiffened, her eyes widening. Even if she wished to release her hold on him, her fingers would not cooperate. "Why would you say that?"

"Your friendship . . ."

She sagged against the frame. *Friendship. Always friendship.*

". . . has begun to change me in ways I did not think possible."

"That's nice," she whispered, hoping her disappointment did not color her voice.

"I have been thinking back on Paris, you know." He smiled. "A wonderful week, wasn't it?"

It seemed Teddy recalled their fleeting time together with fondness, while she remembered being left alone that last day in the coffeehouse they met at each morning, trying not to cry into her novel as she read his note over a second and a third cup. She could still recite those scrawled words that he had been called to return to New Orleans at once. He didn't say farewell in person, as if she were merely someone he had run into and not the dear friend he had confided in about his pain from Bernadette's elopement. She shook herself from the aching past. "Have you?"

"I treasured our time together. Both then and now."

She repeated that in her heart, but it was difficult even to allow the pleasant word to mull in her mind with only six weeks remaining of their time in New Orleans and her father's continual threat to return home early if his daughters did not produce advantageous engagements. Things were about to end with Teddy—for good this time if Clancy proposed, as her father would surely not allow her to reject a perfectly good suit. Even Auntie Violet would wonder at a rejection when she thought of the man as a son. It would not be a match of convenience on Clancy's end and not at all like the circumstances surrounding Auntie's arrangement with Mr. Blum so many years ago.

In the month since her arrival, Flora had spent ample time with Teddy, with him even flirting a bit, and yet he had not once spoken to her of their future, despite that he had been softer than usual toward her, allowing his hand to linger at her elbow, to brush back a curl, not to mention his staring at her on occasion. And because of that, Flora drew back. Father wished for his eldest daughter to be engaged by summer's end, and if Teddy did not wish to court her, then he needed to cease this teasing of her heart and allow her a chance of finding love before being bound to some man she knew nothing about and cared for even less. She suppressed a shudder at the thought of being promised to Mr. Grayson. "What are you doing with me, Teddy?"

"Having a cup of coffee with you. What does it look like?" He rolled his eyes. "Is it too hot in there for you? I don't want you to have a heatstroke on me."

She shook her head, divesting herself of his charm. "Do not play coy with me, Teddy Day. You are no naïve bachelor. And I do not have time for games." She crossed her arms again and closed her eyes, burning from the shame of it all. There was only so much chasing a lady could do, and the constant war between choosing her heart or her head was exhausting. *Is it so wrong that I want to be loved by a husband? To be adored as much as Willow? Is Clancy really my best chance for happiness?* She waited for Teddy to speak, but at his silence she moved to close the window. Others wished to marry her. Well, maybe she would let them.

She couldn't do it anymore. She was a Wingfield. And if Teddy did not want her, she would not be made a fool of again. "It's been a pleasure working with you, but I think it is time I bid you good-bye." She was finished with this whole husband-hunting business.

Teddy slapped his hands down on the windowsill. "Flora, wait."

"I have been." *For years, and it's time I have some self-respect. Father may not love me or respect me, and you may not love me, but I deserve to be cherished. I know it. Even if I never find it in a husband, I know someone who does love me—unconditionally.*

He clenched his jaw. "It was never the right time for us, but now—"

"If you wanted me, you would have spoken weeks ago." *Or years.* But she would not admit to that, not now when her voice already held a tremor and anything could break her. She had been too vulnerable with him already.

Teddy perched on the sill, his feet firmly planted against the oak, the full force of his attention rendering her tongue-tied. "Yet now that I know you care for me, I think it might be the right time."

"Thinking and being are completely different. You either want to be with me or you do not. No games, Theodore. I do not have time to play." Her voice cracked, her father's ultimatum never far from her heart.

"No games." Teddy captured her hand in his.

"What are you doing?" she gasped, her heart pounding.

For his answer, he tugged her to the window and reached his hand behind her neck and drew her to himself, sweeping her into a kiss that was nothing like she had ever experienced before. There was a sweetness, a complete and total devotion to his kiss she had not been expecting. At last he broke the kiss, seemingly reluctantly, but kept his hand wrapped about hers. "I want to be with you, Flora. And *only* you. Do you believe me?"

"I think I may need a bit more convincing," she whispered, her eyes on his lips. She had thought his close beard would irritate her, but it was surprisingly soft, comforting—and all at once alluring.

His lips were on hers at once. She did not dare to fully give in to a kiss again, but Teddy dared, and she soon found herself swaying into him and blinking against the stars that had only moments before been set in the heavens but were now in her eyes.

"How long have you been feeling this way?" she murmured, her head on his chest, drinking in this dream.

"When I first saw you in New Orleans, something happened. I knew it was most likely too soon for my heart to respond to someone again—my family suspects I am in love with the idea of love but have never actually been *in* love . . . which may be true in some sense, but because of my past, I had lost hope in finding the right hands to hold my heart." He lifted her hand to his lips. "And I believe that yours are those hands."

She took comfort in the rapid beat beneath his shirt, until the rumble of thunder followed by a breeze swaying the branches broke their hold as he gripped the window frame for support. His cape rippled free from the oak leaves, flowing in the wind and caressing them, warning them of the impending storm.

"With rain coming, we don't have much time." He took her in his arms once more. "My darling Flora, please don't keep me in suspense. Do you feel the same way about me? Do you care enough about me to give up that Clancy Drake and all other suitors?"

She longed to tell him that there were no others but him, yet Father's warning that no man wanted just her hand, but her purse, blazed to life. But being face-to-face with Teddy, all earnestness in his gaze, she knew that he cared less than nothing about her meager fortune. If he had, he could have courted her much sooner. She shifted back, but his hand lingered on her elbows, keeping her close. "Before I answer, I need you to tell me one thing."

"Anything."

"You say you care for me—that you have felt something

for me other than friendship since I first arrived in New Orleans—but what I am hearing is based strictly on sight." She stepped completely out of his arms, needing some distance to think. She could not allow herself to be caught up in this moment that she had been dreaming about since they were youths. "Beauty and money are fleeting. I need to know *why* you love me before I say another word." *Because I need to banish my father's words once and for all. And know if you are my Ulysses.*

Theodore longed to reached for her hand and pull her to him again, but he felt that his next words would mean the most if he spoke them from his heart and not through his kisses. "It is difficult for me to say what is on my heart after having it crushed too many times, but for you, I'm willing to take that risk again on the chance you will understand how much you mean to me." He smiled. "Since my last engagement, I have been praying and the Lord placed this verse in my soul from Psalm 147: 'He healeth the broken in heart, and bindeth up their wounds.'

"So I've been praying for Him to bind me up, but there were so many broken shards, I feared it would take a long time for me to heal. Over these past weeks with you, however, my heart has been mending. I believe God places other believers in our path for certain pivotal moments. You have always been a sweet light in my life, a star that if I should ever get lost in this world, all I had to do was look up and find you." He turned to the heavens, the crescent moon peeking through the rolling gray clouds, revealing a handful of stars behind them. "I am certain the Lord placed you in the sky for me to find, and even though it took me years to finally see you for more than a friend, I pray you will allow me the chance to hope." At her silence, he found her staring up at him with those luminous blue eyes.

He moved his hand to cup her cheek. "Like the light inside you, there is a light outside as well. Beauty aside, your kindness, tender heart, and brilliant mind captured me this summer. And there is no other woman I respect more than you." He shook his head. "I was a fool not to see you before. And I will never forgive myself if my lack of understanding has made me too late to speak to your father."

"You think I am brilliant?" she whispered.

"As brilliant as the stars in the heavens." He lifted her hand to his lips, kissing her palm, brushing her fingertips across his lips as he lowered her hand once more, rubbing his thumb over it. "If you will give me the chance to demonstrate my feelings for you, I will spend the rest of my life working to make you happy. I love you, Flora Wingfield, and I would do anything to make you my wife."

She reached up and wrapped her hands about his neck, pulling him to her, pausing a moment before their lips met. "I love you too, more than anyone on earth."

And with those words, he felt that last bit of fear within him crumble. He clutched her hand to his chest above where the pain he had been harboring vanished in that instant. She loved him, and he could tell from the shine in her eyes— which had not been in Bernadette's or Willow's—that she was completely his. No other man was in her thoughts. He was not a secondary option. Reveling in the closeness of each other, they spoke under the giant oak tree with the dipping moss shielding them from the eyes of passersby below. He held fast to her hand until at last the rain began to fall.

"You best go before the bark gets too slick for a safe descent," she whispered. "Though I am loath to see you depart tomorrow with your steamboat delivery to the Tyndalls."

He lifted his palm to her cheek, and she turned into it, kissing it. "I wish I didn't have to go tomorrow." He sighed. "It will take at least two weeks to get to St. Louis and back. Hopefully you won't change your mind about me by the time I return." Theodore kept his tone light, though the old habitual thoughts would take some time to conquer.

"I know that your previous fiancées hurt you, but I am not them. And I will do my best to alleviate your fears. But unlike them, I have turned away all because of one simple fact."

"Which is?"

"They are not *you*. You are the only man in the world for me."

That statement required a few kisses that left them both breathless. She gently pushed him back when he came for another.

"I'm afraid you will have to wait for more, sir, but before you go, I want you to realize that I understand how important your trip to St. Louis is for your business."

"For us," he corrected her. "With this delivery, I know I can secure a few more orders from the Tyndalls' friends and will be squarely in the lead. With your help, we will win this competition and our future will be secured." He squeezed her hand. "And the moment I return, I will be speaking with your father—if you are willing, that is?"

Flora laughed. "I wouldn't have let you kiss me like that if I was not going to make you my husband, Teddy Day."

He grinned and kicked his cape out of the way and slowly began his descent as the rain grew heavier, pausing at the base of the tree to look up at her with her braided hair trailing over her shoulder. Casting prudence aside, he called over the thunder, "Order your wedding trousseau, my darling, because I don't want you to leave me for New York at summer's end. We have spent enough time apart. It's time for our *happily ever after.*"

Seventeen

Flora leaned dreamily against the closed window. This had to have been the swiftest answer to prayer on record. She rubbed her finger where an engagement ring would soon encircle. She laughed and twirled, bursting with the secret of all secrets. She could confide in her family, though Father would consider it out of order with Teddy speaking to her before formally asking for her hand. But Mother, who had always been eager for her eldest daughter to marry, would surely wish to know prior to Teddy's return, to make some sort of arrangement for an engagement ball. And if that was going to happen, Flora would need to write Willow to give her time to make travel arrangements, despite the awkwardness it might cause to have her and Cullen at the ball.

She sat at her writing desk in her room's little turret and jotted down a note, thinking that perhaps since Teddy did not want a long engagement that maybe it would be a wedding Willow attended. She sighed at the thought, her pen lingering too long over the page and leaving a splatter. "Blast."

Shaking the paper, it left a long trail of ink as it dried,

but as everything was still legible and time was of the essence, she stuffed it into an envelope and dropped it in the bronze mail tube in the hall on the second floor when she spied Carlisle gathering his hat and cane at the front door. *What on earth? Why would he possibly be calling at this hour?* She clutched the front of her robe, stealing toward the third-floor staircase, the floorboards creaking underfoot.

He must have heard her, for he lifted his gaze, his smile spreading at the sight of her. "Miss Wingfield."

"Is something amiss, Carlisle?"

"Your father sent for me, but as I have found you in, uh—" he paused and focused on his hat, his ears ruddy—"in your current state, I will take my leave. I look forward to seeing you tomorrow."

She ignored the odd statement, still too dazed from Teddy's declaration to think of much else. "Until tomorrow then. Good night, Carlisle."

Being a true gentleman, he did not look her way but instead lifted his hand in farewell and departed.

"Ah, Flora dear, you are still awake." Mother appeared at the parlor door, still perfectly attired in her dinner gown, almost as if she had expected such a late-night visitor . . . even though Carlisle only usually visited with Father. "Come join your father and me."

Why did Mother and Father have such a late caller, and why am I needed? "Of course."

As the door shut behind her, Mother flung her arms around Flora. "My dear girl, I am so happy. Such wonderful news!"

Her heart stopped. Did Carlisle tell them of her attachment with Teddy? Had Teddy spoken to Carlisle prior to her? "Mr. Day told you, then?"

"Yes, and I could not be happier!" Mother drew her farther into the parlor, where Father motioned for her to take a seat on the chaise lounge.

Flora returned her mother's smile, feeling lighter now that she knew her Mother approved and nothing would prevent them from marrying. *Perhaps I won't have to keep the engagement a secret after all, especially since Father made such a display of my being engaged so soon.*

Father sat in his wing-back chair before the dormant fireplace, opening and closing his pocket watch, a habit that betrayed his nerves. Her heart softened. Despite all his words, he really would miss her.

He cleared his throat. "There comes a time in every young woman's life, especially when one is considered an American princess like you—"

Flora laughed, unable to keep her happiness at bay. "I'd hardly call myself an American princess when you compare me against Will—"

"It is late." He held up his hand, cutting her off. "Let me finish. This is not about Willow, but if it was, you know as well as I do that just because we do not flaunt our privilege with garish mansions on Fifth Avenue, our wealth rivals the Duprés' fortune and it is rapidly growing. And with Willow on the throne, I will most likely surpass them in a year's time."

Flora ignored this little jab toward her dearest friend, but she kept silent, the promise of Teddy warming her heart. She folded her hands to keep herself still, waiting for the praise that she had listened to Father's express wishes, even though Teddy's proposal had been out of her control. It was too miraculous to have been by her orchestration.

Father stood and picked up one of Auntie's twenty-odd porcelain bunnies decorating the fireplace mantel. He passed it from hand to hand as if fascinated by the peculiar piece. "As I was saying, European royalty are more often than not expected to marry to shore up the family's legacy."

He knew about her engagement and he was angry? Though Father was forefront in modern thinking, where his daughters' hands were concerned, he was a traditionalist, and Teddy had failed to seek permission first. "Father, I can explain."

He held up his hand again. "Flora, you really must allow me to speak without your constant interruptions. While your loquacious nature is found endearing by most, at this moment it is a hindrance, especially when you do not know a thing about what I am attempting to say."

She pressed her lips together and gripped her hands in her lap, determined not to speak again for fear she would anger him further on the matter of Teddy. *But I obeyed him. How can he be* so *angry with me?*

"So, as I was saying, much like the European princesses, your being American royalty is meant to further strengthen the family's kingdom."

Teddy is from a good family, so why . . . ? She suppressed her opinion of this being the oddest of conversations and simply nodded.

"And as the eldest son is always heir to the kingdom, I have arranged for you to wed Mr. Day next month."

She rose, clasping her hands to her heart, elated until the words registered in her mind. "Wait—did you say the *eldest* son? But Teddy is not the eldest."

Father clutched his hands behind his back, staring down at her. "As I said, the eldest son is always the heir."

"You can't mean . . ." She pressed her fingers to her temples. All the meetings, all the little hints made sense now. No. *This cannot be happening, not when Teddy has finally declared himself to me.* She had to make Father see reason before the idea solidified in his mind. "B-but the Day brothers are having a competition at this very moment to determine the head of the company—"

"Which Carlisle will win. He has shown me what he has done with the company, what he is doing, and his plans for expansion. He is far more experienced, and I have decided to invest heavily in Day's Luxury Line with Carlisle as the head. And you are to be at his side, ensuring an everlasting good relationship in this investment."

She clenched her fists at her sides. "No."

His eyes narrowed behind his wire-rimmed spectacles. "What do you mean 'no'?"

"I mean, no. Ask one of your other daughters to take his hand. I will not."

"One of the others will not do. It is best that the eldest daughter is married first, as I believe I have explained my reasons in depth not two hours ago."

"Not in this century, they aren't." Flora's voice shook as she rose. "I have done everything you have asked of me for years. But this? I will *not* marry Carlisle, especially not when Teddy loves me and has asked me to marry him."

"Another proposal?" Mother gasped, flapping her hands over her jabot. "Imagine receiving so many invitations for *eligible* marriages in a single day. We should've come to New Orleans the moment she turned of age, Florian. I'd have several grandbabies hanging on to my skirts by now."

Father softened his expression as he clasped Mother's

hand. "Yes, my dear, but Theodore Day is unfortunately *not* eligible anymore, not in my eyes that is."

"But, Florian." Mother glanced to Flora and lowered her voice. "What's changed? You knew she had inclinations toward the young man before we even arrived."

"Because I discovered that Carlisle is the best candidate of the two, and *he* is the one I am partnering with in this investment. And he asked me for my permission, which I have granted. Theodore has not. The plan is in motion. She will be a bride at last."

Flora pinched the bridge of her nose to keep her tears at bay, for he would only see them as a display of emotion and not logic. *I won't do it. I can't.*

"Are you truly choosing to go down the path of the privileged, petulant child?"

"One is not considered unreasonable when turning down a loveless marriage in favor of one founded on love. Besides, you never needed a daughter for your investments before. Why would you start now?" Flora's voice shook, much to her dismay. "Father, you have always been at the forefront, setting the tone for society, and here you are reverting to medieval times." She crossed her arms over her robe in an attempt to bolster her voice. "I won't do it. You'll wake up tomorrow and see that I am right."

Father withdrew his pipe and tobacco pouch, meticulously tamping the leaves down in the bowl with his thumb, making her wait. "You *will* marry Carlisle Day, and if you would sit still long enough, I will explain my reasoning. It is either him or Mr. Grayson, and I think we all would prefer Mr. Day. But there have been threats, things occurring outside of my control, and—"

"There have always been threats, and if you refuse to hear me out, I will not extend you the same courtesy." She pushed past her mother and ran from the room and out the back door into the rose garden, desperate for fresh air as the elation from only moments before turned into gut-wrenching sobs.

She sank to her knees before the garden's marble fountain, the goldfish swaying beneath the lily pads as the rain soaked through her hair and robe, chilling her through to her soul, until at last the verses her auntie shared with her rose to mind once more. She buried her face in her arms. "God, help me. I am just one, nameless asset to my father, but you have called me by my name. I am yours. I am precious is your sight. You have given a ransom for me." She wiped her face with the back of her hand. "I am worthy of love. Show me the way."

Theodore turned the wick up in the hurricane vase and leaned back in his leather chair in the spare room he had commandeered for his own private office, his mind spinning with the events of the day. He needed to focus on the task at hand, writing up his advertisement for the papers to work for him while he was out of the city, but it was rather difficult with the knowledge that Flora loved him. She really and truly loved him. In all his years of courting, the women seem to be drawn to him for a time before someone else caught their eye. Yet he didn't think Flora would be the same.

A knock sounded on the open door, and he looked up to see his father in his dressing robe, gripping a book, his brow furrowed. "I just had an interesting conversation with your brother, who was returning from the neighbor's house." He rubbed his hand over his face and sighed. "And I don't know what to say."

"What's wrong?" He sat up, the chair legs thumping against the floor. *Is Carlisle backing out of the competition?*

"Carlisle informed me of an engagement."

He blinked. "What? But he hasn't been calling on anyone. The only ladies he's been around are . . ." He thought of the time Carlisle spent in Flora's parlor. Always inclined toward her. Always present or just leaving when Theodore arrived. Of how he held her that day in the gazebo . . . and of his flirting. Flora had never mentioned Carlisle courting her. *And she certainly did not mention it tonight. What happened between when I left her and now?* "Who?" his voice rumbled, filling the room. At Father's silence, Theodore rose, his fists curling inward. "*Who* is he to marry?"

"I'm as baffled as you are at the news." Father shook his head. "It's a messy business. But I think you know who it is, Son."

Theodore clenched his jaw, the muscles in his shoulders twitching. This could not be happening. Not for a third time. *Do not say it.*

"Your brother has just returned from speaking with Florian Wingfield about marrying his eldest daughter, and Florian agreed to his terms. He and Florian are in the process of drawing up the papers apparently, and most everything seems to be arranged now. And not to add insult to your injury, but Carlisle informed me they are to wed next month to secure the investments from Florian once Carlisle wins the competition and takes over as head of the company. With his large order from Mr. Wingfield officially under contract, Carlisle seems to believe it is only a matter of time before you admit defeat."

Theodore tightened his fists and turned to the window, attempting to hide the rage threatening to overtake him. "I can assure you that Carlisle did not ask Flora her opinion on the matter. For if he did, he would quickly discover that Flora is engaged to *me*." He turned on his boot's heels and faced his father.

"Truly?" Father blinked. "*Another* engagement. Already? It hasn't been but a few months since your last."

Theodore had guessed this would be his father's reaction, but it stung nonetheless. "Yes, sir. I am indeed engaged."

"Well, if you have your heart set on her, it's a relief that you asked her first. But, uh . . ." He scratched his temple with his forefinger. "Did you ask her father for his blessing? Because then Florian would be in breach of promise, which doesn't sound like the man in the least."

Theodore shoved his hand into his pocket and leaned his wrist against the fireplace mantel, picking at the gash in the carved wood from his childhood when he and Carlisle were practicing with their father's forbidden Scottish dirks and Mother walked in, startling them. How could a brother act so against the other, to steal the other's love?

"Son? You didn't ask Florian, did you?"

Teddy shoved off the mantel. "No. I was going to after this delivery, as I thought it would be perfectly acceptable, but I will go first thing in the morning and speak with him and get this misunderstanding sorted."

"Which would work if he were home to receive you. The man keeps abominable hours. The Tyndalls' steamboat must leave at dawn. When you promised to have the boat ready by such an expeditious date, I was wary, but now our reputation is at stake. We cannot be late on this delivery, Son. You went a week past the agreed-upon date, something we never do, to secure all those baubles and furnishings, which canceled any extra time we typically reserve for delivery. If we delay the delivery any further, it could hurt our chances of future business with Mr. Tyndall's family, not to mention—"

"Then I will go speak with Mr. Wingfield now."

"Carlisle said that Florian and his wife have retired for the evening. And calling on a man after he has retired will not turn the tide in your favor. He may dismiss your suit on principle."

"Then I won't pilot the delivery and speak with Mr. Wingfield at the first opportunity. I cannot leave, not when Flora's and my future is at risk."

Father nodded, chewing the inside of his mouth. "I will respect your decision, but you do realize . . . if you do not pilot this boat, I will be forced to have another Day present to deliver it, and according to the written rules of the contest, he who *delivers* the boat and collects the payment will receive the credit. Carlisle will take the lead, and I doubt you will have time to catch up."

Theodore crossed his arms. "Better to lose the chance of running the company than to have a broken heart for a third time. I cannot bear another disappointment, Father."

"Very well. But if you lose, you could lose Flora as well, as Florian wishes for her to wed the owner of Day's Luxury Line. You could be sacrificing everything for a chance to be with Flora. Are you willing to give up everything for her?"

"That's a risk I have to take. Besides, Florian Wingfield is not an archaic man. I know I can make him see reason."

Father sighed. "One can only hope."

Eighteen

Having no more tears, Flora returned inside, leaving her rain-soaked robe in a heap at the back French doors. Trudging to the third floor with her damp nightdress slapping against her calves, her heart weighing down her every step. Father couldn't truly expect her to willingly give herself to a man when she was in love with said gentleman's brother, would he? She clutched the doorframe, staring into the little room, hem dripping on the floor. She would be leaving this room a bride . . . but not to the man she loved.

She clenched her fists. *No. I don't have to stand by while being made a pawn in a man's game for power.* She threw open the ancient armoire, cringing at the squeaking hinges, and dug out her carpetbag. Tossing her traveling shoes in the direction of her bed, she winced when they hit the shared wall with Olive. At the telltale creak of the bed sounding through the wall, Flora knew Olive would appear in a matter of seconds.

She stripped off her nightgown and drew on a fresh chemise and drawers. She knelt and reached into the farthest corner of the armoire and withdrew her reticule with opera glasses tucked inside and stuffed her notebook and the rest of her savings in as well. She had been a fool spending almost all her pin money on a gown that was only to be worn once, but how could she have known she would need funds to run away? She almost paused at that phrase, but she knew if she stopped, her courage would flee and she would stay.

"What are you doing? It's past midnight." Olive yawned and sank onto Flora's feather bed, pushing aside the mosquito netting and resting her head on the carved mahogany bedpost.

"Packing." At her sister's frown, Flora sighed and quickly recounted Father's demand.

"After what Father said, I do not blame you for wishing to return home. But being the bride of Carlisle Day is hardly a burden when faced with the option of Mr. Grayson."

Flora rested back on her heels, looking up at her sister and noticing the red rimming her eyes. She rose from her place on the floor and sat beside her. "You are sweet to worry for me, but I'm not going to marry Carlisle, not when Teddy has finally proposed to me and I have accepted his hand."

"Teddy what?" Olive's pinched expression transformed into a brilliant smile. "When?"

"After the ball, he climbed the live oak outside my window and professed his love," Flora admitted, her cheeks tinting at the thought of their shared kisses in the moonlight.

Olive squealed and embraced her before she gestured to the open bag, clothes spilling out of the chifforobe. "But if that's the case, what on earth are you doing?"

"I'm leaving." Flora returned to her wardrobe and selected a day gown and a dinner gown, tossing them over her arm.

"I see that, but *where* are you going? If you go home to New York, things will only escalate with the reporters sniffing around for the biggest story since Willow's wedding. I don't think it is the wisest plan to return without us to avoid Father's wrath if you still wish for his approval of your marriage to Teddy."

"Which is why I am not heading to New York," Flora said, rolling up a chemise and putting it in her bag. "Teddy is leaving to pilot the Tyndalls' steamboat, the *Marigold*, to St. Louis in the morning, and I know where it is docked."

"Flora." Olive's tone held a warning. "You can't possibly be thinking of joining him. It is beyond scandalous for an unmarried couple to travel together unchaperoned."

Flora shoved the gowns into the carpetbag, the overskirts making it difficult to fit much else. "What is my alternative? It's scandalous if I leave for New York, and if I'm left here and I make a show of compliance, or heaven forbid resist like I wish, Father will surely have the engagement announced, and I will be as good as married to Carlisle before Teddy returns to make this right and I'll be forced into a marriage I do not desire." She returned to the floor of the armoire to retrieve a hatbox.

"Or you could just speak with Carlisle, as a normal young lady would, instead of becoming a"—Olive's voice lowered into a horrified whisper—"runaway bride. You would likely never recover from such a scandal."

Flora snorted, which brought up a cloud of dust that made her sneeze and smack her head against the bottom shelf as she tugged the box out. She rubbed the sore spot. "Do you honestly think such a conversation would make a difference?"

"Carlisle is a reasonable man, but then when it comes to business . . ."

"So you understand I cannot take that chance. By him speaking with Father and securing my hand behind my back, it displays a shocking lack of respect for my opinion, unless he is planning on asking me. Even so, if he knew me at all, he'd know I am not interested in him." Pushing back the tissue paper, Flora lifted out the crêpe silk ebony gown with its heavy veil and matching bonnet.

Olive wrinkled her nose. "I don't know why you insisted on bringing Aunt Gertrude's old widow weeds everywhere we travel."

"Because one does not know when one needs to move about undisturbed. People treat you differently in them. They move respectfully aside, only nod at you, and more importantly, they don't speak to you in deference of your mourning."

Olive gaped at her. "But it is wicked to pretend—"

"I know it's a bit untoward, but what I need right now is anonymity." She clasped Olive's hands. "You can't tell anyone I've departed. It is vital I get away without anyone taking chase."

"Now I am adding lying to your subterfuge?" Olive shook her off, frowning and crossing her arms.

Flora shrugged. "It is difficult to have one without the other. Consider yourself like Rahab, protecting the spies of Israel."

Olive lifted a single brow. "So, in this scenario, I'm a harlot?"

"No, of course not. It's just difficult to come up with a biblical example off the top of my head to convince you it is sometimes okay to lie for someone you love."

Olive groaned into her hands, sinking to her back on the bed, the mosquito net loosening from Flora's halfhearted tie and enveloping Olive in a foggy veil. "What about your reputation, Flora?"

"There will be members enough among the crew to protect my good name." She reached for the black crêpe. She would need to dress quickly.

"But no *women*, which is the most important detail you are trying to make me forget." Olive propped herself up on her elbows, scowling through the netting at Flora.

"Teddy will not have my reputation compromised. He would elope with me before that happened." She motioned for Olive to help her with the row of buttons from her neck to her bustle.

She pushed through the netting and stepped behind Flora and slowly worked at the buttons down her back as if trying to bide for more time. "Mother would never forgive you, and this certainly is not the way to gain Father's approval for your marriage. I can see Tacy pulling something like this, but you?"

"I never thought I would elope, but I am being pushed into it. Promise me that you'll keep quiet?" She caught a glimpse of her sister's disapproving expression in the floor-length looking glass standing in the corner of the room.

"I would never betray you, especially not when your future happiness is at stake. Though Carlisle is a *wonderful* option for a husband, I know how much Teddy means to you. Even if our parents do not," she whispered. "It seems that while they are always looking out for what is best for us, they seem to miss what actually is in our best interests."

"Thank you." Flora squeezed her sister's hand and returned

to stuffing stockings into the only remaining crevice in her bag.

"Which is why I am coming with you."

Flora whirled about. "Olive. You cannot be serious."

"If you want me to stay silent, I'm joining you. For while you may not value your reputation at this exact moment, you may find yourself filled with regret in a few days' time when the thrill of running away has faded and Teddy has been trapped into a marriage." She planted her fists on her hips, pursing her lips. "If you protest a single word, I promise you I'll raise such a ruckus, you will never leave this house alone again."

Irked, Flora pulled out the top gown in the bag and focused on wrapping her silver hand mirror inside it. *She has a point.* Elopement and scandal were not how she wished for their fairy tale to begin, especially if the groom felt at all trapped into marriage. The shame of their elopement would follow them for years, if not a lifetime. "Fine. If you must join me, put on your plainest gown befitting a companion to a widow. Perhaps a rich plum or violet to signify your mourning period is ending?" She removed the delicate black lace mantle from her shoulders and placed it in Olive's hands. "And do wear this atop it."

Olive rolled her eyes. "You are incorrigible, but I'll see what I can do."

Within a quarter of an hour, judging from the timepiece on the mantel, Flora stood by her window tapping her foot under yards of widow's weeds with her bulging satchel at her feet. If she found need of anything, she would have to stop at a port along the Mississippi. Checking the clock, she gently rapped on the adjoining wall before slipping most of her money into her bodice, buttoning it inside, then tucked her coin purse at the top of her carpetbag as a decoy should they be overtaken by robbers.

She threw open the window, heaved the bag onto her hip and tossed it over the ledge, closely followed by her widow's bonnet, the ebony veil fluttering out, ghoulish in the night as it disappeared.

"Please tell me we aren't going to climb that flimsy trellis. It's stopped raining, but that doesn't make it any safer." Olive dropped her carpetbag atop Flora's coverlet and crossed her arms, her dark purple sleeves peeking out from beneath the mantle. "It may work in the novels, but we will fall to our deaths on that rotted thing. It was built ages ago and wasn't meant to be used by the guests as a means of escape."

"Of course not. The servants have gone to bed, so we will sneak through the back door. I'm tossing our things out in case we are spotted. It would be nearly impossible to explain those away."

"And your widow's weeds would be so much easier to explain, I'm sure."

"If asked, I'll think of something." Flora pulled Olive's bag from the bed, grunting at the weight of it as she moved toward the window. "I hope you don't have anything breakable in here, like an anvil."

"Only a few books to keep me occupied while you and Teddy converse. Just because I'm willing to chaperone doesn't mean I'm willing to subject my ears to all your sweet nothings to each other on your honeymoon." She winced as Flora unceremoniously tossed the carpetbag out the window. "Are you certain you wish to go through with this outlandish plan? As I said before, I would've expected this behavior from Tacy, but never you."

Flora flinched at that and scrounged about her desk for an unused piece of paper, scratching out a note to her family. "This is different."

"How?"

"Because I have loved Teddy since the summer I turned sixteen. It was only in Paris that I truly got my hopes up that we actually might marry when his engagement ended." She scored the folded paper and set it atop the mantel. "Hopefully, the servants won't come for us until after breakfast tomorrow, and by then we will be long gone." Her stomach growled, but as she didn't dare to send for a tray, she lifted the lid of the crystal jar on the stand beside her bed and handed Olive a *baci di dama* hazelnut cookie, taking two for herself. "Best eat it because I don't know when breakfast will be tomorrow."

Not hearing any movements in the house beneath them, Flora and Olive crept down the stairs, being careful to skip the second to the bottom step that would alert the entire house of someone out of bed. They slipped through the dark hall of the servants' entrance, feeling their way along the wall, using the chair rail as a guide, until Flora tripped into the hall tree, banging her shin. She sucked in a few choice words and limped out of doors, waving off Olive's concern. They snagged their bags out of the yellow rosebushes, leaving quite a few petals scattered about, and plucked Flora's veil from the gravel, which thankfully hadn't acquired a tear or landed in a puddle. She settled it on her hair and drew the slightly damp, dotted veil over her head, which made things even more difficult to navigate in the dark, then hurried to the avenue, hoping she could hail a cabriolet. Given the time, however, that might prove rather difficult.

"Are you certain a driver will be coming by?" Olive groaned after trudging down St. Charles Avenue toward the port for a quarter of an hour.

Flora's courage faltered as they walked beneath the gas lamps. She had not considered this part of the plan. *Lord, we need transportation. I know I acted before asking, but please send us something, anything that would get us to the docks without being caught.* At the sound of laughter coming down the avenue, she pulled Olive into the shadows and found the Misses Pimpernels two doors down, returning home from Penelope's ball in a hired cab, their brother stumbling out from behind them.

"Seems to have been quite the party," her sister murmured.

"And thank goodness for that. Come along, Olive." She rustled down the road to the cabriolet. There would not be another on St. Charles at this hour. The two-wheeled, hooded carriage positioned to circle back from whence it came, but Flora clutched her skirts in one hand and hauled her bag in the other and ran up to the cab. "Excuse me! Sir? I need to get to the docks."

The man in the hooded carriage with a whip and reins in his fists stared down at the pair of them, pulling back on the reins. "You certain, ma'am? It's rather late to be going down there, especially *alone*, ma'am."

"I have my companion." She gestured to Olive, who stumbled to her side, panting from the weight of her books.

"I meant without a gentleman to guard you." He motioned to the dark streets. "It is no place for ladies at this time of night."

"Well, it cannot be helped. I am traveling to meet with the gentleman who will be offering us his protection . . . now that I am alone." Flora gestured to her black gown, even as Olive poked her in the corset stays at her white lie. "And we have passage on a steamboat that leaves abominably early."

The driver at once swiped his hat from his head, nodding and moving to dismount to take their bags. "Is this all you're taking, ma'am?"

She gripped her carpetbag tight to her chest. She would not release the entirety of her worldly possessions, and her coin purse was too accessible. "I'll be sending for the rest of my things later." *Goodness, this fellow is talkative.* "Can you take us to pier fifty?"

"Of course." Finally, he helped them into the carriage and started for the docks.

Flora settled back into the worn leather seat, her arms loosening their grip on her carpetbag, and looked to Olive. They released their nervous giggles.

"We did it." Olive fanned herself with her hand, whispering so as not to be heard over the steady hoofbeats. "I have never been so frightened in my life. And you should be ashamed of your insinuations."

"I know it's wrong, but we are desperate—and you were splendid playing the quiet companion," she returned in the same hushed tone and beamed at her sister, though she realized it would be hard for Olive to see her smile, what with the thick veil and dim light. Her sense of mirth quickly faded.

She pulled off her gloves and fanned herself with them. *I must have taken leave of my senses to think I could pull this off, but I did!* She had *never* thought of eloping, but the threat of a marriage to the wrong man was too much to bear, even though she almost stopped the driver half a dozen times to put an end to this madness.

The cabriolet at last pulled onto the wooden dock, the flickering gas lamps illuminating bale after bale of burlap-bound cotton and stacks of wooden barrels, ready for loading in the morning. The ethereal outlines of massive ships, steamboats, tugboats, and yachts bobbing in the river sent a tremor of doubt through Flora. Did she know exactly where the *Marigold* was docked? What if Teddy had moved the steamboat? Or, heaven forbid, left early?

Olive clutched the sideboard, her gaze flying from object to dark object. "Flora, I take it back. *Now* I have never been so frightened."

Flora wished she could refute her sister, but she had to agree that the docks seemed even more ominous in the dark with every shadow posing a potential threat. It was little wonder the driver was hesitant to bring them here. He probably did not want their deaths on his hands. The carriage halted, and the driver hopped down and held out his hand to assist them.

"Are you certain this is where you wish to be left, ma'am?" he asked, glancing about from beneath his top hat, scratching his muttonchops. "Some sailors ain't as, uh—" he coughed— "gentlemanly as they should be."

She glanced about, judging the distance between them and the steamboat. Of course, she would have preferred that the driver drop them exactly where they needed to be, but it couldn't be helped. What if he went back to St. Charles Avenue, found her home, confessed all to her family and brought them to the exact steamboat where she and Olive were stowed? She squinted at the row of vessels to where

Teddy's steamboat was anchored a few spots away. The *Marigold* was still there. She exhaled. *Thank you, Lord.* Flora lifted her chin and assumed her character. "Absolutely." She dropped a few coins into his open palm. "Thank you."

He tipped his hat at the generous amount. "May I see you aboard?"

"That will not be necessary." She gritted her teeth against the man's insistent nature. Motioning Olive to follow suit, she hefted her satchel to her hip and made her way to the steamboat directly in front of them, waiting for the carriage to roll away before snatching Olive's hand, veering to the left and ducking behind a pyramid of cotton bales, keeping to the shadows in case any wayward sailors happened upon them.

"Flora, I don't like this," Olive whimpered, her back pressed against the burlap, the stench of its heavy weave making them both reach for their perfumed handkerchiefs to place over their noses. "Where is the boat?"

"Not far."

"Not far?" Olive's voice rose. "We cannot stumble around in the dark. Anyone could happen upon us, and no amount of promised money would save us."

A crash came from behind. Flora whipped around and spied a tin pail roll in a circular pattern where it fell, a flash of red catching her eye. Her heart hammered. "Someone is out there."

Olive gripped her hand. "Good heavens. Do you see a man?"

"No. Maybe it was a dog?" She knew it wasn't, but what other explanation could she offer that wouldn't worry Olive senseless. "Stay close," she whispered when she heard it— the steady thumping of a cane against the dock. She froze. There was only one man she knew of who carried a cane at all times, and he was in the employ of Heathcliff Wellington. Had Mr. Grayson dared to follow her again? Surely her imagination was running away with her again.

At a carousing song growing louder by the breath, Olive gripped her arm, pointing down the dock to a trio of swaying, stumbling sailors advancing toward them, dressed in odd clothing . . . almost like the pirates from Penelope's play. "Flora, what have you gotten us into?"

She snatched Olive's hand and bolted for the ship, the song mounting, but her long widow's weeds skirts were hindering her as much as her heavy satchel. She dropped her hold on her sister and scrambled up the unguarded landing stage, swallowing a cry as she slipped to her knees on the freshly mopped deck. Gripping the railing, she kept low and listened for pursuit as Olive crouched beside her, but only the sounds of the crew from below caught her ear.

Olive shivered. "The crew is aboard already? Are we safe with them?"

Flora nodded. "As per their usual order of business, the Day family has their crew stay aboard the night prior to the journey to avoid overindulging and sabotaging the trip in the morning, which means Teddy is already here, supervising. We are safe. But because Teddy would make me return home, I think it is best we wait until we leave the port before announcing ourselves."

Olive exhaled, rose, and sagged against the rail.

Flora refrained from following suit for fear she would allow Olive to see how rattled she had become. Flora dared to look for the trio of sailors, but instead of seeing their backs, she found a man emerging from the shadows on the dock, the unmistakable shape of a cane gripped in his hand, his form inclined toward them. Even in the moonlight, she could tell it was Grayson, and he was looking directly at her. With a whimper, she tugged Olive's sleeve and ran for the ladies' wing, locking the door at once behind a pale Olive in what would be Mrs. Tyndall's chamber.

"You saw something." Olive dropped her bag and bit her knuckle as if to keep herself from crying out.

Flora threw her veil out of her face and slid a chair beneath the doorknob. "You remember that Mr. Grayson uses a cane, yes?"

"How can I possibly forget the unnerving gentleman and his cane that he doesn't seem to need?" She shuddered. "I try not to think of him, but he keeps popping up at the oddest of times. You think it is *him*? Why would he be following us?"

Flora shivered. "I've been seeing him about the city . . . as if he is following me."

Olive gasped, her hand flying to her throat. "Flora, you should've informed Father! He would have—"

"I tried. But he is always so busy. Always dismissing me. Besides, what would Mr. Grayson want with me? Surely it is a coincidence, since we run in the same circles, and if it isn't, I can handle it on my own." She opened her reticule and withdrew her pearl-encrusted opera glasses and set them on the nightstand.

Olive groaned into her hands. "You think you can use those for self-defense, don't you? That is ridiculous, Flora. You should have told *someone*, namely *me* before I agreed to this ridiculous scheme of yours, that you have been stalked since coming to the city, which is making those little black spotted handkerchiefs you've been receiving far more ominous than I originally thought."

The thumping sounded on the deck, coming toward their door. The sisters exchanged glances, and in that moment Flora realized she could see her sister's terrified expression all too well in the moonlight streaming into the room. "The windows! There is nothing to secure them but these flimsy locks."

"They'll have to do." Olive surged into motion, securing the latches on the windows and drawing the heavy silk curtains to a close, blocking out all light.

Flora tugged the ribbons at her chin and freed herself from the cumbersome bonnet. She hurried to the desk, drew out a silver letter opener and matchbox, and lit the violet flower-painted hurricane lamp on Mrs. Tyndall's desk, basking in the comforting glow of the milk glass. She slipped the letter opener into Olive's hand and grasped her opera glasses by the handle. "They'll work in a pinch," she reassured her sister, standing at the ready, until another *thump* sent them scrambling behind the bed to the floor.

The two waited in silence, and after a terrified quarter of an hour spent hovering in dreaded anticipation, Flora sighed, glancing up at the beautiful comforter. "Perhaps we should attempt to get some rest?"

"Attempt?" Olive followed her gaze past the bed to the pair of chairs. "Please don't tell me that we cannot actually use this bed?"

Flora grimaced. "I dare not use the bed for fear that we would mar the handsome silk sent for all the way from France."

"You mean that *you* would ruin it with your night drool." Olive smirked. "I, however, do not drool." She kicked off her shoes and settled into the bed, keeping the letter opener within reach on the nightstand.

Flora sank into the Louis XIV armchair, setting the heavy glasses on her lap. The chair was a bit stiff, but it would suffice until morning when she could safely travel the long passage to the guest rooms after finding Teddy. *But what if Teddy doesn't wish to wed you?* She sat up straight, looking to Olive for comfort, only to find her sister fast asleep. *He does. He said so. This isn't like before when I had no hope from him.* She settled back in the chair and closed her eyes, tears streaming down her cheeks. *Lord, let my plan work. Let me not have sabotaged my future for love . . . and please protect my family's hearts and let my parents see reason. I never wanted to be the disobedient daughter, but I cannot marry for anything but love. Help me forgive Father for his cruel words, and let him forgive me for running.*

Nineteen

Flora snorted awake—a bit surprised at finding herself stretched out on the Persian rug when she had fallen asleep in the chair so soundly. At the steady lapping against the boat and the hum of the churning rear paddle wheel, she sat bolt upright, wincing at her sore back. If they were moving, that meant they'd left the port, which meant Teddy was piloting!

She scrambled to her feet and, seeing that Olive was still sleeping soundly, quietly stripped off her widow's weeds and stepped into the lovely canary silk gown that Olive, thankfully, had the wherewithal last night to lay out to give the creases a chance to smooth. Flora tamed her wild curls into a tight, low coiffure, as her hair had taken on a nature of its own, seeming to grow in volume and crimp since her arrival in New Orleans. She affixed her jeweled comb to the bun, the gold dressing up her simple hair style.

Flora quietly removed the chair they had shoved under the

door handle and drew a steadying breath, straightening her shoulders. *This is it. Lord, let him be thrilled to see me.* She stepped out onto the deck, basking in the warmth after the petrifying night, but now, in the light of day, it seemed her plan was more than a bit flawed. Thank the good Lord that Olive had insisted on coming with her, even though Teddy had already said he wished to marry her. How poorly could her scheme end? Not wishing to know the answer to that little question, she trailed her hand on the freshly painted rail and took the stairs up to the open-air pilothouse, her eyes on the narrow steps, not wanting to fall flat on her face when she faced Teddy. She lifted her gaze, her smile faltering when she did not see Teddy's broad shoulders at the massive pilot's wheel, but— Flora gasped as the pilot turned.

"Flora? What on earth are you doing here?" His rumbling voice woke her from her stupor.

The second pilot, seated on a wide bench along the wall before the dormant potbellied stove, blinked at her from behind a map as if she were an apparition.

She escaped back down the steps, rushing to the railing, hoping to catch sight of the New Orleans port, but of course they had departed at dawn and she had slept far too long and now all that met her eye was the winding, powerful Mississippi River, with cypress trees lining the giant cane-reed-filled banks that no doubt housed alligators, snakes, and Lord knew what else. There was no escape. "Oh, God, help me. What have I done?" she whispered, clutching at her ruffled jabot that was suffocating her. She ran for the ladies' parlor, desperate to lock herself away again, but her toe caught on her hem and nearly pitched her to the deck when a steadying hand grasped her arm.

"Flora?" His voice was gentle but questioning. "What are you doing here?"

"I thought Teddy was—" She focused on the river, attempting to still her emotions, her gaze on the trees dripping in Spanish moss that swayed in the almost-nonexistent breeze as a murder of crows circled in the sky, cawing at each other. "Father would not listen to reason, Carlisle. I had no other choice."

He gritted his teeth and ran his fingers through his hair. "I see. So you ran to Teddy to avoid a marriage with me?"

"My time together with Teddy hasn't been a secret." She dared to face him and crossed her arms, whispering so that the crew would not overhear her. "And as for your so-called proposal, I had no idea that you had such intentions toward me."

"This is not how I wanted our engagement to finally begin," he murmured, leaning with both palms on the rail.

"Finally?" Flora shook her head, confused. "You make it sound as if we have been courting."

He gave a mirthless chuckle. "Well, I thought I was clear about my intentions, as I called upon you every day for the past few weeks after my meetings with your father, and you *received* me. Besides, I thought you and Teddy were only friends, as you *always* have been, especially after his courting your best friend, where you played the chaperone on countless occasions."

She dropped her arms to her sides. When he said it like that, she could see how the misconception came to be. "While we may seem like only friends, your actions did *not* speak to me of anything but friendship. I thought you were calling upon Father, and when you weren't, that you were just being neighborly. Isn't that something you Southerners pride yourself on being? Hospitable?"

He leaned his hand above her head against the column, hemming her in between the rail and himself. "True, but where you are concerned, friendship has never been on my mind since you first arrived in New Orleans. I had always found you to be a sweet and kind person, and then when I found that you had blossomed into an accomplished lady, I knew I couldn't let you slip away."

He thinks I am sweet? She chewed on the inside of her mouth, feeling remorse for her earlier judgments. Carlisle had been nothing but gentlemanly toward her and she was treating his heart with disdain. She ducked under his arm, putting a pace between them. "I thank you for your kind words, but you must know that friendship with Teddy has only been on my mind *twice* when I was forced into seeing him as a friend during his engagements. And during that time, it was a struggle to see him as such."

He nodded, his jaw clenching. "And where does that leave us, my dearest Flora?" He captured her hand again, weaving his fingers through hers in such an intimate gesture it caught her off guard. "Because I think I'm in love with you and I truly believe that you care for me. So, as you can see, we have a little bit of a problem."

"And I love Teddy." She whispered, not wanting to hurt him, but if she had not been clear that she wished to end this farce of an engagement, she needed to be once and for all. She pulled away from him. "I'll ask you to release me from the ridiculous agreement you made with my father."

He rested his hands on her shoulders. His eyes, so like Teddy's, pleaded with her. "It is not a ridiculous agreement to me."

She twisted her hands, averting her eyes. *No, of course it isn't.* Heartless. That was what she was being. "My apologies, Carlisle. I am, of course, honored that you wish to marry me, but you never asked *me* of my wishes. Therefore, I do not think you should hold me to a promise I never made."

He lifted his hands. "Do you wish for me to apologize? I thought my actions were well defined as concerns you. You received me every single time I called. And besides, it is not as simple as breaking it off now. I have allowed you into my heart, and your father and I made a gentlemen's agreement, which is as good as contractual."

She remembered well the scandal following Emma St. James's breach of promise to a gentleman of middling means and the lawsuits that followed. Flora did not think Carlisle was the type of man to sue for breach of promise, but it was well within his rights.

She rubbed her temples. She had the courage to run away to Teddy, but now that he wasn't here, her reasoning was blurring as it always did under duress. Willow had never balked at the board's displeasure, which was solely comprised of men—well, until recently. Flora forced her shaking knees to still. "But *we* did not come to an understanding. You and Father did without me, a key element to your arrangement that you sorely neglected."

"I don't mean to force you into anything. I truly don't, Flora." He propped his fist against his hip, the other returning to take her hand as if he could not keep himself from her, his eyes sad. "Honestly, I am astonished by your reaction. I thought you'd be pleased. I do not want to fight with you, my darling, especially not about this."

She stiffened at the endearment but did not pull away

from him again. She met his gaze, trying to infuse as much determination into her expression as possible, yet her words came out in a whisper. "Then release me, and we won't have to fight."

He brought her hand to his lips. "I don't mean to coerce you into a marriage, Flora, especially since I care for you, but you have given me little choice but to have to force you into an elopement, for you have threatened *both* our reputations by being here."

"You know I did not intend to hurt you. And besides, our reputations are safe."

"I doubt that, as I will surely be made a pariah for making off with a daughter of the New York Four Hundred and *not* marrying her." He dug in his pocket and withdrew his watch, flicking it open. "You must be starving. Let's get you some breakfast. I hope you enjoy grits and bacon."

"I am not hungry." Her traitorous stomach chose that moment to growl. She pressed her hand to her corset stays.

"Well, *I* am, and I think it is best for you to join me now that the men have been alerted to your presence. We need to discuss how to save your reputation."

She stiffened. "I'm afraid nothing you say will persuade me to agree to an elopement. My heart has and always will belong to Teddy."

"Then I will have to content myself with having your hand, if not your heart, for now." He kissed the top of her hand with such gentleness that she did not pull away at once.

"As I said before, our reputations do not need saving. Olive is with me. She is still sleeping because our flight last night was a bit frightful."

"Olive is here? Well then, I shall have a note slid under her door, inviting her to break her fast with us." Carlisle held his arm out to her. "Come, Flora. I promise you will be safe."

As much as she did not wish to take his arm, she had no other choice, for he was right. If she was not with Olive, the only truly safe space aboard the *Marigold* would be at his side. No matter that her sister was with her, when word circulated that they were alone with a gentleman, there would be no escape from the scandal but through marriage as she was the eldest. *Lord, what is happening? I am supposed to be marrying Teddy!* She swallowed hard and placed her hand on his arm. Three more days to evade marriage or her dream of a happily-ever-after would turn into her worst reality.

Knowing he had to wait until a decent hour to approach Mr. Wingfield, Theodore slipped on a pair of boxing gloves and climbed into the ring of the athletic club, eager to sweat off some of his building anxiety. Since meeting Cullen, the sport had gotten his interest, and although he was terrible at it, he welcomed the feel of stretching his limbs. The instructor ducked under the ropes and joined him. After tapping gloves, they began to spar, Theodore reveling in the distraction.

"Theodore!" Gale Thornton shouted, distracting Theodore and earning him a punch to the gut.

He grunted, doubling over.

"Sorry about that." Gale sucked in a breath through his teeth. "But I just received news about Grayson that I confirmed after following him about the city . . . and it isn't good."

"Excuse me," Theodore said to the instructor and, wiping the sweat from his eyes, jumped down from the ring. He tugged at the laces securing his gloves with his teeth and, tucking a glove under his arm, pulled his hand free. "What did you learn?"

"To start, he has a wife in Illinois." Gale crossed his arms. "And that's just the beginning. He is a tricky fellow to follow. Covers his movements well, which leads me and the agency to believe there is far more to him than meets the eye."

"The cad," Theodore growled. "He was *courting* Miss Wingfield!" He charged for the men's chamber and got dressed while listening to Gale's findings.

Within the hour, Theodore stood in front of the Dubois mansion. He straightened his shoulders and dropped the brass pineapple knocker against the door at the perfectly respectable hour of ten of the clock. *Be calm. Do not forfeit a chance with the woman you love by losing your temper in a moment of passion to a man of logic.* He straightened his neckcloth. Logic. That was the only thing Florian Wingfield would respond to when millions in an investment were on the line.

The door jerked open, Mr. Wingfield grasping the frame, his eyes wide behind his wire-rimmed glasses, his beard in need of a good combing.

Theodore nearly dropped his hat, taken aback that the butler had not answered the door. "Mr. Wingfield, sir, I—"

"Theodore Day. You have received my note already?" Mr. Wingfield ran his hand over his jaw.

"Note? No, sir, I came to discuss—"

"Have you seen Flora?" His brows lowered to a point.

His speech died on his lips. "She's missing?"

He nodded. "Mrs. Wingfield is beyond consolation and has kept to her bed. My daughters are with her now." The man's shoulders sagged as he retrieved a crumpled note from his pocket, thrusting it at Theodore. "She and Olive haven't been seen since last night. I had feared that Flora went to be with you and took Olive to act as witness to your elopement, but now that I know they did not, I fear more what could have happened to them." He withdrew a collapsible cup from his pocket, absentmindedly running his finger and thumb over the gold and the etching *F. H. W.*

He did not know Mr. Wingfield's middle name, but Flora's was Hyacinth. Why would he have Flora's cup?

"Lord, don't let them have been taken." He snapped the cup closed and slipped it into his pocket.

Taken? Theodore's heart raced as he unfolded the note in Flora's crisp, clear writing.

> *My dearest family,*
> *I do not wish to leave you all, but with a marriage being forced upon me, I see no other way. I am safe, or I will be by the time you find this letter. Olive is with me, so you need not fear for our reputations.*
>
> *All my love, Flora*

He slowly folded the note. "She ran away . . . because of your arrangement with my brother?"

"So it seems." Mr. Wingfield motioned Theodore inside and into the front parlor. "If she had only waited to speak with me this morning, she would have been pleased to know that I changed my mind on that front."

Despite her being missing, his pulse raced. "Indeed? Sir—"

"I've decided that my daughter shall wed the *winner* of your little race, which is more than what most daughters would have been offered from their fathers after they had already made up their minds." He retrieved the gold cup again. "But my daughters have made me soft."

Theodore's stomach twisted. He had relinquished the lead to come here. And now he would lose her and the competition just as his father predicted? "Sir, I implore you to reconsider. To gamble a lady's heart on the outcome of my family's competition, well, it's rather untoward."

"Not at all, considering the competition you yourself participated in months ago where you promised yourself to Flora's best friend." Mr. Wingfield looked pointedly at him, but Theodore refused to back down. "It is more generous than you two deserve, as you spoke to her before me. And that, young man, is not acceptable."

At that, Theodore nodded. "I agree, sir. And on that score, I sincerely apologize. I was going to speak with you as soon as I returned from my trip, but when I heard of your plan to marry her off to Carlisle—"

He waved him off. "I do not have time to listen to your reasoning. I need to summon a Pinkerton man and find my daughters before something happens to them, if it hasn't already." Mr. Wingfield absentmindedly opened and collapsed the gold cup, then held the parlor door for Theodore.

"Sir?" The butler appeared with a silver tray, the writing on the note *not* Flora's. "Another message has arrived."

Mr. Wingfield scooped it up at once, his hands shaking as he scowled at the crimson seal before he caught Theodore staring at him. He stuffed the note in his pocket and motioned him toward the door.

"Before I go, you should know that Mr. Bradford Grayson is not who he claims to be."

Mr. Wingfield's gaze shot up, his hands shaking. "Do you have proof of that?"

Theodore nodded. "I have a Pinkerton man of my own gathering information on him as we speak. What we know for certain is that he has a wife."

Mr. Wingfield grabbed the back of a nearby chair. "Good heavens. He hid that well."

"So, you are looking into him as well?"

"I have no further use of you, Mr. Day. You may take your leave now."

His anxiety over Flora mounting, Theodore nodded his farewell, nearly bumping into Cornelia, who appeared to be on her way out as she pinned on her chapeau, but Mr. Wingfield was too distracted tearing open the note to notice much of anything. *What on earth is in that letter that has the great Florian Wingfield so rattled?*

"Teddy?" she whispered, pulling him outside. "What are you doing here? I thought you were piloting the *Marigold*?"

"I was going to be until last night when I heard about this absurd proposal and then decided to come here straightaway instead of to St. Louis." He ran his fingers over the brim of his hat. "Do you have any idea where I should start looking for Flora?"

"Oh dear. Oh dear . . ." she murmured, her hands resting on her abdomen. "This is not good. Not good at all."

He took her elbow to steady her. "Tell me."

"Don't you see the problem with your not being aboard

the *Marigold*? Flora thought *you* were piloting the boat, and I believe that is where she and Olive are hiding."

His forehead beaded with sweat. "She stowed away with Olive?"

Cornelia nodded. "I'm guessing so, yes. She must have thought their reputations were safe in your hands."

He steered her down the front steps, whispering, "*Carlisle* is piloting the steamboat. And if he discovers her aboard . . ."

She twisted her hands. "Then they will likely be wed by the end of the journey, for he would never sully her reputation with rumors, especially when he wishes to marry her already. Last night I overheard his conversation with Mr. Wingfield as I was fetching a book from the library. He fancies himself in love with Flora."

His heart dropped at the news. His brother, in love? A movement on the porch caught his eye and he found Tacy rocking on the veranda, a thin smile in place, her attention on her embroidery hoop. But he did not have time to worry over how Flora's conniving younger sister would use this bit of information.

At the squeak of the iron gate, he glanced over his shoulder to find Clancy striding up, his broad-brimmed gambler hat in hand, his expression dark. "What's this I hear about Miss Wingfield?" he called up to them.

"Mr. Drake? How did you hear about it?" Cornelia's eyes widened as Tacy flew from her perch, dropping her embroidery into a basket at her feet.

"Oh, my sister is only having a bit of fun at Father's expense. There is nothing to worry about, Clancy." She drew out his name on her tongue like a piece of chocolate-covered caramel. "Shall I send for some tea—?"

He lifted a crumpled note. "Not according to your father, Miss Tacy. He's asking if I had anything to do with her disappearance."

So, Mr. Wingfield sent a note to every suitor who has crossed this threshold? Theodore's hands clenched into fists. Without another word, he jogged toward home. He would not lose another love—his greatest love—to another man. Not again.

Twenty

Flora gripped her cup of coffee between her hands, studying the delicate blue floral pattern rimmed in gold that she had personally selected from New Orleans's D. H. Holmes Department Store for Mrs. Tyndall, desperately wishing this were only a nightmare. The steamboat had left port nearly six hours ago. Surely Father would have discovered her missing by now?

"We should be in Natchez by nightfall, but instead of heading into port there, I think it might be best to continue on to Providence." Carlisle traced the circumference of his coffee cup, observing her from the head of the long table that had been set with three places over the linen and adorned with delicate pink swamp roses in the center crystal vase.

She knew they were swamp roses because they had already covered that topic over their grueling brunch that was never-ending, but as Carlisle had stated, there was not much else for her to do until they had everything sorted. Flora took a long draft, enjoying the chicory root flavor despite whom she was sharing breakfast with at the moment. "Oh?"

"Yes. I am mentioning this because Providence will have

less of a chance of our running into someone in our acquaintance, and we can wed in private with our reputations intact." He rose and refilled her cup.

She plunked a single cube of fine sugar into the dark liquid, wondering what her friend, the famed sugar queen, would do in this situation. *Willow wouldn't be in this predicament, because her father actually values her and his daughters above all . . . unlike my father.* She grit her teeth against the lingering pain of the realization that she was nothing to her father but a footnote in a business deal. She had thought his not pressuring her into marriage before now was a blessing, that she would be allowed to choose her own husband or none at all if she wished. But no. All he was waiting for was the right deal to come along to use her hand to his advantage. As she was about to fall into the comfort of her self-pity, Auntie's verses flittered in her heart: *"Thou wast precious in my sight, thou hast been honourable, and I have loved thee: therefore will I give men for thee, and people for thy life."*

"I will be a loving husband, Flora. You will want for nothing. And just because I am not the man you first desired, that doesn't mean we can't have a full, wonderful life." He gave her a tender smile, his hand finding hers. "Come, Flora, I'm not all that repulsive, am I?"

She studied his perfect, dark blond curls that fell to his collar. While he was a handsome fellow, there was one vital element missing. "No. But you are not Teddy. And while I have no doubt that you would be a kind husband, how do you envision the holidays with Teddy? He will always be around, Carlisle—always in my heart."

"I had hoped that . . ." Carlisle cleared his throat and

shrugged. "Well, I suppose that is the risk of opening one's heart to hope, isn't it?"

Flora glanced up in time to see him cough into his napkin, as if her observation had struck a chord, yet he disguised it as he leaned back in his chair, arms behind his head in a boyish fashion.

"I like what you two have done with this model steamboat, Miss Wingfield. You have performed a bit of magic with your choice of colors and furnishings. Given the extensive thought it took to put all this together, I imagine you and my brother are collecting quite the commission on this project, as you've marked up the price for each trinket included." He nodded as he considered the room. "I can see the French masters' influence in your taste of palette. I suppose both of you have spent much time in France studying. When you and Teddy are married—" he paused, his eyes on the fresco above the table—"perhaps I can see if it is not too late to have you admitted to the committee for the World Cotton Centennial in Upper City Park next year. I hear it is going to be quite the fair, and I'm certain they could use someone with such an eye for beauty in the arrangement of the displays."

"I would be honored to be on their committee," Flora answered, breathless, afraid he might change his mind. "Then you agree to releasing me?"

"I cannot compete with 'always.'" He settled his chair firmly on all four legs again and lifted his cup to her as if in a toast. "Consider it a wedding gift."

Flora reached across the table, seizing his hand. "Thank you."

"Carlisle Day? What on earth are you doing here?" Olive appeared in the doorway in a fresh gown of rose.

He shot to his feet, freeing his hand from Flora's. "Olive! I was beyond thankful to hear that you were aboard. Please allow me to assist you." He hurried around the table and held the chair on his left for her, taking her hand and pressing a kiss atop, earning a smile from her.

"Thank you! It is a pleasure to see you, but . . ." She turned confused eyes to Flora. "Where is Teddy?"

"There has been a slight hitch in my plans, dear sister, and I'm going to need your help in sorting out a new strategy."

Before noon, Theodore had his things aboard his private steamboat the *Horizon*, which was much smaller than the *Marigold*, but he hoped would prove to be swifter, giving him a chance at catching up with Flora, Olive, and Carlisle by the time they reached Natchez, where Carlisle would likely attempt to press Flora into a marriage. And if not there, then Providence or Memphis. If Theodore knew his brother like he thought he did, Carlisle would be asking for her hand at every port and trying to gain Olive's support to convince Flora that it was for the best.

He checked his pocket watch in the pilothouse and rubbed his thumb over the engraved words he had read countless times. *Some Starry Someday. Lord, let us have our someday at long last. Don't let it slip away when it is finally in view.* He snapped the lid shut. "Mr. Mason! Swing 'round the landing stage. Sound the whistle!" He moved to speak into the bronze tubes, to communicate to the engine room that he was ready, when he spotted Clancy ambling up the landing stage onto the deck.

"Day! There you are. I was hoping to catch you before

you left," Clancy called up to him, pausing to lift his cane in greeting. "I wish to join you in recovering our dear Miss Flora Wingfield."

Theodore growled at the delay as he headed to the stairs to meet him. Then a flash of orange skirts caught his eye.

Tacy waltzed up the landing behind Clancy, twirling her parasol and beaming to them both. "Mr. Drake, imagine finding you here so soon after leaving my home. I was just coming to convince Teddy that Flora is only having a lark and not to waste his time chasing after her."

Theodore recognized a flicker of annoyance in Clancy's expression before the gentleman turned to her. "Miss Tacy, you should not be alone on the docks unescorted."

"Well, then I suppose you will have to escort me home and keep me safe from any unscrupulous passerby." She batted her stubby lashes at him, her attempts in captivating Clancy making Theodore inwardly cringe.

"This is not a game. Your sisters are missing," Clancy snapped, his knuckles turning white on the carved cane head. "Now, I suggest you go and find a carriage and return home like a lady lest you disappear as well."

Though Theodore had always found Tacy to be a solid creature, her eyes filled and her bottom lip trembled. "No cause to be rude, Mr. Drake," Theodore admonished. "Miss Tacy, I thank you for attempting to save me time, but I fear I will not rest until I see for myself that your sisters are safe. Though we both know that our dear Flora does enjoy a bit of adventure now and again."

His words seemed to calm her as she pulled her crushed scowl into a smile. "True. And since I cannot dissuade you, Mr. Day, perhaps Mr. Drake will see me home?"

Clancy ran his hand over his jaw and exhaled. "Miss Tacy, this is not the time for flirting. Your sisters have left the protection of your father and must be found without delay, so you'll forgive me for being blunt, but *please* go home before my worry manifests itself in anger."

At Theodore's glare, Clancy shook his head and lifted his hand as if about to offer an apology. But Tacy was already weaving her way through the mounds of cotton bales, hogsheads, and barrels of goods to a waiting closed carriage, the canary livery of Mrs. Dubois's servants stark against the sensible, earthen tones of the dockworkers.

Theodore crossed his arms. "That was callous and uncalled for to treat Miss Tacy so."

Clancy ran his fingers through his hair and fitted his gambler hat in place. "I will apologize to the lady later, yet you have no idea how aggressive she has been when I have been clear of my intentions from the very beginning."

Thinking of the belles following him about the city, Theodore smirked. "You'd be alarmed at how familiar I am with aggressive ladies trying to lay claim to my hand. But that is beside the point. You have been paying call to the Wingfields for the entirety of their visit to New Orleans. It is little wonder that Miss Tacy—"

"She *knows* it is Miss Wingfield and not her who has captured my attention. While I did try to explain that in a more tactful fashion, there is only so much forwardness a man can bear before having to become blunt to avoid being ensnared into a marriage by a scorned belle and her irate father that said gentleman never desired or solicited attentions from since the beginning of their acquaintance."

Theodore scowled, shaking his head, thinking of the notes

Mr. Wingfield had sent out this morning. *Just how many young men think they are courting my Flora?*

"So, may I travel with you? I can have my bags ready within the hour."

The old Theodore would have agreed out of an innate sense of politeness, but now was not the time to play nice when his fiancée was under the protection of his brother, who wished her for his own bride. "No."

Clancy flicked back the brim of his hat as if he would find something in Theodore's expression to show that he was merely jesting. "No?"

"It is not necessary for you to come, and besides, I'd have to wait for you to pack and time is something I do not have. Go find Miss Tacy and apologize. Leave Miss Flora and Miss Olive to me."

Clancy clenched his jaw and his fist. "You may want to reconsider tossing me from your boat, Day. I can make your business, or I can break it."

Theodore met his gaze and signaled to the first mate to swing the landing stage. "Then break it if you can." Not waiting to watch the man's exodus, Theodore climbed up to the pilothouse, calling out orders that his first mate repeated before he alerted the engine room, waited for the answering bell, and gripped the massive wheel, steering the paddleboat into the heart of the Mississippi.

Twenty-One

Flora stumbled through the second half of Schubert's Fantasia in F minor on the pianoforte with Olive in the grand salon of the *Marigold*, wishing now that she had actually enjoyed playing and had paid more attention to the maestro during lessons like Olive obviously had.

During the long afternoon aboard, Flora was hard-pressed to entertain herself without using the lady's things, along with the armoire full of novelty games and puzzles. As she had spent so long curating the items, it would be a pity to soil their beauty before they were even delivered, especially when she would already need to replace the lady's companion room bedding and a few necessary items she and Olive had not thought to bring until she was aboard. After making her plans with Carlisle and Olive, it was decided that they dare not stop at a port for fear of their reputations being compromised. A discord jarred her from her musings.

She sucked in a breath. "Sorry, Olive. I became distracted again."

Olive sighed. "You are simply ahead of the beat. There is

so much beauty in the waiting, in the length of a note held," she chided and pointed to a stanza in the middle of the page. "Shall we start here?"

"Please do. You two create such an enchanting duet," Carlisle called from the back set of French doors, shrugging on his coat, having returned from his shift in the pilothouse where he had thankfully hidden himself away all day.

Flora laughed, her cheeks heating at her lack of musical prowess being discovered by anyone. "It was anything but on my part."

"Anyone who can play Schubert possesses a bit of enchantment, no matter a few trifling incorrect notes." He stood at the back of the piano, fiddling with his cuff. "And I come bearing good news."

"Oh?" She ran her fingers over the smooth ivory keys, hardly daring to hope that Teddy was nearby.

"We are approaching the port at Providence, so we are making good time and should be in St. Louis in three days' time. But I was thinking while piloting that it might be prudent for me to stop into port there and—"

"I thought we agreed it was too risky." She paused in the piece and lifted a single brow, wary of any stop, especially ones that she did not know had access to a train to New York City, where she might escape if the need arose. To disguise her tumultuous soul, she began to play again, Olive following suit.

"I think it may be riskier if your father is kept uninformed. It would be best for all parties if I send a telegram saying that you are safe."

"Very good, Carlisle." Olive rose, smoothing her skirt. "Is it time for dinner yet? Should we change?"

"I don't think that is necessary." He gestured at his soiled jacket. "I didn't bring but one other suit for the delivery to the Tyndalls, which I must keep pristine as I didn't bring a valet. But I had the crew set a table for the three of us on the promenade deck as we are nearing Stack Island, and I think you will both enjoy some of the old stories of the pirates who used to haunt these waters. Are you ready now?"

Olive placed a hand over her corseted waist. "Actually I'm famished."

While stories of river pirates would have usually piqued her interest, having dinner with a gentleman she just rejected was not her notion of a tranquil evening. Yet at Olive's pleading look, she could not refuse her sister. She pulled at her collar, the air even thicker than usual after the afternoon rain. "Let's eat, shall we?"

Carlisle was extending his hand to them when a shot split the air, sending the sisters to clutching each other.

"What on earth?" he ran for the deck, calling over his shoulder, "Stay here!"

Flora could not imagine there being any danger and followed him, wanting to see if the crew were shooting at something on the bank to liven their dinner plates as the crewmen had suggested. She had thought it a jest . . . until now. She burst through the double doors to the deck, ready to cease the injustice, and stopped short, gasping at the sight of a rickety boat at the front rail and nefarious-looking men, crawling aboard the three levels of the steamboat through the fog rolling over the decks. One of them caught her eye and grinned, the flash of silver illuminating his mouth and his rotting teeth. She whirled around and pushed Olive from the threshold.

"They haven't seen you yet," she hissed, tugging her sister to the far end of the hall.

"Who?" Olive gasped. "Flora, let me go!"

"The river pirates." She pressed her hand over Olive's mouth, muffling her squeal. "Quiet. There is a hidden door behind the tapestry here that Teddy had installed in case of an emergency with three days' worth of supplies. Stay in here and you shall be safe."

"What? But where are you going?"

"They've already seen me," she whispered, "and if I do not make an appearance soon, they will come looking for me and tear this place apart, which will lead them to discovering you as well."

"You can't go out there." Olive clutched her arm, digging her nails into Flora's sleeve. "Th-they may hurt you."

"There is no time, Olive." Flora pushed the hidden lever in the wall behind the tapestry and shoved her sister inside. "Whatever you hear, do not make a sound or come out."

"Flora! No—"

Ignoring the fear pulsing through her body, she quietly shut the hidden door and darted down the hall and away from her sister as quickly as she could manage, intent on making her way to the far end of the ship to the captain's quarters, where she knew Teddy had several weapons stashed away. She slipped out of the hall and pressed herself against the exterior wall, inching her way to the captain's quarters, when the fight rounded the bow with Carlisle charging at them. His powerful blows sent pirates over the side until three pirates swarmed him, pinning his arms behind his back. *He must have been trying to make it to the weapons as well.* She bolted for the captain's quarters.

She screamed as a pair of arms locked about her waist, his hold tightening more the harder she fought. "Ah, there you are. Come here, missy and I'll be your knight."

"I doubt that." She kicked at him, making contact with his thigh.

"Leave the lady be!" Carlisle roared and ripped away from the three men. He lunged for her, driving his fist into the man's skull.

Feeling the man fall away, Flora dove for Carlisle, who pulled her behind him, turning to face the group surrounding them, pressing their backs against the rail.

"Tapestry," she whispered, and at his nod, she knew he understood Olive was well hidden and out of danger . . . for now.

Carlisle lifted his fists to the group, who laughed at what they proclaimed were feeble attempts in preventing the inevitable. Flora trembled, thinking of the countless stories she had read of maidens being captured on the high seas. None of these men looked like the rogue hero who would protect her once taken, much less Teddy in disguise. *Lord, protect us.*

Carlisle jabbed at a man, who grabbed at Flora's skirts. "Take what you will, pirates, but leave the lady alone."

"Now, why would we do that?" a voice called from the back of the group. The men parted to allow a short, paunchy man through. "She is worth a fortune."

She gasped at the man with the eye patch. "You? You were the lead pirate in Penelope's play!"

He cackled at her shock. "Didn't think I was anything more than a first-rate actor, did you, Miss Wingfield, with a fake patch to boot? They don't call me *Captain* Lavigne for nothing."

"I thought they called you that after your ancestors," Flora muttered.

"I have earned the title in my own right," the pirate said with a scowl, setting to pacing the deck.

Carlisle captured her hand in his and whispered, "Canoe."

Her eyes darted to where Teddy's canoe was tied to the boat a level down, to the dark waters below that were concealed by fog, and back to Carlisle's panicked expression. The threat must indeed be grave for him to suggest she canoe across the Mississippi River to the island.

As one, the men moved toward her, and without another thought she hiked up her skirts and scrambled over the rail. Shouts erupted as she shoved off as hard as she could manage to clear the rail and, by some miracle, land in the canoe. She fumbled with the ties, jerking both ropes at once as she used to do at the lake as a child, sending the canoe plunging to the river.

Flora was immediately flung to the floor, the wind leaving her lungs as river water gushed in from the tipping side, soaking through her bustle and hair. She threw herself into the middle of the canoe to keep it from sinking. Instead it spun, narrowly missing the churning wheel as the canoe was swept downriver. Not daring to wait to catch her breath, she picked up the slick paddle and attempted to steer the canoe to the island to find help for Olive and Carlisle, but this water was no still lake.

Her muscles strained against the current as she traveled diagonally to keep herself from being turned over, until she drove the canoe into the riverbed and scrambled off into the calf-deep water, the river at once pulling her sideways and onto her bottom. Her skirts weighed her down, swirling her backward. Silt splashed in her mouth in her struggle to right herself.

Gagging on the filthy water, she planted her hands and feet on the muddy floor to keep herself from being swept away, scrambling to grasp hold of a fallen tree, anything to keep the current at bay.

The pirates shouted behind her, but she did not wait to listen for the telltale splash of a man in pursuit. *Maybe they have the good sense to know not to play with death in the Mississippi's currents.*

Slowly she hauled herself toward the bank by grabbing the knobs left from the tree's broken branches. Banging her shins against the cypress knees, she sucked in a breath and prayed she wasn't bleeding for fear the blood would draw predators. She paid the pain little mind and risked twisting around to glimpse behind her, praying she wouldn't see pirates scrambling into their own pirogues, but the clouds had drawn a veil over the moon. She had to get to the bank. Carlisle had said that alligators were most active at night, feeding on anything injured or in their path, and judging by the crimson stain blooming on her stockings, she was certainly leaving a bloody trail in her wake.

She stumbled to her knees over a bunch of sticks hidden just beneath the murky surface, sending a family of sleeping turtles from their perch on a log into the water. She gripped at the cane reeds and grass that was taller than her and pulled herself up. She cast a furtive glance over her shoulder once more to the lantern-lit boat just as Carlisle was shoved to his knees in front of a man brandishing a pistol. She pressed a hand to her mouth in a soundless cry. *Dear Lord in heaven, save us! Protect Carlisle, and keep Olive hidden.*

She clambered up the steep bank to put as much distance as she could between herself and the river, only to trip over a massive log, sending her tumbling down the bank and almost into the water again. And to her horror, the log *twitched*.

Theodore gripped the wheel, focusing on piloting the boat through the heavy fog rolling over the banks, spilling into the river. He found no sign of their ever having been at the port of Natchez, and now, after hours of taking chase again, he could at last make out the glow of lantern light coming off what could only be the *Marigold* anchored near Stack Island in the middle of the Mississippi River. His heart leapt at the thought of seeing Flora when he noticed something along the far side of the steamboat. He squinted. "Mr. Mason, does that look like a boat is anchored beside—?" A percussion of shots made his stomach drop. "It can't be."

His ancient second pilot ambled forward with his spyglass, leaning against the open window frame of the pilothouse and focusing in on the boat. He gasped, swiped off his cap, and gripped it over his heart. "Them's river pirates, Teddy boy."

"What?" He snatched the proffered glass, twisting the lens into focus. The *Marigold* had been boarded. He snapped the spyglass closed. "Cut the engine, Harry," Theodore called into the speaking tubes as loud as he dared to the engineer belowdecks. "Stand by for further instructions." He handed the glass back to his second pilot. "There haven't been active river pirates here in decades."

"Be that as it may, as sure as we are standing here, them's river pirates. I well remember the signs of them from when we were boarded when I was just a lad. Those memories stay with a body for life. Weren't like that play you told me about." He passed his hand over his tobacco-stained silver beard. "It was violent."

Theodore clenched his jaw as Mason took a second look. If Cornelia's guess were true, Flora was on that boat with her sister and his brother. And he could not delay another second. "Get the men armed, Mason. And tell the crew that if they want to avoid a fight, to take the emergency boats now."

Mason shook his head and handed his spyglass to Theodore. "I am not speaking out of cowardice but of reason. Look again and count the men. I think our best course of action would be to turn around and get help from the nearest village along the river. They outnumber us four to one, even *with* your brother's crew. If we get taken too, it won't help the ladies. Providence is right nearby. We could go for help and be back with the law in a couple of hours."

"By then it could be too late." He couldn't see Flora from this distance. *Lord, if they are indeed aboard the boat, let the women be hiding and keep my brother and the crew safe.* "I won't leave my brother and the ladies. I will use the canoe and board alone. Stay in the shadows to ensure we are not spotted, then take the crew and go for help. Can you manage all right?"

"I could pilot these waters with my eyes closed," Mason said.

"Open is my preference." Theodore clapped him on the shoulder and ran for his quarters. His revolver would do little good if it got wet, so instead he took from the wall a decorative pair of Scottish dirks his father had given him as a lad and slid the daggers from their sheaths. The double edges glinted in the moonlight. He snapped the daggers inside their sheaths again, securing them in his waistband, and ducked out of his cabin.

The boat stayed close to the riverbank as Theodore rolled up his sleeves, rocking back on his heels as he studied the distance between himself and the *Marigold* as best he could in the fog. He crawled over the rail and slipped the canoe free and cut through the water. By the time he drew near to the hull of the *Marigold*, his breathing was labored, but he didn't dare stop now. Grasping one of the ropes dangling from the side, Theodore hoisted himself up, the canoe floating away from under him as he pulled himself hand over hand on the slick rope, using his feet to anchor himself to the side of the vessel. At last he hauled himself aboard and landed lightly on the balls of his feet. He crept along the shadows and unsheathed his daggers, finding Carlisle bound along with the rest of the crew.

"Killing you wasn't part of the deal," said a short, stout pirate, who was pacing before the group.

Theodore squinted in the darkness. The man looked uncannily familiar.

"But if you charge me again, my men will be forced to act in self-defense and knock you senseless. Got it?"

A scream sounded in the darkness.

"Flora!" Carlisle shouted in the direction of the island. "You have to let me go after her. She could be hurt. The lady is not used to the swamp."

The pirate snorted. "Like we'd release you after you were the one to tell her to jump." He waved the burliest of the pirates forward. "Hold on to him. And if he tries anything, you know what to do."

"He's bound and isn't a threat. You know why we were sent here, Lavigne. Are you really going to waste it on these *theatrics*? The girl is getting away." The man spat at the last word, leaving a brown tobacco smear on the pristine white deck. "After all, she is the reason we were hired. Commandeering this vessel is chicken feed compared to the lady's worth."

Theodore's stomach twisted, his fists tightening over his knives.

Lavigne flipped his hand dismissively. "She won't get far, Cousin, but you are right. Time to go after her."

"No." Carlisle fought against his captors, who kicked him in the gut, sending him doubling over, his forehead resting on the deck for a second before he lifted his chin, bracing himself as if to fight once more, and then he spotted Theodore. With a single tilt of his head, angling toward the port side, Theodore understood.

The moment Carlisle roared and set to head-butting Lavigne, Theodore raised his knives and used the distraction to slice the Kisbee ring from the wall, run to the rail, and dive for the bank.

The current pulled him backward, but he kept his arm wrapped around the ring and kicked with all his might toward the island. He hissed through his teeth and pushed through the burning in his limbs from the effort of fighting the river. As he neared the shore, the current lessened and he spotted muddy indentions on the bank. But unlike the long sliding marks left from a resting reptile dropping into the water, he spied footholds, a dainty slipper stuck in the mud . . . *Flora. Olive.*

Keeping the ring close, he climbed up the bank and cast a

glance behind him to see four men board two pirogues. He bent low to keep the men in the long canoes from spotting him. He moved deeper into the marshy island, his feet sinking into the ankle-deep swampland. At a low growl followed by a hiss, Theodore jumped backward, narrowly missing the whipping tail of an alligator. His heart plummeted at the sight of bits of canary-yellow silk clinging to the wire bustle caught in the gator's jaw. "Flora!"

The gator whipped toward him again, and having no gun, Theodore scrambled up the low-lying branches of a magnolia tree.

Twenty-Two

"Teddy," Flora whispered, clinging to the top branches of the magnolia tree, the thin branches bending in her hold, the crusty pale-green lichen clinging to them scaly beneath her hands. But she didn't dare to let go to brush off her hands or lower herself for fear the snarling beast at the foot of the tree would finish what he started with her bustle.

"Flora?" Teddy shot his gaze upward, his jaw dropping at the sight of her. No doubt she was coated from head to toe in mud. "How did you climb so far up the tree?"

"When a gator catches you by your derrière, anything is possible. And surprisingly enough, when one's bustle has been ripped away, there is an extraordinary amount of room for your legs to climb."

At the snapping and hissing below him, Teddy swung his feet up under him and used the momentum to climb higher as the creature lunged six feet into the air, missing him by a mere foot and drawing a strangled cry from Flora.

"They can jump, too? This is ridiculous," Flora whimpered. "Next you are going to tell me they can climb trees."

"Well, if there is enough of an incline . . ." At her look, Teddy ceased his explanation. "Thank the Lord you are safe," Teddy added, his voice cracking. "When I saw that bustle—"

"I am well. You didn't see Olive aboard, did you?" She could cry from the sight of him, but she didn't dare give into her tears until all was over. *Please, Lord, let it be over soon.*

"No." He set the ring he was holding on a cluster of branches and looked past Flora as if expecting to find her sister up in the tree as well. "She isn't with you?"

"Maybe they haven't found her." Her throat tightened. "I had to leave her hidden in the false wall behind the tapestry."

"Then do not fear, for no one knows of that feature besides my brother, and he would never betray her. She is safe."

Flora sagged against the tree, lifting her face to the speckled sky. She released a prayer of thanks and smiled down at Teddy. "You came after me."

"Always," he whispered.

The single word warmed her heart. *He left everything to follow me.*

"Did you think I wouldn't?" He reached for the branch above him, slowly inching his way toward her. "Now that I have found you, my darling, future Mrs. Day, I don't ever want you out of my sight again, not after the fright you gave me." He advanced by another branch, until one snapped underfoot that left him dangling in the air, his hold the only thing keeping him from the jaws of the alligator below.

Flora gasped, reaching for him, her hand encircling his wrist. "Stop! Or you'll be the next course after that beast finishes his *amuse-bouche* of my bustle."

He paused beneath her, and she felt slightly self-conscious of her shoeless foot dangling quite close to his head. She tucked it under her skirts as best she could before remembering that a missing shoe was the least of her improper state of dress. But Teddy, ever the gentleman, kept his gaze firmly fastened on her face.

He dared to take another branch and pull himself a little closer. "Are you hurt?"

"A few scrapes and fearful of the pirates taking chase, but now that you are here, I'm feeling much better."

He reached up to her, and she, keeping a firm grip on the branch, leaned down to him, his fingertips brushing against her palm before she wobbled a bit and regained her hold.

"I am so sorry, Flora. I had no idea what my brother was planning. He didn't press you into—into a marriage?"

"He was adamant at first, until I explained there is no one else in this world for me but you, Teddy Day." She looked at him through her lashes. "And if that means I have to survive a scandal of the ages to be by your side for a lifetime, so be it."

The moonlight peeking through the oval, shiny leaves illuminated how much her words touched him. "But I'm afraid we cannot wait here much longer. Alligator or not, I am being followed by four pirates, and they will find us soon enough."

Flora shivered, glancing at the reptile below. "Risk being eaten or kidnapped—not much of a choice, is it? Still, I think I would prefer risking the former than be held hostage by those men."

"My crew went for the law, so hopefully we will have reinforcements soon," he replied, neglecting to mention the most frightening aspect of what could happen before then should they be captured.

"Don't you remember the stories from Penelope's party?"

she asked. "This is Stack Island, *home* of the pirates. And there is no way off the island except through the Mississippi River, and *if* we survive the swim across—"

"We have to try, Flora, for Olive and Carlisle and the men, in case my crew doesn't find help in time."

For Olive. Taking a deep breath, she grasped his hand and slipped down from her perch, her feet finding the next branch and the next until she was facing Teddy. He reached out and stroked a sodden curl behind her ear.

"Thank God I found you." His rough hand cupped her cheek with such tenderness it stole her heartbeat. "I love you, Flora Wingfield." He pressed his lips to hers, their breath mingling as she dared to wrap her hands about his neck and leaned into his kiss, growing light-headed as the kiss deepened. At the rustling of leaves, they parted, his hand at her waist, steadying them.

He squinted at the ground below. "I think the alligator is gone. We best be on our way before we are joined by the pirates."

Flora groaned. "Can we perhaps climb across the treetops? It is pretty dense." *Or perhaps take our chances that the pirates cannot see us in the dark in our perch?* She froze at the sound of branches being shoved aside, twigs snapping underfoot.

He lifted his finger to his lips, and Flora spotted the four pirates, slashing through the tall grass with machetes, when the gator whipped about, hissing at the crew, sending the men scrambling back and one aiming his rifle. At the crack, the beast hissed and whipped again, exposing the back of its head. The pirate took aim, and Flora squeezed her eyes shut. *Lord, save us.*

The rifle fired, and the alligator was still.

"Get down here, girly, or your fellow will meet the same fate as this here gator."

Two daggers. Four men. The odds weren't looking good for winning at hand-to-hand combat, but judging from the conversation he had overheard aboard the *Marigold*, these pirates weren't looking to kill. Flora shivered under his grasp. "It will be well, my love," he whispered.

"Keep calling me your love and I'll believe it." She smiled up at him, the dirt caking her cheeks cracking against her smile.

"We've a schedule to keep." The pristinely dressed shorter pirate of the group announced, who Teddy recognized as the leader, the man called Lavigne. The giant behind him wielding the rifle was far more convincing of holding the title of pirate with his rough countenance than the trio accompanying him.

Theodore snatched up the ring and pressed it into her hands. "Stay close and run for the west bank when I tell you. We will swim for it, but don't try it without me. You would have a better chance with the pirates than surviving the river without a canoe or a strong swimmer at your side."

She nodded, but instead of descending, she pressed her lips to his, causing shouts to spew from below. And when she pulled away, he could see his heart mirrored in her eyes. The moment their feet hit the soggy ground, the men lurched forward to claim them and Theodore wrenched his daggers from their sheathes. "Run, Flora!"

Not waiting to see if she followed his orders without question for the first time in her life, he sprang forward, slicing the arms of the rifleman in just the right place to render him useless and turning his daggers on the others. He whirled, blocked their attempts at using their rather rusty-looking swords, and raked his blades along the ankles of another, sending him howling to the ground, with the final two men lifting their hands in surrender.

"We concede!" Lavigne shouted, squeaking at the final syllable.

Theodore blinked, keeping his blades at the ready. "That is not very pirate-like of you."

"That's because the only one of us here who is a true pirate is Gilmore, and you took care of him." He gestured to the giant on the ground, gripping his ankles. "We are the actors of the troupe."

That announcement almost made Theodore lower the blades, yet he did not trust the rifleman not to attack again, despite his injuries. "Are you saying you aren't *real* river pirates?"

The man shrugged with his hands still in the air. "We sort of are."

"How is one 'sort of' a pirate? You either are or you are not." Theodore twisted his blade in warning.

"What I mean is, we were hired because of our theatrical work. I believe you've met me before. Captain Lavigne, from Miss Penelope Bridgewater's party?"

"Are you saying Penelope hired you?" Theodore shook his head. "Because if that is your story, I'd say you are a liar."

"No, no. I don't know her name, but this lady hired me at that fancy party to outfit a crew to kidnap Miss Wingfield and hold her for enough ransom to split between us. She was emphatic that we *not* injure Miss Wingfield. She said that once we had safely secured Miss Wingfield and she collected the ransom, she would pay us the second half of our fee. We'd never have to act again with the price that young lady would bring. So I accepted the job and was about to pluck Miss Wingfield right off of St. Charles Avenue that night, but she and her sister hopped into a carriage and snuck aboard your steamboat. We had heard of your delivery through our channels, and well, I had no choice but to contact my cousin on the river, Robert Lavigne, to help finish the job. Robert brought together the descendants of the pirates from Stack Island to help take the boat, and we took a faster means of getting here than a steamboat to join him, and here we are."

Theodore stared at the man in disbelief. He pointed a bloodied dagger at Captain Lavigne. "Enough talking. Tie up your companions."

"But what about predators? You're going to leave us here to be eaten?" His voice rose with each question.

Theodore shrugged. "That is not my concern. But rest assured, lawmen will retrieve you soon enough to cart you off to jail."

"While we were easy to vanquish, my cousin will not be and will be here shortly. Despite the lady's mandate of no violence, I wouldn't put killing past him, not with such a ransom at stake. If you let us go—" He drew a breath as if to launch into a second long monologue.

"Tie them up. *Now*." Theodore lifted the dagger in warning. He didn't have time for another speech. For all he knew, this so-called pirate was trying to give his mates a chance at re-claiming Flora while he stood around listening to the man rattle on.

Pirates secured, Theodore ran after Flora, his foot sinking in the occasional, mossy swamp puddle. "Flora?" he called tentatively, sheathing his blades. Had she already tried to swim on her own? His heart hammered at the thought.

She slipped from the trees like a sprite, her golden hair now hanging to her waist in matted, darkened curls, her hand firmly clutching together the fabric at her backside. He kept his eyes on hers, ignoring the large patch of missing skirt where he'd glimpsed a bit of powder-blue silk chemise and bloomers.

She seized him in an embrace, forgetting her hold on her skirts. "I half thought I'd have to swim across on my own to fetch help for you."

"I have no doubt in your courage to save us, but I am so thankful you did not try." He pulled back, grasping her hand as her free one clutched her skirt together once more. "We need to hurry. I discovered something disturbing, and I don't want to give the men a chance to catch up with us."

She gave him a quizzical look but followed him down the bank, her foot slipping only once, a whimper escaping her throat.

He glanced sideways at her. Flora never complained. He took the Kisbee ring from her. "Are you well?"

She nodded, her lips pressed into a firm red line against her pale skin.

"Don't be afraid. The swim across won't be too treacherous," he said in an attempt to reassure her, though he had little idea of what to expect. *Lord, please calm the waters.*

"It's hard not to be afraid when a gator almost gobbled me up for his dinner and a band of pirates almost killed you," she whispered, her voice catching.

"We held our own." He stroked her cheek with the back of his hand and helped her down the bank and into the river, the motion of the water pushing against his ankles at once alerting him that the current on this side of the island was not quite as strong as the other. "Slip this over your head." Theodore held the ring above her, but she shook her head.

"I won't take it from you."

"Flora, I am a strong swimmer, much more than you." He lifted the ring again.

"We either both use it, or I won't use it at all." She crossed her arms.

Not having time to argue with her, they both took hold of the ring on either side and forded the water until his feet no longer touched the riverbed. He looked over to Flora, kicking with him as best she could, and he gave her what he hoped was an encouraging grin . . . when the water tugged at him, breaking his hold on the ring, sending her spiraling downriver without him.

"Teddy!" Sputtering against the river, Flora gasped, grappling to get a better hold on the ring. "Dress."

He dove for her and, in a few strokes, caught up with her and pulled the ring toward him, then wrapped his arm around her, feeling the weight threatening to drown her. Reaching for his dagger, he dove under and sliced through the waistband, freeing what was left of her skirt. He broke the surface, gasping and accidentally drawing in water. He hacked the river from his lungs, never releasing his hold on Flora as they swam toward the bank, Flora keeping better pace with him now that her skirt was gone.

Grabbing fistfuls of marsh grass and stalks of scarlet

spider lily, they crawled up the bank where the pair collapsed, her cheek resting in the mud beside him.

"Teddy?" She felt for her skirt, jerking her head up. "Did you cut off *the entirety* of my skirt?"

He gritted his teeth, stood, and tossed aside the ring. "Better to be in bloomers than be a drowned beacon of modesty."

She buried her face in her hands and groaned. "Could this night get any worse?"

"I would offer you my coat, but I'm afraid I left it aboard my boat." He tugged off his suspenders and unbuttoned his shirt.

Flora's eyes widened behind her splayed hands. "Theodore Pierre Day! Whatever are you doing?"

He shrugged out of the soaked linen, handing it to her. "Offering you my shirt to wrap around your . . . uh, well, you won't be warm, but you'll be covered."

She whipped her back to him, the blush staining her ears showing even in the moonlight as she scrambled to her feet to put some distance between them. "Oh, that would look completely appropriate, a half-dressed man with daggers in his belt and a woman in *his* shirt over her bloomers. No, thank you. Keep your shirt or I fear my reputation will *never* recover."

He laughed softly.

"I mean it, Teddy. I will never be received in polite society again."

"It's not ideal, but I thought it was better than wearing nothing over your pretty bloomers."

She gasped. "You keep your eyes on mine and nowhere else!"

"I didn't look on purpose." He laughed again and shrugged

back on the shirt, shivering a bit at the damp cloth against his skin once more and gave her his hand. "The river's current put a good distance between us and the island, but we need to keep moving north to make it to Providence. Are you able?"

"Of course. I could run if need be." She tugged at the waist of her blouse as if she could magically make it longer to cover her bloomers, which were embroidered with little pink roses at the knee. She caught him staring and lifted a single brow.

He quickly averted his eyes while extending his hand to her, hoping he had not offended her by forgetting himself momentarily, but truly it was difficult.

Her fingers laced into his. "Not a word of this to a single soul."

"I am losing track of embarrassing moments of which you are swearing me to silence, but you have my promise. Though, if we are spotted, word will spread well enough without my helping it along." Theodore smiled, keeping her close as they climbed the bank to find a dirt road. Meanwhile, he filled her in on the pirate's confession.

Flora shook her head. "I cannot believe another woman would arrange all this just to get me away from you."

"Well, it wasn't Penelope who hired them, so we don't know it was about me necessarily."

"It was *certainly* about you. What other woman could have a reason to wish me so ill as one of your admirers?" Flora crossed her arms over her yellow bodice, murmuring under her breath something pertaining to Penelope's little group of friends.

At the steady hoofbeats rapidly approaching, Theodore

tugged her into the underbrush on the side of the road, his left hand at her back and his right clutching a dagger. He squinted in the darkness, hoping to see his crew arriving with the law, yet he did not recognize the paunchy man atop the equally stout horse. "Stay down until I discover if he is an ally."

"Teddy! No. It's too dangerous."

He kissed her hand. "It's too dangerous not to seek help." He sheathed his blade and rose, stepping out into the road and waving. "Good evening, sir. How far is it until I reach Providence?"

The horse threw back its head as the man pulled on the reins, his eyes widening, no doubt in shock from someone darting out of the brush. "You gave me quite the start."

Theodore lifted his hands, palms out. "My apologies, sir."

"Only a couple of miles." He bent down and reached into his coat, which was folded over the saddle horn.

Theodore tensed, readying himself for a fight.

The man tossed him a paper sack. "You look like you could use a bite to eat. I always keep a little something on me when I do the rounds with the parishioners. I'm Pastor Young. If you are needing shelter for the night, my wife will make you a bed up right quick. My home is only about a mile out. Right by the church."

Theodore checked the sack lunch and found a slightly smashed sandwich and an apple. Surely no pirate would be impersonating a friendly pastor? Theodore decided to trust him. He motioned Flora to join him. "Then maybe you'll be able to help us."

"I shall do my best." He nodded, pausing in the action. "Wait, did you say *us*?"

Flora groaned quite loudly from the bushes, making the pastor's eyes widen even more.

Theodore would've laughed at the ridiculousness of the situation if it wasn't so dire. "Come, Flora. We have to trust him."

At her emergence, the pastor's jaw dropped and he instantly turned his horse, putting his back to her. He snatched up his coat and tossed it behind him to Theodore and began digging in his saddlebags. "Whatever has happened to you and your wife, sir?"

Theodore held the coat out to Flora, who was in it in a flash, the girth enough to wrap around her thrice over. "We aren't married," she supplied.

Theodore stiffened and whispered, "You didn't *have* to tell him that."

"And lie to a man of the cloth? I think not." She pursed her lips, tying the sleeves firmly around her waist, the coat falling to her knees in front and her shapely calves at the back.

"Running away and sneaking aboard a vessel is acceptable, but not omitting the truth?" he muttered.

"You are fortunate that I was making collections for the poor box and I have these on hand." The pastor tossed back a pair of pants that looked like they were for a growing boy. "Now, you must tell me, what happened?"

"We were set upon by pirates," Flora answered, stepping into the pants, which had Theodore's neck heating as he too turned his back to Flora.

"Pirates? Lord help us," the pastor said, his voice shaky.

"I'm presentable," Flora called to the men, her hands on

301

her hips as she studied herself in pants, grinning. "Thank you, Pastor Young."

"It is nothing, miss." He dismounted and waved her over to the saddle. "Come, my poor child. My Martha will see to you while I prepare your certificate and wedding vows to be taken within the hour."

Twenty-Three

Flora dug her fingernails into the rail as the lawmen's tugboat chugged up the Mississippi River toward Stack Island. She fought the urge to check the security of the rope holding up her pants, but she didn't wish to draw any more attention to herself among the group of men than a woman in trousers already garnered. After donning the pants, she had set about convincing Pastor Young that time was of the essence and that they needed to stop at the police station instead of the parsonage. It had taken a bit of her best work, but at last he agreed that the lives aboard the boat were more important than her state of matrimony or lack thereof.

As they rounded a bend in the river, Theodore's hand enveloped hers. "Lord, let us find the crew, my brother, and Flora's sister unharmed."

Her breath caught at the sight of a stranger's tugboat next to Teddy's steamboat the *Horizon*, and the pirates' vessel alongside the *Marigold*, with no fighting visible.

"Mason beat us!" Theodore let loose a holler. "He must have found help!"

"Lord, let it be so!" Flora clasped her hands to her throat, fearful that the second boat belonged to the pirates.

"Why ain't they slowing down, Sheriff?" a scrawny deputy asked, twisting his spyglass into focus.

Teddy snatched the glass from the young man's hands, paling as he focused on the pilothouse, seeing not his brother but that fool of a pirate. "Because Captain Lavigne is piloting it." He snapped the spyglass closed. "Sheriff, can we get there any faster? That man doesn't know a thing about this river."

They were but half a mile from the steamboat when shouts erupted from the vessel. Flora could see that the two crews were fighting one another on the lower decks as another group attempted to breach the pilothouse, where a pirate stood, a pistol in each hand, stopping Mason from advancing. The commotion at the pilothouse seemed to have distracted Captain Lavigne as the steamboat began to steer toward shore.

Flora screamed as the *Marigold* struck something in the river, the hull crumbling under it, and the boat began to take on water. "Olive!" She felt arms wrap about her, but she could only sob, staring as the boat slowly began to submerge, the pirates abandoning the steamboat for their own that had come alongside it. "Olive!" she screamed.

"Rifles at the ready, men!" the sheriff called out. "We do not know if any of the pirates are still aboard, but we need to help evacuate the boat." He turned to Flora. "Don't you worry, miss. Though the engineer may be injured, unless your sister was in the hull with him, she will more than likely be fine. Looks like they hit a sandbank and won't go sinking to the bottom of the river."

Teddy squeezed her hand as the tugboat swung into place alongside the steamboat's ladder. "Stay here, Flora, I'll see—"

But before he could finish his thought, Flora flung herself across the rail and climbed up the ladder into the boat. She charged down the promenade deck, throwing open the doors to the grand hall to find Carlisle, knuckles bloodied, opening the false door, and Olive flying into his arms, sobbing.

"Olive!" Flora cried out, running to them, Teddy not far behind.

Olive slipped her arms from Carlisle's neck and reached for her, limping. "Thank God, I was so frightened. I thought they had taken you—that they had taken everyone. And water is seeping through." She turned back to Carlisle, her eyes lingering on the gash on his cheek. Her fingertips traced his jaw before she snatched her hand back.

"They nearly did take us all." Carlisle brushed at his cheek, his gaze resting on Olive. "Is your foot injured? You seem to be favoring your right side."

"I was standing on a stool, reaching for some rations in that tiny room, when the steamboat struck something and I tumbled off."

He shook his head, drawing her hand through his arm to lend her support. "We need to evacuate."

"Is it that bad?" Olive gasped. "Is it going to sink?"

"If the hull is severely damaged, the boat most likely isn't salvageable, but first we need to get everyone *off*." Teddy wrapped his fingers about Flora's wrist and pulled her toward the door.

Olive cried out, and Flora glanced back over her shoulder to see Carlisle sweeping her into his arms, followed by Olive's tender thanks. Did her sister have feelings for the gentleman? She didn't have much time to dwell on that thought over the pandemonium as the lawmen searched frantically on all levels, shouting out, trying to locate any trapped crewmen. The engineers staggered from the bottom level, soaked and bloodied but not broken. Through the chaos, Teddy's hand remained firmly clasping Flora's, Olive in Carlisle's arms, until at last they were safely aboard the *Horizon*, where they stood on the deck watching and waiting to see the fate of the *Marigold*.

Wrapped in a quilt from Teddy's bunk, Flora embraced her sister, tears flowing. "Thank God that Carlisle got to you in time."

Olive nodded, stepping out of her arms and wiping her eyes. "It's a shame that the Tyndalls will never see your work. I know you both toiled so hard making it the floating palace it was."

Flora cast a glance at Teddy, whose eyes were fixed on the boat, his jaw tightening.

"It is a blow indeed, but with your father's investment, we will be able to hire a second group of builders to help us fabricate the *Marigold II* in a timely manner," Carlisle said, coming to stand next to Olive. "Until then, we need to continue upriver to deliver this news in person to the Tyndalls to ensure the rebuilding."

"Did you catch the leader responsible?" Olive inquired.

"I spoke with Mr. Mason, and apparently the moment the pirates saw my crew coming, along with the second tugboat's crew that the *Horizon* came across on their way downriver, they all but abandoned their mission, and the rest escaped in the chaos of the wreck. But never fear, the law has alerted the nearby parishes and the states along the river. They *will* be apprehended and brought to justice for the terror they have caused you both." Teddy clenched his fists.

Flora nodded. "I pray it is sooner rather than later."

Olive pressed a hand over her mouth, a giggle spilling out. "Um, where are your skirts, Sister?"

"It is a long story that warrants no embellishments." Flora pulled the blanket tighter to hide her trousers from the gentlemen's eyes. "I will tell you about it at great length, but what's important is that we are all safe despite their best-laid plans, whoever *they* are."

"Amen," Teddy agreed, though Flora could see his gaze traveling over the length of the ruined boat, silently analyzing the damage. She scooted to his side, leaving Olive with Carlisle, who was filling Olive in on all the details.

"Is anything salvageable?" she whispered, shoving her filthy locks out of her face.

"The men were able to save your carpetbags and a few trinkets, but unfortunately we don't have time to save the rest. What's most pressing now is that we speak with Mr. Tyndall and draw up new designs, something even grander than before, and at no additional charge in order to tempt him into waiting." He ran his hand over the back of his neck. "It's going to take the entirety of the journey to St. Louis, not just to re-create but to *reimagine* the order."

"Then we best put on a pot of Mason's chicory coffee and get to work."

He turned to her, keeping one hand on the rail. "I cannot ask you to do that, not after what you have been through."

"You aren't asking, and besides, if we are to be married, your problems are my problems. Your dreams, my dreams."

She sidled next to him and rested her head on his shoulder, his arm stealing about her waist. "And I have no doubt that after Olive has been locked in a room for hours on end, she will be more than happy to stretch her mind and help us. I didn't stay up until midnight for weeks designing, only to see a bunch of rowdy actors ruin the sale of one of the best boats of your career just days before delivery. This is too important. Think about if word circulates in St. Louis about *your* boat designs, one that we will design from scratch now. We could generate enough orders for you to actually win the competition."

Teddy sighed. "And *that* is far more important than you realize. I spoke with your father, and he has some strict conditions for his permission for us to marry."

Twenty-Four

Flora finished brushing her wet locks at the *Horizon* guest room's vanity and reached for the bottle of perfume salvaged from Mrs. Tyndall's room. With their arrival in St. Louis tonight with a possible meeting with the minister, she dabbed it liberally at her jawline, frowning at her reflection in the gilded looking glass affixed to the burgundy-and-gold-papered wall. She traced a long bruise she had acquired during her escape, no doubt when she ran into that branch in the woods. The bruise was just now beginning to fade into a sour yellow after four days aboard.

Her stomach rumbled as she braided her hair into a low coiffure and slipped into her crimson dinner gown that had thankfully still been in her carpetbag when the steamboat wrecked. With everything that had happened since she had left Auntie's, she could see the folly in her attempt at elopement. Mother would be in a frenzy over her daughters' reputations, especially with the news of the wreckage that was surely already circulating in the papers. She would send a telegram as soon as they were married tonight to ease her family's worries on that front. She sighed. *I cannot change the past, but I can surely try my best to make wiser choices in the future.*

"Can you help me with the buttons?" Olive asked, standing behind her, peeking into the small mirror. "I don't know how you managed yours."

"You have to dislocate your shoulder a bit to work all the buttons is all," she teased, happy that Olive was attending dinner at the table. Olive had taken to seeking solace during the past three days whenever possible, so much so that it made Flora question what else happened when she had left her sister alone in the hidden room.

Olive sent her a weak smile. "Has Carlisle spoken with you again?"

"He has been avoiding me, which is quite the talent given the size of the *Horizon*."

Olive slipped on her gloves. "Well, just know that when he hides from you, he seeks me out to confide in regarding his feelings for you, and it is exhausting."

Was that the source of the dark rings under her sister's eyes? "I'm sorry, Olive. I had no idea."

Olive nodded once, her silence betraying the burden more than her confession.

Flora grasped her sister's elbow. "How long have you liked Carlisle, Olive?"

"Well, whenever he was waiting around to see you, I would entertain him." She shrugged. "I didn't want to say anything lest I sounded like Tacy with the gentlemen only wanting you and all."

"If you had said something, I would have helped you—"

"But that's just it. I didn't want your help. I wanted him

to want me without anyone's prodding." She frowned at her flaxen hair and reached for the silver combs, tucking and brushing it into submission.

Flora kissed her on the cheek. "Allow me." She took the brush and removed the pins securing Olive's hair, then rearranged it in a charming, braided coiffure, finishing it off by pulling a few tendrils to frame her sister's face.

At the knock at the door, Flora adjusted her puffed sleeve of rows of white lace with a crimson velvet ribbon bracelet edge and a diamond buckle and turned in the tall looking glass of the guest room, admiring the pointed flounces of her crimson short-trained, round skirt. "Ready?"

"You go ahead. I'll be out directly." Olive gestured to her rose-colored stockinged feet, her left ankle's swelling having gone down considerably. "They weren't able to save my dinner slippers, remember? I have to lace my boots."

Flora stepped out onto the moonlit deck and found Teddy waiting for her, his eyes sparking the moment she met his gaze.

"You're lovely." He gently grasped her gloved hand and kissed it.

Her heart skipped at his compliment, as she was certain her heart would continue to do forever with a man like Teddy as her husband. She would never get used to his *finally* loving her, though she wished he'd kiss her like he had in the magnolia tree on the island. Yet such kisses could prove too risky for a couple traveling together, chaperoned only by one's former fiancé and sister.

"Good evening." Carlisle ambled toward them, smiling as Olive appeared in the threshold, her cheeks tinting at the sight of him.

He bowed to Olive and extended his hand to her. "May I have the honor of escorting you to dinner?"

At Olive's timid nod, the couple disappeared on the promenade deck, Teddy and Flora leisurely following.

"We will arrive in St. Louis after dinner, yes?" Flora prompted.

Teddy nodded, scrubbing a hand over his beard. "Yes. I've been thinking of your father's stipulations, and while our designs may help us secure the Tyndalls' order again—which will have us nearly tied for the running—I've been thinking that during these last few weeks of the competition, we should try advertisements, moderate discounts, and . . ."

She had been waiting for three days for him to mention marrying at the port of St. Louis. *Is he really going to make me say it?* "But as Carlisle has freed me from any obligation of marriage, the answer is glaring us in the face."

He blinked.

"We elope."

His jaw dropped. "Flora . . . we can't, not without at least attempting to secure your father's blessing by winning the competition. Your mother—"

"Will have to understand," she interjected. "And she will. She likes you and thought you were a perfect match for me before Carlisle spoke his mind. We can make my parents see the value our union will bring after we are married. And if we cannot, then we will have to accept the consequences. But I cannot risk putting myself at the mercy of Father's whims. For all we know, he could have me promised to Clancy upon my safe return after Carlisle sent that telegram in Memphis!"

"I doubt that, as he immediately telegraphed back that he was taking the family to New York City to meet us there."

He rested his hand on her arm, brushing her cheek with his lips. "Nothing would make me happier than to call you my wife, but, Flora, we have to do this the right way. I have striven my entire life to be a man of honorable reputation, and I will not act like a thief in the night."

She stepped away from him, her eyes welling at the familiar sentiment. Father had made it clear concerning her value, but Teddy? "Like a thief? I am *not* property to be bartered or stolen, Theodore Day."

"Don't be like that, Flora." He reached for her hand, but she jerked away. "I mean, you and I belong with each other. And because we belong together, we must marry in the correct manner *with* your family's blessing. I know how much your sisters mean to you, even if you say the youngest three plague you. If we do this, there is a good chance your father will have you cut off and you will not see them again. Are you prepared to do that?"

She thrust her chin up. "If he feels so inclined, then I will see them once they are married and out of my father's house."

"What if he threatens to withhold the entirety of their inheritance from them if they do not agree to shun you? Are you prepared to wait until they are fifty to speak with them again after your father's passing?"

Does he care if I am cut off from my family, or is it my fortune he's worried about? She hadn't thought that the money was important to him. "Even if society never discovered my running away with Olive and we proceed with a traditional courtship, Father will never give his consent, especially when I have forced him to break his word as a gentleman to Carlisle." *Please, Teddy. Don't do this.*

"Flora, I love you, but I want us to meet with your family in New York and at least try to—"

"Apparently your love is not strong enough to actually marry me," she whispered and retreated from him to her room. She closed the door between them, rested her head against the polished wood, and allowed herself a moment of tears before retrieving the carpetbag from under the bed.

She withdrew her widow's weeds from the bag and began to dress, packing her things and then Olive's. She had not been almost kidnapped and eaten by an alligator only to be forced into a marriage with Clancy, or any other gentleman, in the end. If Teddy would not have her, then it was time she made her own way in the world—without her father's fortune or a man's protection.

Carlisle lifted his glass in farewell to Olive, bidding her good-night, and leaned back in his seat, crossing his feet atop the brilliant white tablecloth. "What did you say to Flora that has her missing dinner?" He sipped the amber liquid in the glass. "It must have been something significant to keep her from missing a meal."

Theodore clenched his fists at his brother's callousness. "Don't treat the matter so flippantly. This is my heart on the line, not to mention Flora's heart."

"Your heart?" He kicked off the table, the chair legs landing with a thud. "You have been in love *three* times in the span of eighteen months and engaged, well, I suppose three times now. If Miss Flora has rejected you, I have no doubt you will find a new love in a few months' time once the sting of this loss has abated. As for me, a man who has never been infatuated with a lady *before* Miss Flora, I can tell you the matter has me—" he paused and looked down into his glass, swirling the last dregs—"has me feeling things I do not care to admit."

"On that score, I am sorry," Theodore admitted, unhappy with seeing his brother so unlike himself.

Carlisle laughed, finishing off his drink and reaching for the decanter. "Being second choice is not something I relish. Is Flora happy to be your second choice? I doubt any woman could stomach that fact." He snorted. "And Flora is wealthy enough not to have to marry such a fickle man for security's sake."

Theodore snatched the glass from Carlisle's hand and threw it against the wall, the shattering of the crystal against the wood paneling stunning his brother into silence as the drink tricked down the wall, seeping between the floorboards. "You know I loved Willow as a friend for a long time, and the competition aided in me falling—"

Carlisle shot up from his chair, leaning heavily on his knuckles on the table. "*Exactly*. You have fallen for a childhood friend twice now. What makes you think this time it is actually true love when you thought it had been twice before? You have been drunk with the idea of love for years. And who is to say that *I don't* have feelings for Flora? Because I assure you, I do. And unlike you, I have never been in love before and can give the lady more than you."

Theodore refused to flinch at the insinuation that he was damaged goods.

Carlisle pinched the bridge of his nose and exhaled. "I apologize. I shouldn't have let my temper get away from me." He reached into his pocket, retrieving a cigar. "Along with my disappointment, this competition has me on edge, though it is a poor excuse to abuse you so. Forgive me?"

Theodore felt the rage leave his lungs. His brother was never one to admit a wrong. He nodded. "I thought you weren't worried about winning."

Carlisle chuckled, rising and ambling to the door, lighting a match on the frame and holding it to his cigar before stepping onto the deck with Theodore. "I am not. I secured another contract as I departed New Orleans, and my agent is spreading word of Florian's involvement and support of me, so I have no doubt I will secure more upon my return. Unless you manage to beat the odds in St. Louis, the competition is more or less over . . . though I do not like the idea of our being enemies just because I happened to acquire more contracts than you."

"Hold on now." Theodore grinned, leaning against the rail on his forearms. "I haven't given up hope yet, but win or lose, you could never be my enemy, especially not when you have proven yourself by sacrificing a chance to be with Flora."

"Yes, Flora," Carlisle murmured, lowering his cigar, his eyes fixed on the glow of St. Louis as the *Horizon*'s long, bellowing whistle sounded two times, followed by two short blasts in the foggy night, letting the city know their boat was approaching. "Olive mentioned to me that you haven't addressed the marriage at port yet. What are you waiting for, you dolt?"

Twenty-Five

Flora gripped her carpetbag as the train chugged into the station in New Orleans. After two grueling days of traveling in coach, thanks to their limited funds, she was glad for the heavy veil that kept passersby from seeing her mottled cheeks and matted hair. Unlike poor Olive who had to make do with the dust of travel by splashing her face in the train's third-class water closet for the entirety of their journey from St. Louis, which was so dilapidated that it was almost worse than being unwashed for two days—almost.

The hum of the passengers on the train's platform threatened to overwhelm her. Normally when traveling, Flora was escorted and ushered about, but in the humid train shed, she was growing disoriented. She glanced at the windows at the roofline and took a deep breath, only to have the veil cling to her mouth. She sputtered it out and, peering through the passengers, spotted Auntie Violet standing at the front of the iron gate with a manservant behind her. Hefting her carpetbag on her hip, Flora motioned for Olive to hurry as she bustled over and kissed her aunt's withered cheek. "Auntie, thank you for coming to fetch us."

"Of course! I couldn't send a servant for something like this. I brought someone who is quite anxious to see you." Auntie gestured behind her as a flash of navy brocade charged at Flora, arms wide.

"Willow? What on earth are you doing here?" Flora gasped, wrapping her arms about her dearest friend, even as people turned, whispering and pointing to her, obviously recognizing Willow from the society and business columns of the papers.

"I feel so special." Willow rolled her eyes. "Did you forget that letter you sent to me? Cullen and I are staying with Mrs. Dubois, as your family has already departed for New York."

Flora smacked her hand to her forehead. "The letter! Oh no. Willow, I am so, so sorry. I—"

"We can't discuss anything here, my dear," Auntie Violet said, her hand about Flora's waist. "Are you well? I can't tell with your veil and all." She gestured to the heavy material. "What is with all the theatrics?"

"Thank you, Paxton." Olive dropped her satchel into the footman's hands, giving Auntie a kiss in greeting before pressing her hands to her lower back and arching. "Two young women traveling alone warrants a disguise, though I do not have the best of disguises with only this lavender gown and wretched netting over my chapeau that does nothing but impair my vision."

Auntie patted her arm. "Let's get you both home. You will feel much better with a bath and a change of clothes after your ordeal." She shook her head. "I'm sorry. I should have thought to disguise us as well."

Flora laughed. "I didn't have enough funds for a longer telegram to include that."

"A fact which you will be explaining in detail later." Auntie motioned for her servant to procure Flora's carpetbag as well and ushered the ladies through the crowds and onto Magnolia Street. Once inside the carriage, Flora divulged everything to Willow and Auntie from beneath the veil to keep herself from being recognized by anyone on the street while Olive kept her face hidden by her fan.

By the time they pulled up to Auntie's mansion on St. Charles Avenue, Flora was parched from speaking so quickly, Willow in shock, and Olive sullener than she had been in days, which was quite disconcerting.

"He really refused to marry you? After all that happened? And that kiss in the magnolia tree?" Willow shook her head as the driver held the door. "That doesn't sound like Teddy."

Flora followed Willow and Olive out of the carriage. "He said he wanted us to marry in the right way."

"Ahh." Willow gave a knowing nod and handed the butler her wrap in the grand foyer, smiling her thanks to Harold and seeming quite at home.

Flora greeted Harold before hissing to her friend, "What do you mean by that, Willow Dupré, I mean Willow Dempsey?" While she realized that Willow and Teddy had a past, it still irked her that Teddy fell for Willow *before* her.

"I mean that while our dear Teddy Day is a romantic, he is more so a man of character. I know he may not have professed his plans to you in the manner you wished, but his heart was in the right place."

Olive arched a brow. "What did I tell you, Flora? Once again, you acted without thinking and dragged me along."

She scowled. "If it is all right with Auntie, I'd like to be shown to my old room and have a nice long bath drawn."

"Of course. Mabel, would you mind seeing to Miss Wingfield's needs?" Auntie pulled off her gloves and waved Olive up the stairs with the maid following closely behind.

Flora wrung her hands at Willow's words. No one knew Teddy like the two of them. Had she run too soon? "Should I send him a telegram direct at the port of St. Louis? Or perhaps send a note to his St. Charles residence?" Her stomach twisted at the thought that she had once again cost him a massive sale if he had chosen her over his work . . . She hadn't thought of that before. He had chosen her over taking the lead and securing his place as head of the company, and how had she repaid him? Running. Again.

Willow grasped Flora's hand. "If you wish to have a relationship with him, I think you should try both places."

"And I think you had best send word to your parents of your safe arrival here as well. I didn't let them know yet, as I received your telegram after they had already left for New York and wouldn't receive my telegram until after you arrived anyway," Auntie said, ushering them into the parlor and taking a piece of paper from the corner desk along with a pencil. She jotted down a note and handed it back to the butler. "Please have someone send this telegram right away to my nephew."

Flora dipped her head, shame burning her. "Thank you, Auntie."

"Think nothing of it." Auntie wrinkled her nose. "Let's have someone draw you a bath and I'll ring for an early luncheon. It is hard for anyone to think in this heat, especially under a veil and yards of crêpe, lightweight as it may be, filthy and starving."

Within the hour, Olive took luncheon in with Auntie in her room while Flora was seated at the dining room table, devouring her first course with Willow, when the butler extended a silver tray to her.

"A telegram already?" Flora nodded her thanks and cringed at the contents that were certainly going to be dreadful . . . and she deserved every word of it after the trouble she had put her family through.

Willow set down her soup spoon, leaning toward her. "Do you want me to read it first?"

Flora closed her eyes and shook her head as she tore open the envelope and read aloud, "'Flora and Olive, thank God you are well. Received ransom note. Then a telegram from Teddy stating you were missing. Stay inside. I am returning to New Orleans. Pinkerton man will be arriving shortly to protect you. Will explain more later. F. W.'"

"Well, that wasn't too bad." Willow leaned back in her chair, exhaling.

Flora screwed her lips to the side. "Oh, it *is* bad. Father returning the family to New York means Tacy's attempts to ensnare Clancy Drake in a courtship were cut short, and Father's returning here means his New York business will be delayed yet again by me." She sucked in a breath. "It will not be an easy reunion."

Willow reached for her glass. "Why then would your father want a Pinkerton man to watch you when you are staying with us? Cullen is a champion boxer after all."

"Where is Cullen, by the way?"

"Cullen went to the Young Men's Gymnastic Club yesterday where he heard about a boxing match occurring today, where both of the fighters were trained at the club." Willow fairly glowed at the mention of him. "My sweet husband was so enthusiastic about viewing a match in the ring capital of the world, I didn't have the heart to attempt to stay him even though such matches are still illegal in New Orleans."

"Well, I'm glad to know that the trip to New Orleans wasn't a complete waste for the two of you, even without a wedding to attend." Flora picked up the telegram again. "A Pinkerton, though?"

Willow tore her roll, spread a generous amount of butter over it, and took a bite. "Well, I think we can both agree that you put your father through quite a few levels of Dante's inferno, and the least you can do is abide by his wishes to let a Pinkerton man watch the house." She brushed her fingers free from crumbs. "So, we had best enjoy these last two days of peace before his return. Shall we bypass the rest of the meal and go straight to dessert?"

True to Father's word, a Pinkerton agent was stationed outside of Willow's house within the hour with a consistent rotation every eight hours for the next two days, when a cabriolet arrived just as Flora, Olive, Willow, and Cullen were readying for their evening promenade before dinner. With a single glimpse out the parlor's floor-length window, Flora found not her irate father descending but a blond gentleman. Her soul drank in the sight of him. *He followed me. Again.* "Teddy is here."

Willow straightened, Cullen's hand encasing hers as Olive bounded up beside Flora. "Is Carlisle with him?"

"I'm sorry." She squeezed her sister's arm.

Olive's eyes watered. "I shouldn't have even hoped."

"Don't give up yet," Flora returned, the thought blooming that maybe if Father still wished to shore up a deal with Carlisle, maybe he could offer Olive's willing hand in marriage.

She turned to find Cullen whispering away to Willow, "We always knew it would be difficult the first time we saw him, Willow, but he is one of your oldest friends. It's time to make amends," Cullen reassured his bride. "Especially since your dearest friend is in love with him, which will mean frequent visits. And out of all the other gentlemen who paid you court, I would call Theodore Day and Kit Quincy my friends."

Flora sent Cullen an appreciative smile. This couldn't be much easier for him than it was for any of them.

Willow smiled to Flora, her discomfiture evident in her tugging at her collar. "It's been wonderful visiting you, and of course I expected to see him. It's just that the last time I saw him—"

"Oh, we know, *macushla*." Cullen gave a soft laugh. "After all, my darling, I was the one who ended your relationship at your and Theodore's *engagement* ball . . . with Flora's help. But if we do not face this now, it will only be more awkward later."

"Are you ready?" Willow smiled at Flora, firmly lacing her hand in Cullen's.

Flora gulped and smoothed her flawless mint walking gown. She glanced up at Willow, who had gone a shade paler. Flora bit her lip against the uneasiness filling the parlor. *You knew this was going to be challenging when you had feelings for one of Willow's old beaus. But I suppose when thirty suitors paid call on my best friend all at once, it would have been a challenge to receive a suitor Willow did not see first, even if it wasn't Teddy I loved.*

Olive ran her hand up and down Flora's arm in quick succession. "Be brave. There is no call to run from him again, not when he has proven himself to be so steadfast."

Part of Flora wished to flee the room and receive him elsewhere, especially since Flora had never confessed to Teddy her part in Willow's rejecting him, but Willow needed this meeting as much as she did. Flora just hadn't considered until now that perhaps he could change his mind about her because of her meddling . . . which she needed to confess to Teddy before another moment passed.

The group waited in silence as the butler's voice filled the hall, followed by footfalls leading to the parlor, each step sending her head to pounding. She had behaved poorly by running away instead of voicing her grievances with Teddy, and the shame of her cowardice burned within her. But she had been so terrified of being forced into a marriage if she returned to her father's house. She had prayed daily that Teddy would forgive her for not trusting him and that she could forgive him for not wanting to marry her right away, yet the fear of being second choice was a difficult one to surrender, especially since she had always been treated as just one of the many daughters of Florian Wingfield, never quite seen as special enough to warrant enough attention as to stand out.

"Mr. Theodore Day to see Miss Flora Wingfield."

Teddy stepped into the parlor, his gaze flowing over the group and finding her at once. She began to curtsy but found herself being lifted into his arms.

"Flora. Thank the Lord you are safe," he murmured into her hair before setting her down, his hands resting on her shoulders, brows lowering to a point. "Do you know how worried you made me?"

"I'm so sorry. I shouldn't have run." She pressed the back of her hand to her cheek to cool it. "I was only tired of not being in control. For once in my life, I wanted to make a decision for myself and not wait on a man to make up his mind. And while marriage is an agreement between two people, it felt as though you were taking that away from me and leaving me to the mercy of my father's whims."

He winced. "I guess I deserve that."

At the throat clearing behind her, Flora turned to the rest of the group that had all but melted away from the room the moment Teddy's arms were about her. She drew in a shaky breath, thankful for a moment to gather herself, when Cullen crossed the room with Willow on his arm.

"Theodore, it is good to see you again." Cullen nodded to him, clapping him on the shoulder.

Teddy gave him a distracted smile as he clasped Cullen's hand.

"Teddy, I am so happy to see you." Willow slipped from her husband's arm and embraced Teddy, quickly moving back to her husband's side.

Teddy brushed a lock of hair from his eyes that had come loose from his pompadour during his embrace with Flora. "I'll admit that I did not think I would be seeing the two of you for a good many years, but"—Teddy nodded to Cullen—"was she worth the trouble she put us through?"

Cullen grinned at Willow's gasp. "Every bit."

Teddy laughed. "Good. I can honestly say that I am sincerely happy for you both and I would like nothing more than to move forward in friendship."

Willow pressed her hand to her lips, unshed tears filling

her reddened eyes. "You cannot know how much that means to us."

Flora squeezed her friend's hand, reaching with the other to Olive. It was so good to all be together again despite the awkwardness that had so recently lingered between them. But Cullen was right. Time would make it dissipate. Their friendships were too precious to sacrifice to discomfort.

Teddy turned to Flora. "Your father and mother should be here by this afternoon. Until then, I was hoping we could have a moment alone to discuss how we shall be going forward."

"Please feel free to use the conservatory," Auntie Violet called from the tubes at the top of the stairs into the parlor, sending the group into laughter when she offered tea.

"Perhaps a walk?" Flora countered to Teddy. Her limbs needed to be stretched, and as the topic was sure to be a difficult one, she did not wish to be overheard.

Olive twisted her hands. "Flora, you know what Father said about going out of doors without protection. If Cullen is staying, then—"

Teddy clutched his chest. "Well, that stings."

Cullen laughed and rolled his shoulders. "We can't all be champion boxers, Day." He winked.

"Father is just being dramatic because of the attempted kidnapping, which we all know was arranged by a mystery *lady* and therefore is not a threat with Teddy by my side." Flora snapped her fingers. "I forgot my gloves. Let me fetch a pair and then we can take a promenade down the avenue."

She hurried upstairs, her heart hammering. She had acted cowardly in running from a good man like Teddy, but she couldn't help but feel justified in her choice when he hadn't listened to her . . . or maybe she didn't take the time to listen to *him*. She dismissed that thought with a scowl. Men had been making too many decisions about her life lately. It was time she made a few of her own. Willow didn't really understand, not with her father's and husband's unwavering support.

Flora refitted the pearl-handled hatpin through her new cream chapeau with its clusters of dried baby's breath and yellow silk roses and darling mint silk ribbons. She paused in the looking glass, pulling on her gloves, and once more regretted that her hair had lost its naturally delicate curls and was instead eternally frizzy due to the New Orleans humidity. She closed her door behind her and, at the second-floor landing, paused at the banister, spying Teddy and Willow speaking at the foot of the stairs.

"You have been well since I last saw you?" Willow ventured.

"Surprisingly so, especially since Flora appeared in New Orleans."

She pressed her hand over her heart. *To admit such a thing to a former fiancée? He must truly love me.*

"I know it is not my place to say anything, but if you love her and she you, why are you waiting when you are aware of her father's contingency on his blessing? I know running away wasn't exactly the best reaction, but if I were in Flora's situation . . . I cannot say I would act any differently."

Relieved at her friend's confession, Flora descended the stairs, her heeled shoes sounding her presence. She smiled to Willow, and then she and Teddy slipped outside. Their walk was nothing like their previous time in New Orleans. After a few attempts at stilted conversation, the pair fell into silence for nearly an hour, until Flora looked up and found them nearing Upper City Park.

"Oh my, we had best be turning back before night falls." Flora checked her ladies' watch pin at her waist.

Theodore grasped her hand in his. "Not before we take a walk in the park? We have to settle this between us," he pleaded. His thumb rubbed over her hand. "On the island, everything seemed so much simpler, didn't it?" He caressed her cheek with his palm. "There was you and I, love, and life versus death. I was a fool not to marry you then and there like you asked."

She stepped into his arms, stopping short at the sight of the man leaning against a nearby lamppost, and gasped.

"What's wrong?" Teddy tensed at once, but she held him to his position.

She shook her head as if in doing so she would clear her vision and not see the man who had been dogging her steps since her family first traveled to New Orleans. "I cannot believe it."

"*What?*" Teddy twisted around to see what had her looking so shocked, but she pulled him back to face her. "Honestly, Flora, if you do not speak now—"

"Do not look!" She lifted her hand to her chapeau to further obscure her face. "Grayson is here," she hissed. "He's been following me ever since my steamer trip to New Orleans . . . and occasionally about the city at one function or another." *If by occasionally, one means daily.*

"All summer? Why on earth didn't you tell me?" Panic laced his voice as he seized her elbow and steered her behind a live oak. "Flora, the man is not who he seems."

"Well, when I tried to bring it to Father's attention, he

dismissed me so quickly, I thought I must have been over-reacting. And what do you mean? That he's a thief? Because I know now that he indeed took—"

"I mean that Grayson is *married*."

Her throat tightened. "And yet he was courting me? What on earth could he possibly gain from that?"

"An attempt to ruin you? I'd say it was revenge. Thornton works for the Pinkertons, and he discovered that Grayson has been working for Wellington for years. And the appointment to vice president came with explicit instructions on taking down your father."

She pressed a hand to her mouth. "The despicable man." She dared to peek around the trunk, and to her horror, Grayson straightened and looked directly at them, his grin spreading. Flora, not certain what to do, seized Teddy's hand and wove around the line of oaks toward the sidewalk-turned-boulevard in the park, hoping that if she stayed near the houses, they would be safer than taking the long walk home in the dark.

"Oh yes, let's isolate ourselves. That is always a good idea when evading a potential killer," Teddy muttered.

"A killer? You never said he was a murderer, too! I thought it was a good idea, and you could've said something sooner." She pulled him to the left path that was usually more popu-lated, but instead of couples and families strolling about, she found no one, and the lights usually blazing from the houses were dimmed. Her stomach growled. *Dinner. Everyone is eating or out to dinner!* "Let's go the other way." She whirled around and stifled a scream at the man standing behind them.

"Grayson?" Theodore growled.

He bowed to him. "What an honor that the esteemed Mr.

Day remembers me. Miss Wingfield, I have missed our little tête-à-têtes." He flashed his crooked, yellow-toothed smile.

"Mr. Grayson, so lovely to see you, but we were just heading home, and unfortunately I cannot stop and chat." She gripped Teddy's arm.

"No?" He opened his jacket to reveal a row of knives affixed to the interior. "I call them my conversation openers. For if you do not speak with me, I will *open* the conversation in a more painful fashion, if you catch my meaning."

Her knees locked as she looked from Grayson to Teddy. Teddy at once stepped in front of her, arms outstretched, shoulders turned as if ready to grapple with the man.

"Is this because of my refusing your suit, Mr. Grayson?" she asked, afraid of the answer, but she had to keep him talking. Anything to keep him from using his weapons. "Please forgive me if I caused you any distress when I refused to meet with you after my mother promised—"

"It was never about securing your hand," he scoffed. "It was only about providing for my wife. Heathcliff Wellington is nothing if not generous to his supporters."

"If you did not wish for marriage, then why did you attempt to get close to Flora so many times?" Teddy clenched his fists.

For something far worse. Flora's limbs weakened, and she grabbed at Teddy's arm, keeping him from advancing on the man.

He laughed. "I needed something off of her person to send a final warning to Florian Wingfield that I meant business."

"The gold cup," Teddy murmured. "You took it from her purse!"

"And sent it along with another death threat pinned to his

very daughter." He chuckled. "I got a little inspiration from Miss Bridgewater's pirate-themed party and could not help but revitalize the old sign of death in the form of a black spot. Mr. Wingfield was warned to step away from the sugar deals too many times to allow his daughters to go roaming about without a guard. Now, we can do this the easy way or the enjoyable way." The man grinned and removed a long, deadly knife from his coat and turned it over in his hand.

"You'll have to kill me before I allow you to take her from me." Teddy lifted his fists.

"Well then, I vote the enjoyable way," Grayson said with a maniacal laugh.

Twenty-Six

In a fluid motion, Grayson flicked his wrist and a flash of silver caught in the flickering gaslights along the path as Theodore dodged the blade, but not far enough to evade it slicing his scalp and then a second planting itself in his outstretched hand, keeping the blade from striking home in his chest.

Flora's scream pulled him from the haze of pain, and he yanked the blade from his left hand, flipped it in his right and grinned, his body numbing and his mind sharpening. "I said that you'd have to kill me. You should have when I gave you the chance."

Flora pressed her hands to her heart. "Teddy. No—"

"Trust me." He kept his stance in front of Flora, pacing back and forth, weighing his options. In a knife-throwing contest, he would surely lose against a professional like this man, but hand to hand . . . that was another thing entirely. Thank the good Lord for Carlisle's obsession with wrestling and constant need of his brother acting as a sparring partner. It would finally come in handy. Theodore lunged at him, but

Grayson blocked him with a dagger that Theodore caught against his own. He bore down on his assailant, instantly sensing the man wasn't as strong as him.

A mint skirt flashed in the corner of his eye, and the next moment Flora was standing behind Grayson with her reticule lifted behind her head. She smashed the reticule to the man's head, and he crumpled to his knees with a moan, his hold loosening at once. Theodore seized his arms, pinning them behind his back, unwilling to release him until he was certain he was no longer a threat.

"Is the man unconscious?" a voice boomed, the owner of it undeniable.

"Father!" Flora rushed to Mr. Wingfield with open arms.

"Keep your distance, Daughter!" he snapped. "I am an excellent shot, but I wouldn't want to take the chance of hitting you. Theodore, on the other hand, I might not mind as much."

Theodore couldn't turn his head to see if he was jesting, and at the click of the revolver, he stiffened.

"Agent Thornton, apprehend the man."

Grayson smashed the back of his head into Theodore's nose, and with a roar he pulled his arms free and slashed at Theodore with another blade, grazing Theodore's chest, divesting him of a gold button, and carving his skin. The cut broke his body's stupor, his bloodied hand and the pain flaring at once.

Flora screamed again as Gale dove into the mix, Theodore falling to his knees while Gale wrestled Grayson to the earth and pried the weapon from his hands, securing him in cuffs at last.

"Calm yourself, girl. It's just a flesh wound. Stay back,"

her father growled, his finger on the trigger of his pearl-handled revolver. "Grayson, you've been following me long enough to know I'm a good shot."

The man ceased his struggling, his eyes flashing. "When my boss gets wind of this—"

"Heathcliff Wellington will be able to do *nothing* now that I have secured his final suppliers. He no longer has his wealth to protect him."

"And Mr. Wellington is to be moved from his private residence to a more secure prison where he cannot pass messages to his minions. That's what," Gale added with a grunt, shoving off Grayson's shoulder to push himself to standing. "You should have accepted Mr. Wingfield's offer when you had the chance."

Flora knelt beside Theodore, assessing his wound. She pressed a hand to her mouth as if to keep from tossing her accounts and looked away from his bloodied hand, shifting her gaze to his face. But as he was fairly certain the cut at his crown was trickling down far too much, she looked to his lips, which brought forth a grin that immediately turned into a wince.

Gale glanced at Theodore's wound. "Not bleeding a lot, but we best send for the doctor to avoid poison setting in from the wound."

Flora gasped, gently cupping Teddy's injured hand in hers, pressing her handkerchief to the wound. "Poison? Surely, Mr. Grayson would not—"

"Of course he would, Daughter. He's Wellington's hired assassin, albeit a poor one, as your beau is still breathing. Now, come along, Flora. I will explain all once you are safely indoors with your mother and sister. It is time we discuss your future." Father flipped his hand out to his daughter, and to Theodore's satisfaction, she did not relinquish her hold on him but rather clung to his good arm all the more.

"It will be well," Theodore whispered, even as pain blurred his vision.

Father shot the bolt of the front door the moment everyone was inside, the bang bringing gasps from those in the front parlor. Mother strode out into the hall and released a strangled cry, flying to Flora in a rare show of matronly love and worry. Flora allowed herself to return the embrace and leaned her head on her mother's lacy puffed sleeve.

"We were so worried." She held Flora at arm's length. "How could you do this to us? I have come to expect such a thing from Tacy—" She choked on her daughter's name, pressing a rather wet-looking handkerchief to her eyes, which Flora found quite puffy, as if she had been crying for days.

Flora's heart dipped. She had not meant to cause them such distress, yet it was oddly reassuring that despite their opinions on their daughters' futures, they did care for her.

"Out of the hall and into the parlor." Father spread his arms, herding them into the room, Teddy following. "Hyacinth, draw the curtains. I don't want anyone to see us from the street and come calling."

"But it's evening, Florian, and the air is finally cool—"

"Do it!" he fairly shouted, sending Mother scurrying to carry out the task. "Olive, fetch a servant to light the gaslights. Cullen, send a footman for the doctor. Poor Mr. Day is bleeding all over Auntie's imported rug."

Olive squeezed Flora's hand in passing, murmuring a

greeting. But before Flora could even take in the strange events, Mother's arms were around her again. "Oh, Flora, thank the Lord you are safe."

"I had Olive with me the entire time, Mother. You have nothing to fear for my reputation."

Mother pressed her lips into a thin line and nodded, barely keeping her sobs in check. "I know, she told us everything, but after you left New Orleans, Miss Penelope Bridgewater began to spread such salacious gossip—" She stopped short, pressed her handkerchief to her forehead, and sank onto the settee.

Flora sent her sister a confused look. "What happened?"

"It took a while for me to piece together the story, but apparently, shortly after we left, they received a ransom note for *millions* in exchange for our lives. Unlike the threats of the past, Father believed this one at once and was in the process of having the funds sent when word began to circulate that you had willfully absconded with Carlisle."

"What?" Flora gasped. "Penelope did this, didn't she? She had me kidnapped?"

Olive shook her head and grasped her hand. "That is the worst of it and what has Mother in such a state. And Father too, desperate to keep that part of the mystery quiet. I am still in shock."

"*Who* was it, Olive?" Teddy grunted, repositioning himself on the couch as Auntie fluffed and plunked pillows behind his head.

"Apparently, Tacy spread the gossip to Miss Penelope Bridgewater to damage your reputation and further her chances with securing Clancy's hand," Father admitted, sending Mother into a wail and him to patting her shoulder.

"That doesn't make any sense." Flora rubbed her temples. "Tacy may not care for me because of Clancy's pursuit of me, but she would never hurt me."

"Finish the story, Auntie." He ambled to the refreshment cart, pouring himself a cup of coffee.

"Later that same evening, I received a note from Clancy Drake requesting that Tacy cease her pursuit of him and that no amount of dowry would cause him to forget you, dear Flora, so quickly . . . the amount he mentioned was the *exact* amount of ransom requested merely hours before."

Dear God, no. Flora swayed, resting her hand against the settee. The pirates had mentioned a lady had hired them . . . a lady who explicitly stated that no harm should come to the Wingfield sisters. Her gaze flew to Teddy and at once she knew. The diamond necklace that Tacy had given the pirates at the party had been real. It had been the first payment. "It was Tacy. Tacy hired the pirates in order to collect enough funds to bribe Clancy into marriage."

Father nodded, leaning against the fireplace mantel. "But when Clancy's letter arrived shortly afterward with the ransom note, she discovered her little desperate scheme had failed, she confessed all, and I alerted the lawmen along the river of a potential threat coming from Stack Island, but by then—"

"The pirates had already acted," Teddy interjected.

"Yes." Father kicked at a log in the fire, sending sparks flying upward and skittering out to the rug. "Foolish, foolish girl."

"Florian, the rug!" Mother sat upright, her grief momentarily replaced with annoyance. "We just purchased that as a thank-you for Auntie hosting us!"

Father stomped on the embers.

"Because of Tacy, the steamboat sank . . . and my reputation is ruined?" Flora moved to the settee and buried her face in her hands, feeling light-headed. *Does Tacy truly hate me so much?*

"So where is she?" Olive asked, joining Flora and rubbing her back.

Father pursed his lips. "I had to do my best to salvage what I could of our family's reputation, so I had Miss Bridgewater recant the gossip with a subtle threat to her father of financial ruin and married Tacy off to Lord Peregrine for an unearthly sum. She is on the ship to England as we speak."

"Lord Peregrine?" Willow straightened. "I didn't know he was still looking for a wife in the States."

"He was about to leave when I approached him with a dowry of ten million now and a million every year until my death when she comes into her full inheritance." Father snorted. "Greedy man readily signed the special marriage certificate and Tacy was aboard within the hour."

Mother sank back into her mound of pillows. "And I will only see her on visits now."

"Our daughter made her choice the moment she took up with that pirate and unwittingly put her sisters in danger." Father flipped open his gold tobacco box and tamped his pipe with fresh tobacco. "Lord Peregrine's title will act as a balm to Tacy's sore heart. And under contract and threat of losing funding, he will be good to her. And I have no doubt she will be fond enough of him before long."

Teddy shifted from his position, his gaze finding Flora's, most likely thinking of his time spent unchaperoned with Flora on the island. Flora squeezed Olive's hand, silently thanking her once more for protecting her when she was blind with fear and love.

"And given Flora's choice to run away to you, Mr. Day, for an elopement, and your honorable decision to wait for permission to save her from scandal, I hereby rescind my offer to your brother and you have my full blessing to marry my daughter." He lifted his pipe to the pair of them in a salute.

Flora's eyes locked with Teddy's, uncertainty flitting through her heart for the half second it took for him to cross the room and kneel before her, taking her hands in his uninjured one. "Flora, my darling . . ."

"Teddy. Wait."

His look of love melted before her. "You don't wish me to propose?"

She shook her head. "It's not like that. I must make a confession. That night of your engagement ball for Willow, I let Cullen inside to speak with her alone. I was the one who put doubts in Willow's mind regarding your relationship." She swallowed, finishing in a whisper, "I was the one who broke your heart for a second time."

His expression softened. "I had my suspicions."

"And? Do you . . . despise me for my actions and are only marrying me out of a sense of honor?"

He pressed a kiss atop each hand. "Since you lost me a bride, it is only fair that you hear me out. Will you make me the happiest man alive and be my partner in business and life and love? Will you be my darling Mrs. Day?"

With a cry, she flung herself into his arms, kissing him. "Always, my dearest Teddy. Always and forever."

"Then what are we waiting for?" Father clapped his hands

once to garner the group's attention, rallying Mother at once, as Cullen returned with the doctor. "Cullen, fetch a minister. They must be married before any more gossip circulates."

Cullen shouted his congratulations and sent Teddy and Flora a grin as Auntie pulled him into the foyer, who prattled off directions while the doctor examined her fiancé's wounds on the settee. Warmth filled her at the lovely name. *Mrs. Day.*

"Put on your best gown, my dear. You will be married within the hour," Mother exclaimed, shooing Flora away from Teddy, and then she shrieked for a servant to send for a decent suit for Teddy from his residence.

Flora smiled over her shoulder at Teddy, in a daze as she was ushered out of the room by Willow and Olive on each arm on their way upstairs.

"*What happened* on that walk?" Willow giggled, flinging open the armoire in Flora's room.

Flora seized her dearest friend's hands and twirled her around. "Wonderfulness! Well, besides Teddy being stabbed in the hand, but other than that, it was simply a marvelous evening. And will you stand by me?"

"You will have to tell me all about that later, because a stabbing is only eclipsed by the fact that you are getting *married* today to the man of your dreams!" Willow squealed. "If there is one thing I learned during our short visit, it is that you and Teddy are made for each other. Of course I'll stand with you, Flora."

At Mother's shouting a warning about the time, they readied one another in a flurry of ribbons, lace, and hair combs, laughing all the while, for she, Flora Wingfield, was marrying Teddy Day.

"When I woke this morning, I had no idea this would be

the happiest day of my life." Flora ran her fingers over the crown of pink roses Olive had woven in her coronet braid, half her locks falling to her waist in a waterfall of golden curls as Willow created a nosegay bouquet with the leftover roses, adding lace and ribbons for fullness.

"You look like a vision." Father smiled from the doorway. "Olive and Willow, you had best head downstairs for her grand entrance and give me a moment to speak with my daughter in private."

Surely he isn't going to berate me now for my flight . . . not moments before my wedding. She felt his fingers on her chin, lifting it to meet his gaze.

"Can you forgive me, Flora, for not listening? For not considering your feelings?"

She blinked. Was her father actually speaking of *feelings*?

"When I made that deal with Carlisle Day, I had no idea where your heart lay. I only meant to protect you, to keep you from the clutches of Wellington. When I was receiving those death threats, I thought little of them. A man in my position does not become so wealthy without making enemies on the way to becoming American royalty. But when I received your gold drinking cup, taken directly from your reticule. I knew the threat was all to—" he paused and swallowed—"I could not risk Wellington asking for your hand in marriage as compensation for my actions, not after how close your Willow's Cullen came to being in the man's pocket. So that's why I was rushing my eligible daughters into marriage."

Flora stared at her twisting hands. *He wanted me to marry Carlisle because he actually cares for me.*

"And when you disappeared and I received that ransom note—" his voice caught again—"I thought I had lost you

341

forever, that he had taken you, and in that moment I realized I had put treasures before your well-being."

She jerked her head up, unable to speak.

"I treated you like a piece of my property that I needed to shore up, thinking I knew what was best despite your protests." He ran his fingers over his beard. "And now I find I have done that with not only you but with your sisters as well. If I had listened to Tacy and simply increased her dowry after she had begged me to, none of this would have happened. You would have never been in danger and my little girl would not be married to a stranger, a titled gentleman but a stranger to her."

She grasped his hand. "I forgive you, but I want you to know that what happened to Tacy was all *her* doing, Father. What happened to me was also her doing . . . well, besides that escapade in the park."

"Escapade." He laughed, shaking his head. "Flora, I never knew how brave you were until this all began."

"Brave, or foolhardy, which has yet to be determined." She winked.

"Brave." He took her hand and threaded it through his. "Now, there is a young man waiting for you downstairs, eager to make you his bride."

EPILOGUE

Sea gulls called to one another overhead, dipping low over the steamboat promenade deck on the chance there were bits of food for the taking. But Flora hardly noticed them as she was nose-deep in her sketchbook, working on the interior design. She wove through the French doors into the grand salon and out again, studying the effect of the wall coverings in different lighting, with Theodore beside her as she made notes on slight adjustments to the design of the flagship boat they had built, funded in part by Flora's dowry.

After their wedding, they decided to secede Day's Luxury Line to Carlisle and moved to Newport to open their own business and begin building Flora's dream home. Until it was finished, they rented a lovely cottage by the sea, where Flora taught an interior design class out of their parlor for any woman willing to learn the trade, in hopes of the class gaining popularity and eventually being taught in universities across America. And as she already had ten students, some from high society and others shopgirls wishing to improve their situations, Theodore knew she would indeed achieve her dream.

The secession of the family business had gone a long way in repairing his relationship with Carlisle, that and the fact that Carlisle had agreed to take Olive's hand in marriage as part of a revised contract with Mr. Wingfield. And to his complete shock, though not to Flora's, Olive had been more than happy to oblige him. Apparently, she had fallen in love with his brother in his frequent calls at the Dubois residence and his valiant rescue of her aboard the *Marigold*.

He glanced down to Flora, scribbling away her notes on the grand salon. The thought of having a partner in love and work warmed him to the core. "Have I told you lately how happy you have made me, Wife?"

She clutched her notebook to her chest and stepped up to him, smiling. "I don't think you have, Husband. Can you remind me?"

He wrapped his arms about her waist, not minding the workers milling about. "Before there was you, I did not know what love felt like. I did not know that one could hold the world in one person. I did not know that if you did not smile at me every morning, the sun would not rise. You have taken this battered heart of mine and loved it despite all. And because of God's grace and your love, I have the strength to fulfill my dreams—our dreams."

She slipped her hands into his. "Together."

He pressed a kiss atop each hand, his gaze never leaving hers. "Always, my darling Mrs. Day. Always."

AUTHOR'S NOTE

Dear reader, thank you so much for joining me for Book Two in the AMERICAN ROYALTY series!

The year 1883 was a time of great change for Upper City Park, which was renamed in 1886 to Audubon Park, with the promise of the World's Cotton Centennial occurring in December 1884. So there are a few moments in the park scenes that might be a red flag to history buffs, as it may be a few months off with the naming of Exposition Boulevard and the building of the fair and the duck pond mentioned in the story.

You can still visit "Seven Sisters Oak," the largest oak in the United States, in Mandeville, Louisiana today. Although it was originally thought to have been seven separate oaks merged into one mighty tree, it has now been proven to be a single oak. My mother had her bridal pictures taken there, so I had to include it in the novel!

In the Stack Island scene, I have characters *in* the Mississippi River, which as most of you know, if you fall in that particular river, you are most likely not going to make it out.

But, as this is fiction, and Teddy is basically an Olympic swimmer, I took into account the ever-changing river with its oxbow bends that eventually tapered off over the years, and so I made the 1800s version of the river slightly "calmer" on the west side of the island for the purposes of my story. Please forgive my slight liberty with our mighty Mississippi.

While interior design classes were not available in universities until 1904, I gave Flora the passion for them. I like to think that it only took twenty years for her interior design class dreams to come true.

Want to know more about Teddy Day and Flora Wingfield and what exactly happened during that outlandish competition they are always on about? Check out Book One in the AMERICAN ROYALTY series, *My Dear Miss Dupré*. And stay tuned for Book Three to read more about some of your favorite characters in the series. Happy reading!

ACKNOWLEDGMENTS

D akota, I could not do this without you. Thank you for listening to me plot out my book and for your brilliant suggestions.

To Liam, you are my darling and I thank God for giving you to me every day.

To Cora, I almost named you Flora, but since your daddy vetoed that one, I am giving you a heroine christened after your almost name. I'll always remember this book as the one we wrote together while I was pregnant with you during summer in the South in quarantine. I love you with all my heart, baby girl.

To my family, Dad, Mama, Charlie, Molly, Sam, Natalie and Eli and nephews, thank you for always being so supportive of my writing.

To my beta, Theresa, thank the Lord I have you in my ring! Your suggestions are golden and thank you for always being there with a shovel to help me fill those plot holes.

To my agent, Tamela Hancock Murray, thank you for all your hard work and constant encouragement.

To the team at Bethany House, my acquisitions editor Dave Long and senior editor Luke Hinrichs, thank you for bringing Flora's story to life! I am thrilled to be a Bethany House author!

To the reader, you are wonderful! Thank you for reading Flora's story. I hope you enjoy the series! If you did, please take a moment to leave me a review on your favorite bookish website. If you want more updates on where I am in the writing process and behind-the-scenes news, join my newsletter at GraceHitchcock.com.

And to Jesus, You never cease amazing me. You have heard my prayers, given me dreams, and fulfilled promises beyond my wildest dreams. You are and always will be the reason I write. And while there is breath in my lungs, I will praise Your name.

Grace Hitchcock is the author of *My Dear Miss Dupré*, Book One in the AMERICAN ROYALTY series, as well as a number of historical novels and novella collections. Grace is a member of ACFW and holds a master's degree in creative writing and a BA in English with a minor in history. She lives in the New Orleans area with her husband, Dakota, son, and daughter. To learn more, visit Grace at www.gracehitchcock.com.

Sign Up for Grace's Newsletter

Keep up to date with Grace's news on book releases and events by signing up for her email list at gracehitchcockbooks.com.

More from Grace Hitchcock

Upon her father's unexpected retirement, his shareholders refuse to allow Willow Dupré to take over the company without a man at her side. Presented with twenty-five potential suitors from New York society's elite, she has six months to choose which she will marry. But when one captures her heart, she must discover for herself if his motives are truly pure....

My Dear Miss Dupré • AMERICAN ROYALTY #1

You May Also Like . . .

When Arthur Livingston seeks out the agency to find a missing heiress, Eunice Holbrooke realizes her past has finally caught up with her. In order to avoid Arthur and conceal her real identity, Eunice goes undercover on another case. But will the truth she uncovers set her free or place her—and her heart—in peril's way?

To Disguise the Truth by Jen Turano
THE BLEECKER STREET INQUIRY AGENCY
jenturano.com

On the surface, Whitney Powell is happy working with her sled dogs, but her life is full of complications that push her over the edge. When sickness spreads in outlying villages, Dr. Peter Cameron turns to Whitney and her dogs for help navigating the deep snow, and together they discover that sometimes it's only in weakness you can find strength.

Ever Constant by Tracie Peterson and Kimberley Woodhouse
THE TREASURES OF NOME #3
traciepeterson.com; kimberleywoodhouse.com

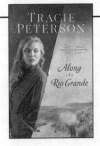

When bankruptcy forces widow Susanna Jenkins to follow her family to New Mexico, what they see as a failure she sees as a fresh start. Owen Turner is immediately attracted to Susanna, but he's afraid of opening up his heart again, especially as painful memories are stirred up. But if Owen can't face the past, he'll miss out on his greatest chance at love.

Along the Rio Grande by Tracie Peterson
LOVE ON THE SANTA FE
traciepeterson.com

⬥BETHANYHOUSE

More from Bethany House

A birthday excursion turns deadly when the SS *Eastland* capsizes with insurance agent Olive Pierce and her best friend on board. After her escape, Olive discovers her friend is among the missing victims. When she begins investigating the accident, more setbacks arise. Finding the truth will take all she's got to beat those who want to sabotage her progress.

Drawn by the Current by Jocelyn Green
THE WINDY CITY SAGA #3
jocelyngreen.com

Harriet Hancock is an experienced meddler, so she realizes right away when she's being set up with Jonas, her friend's brother and a stable hand. As the two work on an artistic project, they begin to see each other in a new light. But will class differences—and Harriet's well-intentioned scheming—get in the way of their chance at a happy ending?

Enchanting the Heiress by Kristi Ann Hunter
HEARTS ON THE HEATH
kristiannhunter.com

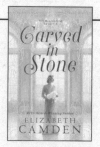

When lawyer Patrick O'Neill agrees to resurrect an old mystery and challenge the Blackstones' legacy of greed and corruption, he doesn't expect to be derailed by the kindhearted family heiress, Gwen Kellerman. She is tasked with getting him to drop the case, but when the mystery takes a shocking twist, he is the only ally she has.

Carved in Stone by Elizabeth Camden
THE BLACKSTONE LEGACY #1
elizabethcamden.com

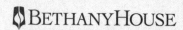